I0632879

The Human Ant

BY THE SAME AUTHOR

The Superhumans (translated by Brian Stableford)

The Human Ant
and Other Stories

by
Han Ryner

translated, annotated and introduced by
Brian Stableford

A Black Coat Press Book

English adaptation and introduction Copyright © 2014 by Brian Stableford.
Cover illustration Copyright © 2014 Mandy.

Visit our website at www.blackcoatpress.com

ISBN 978-1-61227-323-5. First Printing. August 2014. Published by Black Coat Press, an imprint of Hollywood Comics.com, LLC, P.O. Box 17270, Encino, CA 91416. All rights reserved. Except for review purposes, no part of this book may be reproduced or transmitted in any form or by any means, electronic or mechanical, including photocopying, recording, or by any information storage and retrieval system, without permission in writing from the publisher. The stories and characters depicted in this novel are entirely fictional. Printed in the United States of America.

TABLE OF CONTENTS

Introduction

L'Homme-fourmi by Han Ryner, here translated as "The Human Ant," was first published by Les Editions de la Maison d'Art in 1901. It was reprinted in 1913 by Eugène Figuière et Cie., who subsequently published *Les Pacifiques*, the second short novel translated herein, as "The Pacifists," in 1914.

The shorter stories making up the present collection were all reprinted in the collection *Contes* (Les Éditions du Pavillon, 1967). Their original appearances, as recorded in that volume, were as follows: "Le Fiancée du prophète" ("The Prophet's Bride") is dated 1895 but no place of publication is indicated; "Une Transition" ("A Transition") apparently first appeared under that title in 1898 before being reprinted in the *Courrier de France* on 15 January 1913 as "Le Secret de Don Juan"; "Sacrifices" appeared in *La Feuille d'Automne* on 25 April 1902; "La Promesse" ("The Promise") was in *Verse et Prose* on 1 March 1911; "Le Mort vivant" ("The Living Corpse") was in *Touche-à-Tout* on November 1912 and "Un Songe d'Apologistes" ("Apologistes' Dream") was in *L'Idée Libre* in December 1929. Some of the earlier stories appeared under the author's real name, Henri Ner.

L'Homme-fourmi belongs to a numerous tradition of *contes philosophiques* which attempt to reproduce aspects of the hypothetical world-view of an ant, in order to provide a useful standard of comparison for the human world-view. One of the earliest examples in fictional form is a brief sketch included in the collection *Polierge* (1757) by Emerich de Vattel. Ryner's work was by far the most ambitious and sophisticated at the time of its publication, and easily outshines many of the examples by which it was abundantly followed up in the twentieth century. Camille Flammarion included a brief item in one of the stories collected in his *Contes philosophiques* (1911), but it is anemic by comparison. The notion was rapidly taken up by the American science fiction magazines, in "The Ant with the Human Soul" (1932) by Bob Olsen, but with a crudity of thought and method typical of the pulp fiction of the day. The issue was seriously addressed in a more abstract fashion in Julian Huxley's classic essay "Philosophic Ants: A Biologic Fantasy" (1922), which certainly has more claim to intellectual respectability than Ryner's fantasia, but is inevitably lacking in narrative verve.

Prior to Ryner's venture, an intimate fictitious visit to an ant-hill had been paid by human observers in Albert Bleunard's "Toujours plus petit" (1893)[1], which drew upon at least one of the sources that provided Ryner with some of the information that he recycled. The best-known such source was the second series of J.-H. Fabre's *Souvenirs entomologiques*, published in 1879, which includes a chapter on "Les Fourmis rousses" [Red Ants]. Fabre might also have provided Ryner with a model on which to base the entomologist who plays a considerable role in the latter part of *L'Homme-fourmi*, but the experiments described have far more in common with those carried out by the English scientist John Lubbock (later Baron Avebury), who published a notable book on *Ants, Bees and Wasps* in 1881. Much of the information Ryner reproduces originated from Lubbock's book, although it might have been filtered through French secondary sources.

Where Fabre led, of course, several other eminent French entomologists followed, most notably Ernest André, who published *Les Fourmis* in 1885, and which also contains a good deal of information reproduced by Ryner. Although Fabre was a brilliant popularizer, and both Lubbock and André took leave to exploit the melodramatic potential of their investigations, the imaginative range that Ryner added to his own dramatization cannot be regarded as a mere cheapening or perversion of the material supplied by his sources, and really

---

[1] translated as *Ever Smaller*, Black Coat Press, ISBN 9781612270142.

does add a further dimension to it, albeit with the addition of a number of fudges and a few errors.

Literary work dealing with ants stimulated by Fabre and his successors was not limited to earnest *contes philosophiques*. Ants also played a satirical role is such works as *Les Fourmis du parc de Versailles, raisonnant ensemble dans leur fourmilières* (1803; signed "C. L. le Bel" and falsely represented as a translation from the English), the title poem of Charles Woinez's *La Guerre des fourmis* (1870) and Auguste Saint-Yves' pamphlet *La République des fourmis* (1872). More earnest poetic representations are featured in the section of Claudius Popelin's *Poésies complètes* (1891) entitled "Hommes & Fourmis." None of this work, however, has much to recommend it beyond casual eccentricity.

Although not devoid of a satirical element, Ryner's work is much closer to the earnest tradition of philosophical tales, and its method is essentially Voltairean, employing a straightforwardly supernatural facilitating device, but then addressing the fictitious situation thus established with an eye that is as clinical as it is cynical. Ryner liked to think of himself as a cynic in the strictest sense of the word—he published two books of "cynical parables"—and *L'Homme-fourmi* is closer to the that spirit than his later long stories, which increasingly took on a mystical element of which Diogenes probably would not have approved. Like Voltaire too, Ryner is not shy about spicing up his story with melodrama; *L'Homme-fourmi* is probably the most action-packed account of the secret life of ants, and is most certainly the most sex-obsessed, blithely embracing the startling perversity required to accommodate and develop that obsession.

It has to be admitted that the story is by no means the most plausible account of ant life, in spite of the cursory research supporting its hectic plot. In some important ways, it deliberately opposes then-conventional ideas about the organization of hive societies. Its account of the two ant geniuses whom the narrator dubs Aristotle and Hannibal stands in stark contrast to commonplace accounts of the probable working of

9

a "hive-mind." Ryner had a specific political agenda as well as a purely philosophical one, and as a devout anarchist, he was as opposed to popular notions of formic uniformity as he was to popular notions of ant royalty; his notion of the contempt in which his surprisingly individualistic workers hold their egg-laying females, however, is more closely in tune with Edward O. Wilson's classic analysis of the sociobiological rationale of hive society than the traditional notion that made egg-layers into authoritarian "queens"—a term that Ryner refuses to use in the context of the ant-hill. The unorthodoxy of his account, however, serves to heighten even further the didactic contrast he attempts to draw and dramatize between human and hypothetical ant mentality, always to the detriment of the former while recognizing the limitations of the latter.

A narrative methodology similar to that employed in *L'Homme-fourmi* is deployed in an even more robust manner in *Les Pacifiques*. The mildly unsympathetic narrator of the former novel is replaced in the latter by an exceedingly unsympathetic one, whose gradual acquisition of monstrousness, although it parallels the former example in more ways than one, continues to make relentless progress, whereas the earlier narrator reverts to near-sympathy once the issue of sexual attraction is sidelined. While the former novel is a relatively mild admonition to humans to broaden their minds and become more sensitively aware of their limitations, the latter is a full-frontal assault on human vanity and "civilization" that might strike some readers—ironically, in view of its glorification of pacifism—as a trifle cruel.

Les Pacifiques was published on the eve of the Great War, probably a matter of weeks before that conflict exploded—the only review accessible via *gallica* appears in the 5 July 1914 issue of *Les Annales*—and that was undoubtedly not the best timing for the publication a pacifist utopia. The dearth of other reviews probably reflects that opinion, and the novel has dropped out of sight somewhat in consequence, but it is one of the most striking and effective of Ryner's works. Although *Les Surhommes* (1929; tr. as the title story of *The*

Superhumans and Other Stories)[2] is more imaginatively extravagant, its very extravagance gives it a surreal aspect that insulates the reader from its more discomfiting arguments, while *Les Pacifiques* hits a great deal harder, and more often, by means of its sarcastically inverted rhetoric. Although by no means as colorful as the later work, it is more clearly and more tightly focused.

Just as *L'Homme-fourmi* is the most action-packed *conte philosophique* representing the world-view of ants, *Les Pacifiques* is certainly the most violently melodramatic of pacifist utopias. It adopts that strategy, of course, as a means of loading the dice in favor of non-violence, much as Albert Robida promoted his pacifist agenda in futuristic visions of the horrors of 20th century warfare, but it does not shirk the central problem of describing a pacifist anarchist society in some detail and offering robust arguments in its favor as well as leveling scathing criticism at its opposite—a bullet that only a handful of anarchist writers were willing and able to bite, and into which no one else, with the possible exception of Marcel Rouff in *Voyage au monde à l'envers* (1920)[3], contrived to inject as much narrative energy as Ryner.

Les Pacifiques also merits some consideration in the context of a set of French works extrapolating Plato's invented myth of Atlantis cleverly and productively; other notable examples include Hippolyte Mettais' *Paris avant le deluge* [Paris Before the Deluge] (1866) and *Les Atlantes: aventures de temps legendaires* [The Atlanteans: Adventures in Legendary

---

[2] The introduction to the Black Coat Press edition of *The Superhumans and Other Stories* (ISBN 9781935558774) includes a more elaborate overview of Ryner's career and works, which there is no need to repeat here. I hope to produce at least one further selection of his philosophical fantasies, in order to illustrate their full spectrum.

[3] translated as *Journey to the Inverted World*, Black Coat Press, ISBN 9781612270395.

Times] (1905) by Charles Lomon and P.-B. Gheusi.[4] Although Ryner uses the idea purely as a literary device, in the same spirit as his deployment of the wish-granting enchantress in *L'Homme-fourmi*, he always remains conscious that he is working in the tradition of Plato, using a narrative method that Plato had pioneered, albeit with a very different political agenda.

Of the short stories filling out the collection little needs to be said beyond the fact that, seen collectively, they provide a useful illustration of the spectrum of his imaginative fiction and the range of his narrative strategies. The fact that they extend over the entirety of his career also allows them to illustrate something of the development of his thinking, and the gradual complication of the mystical notions whose notional core is set out with some dexterity—and perhaps a little sleight-of-mind—in *Les Pacifiques*.

The translations of *L'Homme-fourmi* and *Les Pacifiques* were made from copies of the Figuière editions scanned by the Library of the University of Ottawa and available via the Internet Digital Archive of Free Books at *archive.org*. The translations of the short stories were made from the London Library's copy of *Contes*.

Brian Stableford

---

[4] I hope to be able to translate both of these Atlantean fantasies in the near future.

THE HUMAN ANT

To Jacques Fréhel[5]

On the day when I saw your generous nature quivering beneath the transparency of your works, I only felt a poor or miserly justice toward you. On first encounter, I like Latin talents and their simple harmony. It requires a longer appreciation for me to comprehend barbarian geniuses. Their liberal fecundity and seemingly crazy prodigality trouble me with an admiration in which, I fear, astonishment takes up more room than sympathy. I get lost at the unexpected bends and the abrupt divergences of their lush creations, and am led to manifest my anxiety more than my wonderment. But it is only a matter of time and familiarization. When I finally know the half-wild forest was well as the park, I sense how more broadly beautiful and more nobly moving it is.

So, with a joyful zeal I am engraving on the frontispiece of this book—a doubtless ruinous monument, alas!—my admiration, more profound every day, for so many pages of *Bretonne*, for almost all the pages of *Déçue*, and even more, if it is possible, for those astonishing poems in prose that you call, with excessive modesty, *contes* and *nouvelles*, and which

---

[5] "Jacques Fréhel" was the pseudonym of Alice Télot (1861-1918). She and Ryner met in 1899 and were secret lovers for many years thereafter, although Ryner published reminiscences of the affair after her death. *Le Précurseur* (1905), the best-known of her several novels, is a philosophical love-story set in a kind of phalanstery. *Le Cabaret des larmes* appeared in 1902, many of the stories having previously appeared in the *Nouvelle Revue*.

you are greatly at fault, Madame, for not having collected in a volume.

Han Ryner

P.S. I have elected to leave this dedication as it appeared for the first time in 1901, but do I not have a duty, my dear friend, to note that your crime of abstention has been repaired? You have collected your delicate and penetrating poems in prose for our durable joy, under an exquisitely melancholy title, *Le Cabaret des larmes*. I would be committing a grave injustice toward the public, and even more so toward you, if I did not indicate how far, since the beginning of the century, you have surpassed your promise and all our hopes, or if I neglected to name those two broad and complete masterpieces *Le Précurseur* and *La Guirlande sauvage*.

I

Before recounting my incredible metamorphosis and the strange adventures of my life as an ant, it appears to me to be good procedure to describe what I was at the moment of the surprise and to summarize my anterior existence in a few lines. I can only explain that period of my existence by recovering the tone in which I spoke then and the rhythm in which I thought.

My name is Octave-Marius Péditant. I was born on 8 April 1875 at Château-Arnoux (Basses-Alpes) of esteemed parents, rich by the standards of our village and proud of their superior fortune. The possessed more than two hundred thousand francs, as much of it in land and other immovable property as in solidly invested money. Unfortunately, sage and sober as they were in all other matters, they were unable to limit the number of their children.

I was the oldest, and from my earliest childhood I showed a considerable penchant for science. They did not have the justice to understand that it was due to my intelligence. However, if I had remained an only son, if I had had sufficient income to live without forced labor, to dedicate all my time to the studies I loved, I might perhaps have become an economist of the first order, the equal of Paul Leroy-Beaulieu or Baudrillart.[6] Alas, I was given six brothers and

---

[6] Paul Leroy-Beaulieu (1843-1916) held the chair in political economy at the Collège de France from 1880 until his retirement. Ryner undoubtedly read and his book *Le Collectivisme* (1885), and did not approve of it. Henri Baudrillart (1821-1892) had previously held a chair in economic history at the same institution; his works were noted for their erudition, which Ryner probably respected in spite of his opposition to Baudrillart's economic theories.

four sisters. Fortunately, my father died young, without having time to complete the dozen.

Although I speak with an inflexible rationality, even when it is a matter of my own kin, I would not want to be thought lacking in heart. That judgment would be unjust, and here is the proof:

My father died intestate. I could, at my majority, have claimed my rights. I did not such things. I left my worthy mother to enjoy what belonged to me for as long as she lived, and when my brother Bienvenu and my sister Désirée's husband asked for a division, I showed them there inconvenience there would have been in such precipitation; I told them how we would go down in the estimation of our compatriots and pointed out that our mother, being very ill, had only a short time to live. In brief, I used my authority as the oldest and wisest against my own interests.

I had the annoyance of succeeding. If I had failed, if the bad sons had persisted, everyone, while blaming them, would have praised my noble opposition, and I would have obtained more advantage from a good deed that would have cost me precisely nothing.

At eight years of old I was sent to the Collège—now the Lycée—de Signe. I was soon withdrawn from that inadequate establishment, and I made the larger part of my studies at the Lycée de Marseille. I was always first in my class, but my most brilliant period was that of my studies in law. I was awarded my doctorate with five white balls. I would have liked, after that success, which augured well, to devote myself entirely to the noble science of political economics, the most beautiful creation of the 18th and 19th centuries, to which they will owe the esteem of the future. Alas, my patrimony, overly diminished by the large number of intruders—that is what I called my brothers and sisters, coarse individuals who wanted to leave school early and had never given my parents and me anything but causes for complaint—did not permit me to follow my vocation without hindrance.

I chose a liberal and esteemed career surrounded by security and consideration. I went into the Registry Office. At twenty-eight, already being a receiver at Sisteron, I made a passable marriage. My wife brought me a dowry of fifty thousand francs and adequately fine expectations, which had the disadvantage of appearing rather distant.

In spite of the scant leisure that my professional duties left me, I had published several papers on political economy. Our government—which is too harshly criticized—had rewarded me with academic palms and the Mérite Agricole. My last work, the one that had earned me the green ribbon, was a very careful statistical analysis of the depredations of which a species of ant, *Aphoenogaster barbara*,[7] was guilty in regard to our wheat.

On 11 April 1897 I had gone for a walk on a plateau near Sisteron, at a place named Chambrançon. Lying face down—an inherently uncomfortable posture that can only be excused by a love of science—I was studying the movements of an anthill. A doubt had struck me regarding a detail affirmed in my pamphlet on the authority of another observer. I wanted to verify it, and, in case it was erroneous, to add a note to enrich the second edition of my *Statistics of the Depredations of Aphoenogaster barbara in regard to our Wheat.*

With the patience that, according to the testimony of Buffon, is sufficient to form genius, I examined the prudent insects. Suddenly, without having heard the slightest sound of footfalls, so deep was my preoccupation, I heard words that were strange in their soft sonority and strange in their meaning: "Bonjour, bonjour," they said. "I'm an enchantress."

---

[7] I have retained Ryner's spelling of this generic name, although it is properly rendered as *Aphaenogaster*. His variation might be a simple error in transcription, but the ant society he describes is a composite image rather than a narrow depiction of one particular species, and the label is primarily a matter of convenience.

My mind translated with great vivacity: *You're a lunatic.* I felt hostile to the newcomer. There was an insolent indiscretion in troubling my work with such ridiculous speech. It was embarrassing for me, even in the liberty of a deserted landscape, to be found lying on my stomach by a woman who doubtless did not understand the exigencies of scientific investigation.

I stood up in haste, as if pricked by a spur. With a rapid hand I brushed the dust off my trousers, and I looked at the annoying woman.

Her clothing, outside of all fashion—drapes rather than a dress—followed the contours of her body in yellow pleats. An ignorant person would have thought them merely ridiculous. I felt more keenly than anyone else how ill-suited they were to our modern world, but they did not distress me as much; they reminded me of paintings. Doubtless I would have thought them ingeniously beautiful if, instead of roaming the fields, they had been manifest at a masquerade ball.

From that noble harmony, which would have been charming but for their unfortunate untimeliness, a delightful and incomparable perfume emanated. I would give a very crude and false idea of it by likening to some mixture of thyme and lavender that had been attenuated by some unknown means, rendered light and discreet but simultaneously more penetrating.

The woman who was wearing that caressant atmosphere and those emphatic garments was beautiful, but her beauty was of a disconcerting, futile kind that did not awake any desire. She was too tall, as tall as the Virgin seated by Leonardo da Vinci on the knees of St. Anne, whose excessive height is condemned by most authoritative critics. The fault was all the more evident because she was standing upright, her head held proudly high. Her long sleek hair hung down freely, covering her shoulders like a black cape, juxtaposing with the yellow of her dress in an agreeable harmony. Her visage was quite similar to that of the Leonardo Virgin I mentioned just now, except that it was less full, possessed of an even more youthful, almost puerile, grace and malice. It made a bizarre, charming and yet irritating contrast with the extreme grandeur of her stature and the arrogance of her attitude. I don't like beauty to be so strange. I want it to be composed of symmetry and health, the result of obedience to all the laws of life.

II

I sensed that it would have been impolite to continue my silent examination. With the smile of someone condescending to share a joke, I said: "Bonjour, Mademoiselle Enchantress."

She was already smiling, and her eyes were shining like the eyes of lunatics. My greeting added radiance to her smile, and her gaze became a blaze of joy.

"Ah!" she said. "You, at least, are not a denier." She used the intimate form of address.

I took a step back and looked the impatient individual up and down. In a very dignified fashion, I remarked: "Mademoiselle, receivers in the Registry Office are not accustomed to being addressed as *tu* by..." I hesitated momentarily. I thought: *by loose women*, but I was gripped by pity for her evident folly. I continued and concluded my sentence in a less wounding fashion, although still very firm. "Receivers in the Registry Office are not accustomed by being addressed as *tu* by just anyone."

She frowned and came toward me, imperious and domineering. At that moment her absurd and intimidating beauty made me think: "a mad queen." Nevertheless, she smiled again, with an indulgence that ought to have offended me, as she replied: "Enchantresses are logical grammarians. They do not employ the plural when addressing an individual. If that wounds you in French, I'll speak Latin."

She stifled a laugh, and, plunging her tall stature into a mocking reverence, she said: "*Salve, proeposite publicis tabulis exactor.*"

Then, straightening up again, her expression greatly amused, she added: "Some titles are a trifle absurd…when one translates them."

I was overwhelmed by amazement. She seemed flattered by my admiring silence. In a voice that was almost no longer insolent, she explained: "Respectable receiver of the Registry Office, I never had any intention of offending you. On the contrary; I wanted to thank you for not having denied my title of enchantress, as so many of the imbeciles I encounter do."

Her smile became amiable. Her overbearing beauty recovered a kind of seductive loveliness. Certain haughty faces are thus transfigured in amorous joy. And she said, in a musical and penetrating voice: "Listen, friend. Those of my kind give active thanks; our words are harnessed teams that draw benefits behind them. Express a desire, and my power will grant it in your favor."

Lunacy is contagious. Thus, I—a reasonable man, a receiver in the Registry Office, a doctor of law and an economist—said to myself, momentarily: "An enchantress. Who can tell? After all, we don't know everything." To be sure, it was only a flash of dementia, immediately extinguished in the somber immensity of shame, but I did not have the courage to draw away from the bizarre and poetic individual. I felt incapable of discontenting "the mad queen." I consented to play my part in her game, and to give my reply in the same spirit.

"Forgive the coarseness of the wishes of a mortal, Immortal Lady. I already have health and intelligence; women find me handsome; what could I desire, except a fortune?"

"What do you call a fortune?"

I became specific. "Admire the moderation of a sage or, at least, don't be scornful of the mediocrity of my desires. A mere million will suffice for me."

"You shall have your million," she affirmed.

More keenly than I should have, I asked: "When?"

"In fifteen months."

I pressed her further: "Why not immediately?"

But the enchantress gave an answer worthy of an ordinary woman: "Because." And she said: "Make a second wish."

After long reflection, I made a grimace of indifference, and my arms lifted slightly in a gesture of embarrassment. "I don't see what I could ask..." I hesitated, and then resumed, fearfully: "To be a minister, perhaps."

"You shall be one in five years, if you still desire it."

That promise, even if I had taken it seriously, would not have given me any great joy. This time, I did not ask; "Why not immediately."

The enchantress spurred me on: "Make a third wish."

Although all of it, in my thinking, was pleasantry and chitchat, my natural moderation rebelled and I said: "I have nothing left to desire."

"What!" cried the mad queen. "You're not asking for anything for your soul..."

I protested: "Madame, I've asked for everything for my soul. A fortune will permit me to devote myself without reserve to my beloved political economy. I shall live in Paris, in the midst of an intelligent society. I'll attend premières..."

She cut me off, scornfully. "Ah! That's what you call joys of the soul. Poor man, who isn't even curious…!"

"What an idea! Not curious, me! What about my work in statistics?"

She did not deign to respond. She sat down on the grass, and gave me a sign to do likewise. Delicately, her fingers picked up an ant. She considered it with a strange smile. Then she asked: "Have you ever desired to know what passes through the mind of another animal?"

My human pride expressed itself: "There must be so little passing through it."

"That's where you're mistaken," she affirmed. "Would you like to do the experiment? Would you like me to change you into an ant?"

III

I was gripped by a great pity for that admirable woman, who was mad. I thought I saw a means of curing her: to demonstrate her impotence. I avoided the awkwardness of my first wishes. I began by cutting off all retreat for the presumptuous woman.

In an incredulous tone, I almost hissed: "Change me into an ant? When?"

"At this very moment," she said.

I replied, mockingly: "How will you do it? You've forgotten your wand."

"Do you think that a king is obliged to pick up his scepter to give an order? At any rate, if you want to see external signs of my power, be satisfied."

By means of I don't know what trick of prestidigitation, she had between her fingers a kind of orchestra-conductor's baton. The ant she had picked up a little while before was on the baton, running along it hurriedly, in bewildered terror. It hastened toward the tip and then, as if it had bumped into an invisible obstacle, threw itself backwards.

The mad queen smiled at the ant. "Calm down," she said to it. "I don't mean you any harm."

As if it had heard and understood, the ant stopped. In order to have something to do, it started cleaning its antennae.

Again the strange young woman addressed herself to me: "Do you want to become this little animal?"

"I do."

"And you don't want to impose any other condition?" she asked. "You don't have any reservations?"

"What would be the point?"

"Imprudent!" she exclaimed.

She looked at me with infinite tenderness. Then her eyes lit up with an ironic gleam, and her words were like temptresses drawing nearer graciously, a trifle coquettishly, in hesitant undulations, advancing as if the slightest gesture would drive them away: "And the million that will fall due to the receiver of the Registry Office—what should I do with that?"

I did not want to be the object of mockery, and, in spite of the emotion with which the word *million* caused me to shiver, I retorted: "You've made me promises contradictory for a poor mortal; it's up to you to keep them all."

"It's simple," she said. "You'll only be an ant for a year. Does that arrangement suit you?"

"I accept it."

"And you're not requesting anything else?" she persisted. "You don't have any other precautions to take?"

"I can't think of any."

She burst out laughing. "What blockheads these receivers in the Registry Office are! What advantage would you obtain from the voyage if you forgot to take a little memory with you? You'll also require the faculty of thinking like a man as well as an ant."

"Poor mad queen!" I exclaimed. "From the impossible you fall into the inconceivable. How can the ridiculously small brain of an ant accommodate human thought?"

Insultingly, she said: "The thought of a man of genius might perhaps overwhelm it, but the mind of an ordinary man doesn't weigh very much." After a pause, she added: "I can't guarantee, in any case, that your duplicate thought won't entail considerable suffering. But your two minds will only rarely be alight simultaneously. Ordinarily, only one of them will illuminate your consciousness. And yet, because the second being will still be there, invisible but present, always on the point of confronting its neighbor, cursing, contradicting and denying the other in a howling quarrel, your thoughts will be painful, anarchic and chaotic to the point of madness, or very nearly. Sometimes, human habits will play your ant thoughts false, maddening the thinking ant. Sometimes your ant mind, a precision instrument and not an implement of labor, will grate upon your heavy human thought, like a fine scalpel of which one is demanding the labor of a spade."

She spoke in a distressed fashion, her head bowed. Her arms slack, her hands almost touching the ground. The smile had disappeared from her lips, and her eyes were two flowers of sadness. But she straightened her upper body. Her expression cleared. Her mouth took on a tremor that gradually opened into a valiant smile. Her arms were raised. Her free hand came to support her chin, and she began again, in a voice that was no longer tearful, but already encouraging.

"Be brave. Don't recoil before intellectual dolor, that ennoblement. The limits of thought are unknown, but it is only calm when it gathers itself in, makes itself small, enclosing itself its blind terror. Immediately it emerges, especially when it yields to its instinct to enlarge itself, climb higher and descend more deeply, that is when it suffers over its entire surface, for things enter into its magnification as thorns and nails enter into a body."

She was scornful of my tranquility: "Poor child, your thought is ignorant, not having yet collided with any other thought."

She raised her wand, and extended it toward my forehead in a solemn gesture, which stopped abruptly.

"I forgot…" she murmured. She opened an irritated parenthesis: "But why hasn't this banal individual even thought about that practical detail?" And she insulted me violently: "Imbecile! If I'd transformed you into an ant without any other precaution, the entire hive would attack the intruder and you'd perish amid horrible tortures. It's necessary that you should be an ant from this hive…"

"In case of an accident," I joked, "you'd have resuscitated me."

I don't know whether she understood my remark ironically, but she neglected it in order to continue with her own train of thought.

"And you're not asking, either," she said, indignantly, "how your human brethren will receive you after your long disappearance, after they've shared out your spoils and their serried ranks have closed to efface your position in social life." She reflected momentarily, and then added: "For a year, you'll be the ant that's on my wand—and that ant, for the same year, will be Octave Péditant."

"That's it!" I said, laughing. "A simple permutation."

I said no more. The wand had touched my head.

I was an ant.

IV

It seems that the shock of such a metamorphosis ought to leave a durable memory. It did not. I had been a man the instant before; now I no longer was. But there had been no transition, no perceptible passage, no intermediate point to which the memory could cling. I only remember one thought—or, rather, one amazement:

"Why, it's true: I'm an ant."

And I was much less astonished in thinking: "Why, it's true: she's an enchantress."

But there it was. Other astonishments—or, rather, other insanities—were entering through my eyes, entering…I was going to say "through my ears," but I no longer had any ears. I wanted to flee, to take refuge underground, in the ant-hill, and no longer to see, no longer to hear, all that impossibility. In vain I ran to the tip of the wand, and tried to let myself drop on to the enchantress' garment, in order to descend by the shortest route into the blind and deaf subterranean passages where my insanity would be soothed and go to sleep.

An invincible force attached me to the wand. The enchantress wanted me, in spite of my amazement, to look right away, for me to know, immediately, that the human universe is not the unique and necessary universe, but that it is our eyes that create our world. She wanted such philosophical terms as "relativity of consciousness," which I had pronounced a thousand times, as everyone does, to be something more than words henceforth, so far as I was concerned.

I had no eyelids to protect me against the maddening light that entered into me in spite of me. And my gaze, instead of simply telling me what was in front of me, screamed at me confusedly all of the impossibility that surrounded me.

The rules of language force me to analyze my stupor, to make it, for those who are reading me, into separate, successive, perhaps amusing astonishments. Their simultaneity rendered them overwhelming. It is not disagreeable to drink in small sips, at leisure. The drowning man in whom the water enters irresistibly through every opening he has suffocates and dies of it. I am astonished not to have died at the moment when I was plunged, suffocating, into that other universe as if into an irrespirable environment.

Think about it, anyway. I can only tell you the less extraordinary, give you the less asphyxiating to drink. In the impressions of another animal, everything that is truly singular, without analogy with human sensations, cannot be stammered by any human words, cannot even be rethought by my mind now that it has become exclusively human again.

How can I express what the colored universe became for me, in that minute of agony? All the hues were new, nameless, without relationship with any memory. In order to be able to tell you anything, I am obliged to suppress their astounding novelty, to devote myself from now on to familiarizing explanations that I compiled much later, little by little. I need to destroy, by analyses of which I was incapable at the time, the insane synthesis that crushed me from all directions like a formidable vice, all-encompassing and made to measure.

Innumerable subsequent observations taught me that my ant's eyes were ignorant of two human colors. The black hair of the enchantress and her yellow garment had formed an agreeable harmony for my human taste; now, the vestments were as black as the hair, and that black was none of the blacks that you know. Of that same black, brighter and more vibrant that what you call black, was the grass that had previously been a tender green. And white light, which lacked the yellow and green rays and was illuminated by unknown rays, was not white to my new eyes.

There is a relationship between human sensations and the sensations of an ant that I could not divine, that I know only by virtue of experiments carried out, since I became a man again, on my friends for a year. I know now, like other entomologists, that except for yellow and green, all the colors of the human spectrum affect the retina of ants. But I also know, which the entomologists scarcely suspect, that they affect it quite differently from our retina.

Violet, indigo, blue, orange and red are colors for an ant, as they are for humans, but an ant does not see any violet object, indigo object, blue object, orange object or red object. In the course of my story I will perhaps have occasion to indicate a color with the names you employ—to say, for instance that the amazon is a red ant—but under my pen, the word red will designate the common rays causing two irreducible sensations, not the inexpressible vision of my ant's eyes. In addition, ultra-violet rays of which the human eye is ignorant create numerous colors for the ant that I cannot indicate in any fashion.

The only expressible thing is that the colored universe of ants is more varied and probably vaster than the colored universe of humans. The shades there are innumerable, and when, in order to bring them back to a few fundamental colors, I examined a rainbow, I was never able to count fewer than twenty colors.

Is that extreme richness given to the insect by the unknown part of its domain, or is it produced by a kind of fecund analysis? Does it have a dozen ultra-violet colors, or is the blue part of the spectrum, for example, divided into four or five colors? I have no means to resolve that problem; I shall never know whether, in the realm of colors, the ant knows vast and numerous regions into which your sight does not penetrate, or whether it takes for granted extensive realms that seem to you to be mere provinces.

You will divine without difficulty that the abrupt change in the proportion of creatures and things was to weigh upon me like a frightful nightmare. The wand on which I was agitating was, for my eyes, an enormous tree-trunk. The enchantress, whose slimness I had admired a little while before, had become a formless mountain. She permitted me to walk over her hand. A fine down, which my human eyes had not perceived, bristled like the long grass of a prairie, and the pores sank, disgraceful holes, into the abrupt jags of that rugged terrain. Another mountain was nearby, and I said to myself: "That's my replacement!" I assumed that he was wearing my clothes, and I studied their strange color, thinking: "So that's what gray is to the eyes of an ant!"

I was jealous of the new Péditant. He would not be suffering as much as me. Doubtless he only had human thought, and was not feeling within himself the clash of two beings. He was not pursued, as I was, by a madness resulting from thinking with organs inappropriate to his thought. He was not tortured by a mind transported into another brain and which, in the midst of that agony, like a fish in our overly subtle atmosphere, was thrashing about, quivering and jumping—and which, still gasping, would never have had any nouns with which to name anything in that universe, formless for him, unorganizable, refractory to his emprise: that terrible universe seen with the eyes of another, with eyes so different, so deforming!

Then again—I had the impression, anguishing and agonizing but nevertheless just—the universe that my replacement was beginning to know was less varied than the one that I had to learn. The education of that fortunate individual would be relatively easy, while mine appeared to me to be impossible.

Everything disturbed me.

I saw, toward the summit of each mountain, a frightful abyss that was opening and closing. Behind the battens of the first door, the entrance to the cavern appeared, defended by two superimposed barriers made of strange rocks, which parted and came together as if to cause cataclysms. After long and terrified reflection I deduced that those moving gulfs were the mouths of the two beings, and that the enchantress was conversing with Péditant.

I was alarmed not to be able to hear anything of that conversation, which, it seemed to me, ought to have rumbled like articulate thunder. Their discreet conversation surpassed, as I only understood later, what a physicist would call the ant's *audible maximum*. I was deaf to all sounds perceptible to humans, which were too strong for me—but I could hear enormous rumors too faint for the coarse human ear to be able to collect.

In the veins of the hand on which I was agitating, the blood was running with the din of a torrent. When I drew away from the deafening tumult, taking refuge on the silent wand, that midday hour, so overwhelmingly calm for the people of the countryside, was suddenly populated by cries, crepitations and vibrations.

The sweet odor of thyme and lavender that emanated from the enchantress, and had been charming to my human sense of smell, was now as intolerable to me as the odor of a charnel-house would have been before. I wanted to cry out to my persecutor: "Let me go; I'm dying. Since I'm an ant, let me live my life as an ant. Oh, how weary I am! I need sleep. Don't you realize that this awakening in a hostile unknown world is an agony that I can no longer resist? Mercy! Mercy!" But I no longer had any organ with which to say words that she could hear.

My antennae, with which I would speak henceforth, on the condition that they encountered other antennae, were waving desperately. I had a bizarre inspiration, and, although it seemed absolutely crazy, I followed it. In the prairie that the hand was for me, I chose a few of the most subtle hairs, and, as if they were antennae, I told them about my suffering and my desire.

Enchantresses are doubtless in touch with all worlds and know all languages. The two hairs were, indeed, able to function as antennae, and replied to me, approximately: "Go, my poor friend."

And the malign force that was retaining me relaxed and dissipated.

I ran, fleeing the mad universe. With a great leap I went into the ant-hill. Without looking at anything I plunged into a dark corner, fell down and went to sleep.

V

My sleep, which was very long, lasted all afternoon and then all night. It must have been a profound tunnel to begin with, as deaf and blind as death. Afterwards, however, it rose toward life again, and its insufficient opacity, punctured by days of suffering, was penetrated by strange hours of nightmare.

I remember one of those dreams, which stabbed me like blades of light. I remember that one because it recurred many more times during the year, and because my wakefulness was often wounded by the same pain.

I felt stunned. The entire left side of my head seemed to be in the process of being crushed. In the middle, as if, at that point, two beings were quarreling, like two hostile schoolboys shoving one another covertly, each trying to force the other to move over, and there was a turbulent torment.

I tried to see what was happening in my head. I soon understood: I was suffering from the duality of my thought. Two images surged forth simultaneously and malevolently. To the right of my mind, a dolorous platform, an ant seemed graceful and noble to me; to the left of my thought—so heavy! So gross!—was a human being drawn up to his full height, his gaze distant, whose two feet were weighing upon half my head, causing me to lean sideways, almost to fall over.

The two images, the two thoughts, were only in full consciousness for the time of a lightning-flash. I think I would be dead if that tearing had lasted. Soon, the two enemy beings attenuated, becoming floating phantoms, and then disappeared. Of their momentary presence no luminous trace remained; of their imminent return there was no precise threat. There was nothing but a vague median ache, a dullness of the entire head, and the crushing sensation to the left.

Then my two torturers reappeared, no longer as hypocritical adversaries concealing their struggle, but as shrill enemies battling one another without any concern for spectators. The man, with a movement of his foot that hollowed out dolorous furrows all through my mind, shoved the ant, making it fall to the right, where it clung on desperately. Afterwards, for some time, I thought as a man and erected the tottering architecture of memory, with difficulty.

More often than not, the ant abused the human. The antennae addressed themselves to two hairs of the big toe, and their indignation cried out something like: "Get out, poor creature who only has seven colors for the treasure of your eyes!"

Later, when I was better able to compare the richness of an ant's mind with the indigence of human organization, those arrogant antennae added many other kinds of scorn to that first one. Most of all, they said: "Wretch who has only five senses, go hide your shame in a somber lair with five narrow fissures!"

The man, humiliated by that merited disdain, shriveled and allowed himself to be overturned. But always, alas, with his curved fingers and clawing fingernails, the dwarf interrupted his incomplete fall and remained suspended in the middle of the abrupt precipice where he had stood tall a little while before, and climbed back up to crush me with his brutal weight.

On awakening, it required a rather long time for me to recognize myself. Then I went out, as happy as a child running to see something exciting. My human thought had disappeared. I was in the delight of a unity in formation, a life commencing, a curiosity about to plunge its young organs into the exquisite freshness of a beautiful universe, entirely new, not yet faded by the repeated washing of habit.

A happy day was that twelfth of April when, without looking back, I accepted my new condition and consented to enjoy my happiness!

What a gamut of pleasures was the scale of all those unknown colors, so rich! Some hurt me by their violence; I subsequently learned that they were the ones corresponding to your red and violet—but the others, so numerous and so commonly spread throughout nature, were joys. There was such a penetrating tenderness in them...

To an immodest violet whose brutal color collided with my gaze like a blow, I preferred that of charming daisies with dark hearts—the yellow of humans was for me a dark and lovely screen, a black silk—and luminous petals. I do not say "white petals," for your crude white was abolished, replaced by an ineffable hue, which the Christians among you might perhaps rediscover in paradise.

And how adorable was the morning light. Whether it was a direct, inundating dazzle, or whether it arrived as a fine drizzle of joy, filtered by the exquisite blackness of verdure, it penetrated me with an enchantment so new and so astonishing: the enchantment of someone born blind, who, following an operation, is finally able to see.

I could see! I could see!

I paid for my admirable acquisitions with a few losses, but I was not yet in a condition to count them. Then again, it was so little, that ransom; I was marvelously enriched in spite of it. I could have been aware of it without complaining; on the day I inherited the two millions, I was able not to curse the demands of income tax.

I perceived later that my eye, that receptacle of joys, was weaker than a human eye, compressing the precise spectacle in a narrower circle, and seizing distant forms with a slack grip, but-a compensation that charmed me—I could see in front, behind, to the right, to the left and above me all at the same time. I could not get enough of the miracle of that richly panoramic vision. The entire horizon flooded my eyes like a strange synthetic pleasure, and I was almost breathless with voluptuousness in drinking in all the beauty that surrounded me simultaneously.

The utterly unexpected performance that my original organs created with scenery worn out the day before was an opera. In that unknown and rejuvenating light, the richness of things seen was accompanied by the richness of sounds. The earth, via every blade of grass agitated by the breeze, every pebble warmed by a ray of sunlight and every clod of soil joyful in escaping winter, was singing the intoxication of renewal. And the footfalls of my sisters, the ants, the rustle of wings of our friends the aphids, the flight of butterflies and birds, the march of all the insects that were revealed within me, formed harmonies of sound at the same time as harmonies of color and harmonies of movement. Oh, the marvelous ballet that was nature on that morning of the twelfth of April!

And were the perfumes also not singing and dancing rhythms, bouquets of undulations and melodies? It seemed to me that I could see them floating and I believed that I was listening to them too, breathing them in like music, perhaps more penetrating than the other. To be sure, I could not bear the scents beloved by humans, scents as heavy and bruising as sledgehammers. Just now, leaning over on its stem like a young woman at her window, a violet had caused me to flee by the brutality of its aroma as much as its aggressive color—but the true perfumes, the delicate perfumes of which your gross organs are forever ignorant, inebriated me to the point of enervation.

Some emanations that you know and do not like were cordials and refreshments for me. The odor of each of my companions gave me courage.

But the joy of that day is impossible to describe. It seemed to me that I was having a dream of paradise. I remember the inexpressible, formless debris of it. I recall, vaguely, the sensualities of my sense of smell, my musical voluptuousness, because I still have organs that can savor analogous pleasures—very far, to be sure, from those I enjoyed, but capable nevertheless of recalling something of them, dull echoes of eloquent voices. Here, I am trying, via the shaky weakness of words, to evoke the Venus de Milo for eyes that only know the Hottentot Venus. I am fully aware of the vanity of my attempt.

I shall not even try to describe the feminine beauty of the material of the path, however. By virtue of so many absent senses, you are as closed as stones. What ecstatic babble could indicate to you the joys of senses that you do not have, that you could not imagine by any means? Indeed, now that I am reduced to your condition I can no longer represent them to myself. At the moment of return to human life, the moment of the anamorphosis,[8] I lost my rich ant thought, alas. Today my memory depends on my indigent organs; it has not been able to conserve the memories of organs without analogues. There, I am as poor as you are—except that I have inexpressible regrets, impossible for my mind to specify: horrible regrets devoid of memory, stirring in the obscurity of limbo; regrets of the damned that cannot enjoy for a second, even in the imagination, the architecture of heaven.

I look at my bare, dry hands, and I despair, thinking that an entire fluid treasure has run through my fingers and that I cannot recover a single drop of it.

VI

For a long time, my human thought was absent. I only felt it suspended in the shadow of the precipice two or three times, trying impotently to climb back to the luminous platform. A slight push of the ant that occupied the whole space was sufficient to repel the assault. The efforts of the man of old, like steely fingernails trying to scratch a flint, enlightened my joy with abrupt glimmers of comparison.

---

[8] The narrator is synthesizing this word directly from the Greek to mean "change back." The author, however, might also have in mind one or more of the other meanings for which the synthesis is conventionally adopted, including its biological use for a limited kind of insect metamorphosis and its use in art to refer to a distorted image that requires the observer to adopt a particular viewpoint in order to reconstitute it.

When I was fully sated with the fresh beauty of things, I admired the sleek nobility of my companions. The elongated form of the thorax filled me with joy, and the sudden narrowing that preceded the abdomen, the admirable petiole, narrower than the neck, moved me as a beautiful female figure once had—but no desire sullied my purely esthetic emotion.

I never tired of the marvelous equilibrium of the body. I gazed rhapsodically at the circle of the head, long perfected, and the suave fashion in which the curve was modified to permit the mobile and noble attachment of the neck. Beyond the thorax, after the petiole, a more elegant neck, the regular oval of the abdomen stood out, forming a counterpoint to the head.

The long and powerful grace of the limbs, the harmonious movement of the six feet, also penetrated me with a sensuality that I never obtained from the most beautiful feminine human gait. If Virgil had been able to see what I saw, he would subsequently have scorned as leaden the revelatory stride of goddesses and the hectic pace of his Camilla.[9]

Most of all, I contemplated the head: the radiant and fascinating beauty of eyes with a hundred facets, and also the beauty of the antennae, long stems perpetually agitated by the wind of thought. Numerous motionless radiations made physiognomies as profound as shafts of sky, and the continual movement of the antennae, sometimes as slow and grave as meditation, sometimes as rapid as fencing thrusts, gave them expression and eloquence.

Now I made a prideful return to myself. After having said to myself many a time, enthusiastically: "How beautiful they are!" I thought, radiantly: "How beautiful I must be!"

I hid in a paradise apart, in the middle of a little forest formed by a clump of daisies, and set about studying and glorying in the marvelous body that was mine.

---

[9] In the *Aeneid*, Virgil claims that Camilla, an Amazon who opposes the Trojans in battle, can run over a field of wheat without breaking the ears.

In the hollow of a leaf, a few drops of dew had aggregated. I leaned over that mirror and admired the spectacle that I was. My eyes seduced me first. At first sight they formed two luminous spherical skullcaps, like two convexities of sky. On considering them attentively, however, they decomposed into innumerable hexagons, each of which was a complete eye, sufficient to see a portion of the horizon. Each of those facets—to employ the scientific term—was a hole through which images penetrated all the way to my brain. I tried several times, but in vain, to count those enriching holes; I always got lost in the mosaic of light.

Then I amused myself moving my antennae, mirroring the eloquent grace of their gestures, their flexibility and their rare finesse. They were divided into twelve sections, all mobile. The first—the one directly attached to the head—is very long; the others, much shorter, form a joint with it, like the cord of a living whip of which it is the shaft. Your scientists have five the two major divisions of the admirable organ ridiculous names; for them, the living thong is a funiculus, and the movable stock is a scape.

Those antennae, insulted by two grotesque names, are not only adornments—slender, quivering plumes—but the most noble and the most useful of organs. They are inquisitively and tremulously tactile; they are the instrument of the sense of smell; and finally, they are the instrument of language. I agitated them less to see beautiful movements as to enjoy my faculty of speech and to make my thoughts more precise. You think in words; I thought in movements of the antenna. And, as a southerner who does not fear being overheard gives voice to his joy, his dolor or his astonishment, my antennae trembled, as if before a confidante, all my pleasurable passions.

I also marveled at the two triangles of my mandibles. I worked them, separating their edges and bringing them together. The disposition of their teeth made them resemble two saws. I told myself that those pincers must constitute a powerful weapon, and tried out that astonishing instrument of labor, which was able to saw like a saw, cut like scissors, tear like pincers, dab, scrape, smooth and compress like trowels, remove debris like shovels and, like hands, grasp, transport and rip.

I also brought into play my long, mobile lips and my singularly elastic tongue, so rapid in lapping or licking—a tongue which, like that of a cat, passed over my entire body with a caress that cleaned and embellished.

Beneath my lips, my palps stirred coquettishly, like frail and exceedingly unequal fingers. The two outermost palps, the long maxillary palps, were agitating almost like antennae, while between them, the two small labial palps were quivering more slowly. The joys that I aspired through those four siphons I cannot describe and cannot even remember. Those slender organs hidden under the mouth are the seat of a sense unknown to humans. I remember, as in a vague dream, that they often brought me paradisal sensations, and sometimes infernal tortures, but having returned to earth, I cannot recover any of the pleasures and sufferings of a world that is too different.

After a few glances at my forehead, my cheeks, and the immobile plate covering the mouth that scientists call the epistome, I drew away from the liquid mirror and examined my thorax and abdomen directly. The abdomen was a very pure oval. It comprised five rings overlapping one another and slightly mobile. The elongated elegance of the thorax made me smile beatifically, but I examined the mystery of my feet at length.

I liked my claws, so prompt to grip, so skillful at scraping the ground and throwing debris away, so strong in holding on to prey, so adroit and drawing a useful object closer or moving an obstacle aside. On the anterior legs I studied the curved combs that served to clean my antennae, smooth my hairs and groom my entire body. But the strange little balls between the claws, bristling with hairs, interested me more than anything else. Thanks to them. I could scale the sheerest and most slippery rock faces. Thanks to them, victorious over weight, I could sustain myself in any position, walking on ceiling as on floors—for each of those countless hairs emitted a droplet of oil when I was climbing or when my legs carried my body beneath them, the multiplied adhesion of which sufficed to sustain me, without harming either the rapidity or the grace of my movement.

VII

I rejoined my companions in order to involve myself with their labors. They were very unequal in size. Some appeared to me to be extraordinary giants, others improbable dwarfs. Between the two extremes, all the possible dimensions existed.

The proportions of the body, admirable in the small and medium-sized, were less so among the giants. The latter displeased me by virtue of their enormous truncated cylindrical heads, formidably but heavily armored. Their gait, more rapid than mine, nevertheless had some awkwardness. They carried their head like a burden, poorly placed and established on the disproportionate, ugly, embarrassing body. One would have liked their palps to be transformed into feet in order to sustain the ill-placed weight and reestablish a little harmony and equilibrium to the disproportionate body.

I was led to scorn the smallness of the dwarfs as an inferiority, albeit an exquisitely graceful one. The ants that were nearly the same size as me were the most agreeable to look at.

I must have measured six or seven millimeters.

Some were only three millimeters long, while some of the big-headed ants reached twelve millimeters.

Those differences in size did not establish any social hierarchy; we were not divided into commanding and obedient castes. Each of us worked as was convenient for the good of all. If a task or a project required the concerted effort of several individuals, one asked for the assistance of the first comers, great or small. Some, however, gladly worked together, being visibly linked by a particular amity. They also had more intelligent and more skillful personalities, to which one accorded more confidence. Whoever solicited it, however, aid was very rarely refused, and then it was always explained, by means of two or three strokes of the antennae—I was going to say in two or three words—either that one did not believe the enterprise would succeed, or that one was hastening to a more cherished project.

The marvel that struck me most of all was that of our muscular strength. Astonished by the enormous burdens that some of the workers I encountered were maneuvering with ease, I carried out a few experiments, timidly and tremulously at first. Gradually, however, I was emboldened by an increasing pride. I had no difficulty displacing a weight twenty times greater than that of my body. I even succeeded in lifting a pebble that surely weighed thirty times as much as me. I soon ceased that final effort, which exhausted me and might have been dangerous.

At that moment, the left side of my mind was subjected to an aggression of my human thought. It succeeded in rising up to consciousness, standing up proudly, for a second. But I loaded that presumptuous man with a weight proportional to the one I had just lifted. I said to him: "You weigh seventy kilos; here's twenty quintals on your shoulders." Because I loaded it slightly to the rear, he did not fold up like a compressed spring; he fell backwards, a feeble insect carried away by the fall of a rock.

An ant came over to me. Her antennae brushed mine. In an affectionate reproach, which, by a bold use of analogy, I shall risk calling a smiling reproach, she said to me: "Hey, idler, come and help us. We've discovered an astonishing prey, but difficult to capture."

I followed her hastily and this is the spectacle that I soon beheld:

An enormous earthworm had half-emerged from its hole. A hundred workers were holding it with a crazy and futile ardor, like humans trying to uproot an old oak tree with their bare hands. It was writhing desperately, and the obstinate hangers-on were exhausting themselves without making any further progress.

I stopped, gazing at the great absurd effort, and said to my companion: "There's nothing to be done."

"You're mistaken," she replied. "They're certainly not doing much good, but come with me; we're going to unearth the monster's root."

We began clearing a space around the mulish prey. Comrades saw what we were doing, understood and came to help us. Little by little, the majority of the workers joined us, while thirty remained attached to the earthworm, preventing it from retreating.

Our mandibles and feet work vigorously. Grain by grain, the soil is excavated; the small cylindrical hole broadens out into a funnel and a few more millimeters of the body of our prey are invaded.

Oh, the rude, long task! When we began, the sun was in the middle of the sky. Now it is setting, and the work is not finished. I feel weary, impatient, enervated—but none of my friends is discouraged, none thinks of taking a moment's rest. The work has to be completed in one go, under penalty of being futile; that great interest prevents them from thinking about fatigue. I am ashamed of my lesser valor, and my feet and my mandibles, dolorous by virtue of repeating the same action too often, continue their earthmoving labor mechanically.

Finally, the whole of the monster is disengaged! It only remains to transport the enormous captive. A numerous company is harnessed to the fore and tugs; another is at the rear, shoving; a few direct the mid-section of the burden. I am part of another band, one of the scouts clearing the route, removing small obstacles. At intervals I look back to see the colossal and harmonious work; I devote myself to calculations; I think about humans carrying a sausage a hundred meters long and ten meters in diameter.

All went well; the porters were relieved several times, and the caravan advanced, slowly but regularly. A thicket of grass was encountered that was too long but would have taken an interminable time to go around. The march through that forest became extremely difficult. On contact with every leaf and stem the worm writhed. A time came when all its sinuosities were engaged with inextricable undergrowth.

Then, it being impossible to continue the transportation, there was a long hesitation. The ants hardly ever resigned themselves to abandoning an enterprise, and their perseverance was obstinate for a long time before renouncing the means initially employed. When a few proposed cutting the worm in two, there was proud resistance. Twenty times, before deciding, they harnessed themselves once again to the overly long, soft and supple burden; twenty times experiment demonstrated the futility of that effort against the hostile forest. The night was dark when we resigned ourselves, humiliated, to dividing the sheaf of difficulties that we could not break.

When the two fractions of our prey were stored in a subterranean bunker, I shared a meal with my friends for which we had been waiting for a long time. Soon, sleep came to repair the fatigues and soothe the emotions of that happy and difficult day.

VIII

I am slightly astonished by my boldness in the use of analogy in the previous chapter. I ought to have offered apologies to the readers twenty times over for such involuntary and inevitable lies. When I try to express with human words the thoughts and expressions of an ant, it is very evident that my translations are shameful treasons.

To translate exactly into one human language that which is thought and said in another human language is almost always impossible, and yet, how close is the relationship between words expressed by the same organs and thoughts created by similar brains! On the other hand, between brains as different as that of a human and that of an ant, between languages as various as articulate speech and the movement of antennae, there can only be hostility and mutual incomprehension.

Undoubtedly, although deprived on the indispensable organs, humans have vague rudiments of antennal language. They have the handshake and they have the kiss—but those touches, to synthetic, are merely a sentimental language, profound and imprecise. True antennal language, by contrast, with the twenty-four sections that can be touches, is a marvelous instrument of analysis. For as long as I had two thought-processes, I was able, in spite of the continuous absence of concordance, to attempt the crazy comparison, and the language of the ant appeared to me to be more precise than your own speech.

The other day, I was curious enough to ask my friend Caressan, a skilled mathematician, how many combinations that twenty-four active sections could produce in touching the twenty-four passive sections. After long calculations he replied with a cabalistic or mathematical formula mingling Greek and Latin letters. To give an idea of the crushing result, he had determined the value of one of those letters, the least, and affirmed that that one alone represented a figure followed by seventeen zeroes. Think, on the other hand, about the variety of possible touches, raps or strokes; consider that the meaning differs according to whether two contacts are successive or simultaneous, interior or exterior, according to whether the friction is longitudinal or vertical; consider the various degrees of force and duration—and you will begin to suspect the incomparable richness of antennal language.

The points that an ant wants to specify are rarely details that a man would have noticed, however. The same object or the same event, analyzed in accordance with the two systems, would produce two objects or events a thousand times more different than your most reasonable wakefulness and your craziest dream. The elements attained by one method are of an entirely different order than those attained by the other. Now, every object is a microcosm that reflects the entire universe;

every event, in terms of its causes and effects, contains the history of worlds.

Try to nourish a sheep on meat and a lion on grass, but do not try to introduce the thought of an ant into a human mind. The comparisons I make in order to describe that impossibility are anemic; the sheep can see your meat and the lion can see your grass, but the ant's thought has no more existence for your mind than ultra-violet rays have for your eye.

I know that all too well. I've suffered so often those two thoughts contending with one another without understanding, in perpetual and irreparable mutual incomprehension: here screeching like the deaf, there gesticulating as if in delirium. I've suffered from the impossibility of comparison, the impossibility of creating a unity. The rumbling course of a locomotive and St. Theresa's prayer resemble one another more than the two ear-splitting thoughts that I carried within me.

Let us suppose, however—alas, I believe that I can't imagine what I'm going to say, that I'm only going to write empty, meaningless words—that God could bring together a human thought and an ant thought. Even then, he could not reproduce the miracle of that unity in expression; he could not find a movement of antennae that would correspond exactly to a spoken word.

Sign language, as long as it remains natural and spontaneous, is, in its poverty, that which most resembles the rich antennal language. Try to translate into words the meaning of a natural gesture. Several versions are possible, none of which is absolute.

The language of deaf-mutes is easily translatable into words because it is an artifice that gesticulates words decomposed into letters. It consists of words written in the air, as a missive is speech inscribed on paper. It is, in spite of its initial appearance, vocal analysis. It is not a spontaneous translation of thought.

The spontaneous translation of thought is the necessary expression of that thought. It is the thought itself, the thought in motion. Antennal thought can never be expressed by vocal thought, nor vocal thought by antennal thought. The words of ants that I have reported or will report must be considered as crude symbols of a reality that we cannot express.

The ant that had taken me to uproot the earthworm was to become my best friend. On returning to the nest after the difficult task in which she had shown so much intelligence, decisiveness and activity, I felt drawn toward that superior being and timidly, I asked her name. You will understand that I cannot reproduce the true name, that I can no longer say it to myself, or think it, now that I no longer have any antennae. It is not, however, entirely at hazard that I shall name her. I will give her the name that, within the ant-hill, my human thought had already given her. I will call her Aristotle.

Why?

Aristotle is a human word, a vocal thought, that the antennal image of my friend routinely evoked in the double and monstrous entity that was my mind. Her true name was composed of four touches. The last, fainter than the others, had a vague analogy with our mute syllables. The great wisdom of my friend, her conversation rich in facts, always penetrating and always—yes, the word stammers a distant verity—generalizing, incited me to think of the great philosopher. Every time that my ant thought, my right-side thought, quivered to the three forceful touches and one slight touch, my left-side thought pronounced the three sonorous syllables and the mute syllable: Aristotle.[10] And immediately, I saw myself as a man, because that name, applied to an ant, gave me a desire to laugh, and an ant cannot laugh.

In recounting my first encounter with the ant Aristotle, I said that she addressed an affectionate, as if "smiling," reproach to me. I ought to explain that the analogy here is with a fraternal smile.

Humans have several languages. There is speech, analytical language, practical language, the language of thought—

[10] In French, Aristote [Aristotle] has no intrusive consonant to make the fourth syllable more emphatic.

the speech that expresses everything of which there is a precise consciousness. And they have smiles, attitudes, gestures, handshakes and kisses; they have the movements and touches that express spontaneities and mysteries, the profound and the unanalyzable.

Ants also have, in addition to the antennal and analytical language dictated by thought, means of stammering the soul. The antennae can, like our speech, say: "I love you." But sympathies can be expressed in a less voluntary and more spontaneous fashion by soft stridulations, compared with which the songs of crickets and cicadas are drum-rolls so gross and deafening that ants cannot understand them. It was by means of a note in that spoken, or rather musical, language that Aristotle corrected the aspect of her reproach that might have been wounding, transforming by means of a "smile" the slightly rude blows of her antennae into caresses.

IX

The unhealthy fatigue of the eleventh of April, caused by miraculous and maddening phenomena, had been followed by a long and agitated sleep, vertiginously borne away on the clouds of nightmare, which opened and dissolved continually, letting me fall. The healthy fatigue of the twelfth, the natural fatigue of joy and toil, procured me a good, dreamless sleep that rendered me all my strength in a matter of hours. I woke up cheerful, with a pleasure devoid of fever and astonishment.

In the upper gallery, I encountered Aristotle, who had woken up first. She wished me an amicable good day. I was sad as I returned her antennal caress, because my human thought had woken up too, and was demanding a joy unknown to worker ants, the satisfaction of a need that they do not have: an amour. The vile human crushing me was stamping on the left side of my mind, and saying: "Aristotle isn't a female and you're no longer a male. You're two neutered individuals ignorant of the kiss, ignorant of familial tenderness. What is commencing for you—indigent beings!—is one of those poor particular amities in which two impotent nuns try to console one another, and of which the community is stupid enough to be jealous."

I wanted to expel the insolent individual. I replied to him: "Dare you assert, as a rare joy, the infamous need that leads you, in exchange for a few miserable physical pleasures, so much mental turmoil!" And, in a prideful revolt, my antennae gesticulated the names of senses that he did not have, and those of powerful joys that he would never experience.

He did not understand and repeated to me, obstinately deaf: "You've lost amour! You've lost amour!" He even permitted himself a gross historic insult, and, after having scornfully called me a "eunuch" several times, he finally shouted, just as I succeeded in knocking him down and tipping him out of my consciousness: "Abélard!"

And, as I might express my sadness today by means of a wry smile, or a defeated gesture of falling arms, or one of those shakes of the head that seem to deny all happiness, my pain drew a long stridulation from me, anguished and anguishing, like the interminable and heart-rending sob of a violin.

Aristotle looked at me, astonished, and made consolatory music, as tender and low as a lullaby to begin with, but which gradually rose to encouragement. Her antennae asked: "What's wrong? No ant ever produced such a plaintive chord."

She seemed to me to be so friendly, so maternal that I wanted to confide in her. I emitted melodies of confidence and abandon. It was as if, had I been human, I had lain my overly heavy head upon a sure heart.

And my antennae tried to tell her: "Two days ago I was a man. A supernatural power has turned me into an ant. But my old thought suddenly returned, as cruel as an enemy driven back from a city, who, without every wearying, opens new breaches as recommences the attack. Just now, it made me regret that I'm not a male and that you, whom I love, are not a female. Tell me, my darling, why have we no wings in order to go and make love in the sky?"

She looked at me as one looks at a lunatic. With a music of amazement and pity that might perhaps be translatable as your head-shaking, she said: "You dreamed that you were a man. I've had many nightmares in my life, but I've never had a nightmare as nasty as that."

After a pause, her antennae went on: "But what else did you say? I've seen many ants that have respired or drunk intoxicants, but no drunken antennae were ever as drunk as yours?" She added: "Pull yourself together. Be ashamed of the inferior desires that have followed your bad dream. Wake up again entirely."

She became very amicable again, and, as a human sister might have kissed my saddened face several times, she stridulated a few indulgent and tender notes that seemed to say: *I forgive you your momentary folly and love you as much as I did before your absurd remarks.*

I learned in that cruel and tender moment that any profound confidence is impossible and that, if one does not want to be thought insane by those one loves and to see the greatest affections degenerate into pity, it is necessary not to try to stammer the reality of one's soul.

X

Among all sad moments, I will relate the saddest one I know. One has just obtained from a beloved and loving being all that the other can give. The two have tried by the most powerful means—by means of speech and silence, kisses and gazes, if they are human—to come together, to penetrate one another mutually, to amalgamate, no longer to be more than one. At first they have tasted intense joys, seemingly limitless voluptuousness—but those ambitions have tried to go further, ever further, in joy—and now they have surpassed the region of joy.

They do not weep, as in vulgar pain. Their damned eyes are dry and hot. They smile and they proclaim that they are enjoying life to the full, but they know full well that they are in the worst of hells, the superior hell that their crown of light has made of paradise, and from which they cannot descend again. And in the dolorous nucleus of that sun whose rays create joy a little further away, the two wretched souls think:

Yes, our lips can do nothing but kiss for a long, long time; but the second will come, inevitably, when they must separate. Perhaps our hands can remain united for hours on end; but fatigue or the urgency of a banal gesture of life will ultimately disconnect them. We can repeat words of love, and although one uses them to pronounce so many banalities and superficialities, we will find them sweet for a time; but a bigger wave in the tempest of love will lift us too far above the expressible, and we will become irritated with the impotence of words.

We can gaze into our eyes at the reflections of our thoughts, we can sense that they are traveling at the same pace along the same path; but now the eyes of one of us, with the blink of an eye or the shift of the gaze, have slipped away. We're at a crossroads of the dream. Now, each of us is going a different way, astray, lost, and we know that we're lying in affirming our accord and that our progress is continuing, inseparably.

Oh, all our efforts to unite have just collided, bruisingly, with the metaphysical wall that makes two beings two, so that two minds, like two atoms, are impenetrable to one another. Oh, the distance is still as infinite, since it is inexhaustible, as if we were a thousand leagues apart and were enemies. Our flesh and being believe they can penetrated by one another by way of love, but the same indivisible point in space cannot be occupied by two bodies at the same time, nor the same indivisible point in thought by two minds, nor the same indivisible point of dream and aspiration by two souls.

Oh, nearness is only apparent and victories over mental distance lead to veritable anguish. There is the anguish of feeling eternally, irreparably two. The affirmation of our unity was hyperbole, benevolent in the journey, but devoid of virtue now that we have reached the end, and we know, alas. Let us weep for our mystical dreams. I shall not be you; you shall not be me. It is in vain that we have found one another...

That anguish, humans, is given to you by amorous love alone, because, in you, amorous love is the great effort against invincible isolation, the effort that offers you the best promise of victory, and which, from a higher hope, sees you fall more heavily into inevitable deception. The coarse and material being that I had been before the metamorphosis was ignorant of such falls, because he had had no wings with which to fly toward the impossible. Now, sketches of suffering had refined me, had prepared me for Suffering, and I aspired to love. Love was forbidden to me. But one makes of dolors what one can, and amity is able to create an irrespirable storm around those who cannot climb any higher.

The great dolor, which is still our solitude, was observed to be irreparable. Aristotle, in reproaching me for my desires as well as my abasement, had isolated me within my uncomprehended and incomprehensible self, making an abrupt island of myself, where no one could land.

We have been created by a Defoe who never softens; to none of the Robinson Crusoes that we call our souls does he accord a Friday.

In those profound hours, one experiences the need to descend recklessly and sit down in the depths of one's suffering, as if bitterly satisfied to sense it so complete, so far from the coarser aspects of life. True dolors admit no distractions, wanting to devour themselves.

I quit my friend under some pretext or other. I retired into an inferior gallery, to the most solitary point, and, motionless, I gave myself entirely to my torture, turning it over and over within me, in order to enjoy all the harm it could do me.

How long did my "mortal sadness" last? I don't know. Metaphysical anguish suppresses time.

The first remedy that soothes the surface of that distress slightly is pride: the pride of having penetrated into suffering inaccessible to the vulgar. Then, as time goes by, the too-oft-repeated thought loses its precision: the indecisive daggers no longer strike, and they fold up, phantoms floating and dispersing, to form a mist of melancholy. And those times have their gently cradling tenderness.

One ends up yielding, with an indifferent indulgence, to the necessity of reentering into life. And little by little—oh, to be sure, one does not care about the results; when one carries such a mixture of the inferno and paradise within one, how can one still be touched by earthly concerns?—the superficiality of our soul becomes interested, curious and smiling, before the spectacle.

My grim melancholy kept me away from the work going on outside. For a long time I wandered at random, without knowing why, irrationally resuming my aimless march. By degrees, however, my inaction became observant, and I ended up studying, sometimes with my eyes, almost always with my antennae's senses of smell and touch, the labyrinth that was my new homeland.

XI

The subterranean city was composed of twenty-two layers of streets. One entered it via a crater formed by parcels of superimposed earth, with a slippery and crumbling wall, an excellent rampart against attacks from outside, but fragile and always being repaired. It also protected us against the rain, and the ephemeral lakes and sudden torrents that it creates. It gave access through a long, narrow oblique tunnel that was very easy to defend.

In times of danger, that gallery was guarded by a soldier, one of the twelve-millimeter giants. Its enormous cylindrical and abruptly-truncated head served as a door. It as a cork exactly fitted to the bottleneck. Stings and teeth slid off its smooth hardness. Sometimes, at a favorable moment, the cork moved, advancing toward the crater; formidable mandibles opened and entered into the head of an attacker. Then, rapidly, without even trying to part its jaws again, the soldier retreated slightly to its original post, and, confronted by its obstinate presence, the immobility of death formed a first rampart. But I have no intention of describing in this chapter the scenes of war that I only witnessed later.

The crater and the long oblique entrance allowed little light to reach the galleries and chambers of the first level, even less light to reach the following levels, and none at all to reach the inferior strata. The highly-developed sense of smell told us where we were. We also possessed the precious sense of direction that also seems to constitute part of the treasure of certain birds. My sense of direction, perfect so long as I was marching with empty mandibles, was sometimes in default when I was burdened. I cannot discover the cause of that lacuna; it would require a precise analysis of a sense that I no longer have, the detail of which I can no longer conceive, which I can only define from without, by its general results.

My astonished sense of smell warned me of any error; in grave cases I set down my burden momentarily and immediately knew. More often than not, the rapid touch of my antennae sufficed, telling me exactly where I was and the recent changes brought to the construction.

The twenty-two levels resembled one another. The horizontal galleries were superimposed for almost their entire extent. They were not straight, however. At certain points, most frequently at the extremities, their curves drew closer together, ending up meeting one another. A small number of vertical galleries, irregularly disposed but almost all toward the center of the nest, also connected them. At intervals, pillars sustained the vaults, and long walls sometimes partitioned the galleries. Elsewhere, by contrast, streets broadened into immense plazas, or corridors opened into vast clambers. These vast chambers often occupied the point of intersection of galleries. Their vaults were supported, according to circumstance, by columns, thin walls or robust buttresses. Sometimes, too, a corridor scarcely commenced stopped dead, closing in a dead end, only being a retreat.

The inferior levels were unoccupied. I walked there is absolute solitude. One might have thought them an abandoned city. The ants only retreated there in very hot weather, or if the upper levels of the nest were flooded. Ordinarily, they kept to the first level. During the day, in any case, when the weather was fine, almost everyone was outside. Hunting, harvesting, gleaning, working on roads, or even playing and enjoying life.

Some store-rooms were full of wheat. My sense of smell and my antennae told me that those granaries differed from places of habitation. Their walls were smoother, more cemented, better defended against the damp that spoiled our provisions. Sometimes I encountered a few workers there who were shoring up the walls, for the absolute dryness that permits grains to be kept intact, without the commencement of germination, is only conserved by continual care and constantly-renewed labor.

In one grain store, a slight commencement of germination wounded my sense of smell. My instinct got the upper hand over my sadness and the convexity of my mandibles struck the walls valiantly until everything seemed to me to be in order.

Some grains, however, were in a damp store-house that was to remain damp; that wheat was destined to be eaten shortly. The ants' jaws, powerful and ingenious tools, were not adapted for chewing. We could not nourish ourselves on entirely solid aliments, and much preferred lapping and licking fluids. Before serving as our meal, therefore, the wheat had to be subjected to a commencement of germination, softened, and its starch converted into a delicious fluid sugar.

XII

I went back up toward the light. On the upper level I had a curious encounter. An enormous ant, even larger than the most gigantic of our soldiers, was walking slowly, closely followed by a few workers. I drew nearer to the monster and considered her attentively. The small head had a certain elegance and bore a charming adornment at the rear, near the slender attachment of the neck, like three pearls marking by their limpidity the apices of a triangle. The thorax, however, too round in its form, was dishonored between the first two pairs of legs by the incomprehensible poverty of four stumps. The abdomen, excessively stout, rendered her gait heavy and awkward, dragging along ignobly and grotesquely.

Fully occupied in examining these strange features, I did not notice that I had crossed the path of my friend Aristotle, but she saw me and stopped me.

Her antennae said to me, while her entire body rose up with disgust: "That's what you wanted me to be!"

At that moment, the monster, without pausing in her progress, let fall behind her an elongated ovoid, almost opaque in its whiteness—I am obliged at the moment to name the human color that corresponds to the hue, nameless for you, that my ant's eyes beheld. A worker rushed forward, collected the whitish ovoid preciously, and disappeared with the bizarre treasure

"What's that?" I asked Aristotle.

She looked at me in astonishment, and said: "Your nightmares have killed your memory, then! That monster is a female, and the treasure that one of our sisters has carried away is an egg." Indulgently, she went on: "You're so young, in any case, and so stupid that your ignorance ought not to astonish me." Her antennae softened, as if into a maternal tone.

"I don't know why I always loved you," Aristotle continued. "I don't know why I gave you particular care and felt a particular emotion when you were a poor shivering larva, and when you were a sleeping nymph traversing the kind of death that precedes complete birth. On the day when you were delivered from your cocoon, I was the one who drew you gently from the prison in which your limbs could not unfurl. It was me who tore away the last satiny pellicle that wrapped you. It was me who, with delicate care, disengaged your antennae and freed your palps and feet. It was me who rid your abdomen of its envelope and discovered the rare beauty of your petiole. I taught you the touches that declare our thoughts and the sounds that our emotions sing. I watched over your first hesitant steps and educated your antennae to sense the pathways and labyrinths of our city."

Her antennae paused momentarily, as if crushed by a burden of emotions. Then they resumed, caressant at first but soon sad and almost indignant.

"You certainly remember those last cares, my dear child. Until then, I had always seen you grateful, and worthy of my love—but I don't know what madness has got into you. I had the astonishment, yesterday, of feeling you ask my name. This morning, you were initially affectionate and charming, but then, by virtue of I don't know what aberration, your love was deformed into a vile sensual desire that, fortunately, can have no realization. I've seen in you the ignoble delirium of a male, and you, a noble wingless worker, have been touched by the folly of wings."

Her maternal grumbling went on for a long time. I sensed how much I had wounded that precious friend. I made my apologies. I confessed that since two days ago, in fact, I no longer recognized myself. A shock, a malady, or something beyond my experience, had troubled me with absurd aspirations and had taken away my memory. I had difficulty getting my bearings in the nest. My sisters were all unknown to my changed eyes and I had even forgotten my name.

Aristotle looked at me pityingly. Her antennae beat the air in a monologue, but my eyes followed their movements and I eventually contrived to read what they were saying, which was: "This is a very strange illness."

"I appeal to your affection," I begged. "The strange illness has enveloped my mind with a blinding and paralyzing cocoon like the one in which my nymphal body slept. Free my mind, Aristotle, from the cocoon of ignorance which, by some mystery I don't understand, has re-formed, and teach me to love for a second time."

The gesture of her antennae was an exclamation. "I've seen many extraordinary things," they said, "but the illness that has struck you is more extraordinary than anything else

I've seen." Then, with an abrupt resurgence of suspicion, they quivered the words: "You're not making fun of me?"

I made a dolorous stridulation, which proved my entire good faith. At the same time, my antennae reproached: "Oh, my darling...!"

She was convinced.

"Come," she said.

She led me to a chamber where numerous white ovoids similar to the one that the female had let fall and the workers had picked up were arranged in order. The eggs near the entrance were the same size as the one I had seen laid; as we went further, we found larger ones, and the most elongated dimension was almost double that of the first ones. In addition, the upper extremity was curled back, and all of their mass had become transparent. Workers were caring for the eggs; their tongues were turning them over and over, continually molding them. Aristotle explained to me that they were nourishing them. The liquids spread over the thin shell were nutrient sugars, which penetrated the interior and permitted the egg to develop.

While we were there, the largest egg opened and a minuscule faltering larva appeared.

Aristotle picked up that new being and transported it. I followed her. We arrived in a neighboring chamber, where numerous larvae were asleep, all very tiny.

Aristotle had me examine those blind creatures. Devoid of feet, palps and antennae: poor formless soft masses. They were composed of twelve rings. The head, narrower than the body, was inclined forwards. Some were shivering, almost motionless, seemingly asleep and suffering nightmares. Others were raising themselves up, and the opening that preceded their head, which was the mouth, was agitating anxiously, visibly seeking something. The almost transparent larvae were sated; the turbulent larvae were hungry.

The workers understood the quivering of the mouths and the somersaults of their impotent masses. They ran, mandibles apart, disgorging droplets of nutritious liquid directly into the hungry mouths. One might have thought that they were birds giving the beak to their young—except that here, the nourishment was not collected outside and brought in brutally; it emerged as an exquisite syrup from the crop of the nurse.

Another chamber contained slightly larger larvae, somewhat coarser in their design, a third larvae larger still and better formed. My human mind thought of children distributed according to age in the different classes of a school. Finally, one last chamber contained larvae almost as large as us, and formed the transition with the dormitories of the nymphs.

The nymphs slept motionlessly. A few had prudently spun a sheath and were sleeping their temporary death in a sumptuous silken coffin. The majority had only thin clothing, awaiting life rolled in the spare poverty of a shroud. Their form was already ours, but the feet, palps and antennae were folded up, applied to the body, and the entire being as a soft white. A few workers with rare, slow and silent movements, like sisters of charity in a hospital, were keeping watch on their immobility.

One of them came back from visiting a cocoon. She stroked two or three friends with her antennae and they came to the cocoon.

They examined it at length, doubtless searching for the thinnest point. Tearing away a few silken threads, they thinned it out further. The fabric was tangled and difficult to break. They pinched and twisted. A little hole was pierced; then another, close by, and then a third.

Aristotle explained their operations to me, and what I shall call, for want of a better word, the tone of her antennae was approving.

Suddenly, however, she said: "The bunglers!"

At that moment, they were trying to enlarge the openings by tearing the silk as if trying to rip a piece of cloth. For some time my friend watched them exhausting themselves in futile efforts with an ironic gaze, but when she saw that they were not giving up on the absurd procedure she took pity on the prisoner and ran to help in her deliverance.

She passed one of her teeth through one of the holes and started slicing through the threads, unhurriedly and methodically, one after another. Two workers were enlarging the other two holes simultaneously. The operation took a long time; it was a marvel of patience.

The three holes joined up into a single tear, opening a passage through which the head and feet of the imprisoned individual could be seen, but it would have been dangerous to disengage it through that narrow orifice, the edges of which might have scratched or even torn her soft tegument. Aristotle, till making use of her teeth like a pair of scissors, drew a long fissure from that circle. Another worker proceeded with a parallel slash.

Now Aristotle, standing upright, supported on her abdomen, for which her four braced hind legs seemed to design firm buttresses, used her two front feet to lift up the cover that she had just rendered mobile. And several ants, with slow maternal precautions, drew the newly awakened individual from the coffin.

When she was free, she could not even try to walk, and her trembling nearly caused her to fall over. A shroud still enveloped her, separating her from life and voluntary movement. It was a thin satiny membrane. That paralyzing wrapping was unrolled delicately. First of all, the antennae were unsheathed, stretched out and worked back and forth. The same was done for the palps. Then they release the feet and they were extended, one after the other, placed vertically on the ground. Finally, with the triumphant movements that accompany the successful conclusion of any difficult task, the head, thorax, petiole and abdomen were disengaged. And with a tottering tread, as if drunk, the resuscitated ant walked.

A worker gave her a drop drawn from her crop. The child swallowed it delightedly.

Meanwhile, Aristotle ran to a neighboring chamber, brought back a grain of wheat, ready to eat, all sugar and syrup, placed it in front of the new ant and, marking out the movements as in a lesson, set about licking it. The pupil gazed without seeing in a poorly awakened stupor. Aristotle gently parted the young ant's mandibles, succeeded in making it put out her tongue and passing it over the exquisite meal. And with awkward and joyful gestures, the child licked. A false movement caused the grain to roll out of range. She continued, stupidly, to lick the void in front of her, but Aristotle swiftly brought the food back beneath the maladroit tongue.

We drew away. Aristotle, at my request, explained the future of the worker I had just seen born. In ten days, nothing would distinguish her from one of us. She would go joyfully to free work, outside or inside, according to her whim, according to the temperature and according to whether her intelligence sensed one of the community's needs more keenly than another.

For two or three days, however, an older ant would attend to her education, informing her about the city and the work, teaching her to clean herself and making her antennae repeat the most necessary words. Then, although she would only feel half her strength, as if convalescent from the effort of being born, she would live inside, helping to nourish the larvae and maintaining the neatness if the habitation and the dryness of the granaries.

While my knowledgeable friend was explaining these things to me, we encountered once again the poor heavy progress of the female. I interrogated Aristotle about the beautiful triangle of pearls that ornamented the monster's head and the four short stumps that dishonored her thorax.

The pearls were ocelli, small simple eyes similar to human eyes, of little use to an insect that possesses admirable faceted eyes. The stumps were the attachments of ancient detached wings: the ugly objects were the stigmata of vanished beauty.

Aristotle revealed these facts rapidly, without any reflection. She hastened her steps to get away from the monster and, as you might make a gesture of scorn, her stridulant organs emitted a disdainful note.

XIII

I had encountered Aristotle in the environs of the nest. We had exchanged a brief affectionate harmony, like a rapid greeting, and she had continued walking.

I had stopped and was pensive. My ant thought, frustrated by human habits, could not resolve a problem that was, in fact, very simple.

I had no ears but I could hear. Where, then, was my organ of hearing?

I produced stridulations, listened to them carefully, and asked myself with what I was listening. I could not find an answer.

I applied myself to proceeding methodically, by a kind of analysis. I placed my antennae close to my organs of stridulation and then drew them away; there was no change in the intensity of the sound. I even applied them against the vibrations as one applies an ear to a watch, suddenly magnifying the tick-tock. The sound did not increase when touched.

I repeated those experiments with my palps, with no result. I approached my head to the sound and drew it away alternately. Nothing had changed. The organ of hearing was not in my head!

At that observation my human prejudices were stirred, alarming my ant mind. I stood there stupidly, my mandibles parted like the open lips and jaws of an imbecile, no longer even trying to understand.

Fortunately, Aristotle came back in my direction. I ran to her and asked the question that was troubling me. She played an ironic music and, taking one of my anterior feet, placed it on the stridulant roughness. The harmony became enormous, deafening me and shaking my whole body.

My friend released my foot and drew away without further explanation. On the left side of my mind the man reared up, gigantic in astonishment, arms raised toward the sky. And he said, stupidly: "Come on! My tibias are ears now!"

But I did not have time to devote to his kind of wonderment.

A nauseating odor commenced, drawing nearer, more and more sickening and increasingly unbearable—and I saw ants fleeing toward the nest. Others were sheltering in hollows or under tufts of grass, as if they feared being squashed by some heavy falling object.

"What's wrong?" I asked one of the fugitives.

Her antennae quivered, trembling fearfully, as she stammered an astonished question: "Can't you feel it?"

She passed on, rapid and unsteady, propelled by a wind of terror—and I saw the inexplicable panic continue. The contagion gripped me; it was with a mysterious fear that I interrogated a shivering worker hiding in a nearby hole.

Huddling close to me she said: "Stay here, under cover. A human is coming, who will crush you if you go out."

In fact, she did not say "a human," for I'm being scrupulous to the point of minimum inexactitude in my translation of the untranslatable. For the ants of my nest, human beings were not designated by a single word. They rarely mentioned the vast animals, redoubtable and despicable, and named them by a bizarre definition that I shall try to express. The coward had said to me, approximately: *a mountain walking on two feet, that will crush you.*

I did not stay under cover. I had just perceived the bipedal mountain, and a strange nostalgia attracted me toward it. My human thought had dispelled my ant thought, without a contest, almost without suffering. Memories possessed me, so intense that they suppressed the present, that the moment was conquered by my past.

By what miracle had objects resumed their proportions of old—the proportions they had had when I was a man? My ant eyes were seeing with the habits of a man, and were truly not the eyes of an ant. It was a former self that was judging and comparing, and such is the irresistible power of the mind that in spite of the unintended opposition of organs, I was a human looking at another human.

And I said to myself, in that extraordinary waking dream: *He's smaller than me. He seems weak. With a shove, I could make him stagger back several paces, and then fall.*

He was almost upon me. I shouted: "Hey, friend, change direction!"

But I had no organs of speech; my shout remained internal. With a commencement of horror, I thought: *It's a nightmare. I know that one can't cry out.*

I remember that I also said to myself: *Am I going to go on dreaming that I'm an ant?* And it seemed to me that, by making a great effort, I might wake up.

Too late. He already had his foot raised above mine. Oh, I didn't expect the bumpkin to tread on my toes. So much the worse for the clumsy oaf: one shove, the staggering retreat, the fall!

My arms were raised in hostile fashion. Then, in a flash, I saw that my arms, so tiny and so frail, were the feet of an ant. Again, I thought: *Feet that are ears—what crazy dream, beginning again!*

I thought that a nervous laugh was about to wake me up.

But dark, sinister night suddenly fell. The nightmare crushed me, mortally. Then I no longer felt anything. The mountain that walked on two feet had walked over me.

XIV

How long did my unconsciousness last? I don't know.

The first memory that I can recover is a lugubrious one. I hear mortally sad harmonies, and my eyes begin to see as if through a mist.

One of our giant soldiers is holding me, delicately, in its formidable mandibles. She's carrying me. Where? Why?

Her march is slow, as if oppressed.

As my position changes, I think I glimpse a crowd of workers behind her, marching with the same sadness. It's doubtless them who are stridulating the funeral melodies.

Everything is tormenting me. In my impotent terror, it seems to me that the horrible promenade is interminable, perhaps lasting for hours.

The first precise thought that I can formulate is: *If I were still a man, I'd think that I were witnessing my own burial!*

The strange, slow, sad promenade comes to a halt. The music takes on a more forceful gravity, an unknown dolorous profundity. The drama must be approaching its denouement.

I'm still paralyzed, my limbs splayed, as if in pieces, devoid of articulations, with no communication between them or with my vague will. But my eyes can see normally, and my intelligence becomes as clear and penetrating as ever.

I observe—with what anguish!

I am placed on the ground, lying on my back. I'm at the extremity of a rank of motionless ants, also lying on their backs—surely dead. Behind me are other rows of cadavers.

I sense that my companions are about to leave. The ceremony is over. I shall remain there, abandoned, at the end of that rigid line, the only living being in the cemetery, motionless by virtue of weakness and agony, in the midst of the immobility of the dead.

Thoughts crowd within me, innumerably, marching like a rapid procession in two rows—for each one is double: human thought to the left, ant thought to the right.

What I am trying to describe lasted, probably, a few seconds; but for me to repeat the little that remains expressible in what I saw and thought clearly in those few seconds, I would require hours.

My ant thoughts are about ants; my human thoughts are about women. The antennae of the ants are addressed to my right antenna; the women speak, leaning over, to the tibia of my left front leg. The majority of my thoughts are sad; some console me; but the colors of the former and the latter strike me with equal astonishment.

When the thought is consolatory, the woman who leans toward me is a tall blonde dressed in white, while the ant, the other interpreter of the same joy, is the ordinary black of the ants of my species, and resembles Aristotle.

The women who bend down to tell me sad thoughts are short stiff brunettes clad in black with long mourning veils. The ants marching in a parallel line, whose antennae quiver similar despair in a very different language, are whitened, the color of nymphs: nymphs that are walking without having cast off their shrouds.

I am expressing what I mean very poorly, and I can't put it any better—but the reader will remember, I hope, that my white wasn't white, and that my black wasn't your black. I only want to express this singularity, which astonished me greatly: the color in which my joyful thoughts were dressed for my human mind was the same in which my ant imagination clothed my sadness; and that which formed on the left the lugubrious livery of my chagrins, became on the right the cheerful costume of my joys.

I can recall the sight—truly black and white now—of the double procession. I can't succeed in sensing all that the ants were saying to my antenna, or even hearing all that the women were whispering or shouting at my tibia.

In abstract language, this is all that I can rethink:

Anguish, black to the left and white to the right, said to me: "You're going to be buried alive!" And a long procession of widows and nymphs detailed that horror for me.

Consolation replied: "Ants don't bury their companions. They leave the cadavers to desiccate in the open air. Look. Nothing would prevent your neighbor, were she to be resuscitated, from righting herself, getting to her feet and returning to the nest." White-clad blondes chased away the flock of mourning brunettes, and delightfully black ants bundled the horrible white nymphs into a hole. And joyful blondes and cheerful and active ants each spoke to my two thoughts about the tender convalescent joys of my imminent resurrection.

But the oppressive widows and the spectral nymphs came back, victorious again. They replied to the vanished opponents that the paralysis of the coffin and the stifling of the earth would be quite superfluous in killing me. Abandonment far from the nest and lack of care would be amply sufficient. And they multiplied ironic and cruel questions:

"Where will your body find the strength to turn over?"

"Where will your feet find the energy to carry you?"

"Will your eyes and your discouraged antennae alone be able to guide you?"

And the black phantoms on the left, like the white specters to the left, concluded: "You're doomed! Doomed!"

Because I've tried to express what was singular about my thoughts, I can't move you with my emotion. I regret that slightly. Panics as terrible have been experienced. Other individuals have been abandoned to a lingering death without hope—but none, I assume, has known the black-and-white dualism of my joys, and the black-and-white dualism of my despair.

I have said that those two worlds of thought were juxtaposed within me for a few seconds, at the most. In fact, the white- and black-clad women, and the ants and nymphs, all repeated to me, some in various joyful and lugubrious tones and others by means of sinister or luminous movements: "This is the irreparable moment. An effort might save you. Make a movement that your friends will perceive, or sing your despair, and they'll understand that you're alive."

It seems to me that I succeeded in quivering—oh, so feebly!—the six dolors that were my legs; it seems to me that I succeeded in stridulating a vague: "Help!"

A few ants came closer. I tried to repeat my cry, and also to renew the appeal of my legs, but the novelty of hope was more paralyzing than despair had been a little while before. Perhaps, also, a single effort was sufficient to exhaust me for several hours.

I was dying of weakness and waiting. My half-extinct will was entirely expended in conserving me a residue of sentiment and enabling me to see a little of what was happening around me.

Now the thoughts were no longer the rapid flow inclined whispers. They were all grouped around me, upright women and elongated ants. Their motionless weight, it seemed, was making me descend into a bottomless abyss, without any shock, without any pain other than the horror of sliding into the inevitable. Real beings and things slowly and implacably became distant, and it was as if I were leaning over the edge of an abyss as I saw the rigid cadavers and the grass stirred by the wind. From the midst of a dream that would doubtless never end, I also watched my friends agitating up above, on the strange plateau of a life that I had known.

They were coming and going in a restricted space, as if imprisoned, quivering in an insurmountable hesitation; and their antennae were clashing argumentatively, with persuasive elegance, or abrupt, dolorous and, I dare say, mocking negations.

Finally, one of the ants came toward me. I was inundated by hope, for I recognized my beloved Aristotle.

Her anterior feet lifted up my antennae, which were trailing miserably. It seemed that I rose up again from the depths to the open air.

The dear benefactress said to me: "If you're still alive, show signs of life."

I sensed the agonizing fall begin again, and my entire being was gripped by one idea: *I'm too weak!*

The frightful anguish gave me antennae a tremor of impotence, which was divined by Aristotle's affection rather than perceived by her sense-organs.

She seized me by the thorax and, followed by the others, who were emitting joyful music, she brought me back to the nest.

She deposited me in a chamber on the second level, in lovely obscurity, and cared for me with a devotion that was never in default.

Her care was simple. She slid into my mouth exquisite nutritive drops drawn from her crop. Her tongue licked my wounds, which did not take long to close. With delicate precautions, he folded and unfolded my legs, my palps and my antennae, gradually rendering them the faculty of movement. When I took my first steps, her mandibles, surrounding my thorax like arms, were half-carrying me.

How many times and with that emotion, we recalled that epoch! How many times I repeated the details of my funeral, Aristotle's sadness, her slowness in quitting me, the impossibility she felt of going away, because something told her that I was still alive! Her comrades were tempted to mock when she came back to me to demand that the dead should manifest evidence of life.

She never wearied of recalling her tremor of anguish and hope at the moment she interrogated my immobility, begging it to shiver the frisson of salvation, and the overflow of her joy when she sensed, or rather divined, the feeble quiver that returned a friend to her.

She asked me about my impressions of being transported to the cemetery and my impressions of the abandonment. I told her everything that had stirred my right-side mind, all the ants and all the nymphs that had encouraged or oppressed my antenna, and that the consolers resembled her, with her grave and gentle beauty.

The movement of my antennae avoided, however, clarifying the excessively strange cinematography produced by my left-side mind. I left Aristotle ignorant of the white- and black-clad women who spoke to my tibia. I knew only too well that my human side would have seemed insane to her, and would have saddened her needlessly. But I was very sad myself and being unable to tell everything to the most loved and loving of beings.

Sometimes that sadness was augmented, like one burden placed atop another, by the sentiment that our love was incomplete, but I hid my "folly of wings" with tremulous care.

I often went, in those melancholy hours, to visit the cemetery where my body had nearly perished in abandonment. Not far from the anthill—five strides for a human—there was a clearing surrounded by long grass. A strawberry plant stood in the middle, quivering alone over the rows of cadavers lying on their backs, drying out in a definitive immobility.

XV

One day, as I came out of the cemetery, I was in a melancholy mood. I was saddened by the thought that I would become a man again, with impoverished senses and such a firm mind.

For some time, my human thought, almost disappeared, had permitted me to be happy. When a memory reached me of previous years it was vague and phantasmal, as if reduced to vapor by the passage from one life into another. I no longer accepted it as recent, or even as materially true.

I welcomed as poetry the strange symbolic dream that spoke of the multiplicity of existences and the astonishing stations of our soul in various bodies. But had my soul really inhabited that ponderous abode with five poor windows? I doubted it. Would it return to it one day? The supposition appeared to me to be absurd as it was anguishing.

Why then, today, was the dualism of my thought tearing me, brutal and undeniable? Why was I seeing myself again as a child, on my mother's knees? Why was the remembrance of soft caresses rising slowly within me? And why were violent memories of kisses that agitated and cried out—abrupt memories of kisses that wanted to bite and did bite—also assailing me?

They were ancient, those impetuous kisses. I had received them in the little room I which I had lived as a student. For years, I had forgotten them, the feelings put to sleep by the calm and quotidian regularity of conjugal caresses. Today, in my life of a neutered ant, they were troubling, nostalgic appeals to the opposite bounds of the horizon, splitting me apart between regrets of yesterday and hopes of tomorrow.

I would have liked to become a man again immediately, to return to that universe, so poverty-stricken, but in which one could experience amour, savor kisses sweeter than wheat-sugar.

And I was anxious about the dangers to which my interior dualism was exposing me. What if, the other day, when the bumpkin had crushed me, I had died completely? What if my ant body were now drying out among the little black cadavers, under the sad forest of the strawberry plant? Would Octave Péditant, the man who had known violent kisses and calm caresses, and who hoped to find them again, also be dead?

I shivered all over at that idea: perhaps I had already received the last caresses I was going to receive; perhaps my stupidity would kill me before the end of my year and I would only have in my agony the cold consolations of Aristotle, a neuter like me and proud, in her cause, of being a neuter, as scornful of unknown amour as a chaste nun.

Sometimes, I cursed the enchantress who had not guaranteed that I would get through the year, perhaps wanting, by letting me die as an ant, to release herself from her other commitments. And, summoned by a long despair, the man loomed up haggardly in my left-side mind. The open mouth cried: "Render me amour! Render me amour!"

It also said: "Keep your million!" But the phrase, commenced loudly and clearly, faded away into an indistinct stutter, for the bodies of women appeared, marvels for sale, and I would dearly have liked to be able to pay for them.

The joys of spectacles and the joys of science made my left-side mind laugh. I was no longer unaware that human science studies the universe with very poor eyes and knew that, in becoming a man again, I would be going to a discolored poverty of spectacle. But sexual intercourse, once almost scorned, now appeared to me as an absolute, as the only thing truly good and truly desirable.

I was wandering alone, in my reverie. Suddenly, I stopped, astonished. Two enormous masses, two of the terrible mountains that walked on two feet, were there in front of me, lying on the grass side by side. As soon as the sudden spectacle was noticed, even before its nature was recognized, and doubtless aiding that recognition considerably, the ignoble odor that had already advertised human presences to me twice before, invaded me. Perhaps I had not sensed it sooner because I was only thinking as a human and the perversion of the thought had extended to my senses.

It seemed that the two beings were embracing, and my human soul wept.

The proportions and colors were too different for me to be able to distinguish the most familiar individuals of my previous life. A jealous hypothesis pinched my nerves: *Perhaps it's my wife with my replacement!*

At the risk of getting myself crushed, I climbed up one denuded part of the nearer mountain, and furiously sank my sting into it twice.[11] The gaping double wound received all my provision of venom. The mountain was agitated by powerful somersaults, and a hectic flight carried me away.

When I thought that I was out of danger I reproached myself for my temerity. Life became precious to me, as a conclusive anguish, since it would one day return sexual intercourse to me.

My aimless wandering had taken me into unfamiliar territory. I was getting ready to return to the nest when I perceived, fortunately some distance away, a troop of ants that were strangers. Their odor, brought to me by the wind, although less infamous than the human infection, nevertheless had something hostile about it. It irritated and alarmed my sense of smell, as the uniform of an enemy regiment irritates and alarms the sight of an isolated soldier. I maneuvered as

---

[11] Very few kinds of ants have stings, and they do not include *Aphaenogaster* species. Ant bites tend to communicate a stinging sensation, produced by formic acid—the same substance that is secreted by stinging nettles—thus leading to a common misconception, but it is odd to find the mistake here, if it is a mistake and not merely an aspect of rendering the depicted ant species a composite.

best I could to avoid them: to avoid death, to avoid the definitive loss of amour.

That had, however, been altered to the proximity of prey,
doubtless y my odor. They pursued me doggedly, in a merci-
less hunt. I ran, breathlessly, sensing that I was doomed, hearing the ever more rapid footfalls of the horrible behind me,
drawing ever closer.

Finally, I perceived the reassuring rampart of my ant-hill
in the distance. The menacing noise behind me died away. The
malevolent band had stopped. In front of me, close by, raising
all joys in my double soul, was a troop of my compatriots.

Courage came to me, transforming my fear into wrath. I
stopped and turned round. My attitude was one of defiance.

My friends had seen, sensed and understood. They drew
nearer. Slowly, in several straight lines, the enemy troop advanced.

I experienced a bellicose shiver. I thought that a great
battle was about to be engaged. I wanted to be the first to
strike.

The two troops have stopped, some distance away from
one another. An enemy, detached from the malevolent band,
advances toward me. We are watched from both sides. There
is not to be a battle, but probably a single combat.

My ardor evaporates at the idea that I alone will be in
peril. I feel less brave for isolated combat than for an intoxicating melee.

Besides which, my enemy is bigger than me. I think it
unjust that my friends are leaving me to that unequal struggle.
Ought they not to replace me with a soldier of the same size as
the enemy soldier?

For a second, I abandon myself and resign myself to
death. It seems that my abdomen would be glad to be trans-
pierced by the sting, or that my head, crushed between the
mandibles, would experience some unknown voluptuousness.
But the idea of those strange joys becomes characteristically
human. The mandibles crushing my head are arms embracing
me in order to kiss me—and my courage wakes up, with the

desire to live. I shall fight against the false murderous embrace in order to preserve myself for the true embrace, the embrace that relaxes smiling and recommences more tenderly.

Mandibles open, antennae pulled back, we advance with a wary slowness Suddenly, she launches herself toward me, in a terrible bound, and falling terribly, tries to seize me by the thorax. I have bounded at the same time, and our mandibles collide, clashing like four swords in the hands of two violent combatants.

She recoils in order to gather herself before launching forward again. I do not leave her time for a new attack. I hurl myself upon her impetuously. My mandibles, vigorous assailants, prompt to feint and prompt to attack, clash with her rapid mandibles, always parrying.

I hear the encouraging and intoxicating music of my friends behind me. From the other side come savage harmonies that also intoxicate me, but with irritation.

Anger agitates us both. Our mandibles strike furiously, without being able to reach the body. We advance, we rear up; our anterior feet grip one another, inextricably knotted. We grip, we fall, horribly entangled.

I'm underneath, alas! All over for my eyes, rich and poor spectacles alike! All over for my body, bitter kisses and tender caresses! Emotions of love, my soul will never find you again! The sting is about to pierce me; the venom is about to penetrate me with its burn. After the thrashing of agony, here comes the grim immobility that even orgasm will never again cause to quiver.

Sexual intercourse! I still want to experience sexual intercourse. What nervous force shocks me, lifts me up, redeems me! I am almost behind my enemy.

As rapid as sudden death, I leap astride her and my mandibles sink into her back. Already I am drunk on victory. The long joy I experience grips me, alive and climbing, with a regular movement, to the neck of the one who nearly killed me, who nearly separated me forever from feminine caresses! With the delirious joy that would lift me up in striking a rival in love, I squeeze the miserable neck between my fangs. Already the nerve-cord is severed; already all resistance is dead.

Triumph is not sufficient for me. I need to feel shudders of agony between my joyful limbs; I continue to squeeze. My mandibles come together within the bloody flesh, make contact. The severed head falls in front of me.

My friends run forward with proud songs. The hostile troop disappears, as rapid and furtive as shame.

XVI

After the single combat, we lived in anxiety. Aristotle often said to me: "Don't go far. There's surely an ant-hill too close to us. Beware of being taken by surprise by the enemy."

"*The enemy* is any stranger?" I asked.

My dear Aristotle looked at me with an almost sad astonishment, and the rapid movement of her antennae had something exclamatory about it that I can only translate very poorly: "Of course!"

On an afternoon of overwhelming heat, I was dragging a seed when I saw an ant from the other nest near our crater. She was running back and forth madly, hiding behind blades of grass. Several of our troops were in the vicinity and the poor stray had little chance of getting away without being spotted, without her noxious odor attracting our brave patriots, as the odor of carrion attracts crows.

My right-side mind impelled me to hurl myself upon the evil-smelling stranger and tear her apart—or, rather, to summon my friends and drink the powerful intoxication of the cruel pleasure communally. My left-side mind, however, reminded me of the danger run the other day, confusing my past peril with the present peril, in a compassionate sympathy. The human in me triumphed over the ant. That day, I was human, in the best sense of the word.

I ran to the unfortunate individual. She stopped, awaiting death with resignation. My antennae said to her: "Come; I'll guide you."

Her antennae replied with frictions that were devoid of meaning for me.

Every homeland, I thought, *has its own dialect, which puts a frontier of incomprehensibility between it and other homelands.*

Fortunately, my human thought remembered that only analytical language differs. The people of different nations can say what is indispensable synthetically, by means of gestures, and a kiss has the same significance for all human societies. Doubtless an affectionate music ought to awaken the same glad emotions in all ants. I stridulated pity.

A harmony of amazement replied to me. I marched forward; she did not follow me.

I came back and took the poor thing in my mandibles. She looked at me as a condemned man looks at his executioner, and her body, with a long tremor, gave voice involuntarily to resigned music.

I carried her gently and carefully. The quavering stridulation became astonished again.

The critical moment arrived. I stopped, embarrassed. To the right was the cemetery, where many of ours had gone to transport the cadaver of an aged worker. To the left was a large band of workers, among whom was Aristotle.

· If we got passed those two dangers, my protégée was very nearly safe, but they were so close that they were strangling hope in an exceedingly narrow space.

I thought about getting away from both of them, by going around one or the other. It would take so long, would be bristling with unknowns, surprises and perils! And then again, when one is burdened and one cannot go straight ahead, it's difficult to steer!

I could only see one wise course: to slip between the two bands, staying further away from the cemetery, the more dangerous. If we bumped into the other troop, Aristotle would understand my reasons, or at least yield to my pleas, and no one would rebel against her authority.

The inertia, indifference and suspicious astonishment of my protégée rendered progress slow and difficult. I stopped for a moment, trembling. I looked in the direction of Aristotle. Half raised up on her hind legs, antennae extended toward us, she seemed to be sniffing the stranger's odor. The wind was carrying the infection directly toward her. Soon, I saw her marching toward us, followed by al her companions.

Flight was impossible. My heavy tread would have been very rapidly overtaken.

I set down my burden, and ran to Aristotle. My antennae told the truth and explained that an isolated stranger was not a danger, that there was no reason in this instance to kill.

Aristotle did not reply to me. It was to another that her antennae addressed themselves. The news was rapidly spread, and the band moved off. Their gait was not our ordinary march. A joyful and angry disorder pushed my companions together, throwing them forward, one against another. They ran, overtaking one another and colliding with one another, as if lifted up by an intoxicated swell. Everyone wanted to get there first, to be one of those who surrounded the prey, who would play with her and enjoy her agony, who would have the sensual pleasure of seeing her suffer and die, of making her suffer and die.

More rapid than their bloodthirsty folly, I threw myself in front of Aristotle, who was in the lead. I begged her to have pity.

I said to her: "Perhaps she's a good ant, as gentle, as loving and as intelligent as you. Think how grief-stricken I would be if anyone killed you without any reason, my beloved, as you want to kill this one, who is perhaps loved as well."

She shoved me away, saying: "She's a stranger!"

I returned to the charge: "Perhaps she's the Aristotle of the other nest."

She replied: "She's a stranger!"

I persisted: "In what respect is a stranger any less of an ant than you? Does she not have antennae, like you, always quivering with a thousand joys, a thousand dolors, a thousand thoughts? Does she not have, like you, faceted eyes, sponges to drink in all the surrounding beauty?"

A brutal shove interrupted my Shakespearean enumeration, and the antennae repeated: "She's a stranger!"

But I clung on to my friend desperately, and I continued: "She is, like you or me, a treasure of life. Why destroy her?"

I had slowed down Aristotle's progress. Several others were now ahead of her. She perceived that, and her anger became violent.

"Imbecile! You're holding me back!"

With an irresistible thrust, she freed herself, and her surge carried her once again into the forefront of the ignoble, rapid and joyful rush. At the same time, she gave voice to a hateful music. And the hatred she was singing was addressed, at that moment, to me, who loved her, as well as to the stranger.

They arrived. There was an indescribable scrambling and swarming. They climbed over one another. They all wanted their share of the communion of hatred. All of them were pulling, pinching, clawing at a piece of a leg, a piece of antenna or a fragment of a palp. The patient ant was tortured in every limb by that horde, drunk on cruelty. Aristotle grasped the head in her mandibles. And with slow, repeated, joyful thrusts like strange sadistic kisses, they nibbled, making the voluptuousness last.

I don't know what joyous need was answered in me by the spectacle of all that joy, the spectacle of that pain. I was sickened, and yet, a powerful instinct picked me up, urged me toward the infamous enjoyment, spurred me toward the prey too, in order to torture her.

I did not yield to it, but the fear of yielding to it threw me into flight.

I went into the ant-hill. While going through a chamber of larvae, I said to a nurse: "Why take so much trouble to create life, when other comrades are amusing themselves producing death?"

She replied: "I understood each successive movement of your antennae, but now that they've paused, I no longer understand."

I passed on, with a haughty music. I plunged into the blackest subterrains, and, alone and motionless, began to think.

My head was aching terribly. The human was insolently triumphant there, as if no human had ever killed another because of a difference of race.

Aristotle found me there. She was evidently looking for me. Softly, she asked me: "Did I hurt you just now?"

"Yes. You've killed my affection for you."

"I don't understand. Doubtless I shoved you a little violently, but I didn't have time to calculate and moderate my gesture; you were about to rob me of my part in the great joy."

"It's not because you shoved me that I'm angry with you. It's because you killed without reason."

She was astonished. "Without reason? A stranger!"

"I'm scornful of you for having killed one of your own kind."

"One of my own kind? A stranger!"

"Hazard might have determined that you were born in her nest, or that she was born here."

"You're definitely an inventor of unknown insanities." She added: Your words are absurdity itself. One is of the homeland that one is, and a stranger is always a stranger."

And she drew away, making bellicose music. It sounded horrible to me.

In my left-side mind, strange musical memories were stirring. The man, so proud a little while before of his *humanity*, rose up aggressively now, fists raised, eyes bulging, body straining forward, precipitating himself in his entirety against an imaginary enemy. He was no longer a man; he was a Frenchman howling the *Marseillaise*.

XVII

Perhaps I ought relate all the warrior memories of my life as an ant in one go. They are too painful. I suffer too much in thinking that the enrichment of communal joys, that the more opulent beauty of the universe renders us no less cruel, and that the mind can drink so deep of joy without repudiating the ugly absurdity of killing similar instruments of joy.

I prefer to rest for a moment and rediscover my peaceful memories. Besides which, it seems to me that I would thus be following chronological order, and that a long time passed between the two alerts that I have just related and the real wars that we had to sustain.

It seems to me...but I cannot be certain. For my human mind, my entire life as an ant is a monotonous sea of forgetfulness beneath a starless night. Vague islands of dream float therein, almost unreachable, agitated, as if put to flight by my very attempts to approach them. I don't know how Apollo did it when he fixed floating Delos; personally, I'm a clumsy fixer of islands. I can only succeed in reaching their fleeting instability by ruses that are doubtless too gauche, which always break them into pieces and disperse them in the black infinity. And it's difficult for me to ascribe a precise date to the rare debris that I seize.

I'm almost certain, however, that the great battles began toward the end of the harvest.

Preparations are made a long time in advance for that collection, which has to nourish us all year round. The plants that furnish our grains are scarcely in flower when we are already preoccupied with facilitating the future labor. First we visit the terrains of last year's crop and search all around the nest within a radius of fifty or sixty meters to see whether new fields have been created.

As soon as the various domains to be harvested are well known, they are linked once again to the ant-hill by new roads, and the old roads that have deteriorated in winter are repaired.

The roads are clearly traced, almost always in a straight line. They are established by hollowing out the soil slightly and rising the causeways of all clutter: pebbles, leaves and other obstacles that might impede progress. The blades of grass, scythed down to ground level by our mandibles, are gnawed away again every time they reappear. The width of the road varies according to the importance of the field to which it leads and the difficulties clearing. I know narrow four-centimeter paths and magnificent twenty-centimeter highways.

In dangerous places, everywhere that attacks by enemy ants or carnivorous insects are to be feared, the passages are protected. Most frequently, the road is insinuated between two slippery and crumbling ramparts, constructed on the same model as the crater that defends our nest. Sometimes it is covered by a masonry vault; sometimes it plunges downwards, transformed into a subterranean gallery.

This is the procedure used for the construction of vaults. Parallel walls are erected on either side of the road. As soon as the walls attain a sufficient height, the materials added to them are inclined toward the center. Work on both walls takes place simultaneously and at several points, each ant working freely, wherever it pleases, whenever it pleases, and as it pleases.

The work advances unevenly, depending on the number and ardor of the workers employed at various locations. Soon, the two walls join up in a few places. The first keystones of the vault form points of support for the adjunction of new parcels of mortar.

Other arches are successively welded. The viaduct finally nears its definitive form; only a few holes remain, dispersed in the upper part. These openings are carefully filled in and the fabrication is complete.

The construction of covered roads is rare. The slippery embankments and the walls that crumble under the weight of the aggressor, dragging them to their ruin, almost always seem sufficient. In very dangerous passages the tunnel is adopted for preference, for one can excavate in all weathers, while the elevation of a vault is only possible in fine drizzle and the few hours of humidity that follow showers. We do not have any other means, in fact, of giving any coherence to the earth employed and are obliged to wait upon the good will of nature.

Walls and vaults are formed uniquely of moist earth. Every worker brings a little ball that she has just shaped with the tips of her mandibles. She applies it to the chosen place; then she divides it and pushes it with her teeth, applying herself to filling in the smallest inequalities in the construction. Her antennae palpate every particle of earth, making sure that it is well disposed; then the anterior feet press down lightly to make it firm.

To begin with, these parcels of molded earth are only held in place by juxtaposition, but when rain comes they will be bound together more tightly, to equalize, polish and varnish, after a fashion, the convexity of the vault and the exterior of the walls. The last roughness of the masonry disappears, and one will no longer see anything but a unified layer of earth that the heat of the sun will consolidate.

Sometimes, excessively violent rain destroys the work commenced, even carrying away completed vaults that have not had time to dry, and the work has to be done again. It is always done; ants persevere to the point of stubbornness. They are obstinate not only in obtaining the definitive result but also in producing it by the means originally chosen. Even when initially favorable circumstances turn against us completely. I have never seen the enterprise of a vault abandoned in order to hollow out a tunnel. We recommence ten or twenty times over work destroyed by evil circumstances. An obstinate anger impels us and sustains us. We do not give in. It's necessary that the hostility of circumstances ends up being vanquished.

Although vaulted roads are rare, all roads are bordered, at intervals, by light constructions. They are shelters prepared for workers and the provisions they carry. Those hostelries of a sort serve many useful purposes. When one is tired, one can rest there in security. If one is pursued by an enemy one can take refuge there, hidden and undiscoverable, or at least protected by the walls, able to wait for help or to recover strength in order to flee when the besieger is momentarily inattentive. One can shelter there in a storm. One can spent the night there if one is late returning. In the evening one can store the produce of a collection or a hunt there, for which one can come back the following day and transport at leisure.

When the roads are in good condition, well cleared, the old tunnels unblocked, the old vaults and refuges repaired, everything is ready for the great labor. One looks forward to it with a kind of anxious joy, spending long hours examining the degree of maturity of the grains.

Finally, the happy and tiring epoch of the harvest arrives. To work! To work!

As soon as dawn breaks, the paths, roads and highways are black with ants. In one direction, the rapid column of those who, free in their movements, are running to work. In the other, slower but just as joyful, the laden ants return.

Idly, only awakened by the hubbub of the first departures, I have emerged from the nest slowly, pensively and slightly sad, but the activity of my friends makes me ashamed and excites me. I too run to the crop, my bad mood cradled and put to sleep by the laborious rhythm.

The grains stew the soil, ripe and sonorous. Their elongated form and the grooves that sink into them on one side cause my human thought to smile. Do they not resemble, the precious grains, the crusty bread that was put on my table? While my mandibles pick up a seed, sustain it, carry it to the nest, I sense to my left a man of the people marching along happily, his good loaf under his arm. In a few hours, that easy work is finished; there is nothing more to glean in the small field. Let's run to another domain.

The seeds have not yet fallen here. It's necessary to collect them from the summits of the stems. But they're fully ripe, ready to escape: an easy and amusing collection. I've climbed up to an ear. My feet open the envelope of each grain and my mandibles grip it and cause it to fall. At the foot of the tall stem, shaken by the wind, where I'm working enjoyably, my friends pick up the good things I dislodge and carry them to the house where I shall rediscover my fortifying share. My left-side thought smiles again; I'm a child in a fruit tree throwing juicy fruits down to my friends. Or I'm a little girl threading pearls and smiling.

The pleasant work lasts for several days. Then gleaning and picking no longer offer anything. It's necessary to move on to the veritable crop. The grains, less ripe, adhere forcefully to their envelope. Each one takes a long time to detach. It would be better to do that work inside, tranquilly, at leisure, on ears that lie still. Here we detach the whole ear: demanding work.

I gnaw the stem at the point where the ear commences. Meanwhile, Aristotle has taken a corner of the ear between her mandibles, pincers that do not let go, and, bracing herself with her hind legs, she twists and turns. She is very skilful, but her feet sometimes encounter me, clutching me instead of riveting themselves to the plant, lifting me up, tearing me away from my dangerous position and half-suspending me over a vertiginous drop. Finally, the stem breaks; the useful heavy summit falls. Aristotle only just has time to get out of the way, and I too am nearly drawn into the fall.

Aides run up. We carry away our conquest, an enormous ear whose beards, here and there, sway like overly stiff antennae.

Fatigued by that great effort, we don't come back to the field. We join the workers inside. We pluck our ear, disengaging each grain from its envelope, as we would disengage a young ant from its nymphal cocoon. We store those riches in a dry chamber. We carry the ear, emptied of all its treasures, outside the nest. We abandon it on one of the rubbish-heaps that form a ring of artificial hills around our city.

XVIII

There was a region in the neighborhood of our nest into which we rarely ventured. The soil there was infertile and the excessively uneven rendered all work difficult. Among other obstacles, it presented two steep drops three feet from the crater, something like two steps of twenty centimeters each—twenty centimeters being thirty times my height.

In my hours of human sadness, I sometimes strolled in that direction, like a melancholy poet wandering on a deserted heath.

One day, I discovered an excellent and enormous item of prey there. It was a large caterpillar. It was black to the eyes I had then, and would doubtless have been yellow or green to the eyes I have today.

I could not think of raking possession of that formidable prey alone. I ran to summon friends. We found the powerful prey again at the very foot of those steps of a giant staircase—the two steps that were as high for us as steps of fifty or sixty meters would be for you.

We threw ourselves on to the caterpillar, overwhelming it with our thrusts. It writhed desperately, almost immediately rendered incapable of flight. Our mandibles and stings sank voluptuously into its soft flesh. The convulsions of its agony soon ceased.

The difficulty lay in transporting the cumbersome prey to the top of the gigantic stairs. For hours, working continuously in shifts, we tried to raise it up the colossal height of the first cliff. The caterpillar always fell back at the very start of the ascent, dragging the crowd clinging to its body with it.

As a fault of my human reflection, I was often the first to become discouraged. When Aristotle was there, I was ashamed of my laxity and dared not abandon work, but that day, Aristotle was absent. I drew away with a gesture of indifference, while my comrades obstinately recommenced the futile and bruising ascent interminably, which the same fall renewed indefinitely.

I encountered my friend. I thought that the unfortunate expedition would be the object of many conversations, and that the problem might have been explained to her, with the question: "Can you, who are so ingenious, not find a means?"

Since she was unaware of what was going on, I hastened to tell her myself.

She went to see, mingled with the workers, on one occasion she was one of those who climbed up, heavily laden, and fell back with the rolling burden.

Just once! I was astonished to see her going away after that unique attempt. For some time she stood at a distance, motionless, her antennae extended toward the insurmountable obstacle, in an attitude of profound meditation. I stayed by her side without troubling her reflections.

Suddenly, her antennae quivered, resolutely. Then she stridulated a triumphant song and made movements of strange joy, movements of hectic joy that invoked in my left-side mind the image of Archimedes running through the streets of Syracuse shouting: "Eureka! Eureka!"

"Come with me," she said to me. "Let's take a few comrades with us. You'll see."

Several of us are following Aristotle; she heads toward the ant-hill, goes into it, and marches through the corridors for a long time without our being able to guess where she is going.

She finally stops, antennae taut, turned toward herself. Then her antennae touch the walls, slowly and at length, as if searching for something. Her palps and her anterior feet are studying too.

She turns toward me and says: "Follow me, and widen out the hole I'm going to dig."

I transmit the order, and without any other explanation, we start work on a task whose objective we cannot foresee. Such is our confidence in Aristotle's intelligence that we toil for hours without asking what we're doing, what we want or where we're going.

Suddenly, the light blinds us. The thick wall is pierced. We come out behind Aristotle, and sing our admiration and joy. For we have emerged at the foot of the obstacle, invincible to force and skill, vanquished by our friend's genius. We harness ourselves triumphantly to our prey, drag it into the subterrains, and blithely close the useless opening behind us.

XIX

For a long time, no disquieting incident occurred. We had forgotten the anxieties caused by the mob that had pursued me, renewed by the inexplicable presence of the stranger. We were working, tranquil and happy, entirely focused on the fruitful crops.

"It's an excellent year," Aristotle often repeated to me."

We were not taking any precautions. No sentinels guarded our doors. It happened that we were all outside, occupied in collecting grains.

One day, we were harvesting our last field, the largest and the most fertile, but the most distant. All day we had been working without returning to the nest. We deposited the harvest in the various refuges distributed along the interminable road. In our haste, we even encumbered tunnels and vaulted roads. That evening, on returning, we brought back what we could, which was the most poorly sheltered. The transportation of the rest would take place later.

That day, a storm was threatening and it was necessary to save as much grain as possible before the rain, or perhaps hail, descended on suddenly muddy ground. Besides which, the field, which was vast, with unknown limits, does not belong to us alone. Humans devastated it every year. It appeared that they were already in the process of stripping it in the distance, on the other side. Even if the storm fell further away, it was urgent to harvest all that we could, for the following day, the frightful mountains that walk on two feet would probably be where we were, and with a few strokes of the immense artificial mandibles with which they elongate their immense limbs, they would fell all the ears.

Evening arrived, too soon for our taste. It was almost pitch dark when we decided to return. I went with Aristotle well to the fore. A mediocre grain burdened me lightly. As soon as we arrived at the top of a slope we stopped to rest and stood up to admire the powerful spectacle of that peaceful army on the march, bearing riches in the friendly moonbeams, which were becoming rarer, increasingly devoured by hostile clouds.

One last time, at the summit of the crater, we had proudly contemplated the army on the march when, just as we were about to descend, Aristotle, her antennae suddenly anxious, recommended me to be prudent.

"What's wrong?" I asked.

"I don't know, exactly—but something alarming is happening."

After a pause, she added: "Don't move. Don't make a sound."

Her antennae extended toward the nest, she breathed in. "Can't you smell anything?" she asked.

"It smells bad."

Furiously, her antennae said: "It smells of strangers!"

At the same moment, ants emerged from our nest in numbers, threw themselves upon us, knocked us over and sent us tumbling down outside the crater. We were obliged to flee precipitately. I'm proud that I didn't abandon my burden as I fled.

The enemy pursued us. We ran as far as our first companions. We explained to them what had happened. During our absence the city had been invaded, not even by strangers of our own species but by ignobly designed ants with small bestial heads and inelegant petioles.

Since my anamorphosis I've tried to identify that day's enemies. Confused comparisons between my vision then and my examination today whisper to me that those ants must have belonged to the species that formicologists call *Formica rufibarbis*.[12]

---

[12] The species in question is described in Lubbock's *Ants, Bees and Wasps*, but Ryner's characterization is not derived

Were we, noble *Aphoenogaster barbaras* going to allow ourselves to be expropriated by vile *rufibarbis*?

The plants were quivering, however, at the approach of the storm. In the blackening sky, one side was a dazzling white, in the midst of which a flash of lightening vibrated.

Fury gripped us, and the fear of still being outside shortly, beneath the stinging rain, amid the wildly waving grass, in the hectic confusion of beings and things.

More ants were arriving continually, overflowing at the point where we were from the road, like a river colliding with a barrage, flooding its banks in an immense black lake. From the continual arrival of our comrades, an increasing force surged forth that drove us forward toward vengeance, toward the homeland and the security to be reconquered.

"Forward! Forward!" said all antennae.

"Forward! Forward!" repeated all attitudes.

"Forward! Forward!" sang bellicose music.

And saw once again, in my left-side mind, the violent being who had reared up once before, fists clenched, mouth wide open, bellowing the *Marseillaise*.

Aristotle and I taking the lead, the others five or six lengths behind us, we advance.

But the invaders make a sortie, launching themselves toward us. Marching rapidly, heads held high, mandibles open, they're formidable. My left-side brain remembers an enormous dog that threw itself upon me because I got too close to its pups, fur bristling and teeth menacing. I'm afraid. I look at Aristotle, who hesitates. And abruptly, a lightning-flash that half-blinds us renders the entire scene frightful, arming our enemies fantastically, and precipitates us into a hectic flight.

We flee, and in front of us, the entire troop runs, in a mad panic. We only stop when we reach the first station, the place where we sang so valiantly, a little while before: "Forward! Forward!"

---

from Lubbock, and the name, once again, is allocated as a mere matter of convenience.

And still new compatriots are arriving, laden, wanting to continue their march, obliging us to give explanations, in which, to overcome our shame and also because the lightning really did appear to all of us to be enormous, we magnify our enemies and events.

The rain starts falling, heavily. Every violent drop is an injury. Are we going to stay there're under the commencing deluge, letting ourselves be drowned by the imminent deluge, letting ourselves be crushed by the repetitive fall of the brutal drops?

We sense the futility of a new attack, at the moment when everything is our enemy. We run, in total disorder, to the foot and up the trunk of the nearest tree.

There, there are plaints and fearful lamentations; it is the absolute loss of all self-composure, of any ability to study the situation; it is the disruption of our faculties of foresight and capability.

"All is lost! All is lost!" repeat the antennae.

And music rises up of a poignant sadness.

Is this not the commencement of the death of an entire people?

Beneath the storm our tree shakes, threatening to break. It shelters us from the wind, but the rain is already traversing its impoverished foliage, falling upon us along with leaves, twigs and branches.

And here comes the fall of enormous round rocks of hail.

"Can't we find any means of saving ourselves?" I ask Aristotle.

"I'm searching," replied my friend, the genius.

"You're not despairing of finding one, are you?" I implore, tremulously.

"I never despair..." She adds: "Your words are distracting me. Let me think."

She draws away at a long, thoughtful stride. I follow her at a distance. Soon, she disappears into that frightful shivering crowd. I feel that I'm alone, in the midst of the egotism of despair.

She comes back, the valiant, the ingenious individual with a thousand resources. Her antennae say: "We're saved. Follow me."

My antennae vibrated against the neighboring antennae: "Aristotle says that we're saved. Follow me."

The order is transmitted, rapidly, throughout the crowd. Most of them come. Some have lost all valor, all hopeful strength, and stay where they are, stupidly, waiting for death or a miracle.

Oh, the difficult and dangerous march through the unknown rivers and unexpected seas hollowed out by the storm, under the contusive rain, under the murderous hail, under the flagellation of the grass and the fall of branches, groping through the night, constantly afraid, with the abrupt terror of lightning-flashes. How many of our friends have died, drowned or crushed? How many have gone astray, wandering in isolation through the immense bog of perils?

I have the anguishing impression that our number is diminishing at every step. I dare not look round to see how many we are, how many fewer we are—and I don't know where we're going, an army decimated by the minute, a vagabond army without refuge, an army continually battered without combat.

Now we're going down, in a stumbling, sliding fall, the two gigantic steps toward which we so rarely go; and at the foot of the staircase, in the sticky, clinging mud, beneath the diminishing anger of the rain but beneath the new rage of a cataract, we stop.

The glare of a lightning-flash quivers, showing me Aristotle, who is working. Her mandibles are scraping away the thin layer of earth, reopening the gallery hollowed out the other day in order to introduce the caterpillar into out treasury. I understand. A joy of deliverance and triumph lifts me up, and the music I stridulate gives our companions an uninformed but powerful hope.

We reenter the city from which we thought ourselves exiled in order to die. By means of long and prudent detours we penetrate into the lowest subterrains. The storm has chased our enemies into them. We attack them in the profound darkness, in their sleep or in the frightful starts of an awakening more paralyzing than a nightmare. For a long time, they know, the inundated crater has rendered the entrance to the ant-hill unusable, and they cannot conceive how we come to be there. Stupor delivers them to us almost immobile. A bewildered flight hurls some of them into the obscure labyrinth of night, obscured by ignorance and obscured by terror.

Illuminated by the moving torches of our memories, we pursue them, bitterly joyful, into all the retreats into which fear has dispersed them. The ant-hill is an immense trap, in which there is slaughter everywhere: in the narrow galleries, in the vast halls, in the blind alleys and at the crossroads. Strangers hide behind grains, stupidly, as if it were not dark, as if their odor of prey, already half-rotten, was not the only guide for our pitiless hunt. Other flee, incessantly, before our pursuit, which is tireless, even precipitating themselves into the flooded levels of the city, but not escaping our mandibles, to die impeded by thick mud.

An hour after our entry not a single *rufibarbis* remains.

In spite of the success that fills us with pride, we curse the abominable aggressors; many of our comrades have perished under the storm, and our poor children larvae and nymphs, to which the invaders have given no care, which they have not even brought down, have drowned up on the first level.

Several sad days are spent carrying so many cadavers to the cemetery, and putting the treasure in order—much enriched, alas, by death.

The *rufibarbis* receive no honor. They are thrown on to the rubbish heaps, in the midst of the beards of ears and the empty uselessness of the husks of grain.

XX

The great labor of the harvest was finished. We were in a period of relative repose. After long slumbers, we went wandering in search of some prey or indulged ourselves in interminable conversations. Our toilette also took up a good deal of time. I watched Aristotle licking her thorax, her feet and her abdomen or passing her anterior feet back and forth in slow frictions over her inclined head, and I thought about the attitudes of the two cats that prowled around my human house.

We were also leisured individuals, who played together. In addition to conversation, that joy, our distractions included gymnastic amusements, racing, and especially wrestling. We placed ourselves two, three, or as many as seven or eight abreast on one of our finest and least uneven roads. A comrade stationed a little way in front of us on the embankment suddenly straightened up, magnified even further by raising her antennae like a quivering double plume. Her gesture was the signal to start.

Our six feet always hastened toward the same point. The invariable goal was the crater, in the distance, which promised repose, security and gentle pleasures: the good crater, rising up toward the sky, the architecture of earth and memories, which spoke to us as the bell-tower of a village speaks to the simple man who is born, lives and dies in the same thatched cottage.

More often still, one of us approached a comrade of the same stature and nearly equal strength, and challenged her to a wrestling match. The challenger patted the head of the friends she was challenging and her antennae danced rapidly. Very rarely was the challenge spoken. The attitude, the caress of the feet and the puerile dance sufficed to indicate our desire.

The comrade's antennae repeated the joyful mime, as the arms of a human wrestler, in the polite gestures that precede the opposing efforts, render a salute to the adversary.

Then, promptly, the two joyful ants stood up on their hind legs and seized one another with their forelegs and with their mandibles—but with friendly mandibles that did not bite or inflict injury—and the peaceful combat commenced.

If one ant felt herself weakening, she disengaged with a rapid twist and a brisk slide; but came back abruptly, trying to grip the adversary in a more favorable fashion. Sometimes, for long minutes, the ants grappled, freed themselves and attacked again, were knocked down and got up again with an untiring ardor and a self-respect that would not permit either to recognize defeat.

I rarely fought. I preferred to watch, to enjoy via my two thoughts: the one that saw with the eyes I had then, and the other that remembered. For my left-side mind smiled at pleasant images: nude wrestlers in a tent, and movements that showed off the strong and supple youthfulness of their bodies, pressuring, twisting and lifting one another. As the nocturnal sky is animated by stars, spectacles received a numerous life of many curious gazes, and a long silence of expectation remained vibrant, as if taut, until unanimous applause suddenly burst forth.

XXI

The great storm that had rendered our temporary exile so murderous had also caused us a great deal of material damage. The crater and the upper levels obstructed by the deposits of the inundation, which it was necessary to clear, with difficulty, are barely worth mentioning; that was only work, and we were always ready for work. But the tempest had diminished our wealth in a fashion that was doubtless irreparable; it had flattened in a thick mud the plantains and daisies in the vicinity of the nest, and all of our livestock had perished miserably.

I have not had occasion thus far to describe our pastoral mores and indicate the considerable resources with which livestock furnished us. Certain insects secrete a clear and sugary syrup, which their anus rejects in periodic droplets. These droplets form a restorative and agreeable aliment. It appears that some ants belonging to the genus *Lasius* have no other nourishment.[13] Such a regime would have seemed insufficient to us; what we needed most of all was wheat and the flesh of insects, but that milk of sorts was much appreciated as a delicacy. It brought a welcome element of variety to our diet and, in sum, our herds represented a wealth that was by no means negligible.

The insects that furnish the aliment in question are fairly numerous. Among them, the claviger, a small blind beetle, lives inside the ant-hill. Certain species of aphid also remain underground, attached to roots. The majority, however, aphids or gall-insects, live on foliage or stems, and our pastoral wealth consisted almost entirely of the aphids of plantains and daisies. After the storm, the plants gradually recovered, but were depopulated, poor dirty prairies devoid of herds.

One day, one of our comrades arrived from a distance, running and out of breath; her antennae hung down for hours, never ceasing to chatter to someone or other. She had discovered aphids that the storm had spared because they lived in a big tree, but they belonged to a species of ants smaller than the smallest of us. The little ants had seen our friend, who had had great difficulty escaping from them.

That news was, from then on, the unique subject of conversation. There was keen regret that the aphids discovered were not free aphids, ripe for domestication. Groups set off to gaze from a distance at the large rich tree whose treasures belonged alas, to strangers.

The desire grew to take possession of those aphids. Eventually, we all begged Aristotle to organize the capture of the herd, no matter what the cost.

---

[13] *Lasius flavus*, the yellow meadow ant, occasionally "farms" aphids within subterranean nests; although it is highly unlikely that any species adopting the habit lives exclusively on honeydew, Ernest André did make that assertion. Lubbock also studied the species, employing it in some of his experiments. *Lasius flavus* sometimes lives in seemingly-amicable association with claviger beetles.

The enterprise was not easy. The aphids spend five-sixths of their life sucking the sap of plants, their trunks profoundly plunged into the leaf or the bark. To detach an aphid without breaking its trunk requires patience and precaution impossible in the confusion of battle—and the owner certainly would not allow such precious wealth to be stolen without a battle. In any case, the herds were, for the most part, enclosed in stables—by which I mean that they were protected by earthworks built on the bark of the nourishing tree, into which one could only penetrate by way of a narrow opening.

Aristotle responded to our solicitations by setting out those grave difficulties. She claimed that each stolen aphid would cost the lives of nine or ten of us; in those conditions, the expedition was pure madness.

But we did, in fact, go mad.

The great faults of ants are gluttony and anger, especially a kind of anger of pride: rage in confrontation with an obstacle that remains inertly invincible, as if mocking; irritation when beings and things do not yield to our desire, our effort, and the power of our genius and determination. An ant has a keen sentiment of her superiority and does not understand that not everything bows down before the arrogant gesture of her antennae. She is an authoritarian exasperated by resistance, an individual who deserves a great deal, thinks she deserves everything, and becomes indignant when things are refused, as an intolerable injustice—and who subjects that injustice to furious assaults until triumph or death.

We only know the three capital sins of gluttony, pride and anger—those who accuse us of avarice are very superficial slanderers; we are all generosity toward our compatriots—but our three capital sins are worth all seven of yours, poor humans whose passions are deadened by so much servitude, who mix the already-ungenerous wine of your nature with so much water of the social quagmire.

In this instance, our three follies were pushing us in the same direction, into the utmost depths of an impasse, becoming an increasingly exacerbated fever. At night, we dreamed about aphids. Our antennae were agitated by the brisk alternating movement that caresses the abdomen of the animal to demand the sugared droplet. In the morning, we woke up unhappy, indigent among our disdained wealth. We no longer encountered one another without saying: "We need aphids!"

Isolated or in bands, several of us went to try to steal a little of the milk, the thirst for which was torturing us. They all perished, victims of their covetousness.

In vain, Aristotle preached the calm scorn for wealth that one does not have, and praised the sweet taste of wheat fluidifying into sugar and the savory taste of abundant prey. We only desired when we did not have, and our increasingly exclusive greed spurred us to the worst adventures. All of us would have gone, one after another, to get ourselves killed trying to obtain a drop of milk.

Defeated by our obstinacy, Aristotle finally promised to organize the conquest. She asked for two days to make preliminary studies and begged us to renounced isolated suicidal attempts.

The delay passed, and the expedition set forth.

My friend's genius had probably never been more admirably manifest. She had spent the two days examining the habits of the proprietor ants. We knew that their nest was some distance to the right of the tree where the stables were established and deduced that the tree and the ant-hill must be connected by a broad tunnel.

Aristotle divided our army into four unequal contingents. The first, uniquely formed of gigantic soldiers, went to attack the enemies that were to the right of their ant-hill, soon drawing all defensive efforts in that direction.

Lasius ants—that was the species to which our adversaries belonged—are much weaker than *Aphoenogasters*. Furthermore, they have no military talent and their armies are ignorant of collective maneuvers. However, the population of the ant-hill that we were attacking was extremely numerous.

They precipitated themselves upon our soldiers as an innumerable horde. They clung to their legs and paralyzed their

94

movements. While ten or twelve of them held down one of our giants, another *Lasius* pierced it with its sting and injected its venom. Almost always, however, our victorious feet sent the bruised assailants flying, and our mandibles opened and closed rapidly, crushing heads, heads and more heads with repetitive gestures. Our feeble adversaries lost twenty times as many casualties as us.

Meanwhile, a troop of our soldiers surrounded the foot of the tree. A less numerous battalion introduced itself into the tunnel and several menacing ranks sealed the passage. On the completely-abandoned tree, to which the enemy could no longer send help by any route, our workers seized the aphids, detached them and carried them away. They were installed in the bark of a tree near our nest, where stables were soon built for them, at leisure.

When the entire herd had been removed, Aristotle ran to put a stop to the unnecessary combat. Our soldiers returned in good order, without being harassed.

Aristotle affirmed that if we had continued the battle, the enemy army would not have taken long to disperse and flee. It was only fighting, it seemed, to gain time. Meanwhile, the other *Lasius* had barricades their subterrains with clods of earth and, being rapid diggers, had hastily hollowed out long tunnels in order to install themselves in a new city some distance away.

That opinion seemed quite extraordinary to me. The next day, I was curious enough to go and see. I approached prudently, ready to flee, but I was traveling through a deserted area. I reached the *Lasius* nest, a simple hole at ground level unprotected by any rampart. It was hermetically sealed by a stone. My curiosity was strong and I tried to lift the stone, which was too heavy. Then, renouncing that futile effort, I dug around it and went into the frightful trap, tremulously.

The ant-hill was empty. Freshly-moved earth indicated the channels of communication hollowed out and filled in the day before. I wandered for a long time, pensively, through the dead city, which only lacked inhabitants. While my right-side thought saw our malevolent bands again, my left-side mind perceived a volcano launching lava and flames. I was looking at an abandoned ant-hill, but my memories recalled the engravings in a large book and murmured the melancholy name of Pompeii.

XXII

A human city does not only contain humans. It also encloses useful animals, agreeable animals and harmful animals: horses, dogs, cats, rats and mice. An ant-hill contains the same various kinds of populations.

Some species of blind aphids live on the roots that traverse our tunnels. Clavigers also lead a subterranean life. Both produce drops of syrup analogous to those of outdoor ants, but of a very inferior quality, nourishment for days of famine rather than succulent Epicureanism. But the former please us with their graceful movements and the latter cheer up with their clumsiness, and we tolerate them partly as useful animals and partly as pets.

Certain insects belonging to the order of staphylins are merely agreeable,[14] slightly vibrant things to caress with antennae or on which to feast the eyes, possessed of an elegance different from our elegance, or grotesque and caricaturish visions of life.

On the other hand, our nest had occupants as terrible as mice that eat human children. In the thickness of our walls,

---

[14] Most of the Staphylinid "rove beetles" that live inside ant-hills are predators feeding on eggs and larvae, using noxious chemicals to deter attacks by adult ants. Some, however, are commensals that live on the debris of the nest and help to sanitize it, and a few produce a chemical that acts as an intoxicant sufficiently addictive to cause ants to supply the beetles with food in exchange for it. The notion that some are employed as "hunters" to chase and kill *Solenopsis* thief-ants is, however, fanciful.

narrow tunnels opened, inaccessible to us, which sheltered the ogres. They were very tiny slender black ants—yellow to human eyes—which moved with lightning rapidity, evasive and slippery. Entomologists know the nightmarish monster in question by the name of *Solenopsis fugax*. Almost all of the frightful lairs that the *Solenopsis* hollowed out within the very bosom of our city opened into the chambers of larvae. Under our very eyes, the swift enemies came to tear morsels of tender flesh with a thrust of the mandibles and then flee into their unreachable lairs.

Just as you have cats, guinea-pigs and ratting dogs to pit against mice and rats, however, we have various carnivorous beetles of the staphylin order to hunt down the little ogres, which are useful allies. Those valiant individuals penetrate into the most troublesome retreats, where they lay in wait for hours, in order to engage in obscure combats. As soon as a devourer of children appears, with a single bound, as prompt as vengeance and as inevitable as justice, they seize the infamous creature and, without taking the trouble to kill it first, they eat its flesh while it thrashes about.

Other guests are accepted because, nourishing themselves on all sorts of detritus, they clean and sanitize the anthill. In winter, those sweepers do all the work; in the good season, they render the labor of our housekeepers less onerous.

I shall not describe the different insects, and will not relate any of the scenes in which I saw them play roles. I only wanted to indicate that element of variety in my life as an ant, and I remember with gratitude that in bad weather, when we were deprived of the rich spectacle of life outside, those little animals provided amusing company and furnished an excellent recourse against boredom.

XXIII

The theft of the herds that I recounted in chapter XXI must have taken place toward the end of summer. I remember that the air was very warm and that the males and females were beginning to hatch.

Since the great storm that had killed so many adults and destroyed all the children, we had been desolated by the diminution in our numbers and our power. We had adopted every means possible to repair our losses quickly. Our three females, stuffed with stimulating nourishment, were laying twice as many eggs as usual. Instead of relying uniquely on the staphylins for the battle against the ogre-ants, we posted a cordon of sentinels continuously around every chamber of eggs, larvae or nymphs. Patrols searched for the entrances of *Solenopsis* nests and blocked them, and two soldiers were stationed at each former hole.

Thanks to these extraordinary measures, the *Solenopsis* had almost disappeared, crushed between our mandibles or dying of starvation, and numerous young were beginning to cheer up the city.

Finally, the earth, penetrated by warmth, declared the imminence of the moment of fecundation. A few more days, and we would be enriched by one or two egg-laying females, who would spend their lives populating our nest. In spring, we would be more powerful than before the disaster.

With what joyful care the males and females were freed from their cocoons! It is even more delicate work than liberating workers, for the insect emerges from nymphal sleep with poor crumpled wings that it is necessary to extend without tearing the frail tissue. Those four fans with slender ribs and thin fabric, folded up without precaution by indifferent nature, rolled up with the rest of the body in the tight shroud, almost dig into the thorax and the abdomen, and the pleats of each one are mixed up absurdly with the pleats of the other three. It is necessary to separate them and draw them away from the body, to deeply them without ripping a single section of fabric or twisting or breaking a single rib.

Afterwards, it is necessary to nourish those excessively young individuals, hardly awakened from their birth—who remain awkward, useless for any practical endeavor, incapable of finding anything to eat for themselves—and to bring all aliments to their mouths. In the realm of the ants, where the majority is sterile, the sexual beings are naturally the most inept of specialists.

It is necessary to maintain a strict surveillance over the males. If the females are imbeciles until the day of the nuptial fever, the males are insane from the very first day. As soon as they can walk they set out at hazard, dispersed and lost throughout the ant-hill, emerging when the exit is in front of them, continuing their drunken march at random, ignorantly delivering themselves to all dangers, poor creatures devoid of reason and devoid of stings, ants with noble wings but mandibles deprived of strength and skill, unable to defend themselves against hunger or the smallest enemy. Fortunately, we assemble them in the same chambers, not letting them escape our care for an instant, and, even when they are taken out of the ant-hill to get a little air, they are guarded like a flock of lunatics.

I saw their weakness, their unintelligence, their lack of industry; I knew that they were destined to die, in a matter of days, as soon as they became unnecessary. Even so, I could not help admiring their sleek elegance, their pretty ocelli, and their eyes, shinier than my own, and divided into more numerous facets. I was jealous of their delicate transparent wings. For long intervals I gazed at the marvelous fabric in which each slender rib possessed a beauty that I contemplated enviously.

When Aristotle went by she said to me: "That's the brute that you would have liked to be, some time ago, when, although devoid of wings, you had the folly of wings!"

I did not make any reply, but I was afflicted more than ever by the folly of wings. More than ever, I would have liked to be one of those poor beings with a wretched life, the playthings of all the workers, who would soon die of hunger, or violently, but who would doubtless die in ecstasy, drunk on kisses.

The females appeared to me to be less beautiful, too large and too gross. Their heads did not have the firm sleekness of the male's head; the thorax, and especially the abdomen, was more massive. They too had wings, however, and they would soon return the kisses they received in the sky. That thought excited me. I spend hours prowling around those beings, heavy in the subterrain but whose flight would doubtless have a dream-like beauty.

There was one in particular whose proportions appeared to me to be almost noble, whose eyes were more sparkling, her ocelli more limpid, and her wings more tremulously gauzy. I was always in her vicinity. I fed her the most delicate nutriments, protected her against the coarseness of the workers.

Others were astonished to see my antennae caressing hers for minutes on end in animated conversation. "What are you saying to that imbecile?" I was asked.

Her conversation was, indeed, somewhat lacking. It was me who spoke almost all the time to those gauche, silly antennae incapable of precise thought or expression. But I was as happy as if a beautiful girl, almost mute with timidity, were responding to my amities with moving hand gestures, for the poor thing—whom my awkward thought named Marie because of her naivety—often stridulated grateful music to me.

On the eve of the day that would permit all those poor individuals to couple, I multiplied my attentions. I was, however, harassed by a frightful jealousy.

"What a pity I'm not a male," my antennae said to the poor maladroit antennae.

Marie wept a dolorous music, but her antennae made no reply.

"You don't regret that I'm not a male?" I enquired.

Oh, the beauty of her eyes, charged with a thousand thoughts, a thousand sentiments, and the desire to say so many things that were within her, and with the conscious inability to express any of them. Oh, the gentle tremor of her response! For this time, after a hesitation, the poor antennae, unskillful in language, tried to reply, quivering and stammering.

"I can't desire my friend's death," she babbled.

"What value can a life deprived of our kisses have?" I lamented.

"I love you, my friend," the naïve antennae mumbled.

But my antennae stood up, agitated, as if in a cry of despair. "Oh! The horror of impotent love..."

Motionless, Marie leaned on the wall, as if her feet could no longer support her, weeping harmonies for a long time.

"Tomorrow," I implored, "Fly a long way, very high, in order that I shall not see the kiss that anther will give you."

"Yes," she promised. "I'll fly very high, far from you, in order to submit to the amour that I cannot escape, and which cannot come to me from you."

Crushed between two dolors, however, I went on: "Forget my egotistical words. It's your death that I'm demanding, jealous wretch that I am! But I want you to live, I need you to live, I demand that you live. Rather stay by the ant-hill, within my sight, I beg you. As soon as you're fecundated, it's me that will kill your male. After that vengeful joy, it's me who will carry you, dear burden, into the nest. It's me who will tear away your poor ephemeral wings, in order to be sure of guarding you for life. It's me who will always nourish you and care for you, adored queen of all my thoughts and all my actions. Promise, promise to stay."

With music that was all tears, Marie promised everything I wished. She was so emotional and so proud of the implausible and dolorous love inspired in a superior being, in a neuter!

XXIV

The day of the drama has arrived. The flock of sleek little males has been taken outside into the vast plain that surrounds the nest, followed by the troop of gigantic and heavy brides. Those individuals, so docile and stupid a little while ago, are agitating now under the spur of desire, uplifted by a thirst for the azure. Their wings are trembling to take flight. It is up there, in the blue inaccessible to workers, far from those tormentors, far from the narrow and nasty homeland, far from gazes, that they want to rise for sexual intercourse: up there, in the boundless homeland of amour, in the modest sky that will hide them in the cloak of its dazzling immensity. Oh, how it lifts them up, the folly of wings!

The workers strive to calm that instinct, of which they have no comprehension. They address themselves primarily to the females. Their antennae only stir to offer well-meaning advice.

"Stay," they say, "stay in order to live, for years, as egg-layers in the service of all, to be the mothers of generations and to see your daughters multiply gladly around you. Stay, in order to be those who perpetuate the homeland.

But the females do not pay much attention to all those counseling antennae. The males are making the charming and enervating music of seduction, music that says: "Let's go, let's go, for the sake of free love and ecstatic death!"

The female stridulations reply: "Yes, let's go. Let's make love in the great sky. What does it matter what becomes of us after the divine minute?"

But the prudent antennae resume: "The males are egotists. They are equally condemned to death, whether they make love here, under our gaze, protective toward you, hostile to those parasites, or confront it in the distant and perilous unknown. You, on the contrary, are saved if you stay. Fully certain of perishing, those wretches want to drag you with them to their doom. Intercourse only seems good to them if it is mortal to you. Will you be naïve enough to listen to the ferocious egotism of the males?"

And the exquisite juices stored this morning in our crops stuff the hesitant females. We try to weigh them down with nourishment, to bind them with memories and gluttonous desires.

I am next to Marie. I lavish succulent aliments upon her, and my antennae utter promises and threats, coaxing and furious. For she too, in spite of our amity, in spite of yesterday's promises, is lifted up by the folly of wings; and the music of the males is drawing her into the azure.

"Let me go," she says to me, "and remember me without bitterness. I love you dearly, as much as one can love a neuter, but my nature and amour are stronger than our poor affection."

I persist, obstinately. My antennae, with I don't know what gauche and passionate phrases—poetic too, grazing the ineffable—quaver, as if stammering, the human thoughts that are torturing me. "You mustn't go," they affirm. And the strange tactile babble tries to explain: "The males are frightful demons. Their perfidious musical caresses want to drag you down into the hell that is inevitable for them. Stay here, in the paradise where we shall be together forever."

But Marie's wings are beating the air, about to carry her away. She replies, as if with mocking scorn: "What joy can you give me, you who are not an amorous being?"

My antennae continue to translate ridiculously subtle human thoughts in a bizarre stutter, talking about the grossness of carnal pleasures, the nobility of platonic love.

The winged being, half in flight, replies: "I no longer understand what you're saying." She adds: "It's not us who have the folly of wings; it's you who are jealous to the point of folly, because you have no wings."

"Yes, I'm jealous," I confess. "And I'll keep you here whether you like it or not."

I cling on to her. I feel myself lifted up, too light a burden. Is she going to carry me away into the sky, infernal for me, to make me watch, suspended, the kisses of her lover? Am I destined to die with them, to share the disaster without having shared the joy?

No, I don't want that. To retain her, I brutalize the one I adore and hate. My feet and mandibles clutch her back, brushing her wings, hurling her to the ground, holding her motionless.

Aristotle passes by.

"What are you doing now?" the neutered genius demands. "What's this new madness?"

103

Ashamed, I release my victim, leaving her to get up, insanely annoyed. But I feel glad, for the swarm is already far away. I can hardly see them…I can no longer see them at all. Marie's eyes, better than mine, are still following the flight, invisible to me, with a long nostalgic gaze.

But it's too late. She won't leave, won't deliver herself alone to the enemy winds. She stays, waiting. A male advances, preceded by amorous music. She forgets the others, almost forgetting the distant sky, and on the ground, with a mixture of sadness and joy, allows herself to be loved.

Two other couples are there, close by, also fecundating.

Aristotle is enthusiastic. "Three more egg-layers," she says to me. "The number of mothers has doubled! We're a fortunate ant-hill."

I don't reply to her. At that moment, my soul, all covetousness, is bitterly focused on the intercourse to which Marie is subject. As soon as the male moves away, tottering weakly, tottering with a prolonged intoxicating joy, I hurl myself upon him, and my impotent amorous mandibles, joyful and furious, crush that elegant head.

Rapidly abandoning that agony in order to hurl myself upon my beloved, I brutally tear away her wings. I shove her into the nest, bundle her into a distant corner where no one can see my insanity. There, while my antennae pronounce love and hate, while my cimbaloms sing fury and desire, I hold her and I press her against me, in an ardent deceptive embrace.

XXV

My life was tortured by that shameful madness for a long time. I suffered near Marie; her presence made me feel the deprivation of love and sexual intercourse more intensely. As soon as I tried to distance myself, however, a dolorous bond drew me back to the place where that lumpen brute was walking and laying her eggs.

She was even more stupid than before. It seemed that in losing her wings she had lost everything except the faculties of digestion and egg-laying. Her antennae did not even try any longer to stammer vague responses. In her dead eyes I thought I could see something like a stupid dance of terror and gratitude; she waited, inertly, for me to give her something to eat or to beat her.

No remedy could soothe my malady. I stared for long periods at her abdomen, deformed by continual egg-laying, at the four stumps on her thorax, and her clumsy gait. My left-side thought said to me: "It's a goose!" My right-side thought replied: "It's a monster of ugliness and stupidity!" And yet I followed her heavy march, dragged in her wake by the unbreakable bond of an absurd and hideous love.

I said to myself repeatedly: "Even if I had sex organs, that ignoble egg-layer could be nothing to me. A single sex act fecundates our females for life, and they do not subject themselves twice to the approach of a male."

In spite of that reasoning, an ineffective sedative, and in spite of all Marie's ugliness, I could not keep away from the being that had had wings, the being that, for a moment, had known amour.

What would I not have given in exchange for the emotion that remained in the treasure of her memory; which, undoubtedly, had dazzled her entire future, had rendered her incapable of any other thought, had imprisoned her in an eternal ecstasy?

In vain I tried to draw consolation from the memory of caresses received and given by the man that I had been. They were such vague, deceptive and fleeting memories. Impotent to stir my present organs, they were nights of regret that never ignited the lightning of joy.

In any case, grim guardians loomed up at the gates of the inaccessible past, strange jealousies and strange disdains. Amour, it seemed to me, had rejoiced all my poor senses in that lost paradise—but how much more beautiful was the paradise that I had never entered! The ant with more numerous senses, a palace open to voluptuous in all directions, must be enlightened in sexual intercourse by far greater illuminations than the miserable human cottage, so narrow and obstructed!

I had known a night laden with clouds, and the poor filtered rays of moonlight had penetrated me with ineffable joys. But Marie! Marie had known the great stream of sunlight of a summer noon.

And I was sometimes uplifted as if by a strange caress when our limbs touched, especially when, like the kiss of a bird, I disgorged a few drops of nourishment into her open and contented mouth.

Often, by contrast, I was irritated by the torments she caused me; I was irritated that no true joy could come to me from her; I was indignant at feeling enslaved by an unrealizable desire and a regret devoid of memory. At those times, the temptation rose up within me to kill the infamous female and thus suppress the amorous infatuation that nailed me to the places dishonored by her stupid presence.

Even that bloody satisfaction was refused to my love and my hatred. Marie was the best of our six egg-layers. The community considered her as the most precious treasure. I would not have been forgiven for destroying so much future. The murder would surely be punished by death. Although I would never know the rich caress of winged beings, I wanted to live; I wanted fervently to live, in order at least to recover the poor shadow of sexual intercourse that humans know.

XXVI

The most desperate amours have the recourse of dreams. My amour was deprived even of the most unreal voluptuousness; there was no refuge, in the future, in the past or in hypothesis. I had no organs corresponding to my mad desires, and a damned soul howling at an unknown heaven, I could not imagine the delights whose absence was torturing me.

A languorous malady gradually weakened my limbs, softening my movements. I felt myself falling toward death, but I did not have the courage to climb back, nor even, by an almost-reflexive gesture, to cling on to the edge of the precipice. The shadow of sexual intercourse that humans know was no longer a sufficient promise, could no longer entice me to the slightest effort. Since I could not know the rich caress of winged ants, what did anything else matter to me?

Slowly, without resistance, I allowed myself to be invaded by the lugubrious inertia that would be the definitive exile of all joy, but would also be the end of dolor. If, in that cowardly interval, I did not kill Marie, it was because I was too torpid for the abrupt trigger of fury, because my melancholy was soft and slack, musically lachrymose.

Fortunately, a great war snatched me from the depressing sadness that was crushing me like a tombstone gradually increasing in weight.

A wandering army of *Aphoenogaster barbara* came to settle in our territory. Those insolent creatures dug their nest and raised the threat of their crater about twenty meters away from our city, cutting in two the broadest of our roads, isolating us from the large field whose harvest the human disputed with us every year, and which furnished half our resources itself. And the precious tree that sheltered our dear aphids captured from the *Lasius* was in the immediate vicinity of the troublesome colony.

We could not consent to that impoverishment and continual danger; we could not tolerate that insult. The extermination of the invaders was decided. The war commenced the following day, at dawn.

Our ant-hill was a seething mass of agitation. Everywhere, one encountered feverish individuals; antennae were menacing plumes; heads rose up in indignation, palps trembled with wrath; the movement of rapidly-marching feet had a bold and aggressive thrust. One bumped into ants that had hard grains of wheat between their teeth, with which they were sharpening their mandibles, like human soldiers polishing their weapons. Others were cleaning their stings. A forceful martial madness was stimulating the entire city.

To begin with, my weakness, my disgust with everything—since the sole object of my desire was forever out of reach—and my unhealthy indifference insulated me from the common folly, but I gradually submitted to the contagion. I had a great deal of difficulty sleeping, and murderous dreams weighed upon my slumber.

I will not relate the scenes of carnage of those three days of war, the three great pitched battles. I am slightly ashamed on behalf of the ants for having seen them lower themselves so often to the ignominy of killing. I am proud of having found geniuses among them, but I prefer to remember them applied to engineering works, realizing Archimedean dreams, rather than the hours in which their intellectual power, directed by a bestial human instinct, made them into Alexanders or Napoleons.

The two armies were led by generals of the first order. I remember that every evening, after the battle, we discussed Aristotle's ruses with glorious admiration, and the enemy general's stratagems with hateful admiration. All day we had seen the latter, in the midst of the movements of her troops, motionless on a mound, standing up on her hind feet, her head slightly tilted, gazing at the totality of the conflict. We shivered whenever she leaned forward and passed an order on to the antennae of a passer-by. We knew that some misfortune as about to fall upon us.

In the center of our battalions, Aristotle maintained a similar attitude. When the adversary gave an order, her observation became more intense and more impatient, as if feverish. But the commanded movement had scarcely begun before she had deduced it in its entirety, along with its consequences. With a presence of mind that was never in default, she parried the thrust and riposted.

Her role was difficult. The invaders were three times as numerous as we were, and every evening, we had to admit that the day had gone rather badly

Instead of discouraging us, our impotence excited us to the point of rage. After the second battle, when Aristotle advised abandoning the location, departing by night with our larvae and our provisions to search for a favorable spot further away in which to rebuild the city, we refused with a unanimous fury. If my friend had insisted we might have killed her, accusing her of cowardice and treason.

Our anger was relieved slightly by torturing the prisoners. We obtained profound and infamous joys from it. One of us would use her mandibles slowly to saw off one of the poor captive's antennae; another would enjoy herself cutting off a foot; a third would tear away a palp with little repeated thrusts. When the victim was derived of all her limbs, we often had the cruelty of not finishing her off, of leaving her to die in a long immobile despair, but coming back from time to time to contemplate her anguished eyes, as if plunging into a bath of joy, or, with a light thrust of the mandibles, causing her to shiver in her apparent slumber.

That night, I did not go to bed. After having played my part in the murder of the prisoners I wandered for a long time over the abandoned battlefield. I witnessed a repulsive spectacle there. Little ants of an unknown species—they were doubtless what my books call *Myrmica scabrinodis*—were running from one cadaver to another, like scavengers after a human battle. I watched them for some time without understanding what they were doing. Finally, I approached a corpse at which a group of them had paused, cautiously. Horror! The chitinous envelope that forms a kind of external skeleton for an ant had been opened up, and the flesh devoured.

I could not contain myself. Without asking myself what frightful dangers I might be running, I set out in pursuit of the *scabrinodis*. The ignoble creatures were cowards. In spite of their swarming numbers, they fled. I had the relief of catching up with a few of them and decapitating them with a single thrust of my indignant mandibles.

I was drunk on blood, agitation and horror. I was no longer an ant; I was a monster. My mind was a cinematograph in which violent scenes agitated; my body was an aggressive surge; my weapons were murderous instincts. How is it that in that state of madness I thought about Marie? Immediately, her image exasperated my hateful amour, and since I could not shiver with pleasure, I wanted to feel her body gasping and dying between my furious limbs.

I returned to the foot of the gigantic stairway, and found the entrance to the tunnel of which we had already made use twice. Silently, without leaving the poor female the time to awake with a start, I seized her between my mandibles and, with a single stroke, severed the nervous cord linking the head to the body. Then, slowly, fearful of being caught, I transported the heavy body, which quivered vaguely but soon became still and sinister. I carried it to the battlefield. In spite of the improbability, it would be thought that the heavy egg-layer had also been carried away by martial fever and had died the victim of reckless courage.

I spent the rest of the night next to the ugly creature that had known amour. I sensed that her death would not liberate me. My desperate eunuch thoughts would be populated by her phantom; my mad love would be sharpened by remorse, and I would curse myself for having destroyed forever the strange caress of her open and contented mouth, into which my mouth poured nourishment.

XXVII

The third battle was particularly furious. The death of many of our friends had made us thirsty for vengeance and our two successive defeats had reinforced our hatred of the strangers with a rage of humiliated pride against the offenders. The war seemed bound to go on for a long time, and, save for some scarcely conceivable stroke of luck, it would finish with our extermination. We wanted, at least, to kill a great many of those who were killing us. Perhaps, too, our reckless valor would frighten them and persuade them to an exile.

Our fury, extraordinary from the start, was further exasperated. The increasing heat, the drunkenness caused by the perfume formed by the vapors of blood and venom, and the encouragement of a few partial successes—quickly canceled out, in any case, by the genius of the enemy general—all transformed our natural courage into fervent temerity.

I was conspicuous among the most audacious. The irritating memories of the night spurred me with shame and anguish. I wanted to die, and, before, dying, to kill, kill and kill again. I went forth like a fury, bringing disorder and flight everywhere, only able to seize living flesh on the run, which I made into dead flesh.

I had a few minutes of absolute madness, in which I no longer knew where I was, what I was or what I was doing, in which I was nothing more than a need to destroy, incapable of distinguishing between friends and enemies. I threw myself indifferently upon everything that passed close by, as furious as death. It seems that I killed five or six compatriots. With a mixture of indulgence and rudeness, antennae warned me: "Be careful where you're striking; you've just killed one of ours."

Without listening, I precipitated myself on the adviser, since it was a life that I could seize and destroy. My mandibles crushed her, and it was a long moment afterwards that I sensed her words arrive, still vague, in my consciousness.

Finally, seven or eight of my compatriots threw themselves upon me, immobilizing my feet and mandibles; and meanwhile, antennae struck the being slightly calmed by immobility with energetic reproaches. I was released again upon the enemy when I had recovered consciousness of the situation.

I perceived in the distance, standing up, the general that had heaped so many evils upon us. I resolved to die or kill her. Rapid and direct, without rendering or warding off a single blow, I hurtled toward her through the midst of the enemy battalions. Just as I was about to reach her, several of them seized me and dragged me away—and I felt happy. It was good: that evening I would be punished for my crime. That evening I would die, since Marie was dead, and I would die slowly, in refined tortures that would make me savor death like a voluptuousness of despair.

Now the combat, momentarily hesitant, stops. What's happening? An enemy prisoner comes back from our city, and speaks to the chief that I wanted to kill. The discussion is prolonged. Then the antennae of the two interlocutors turn in my direction. A messenger arrived, speak to my guards. I am taken to the general, enchained—by which I mean that each of my feet is held by a guard.

Slowly and hesitantly, with repeated movements—for we speak two different dialects of *Aphoenogaster*—she says to me, approximately:

"Your general is mad. She proposes that we terminate the quarrel by single combat. Certainly, I believe that I am no less brave and strong than she is, but I have three times as many soldiers and today, again, you're beginning to lose ground. If, as a false point of honor, I accepted her proposition, I would be committing a veritable treason toward my homeland, since I would be gambling a certain victory on equal terms."

I scarcely understood why she was explaining all that to me. She went on: "But I do not want the destruction of your people. We are *Aphoenogaster*, like you. We have been expelled from out former territory by amazon ants, which are much stronger creatures, almost irresistible. We came peacefully to establish ourselves here, where we found room. It's you who attacked us."

I replied: "You've come to install yourselves insolently in our territory. You couldn't be unaware of that, since it's in the very middle of a road that you've hollowed out a hostile city and raised your crater like a challenge and a threat."

"Yes," she said, "but the entire region is abundantly occupied. We stopped in the vicinity of a weak nation of the same race, hoping that its weakness and our kinship would render it tolerant."

"The weak need to be the proudest and most intolerant defenders of their rights. If the strong support what they could easily prevent, others are grateful to them. If the weak submit,

112

it is deemed that they lack courage, and they are justly scorned."

"Those are fine sentiments," said the general, "but you'd do better to let me speak."

With a very noble courtesy, she began by offering a eulogy to our courage, and Aristotle's genius. Then she continued: "You can no longer live alone. If you don't want to be exterminated by our irresistible numbers, you'll be forced into exile, among so many dangers. I've told you that the entire region is occupied, and we chose your neighborhood because you were the weakest people. You will not be allowed to establish yourselves anywhere..."

After a pause that increased my patriotic anguish, the clever ant concluded: "You have only one means of salvation. Make an alliance with us."

I was astonished. "The proposition is strange. Ants hate strangers."

"Unite with us; we will no longer be strangers. Will you take my proposal to your general?"

"My general will not believe that you're serious unless she knows what advantage you find in that."

"I'll respond in all frankness," my interlocutress said. "That alliance, which is the only salvation for you, is not a negligible enhancement of our strength. Amazon armies..."

She saw that I did not understand what she was talking about. She explained. "Amazons are gigantic ants with mandibles ten times as powerful as ours. They do not harvest, do not hollow out their dwellings themselves and do not know how to maintain them. Having no other industry than war, they come to steal our larvae and nymphs in order to make slaves of them."

After that didactic digression she resumed the interrupted sentence. "Amazon armies are nearby, and we can never be too numerous to defend our children against those monsters."

"Is that the only advantage we would bring you?"

"No," she confessed. "And I'd prefer to tell you everything. In the country from which we come, there is more shade, more humidity and less heat than on this summit. At the moment of our flight the harvest had scarcely begun. Here, we find it concluded. Our provisions are insufficient to get us through the year. By contrast, the rubbish heaps surrounding your crater testify eloquently that your granaries are sufficiently well-stocked for you and for us."

"We're certainly rich," I said, proudly.

"We need a part of your wheat."

My antennae made two rapid strokes, as if sniggering. "Ha ha!"

"One way or another, we shall have it," she affirmed. "If you refuse the alliance, we'll kill you all, and your wealth will belong to us without division. If you run away, we'll let you depart into the unknown, fraught with perils, but you won't be able to come back to fetch your provisions; we'll occupy your nest immediately. Burdened by your nymphs and larvae, you won't be able to carry away many provisions."

She concluded: "Now you know that you have to choose between alliance with us or extermination. Now you know that we need to have you as friends, or kill you, or chase you toward hunger and danger of every sort. Go tell those things to your compatriots, and let them choose quickly."

When I had reported this conversation to Aristotle, she was joyful. "We're saved!"

The news spread rapidly. The two armies which had been killing one another a little while before, melted into a fraternal crowd.

We went to visit the new city. The others visited our city, which was much vaster, much more beautiful and much better disposed. The union of the two peoples in our ant-hill was decided. The females were transported there, along with the innumerable future of the populous nation—the nymphs, larvae and eggs—and also its meager provisions. But the second nest was not destroyed. The road that it severed was connected to the right and left, enclosing the crater as a river embraces an island, and it remained there, a sad and abandoned colony, but a precious shelter in case of danger.

The next day, Aristotle, who was intent on her idea of single combat, challenged the enemy general—whose name was composed of three forceful strokes, the first of which had a hesitant quality, like an aspirate, which my left-side mind rendered as Hannibal—to an amicable contest. Hannibal consented indifferently. She brought to the combat far less fervor than our friend, and we were happy and proud, as if consoled by Aristotle's victory.

XXVIII

In spite of the fits of anger to which they are subject, *Aphoenogasters* are friendly and nobly generous ants. According to all observers, the species is one of the most peaceful, and the kind of alliance that had just united two enemy ant-hills is less rare between nations of that race.

Our new friends had been received at first with joyful affection; we had believed that we were doomed and now, not only were we saved, but our number and our power had been increased. On the other hand, we had been flattered by the choice of our nest and the praise lavished on our architectural talents.

Afterwards, however, we were invaded by bitterness. We had been vanquished. The alliance was certainly a great benefit, but, having been imposed by force, it was also a humiliation. We looked at the new citizens with animosity, unready to tolerate anything on the part of the intruders, and it's astonishing that our bad attitude didn't lead to numerous brawls.

The newcomers behaved perfectly. All our actions and gestures were pretexts for flattering eulogies on their part. When we invited them to peaceful wrestling matches they always consented; they fought with exquisite courtesy and didn't complain about the almost hostile violations of the rules by which we routinely obtained victory. Happy to find a homeland, the exiles wanted to be loved by their new fellow citizens.

Gradually, they succeeded in that. Their odor, much less disagreeable than that of ants of another species, became increasingly familiar to us, seeming to us to be much more like our own. Soon, we could scarcely distinguish the larvae emerging from eggs laid by their females from the larvae that came from ours.

The series of misfortunes commenced by the great storm and the invasion of our nest seemed to have been concluded. Once again we were as happy as we had been in spring, or even happier, so quietly pleased to have arrived, after so many anguishing defiles, in the smiling immensity of the plain. And winter was approaching: the war, intimate season, the season of repose and long repasts, long slumber and slow, nuanced conversations.

Among that people, who seemed gradually to be entering into a torpid contentment, I was happy. My human thought, as usual in times of calm joy, was effaced, like an unreal and distant mist, appearing rarely and phantasmally, a vague symbol of possible anterior lives and probable future lives.

Even my crime no longer tormented me. I scarcely remembered it, and only to excuse it. I avoided analyzing my state of mind at the moment when I committed it. I now felt like the other workers, and no impossible amorous dream tormented me. Marie's murder was one of those acts that it would be absurd to try to explain: a movement of madness, the repetitive mechanical gesture of someone who has killed so many times and who kills everything she encounters, of someone from whom martial fury has removed all reason and will, someone who is no longer anything but a killing machine. I expelled from my memory the circumstances that might have given the lie to that theory.

I had become a friend of Hannibal I anticipated great pleasures from her conversation. Her mind, as powerful as Aristotle's, was newer to me, and I liked to draw fresh beauties and pleasant astonishments from the treasure of her memory. We understood one another marvelously; the two dialects gradually melted into a common language, rich and flavorsome, whose unexpected turns were striking and charming. Hannibal's stories about the cold and damp regions of the valley, especially what she said about the terrible amazons that had expelled her from the cold, damp homeland, certainly less beautiful and poorer than ours, but for which she retained a nostalgic tenderness.

The amazons, those great russet barbarians, were portrayed in her stories as inept but formidable creatures. According to Hannibal—since my anamorphosis I have verified that her information was accurate—those terrible beings are incapable of building or digging; they do not even know how to nourish their eggs and their larvae, disengage their nymphs or teach their infants to walk. They have no instruments of labor; their mandibles cannot serve as scissors, saws or trowels. Long and polished, curved and pointed, they are merely weapons, penetrating blades, inappropriate for any other usage than murder, incapable even of picking up nourishment and carrying it to the mouth.[15]

The amazons, therefore, need slaves as larvae need nurses. They spend their lives at war, having no other occupation than attacking their neighbors to steal nymphs, which soon augment the number of their servants.

I interrupted the stories to exclaim: "I'd really like to see one of these extraordinary creatures."

But Hannibal replied, tremulously: "Hope that you never do!"

XXIX

I was alone on the aphid tree. Like almost caressant hands milking a cow, my antennae, by means of delicate touches, had obtained several nice drops of sweet and stimulating sugar. My greed had been excessive, and to tell the

---

[15] The reference is obviously to the species *Polyergus rufescens*, but ignores the fact that it only parasitizes (or "enslaves") the nests of various species of *Formica*.

truth, I think I was slightly drunk. All of nature appeared to me to be bizarre, cheerful and grotesque, astir with awkward and hilarious gestures. I was greatly amused when I perceived, still distant but as rapid, sinuous and vertiginous as a comical crawling lightning-bolt, a column of enormous red ants.

At a run that was almost a dance, I hurried back to the nest. At the entrance I met Hannibal. My heavy and contented antennae spoke to her.

"What joy! We're going to fight. The amazons are coming."

"Woe! Woe!" said her fearful antennae. She climbed the crater and came back in haste.

"Woe betide us!" she resumed. "Quickly, let's seal the city."

Aided by a few comrades who happened to be there, we made a first barricade with the crumbled materials of the crater. Behind it we placed one of our soldiers, whose cylindrical head closed the tunnels so precisely. Others were stationed at the narrowed points of all the upper galleries. Eggs, larvae and nymphs were transported to the deepest subterrains, and, with the anguished of besieged people who cannot even see those laying siege to them, we waited.

Aristotle became impatient. She proposed that we reopen the caterpillar tunnel, make a sortie and, attacking the enemy unexpectedly from behind, driving them away. The motion had no success. Hannibal and her compatriots declared that it would be running needlessly and inevitably to death. According to her, there was nothing to be done but wait. Perhaps the enemy would not succeed quickly enough in forcing the successive defiles, and would go away for the night. In that case, it would be immediately necessary to go into exile, for now that the amazons had located our nest, they would come back to attack it so long as a single nymph, larva or egg remained within it.

If, as was unfortunately probable, the slavers penetrated as far as our ultimate retreats, there would be nothing to do but flee with our children. We would leave the provisions in order that as many of us as possible, with our mandibles free, could slow down the pursuit. Later, when the brigands had lost interest in the nest devoid of nymphs, we would come back prudently and furtively to search for our wheat.

"They're forcing all the doors!" said Hannibal.

The caterpillar tunnel was reopened. Workers picked up the nymphs, the eggs and the larvae and the exodus began. We all got out before the arrival of the amazons. The ants charged with taking refuge in the nest abandoned by Hannibal and her companions barricaded themselves therein solidly.

I remained in the vicinity of the invaded city, with the troop that was to sacrifice itself in order to gain time for our friends—but I had an idea of which I am not very proud today. After having sealed the tunnel through which we had fled from outside, I advanced as far as the crater in order to see whether any amazons remained outside the city. They were all inside the ant-hill. We caused the crater to collapse over the entrance, and loaded that ruin with a heavy stone.

I ran to announce that operation.

Hannibal was delighted.

"They're so stupid!" she said. "They'll search the empty tunnels indefinitely. Then they'll go to sleep wherever they are. They won't pay any attention to getting out until tomorrow, after having made quite certain that there are no children to steal. Let's take advantage of the respite to get away with our family. We're too close here—we'll surely be discovered."

It was difficult to reconcile ourselves to that new exile. At least, when we had quit the old nest a little while before, we had known in which shelter we would take refuge. Besides which, we were remaining in our own territory, close to our fields and close to the aphid tree, in the midst of the region to which we were attached as daughters to their mother, and as mothers to their children, for its contours, its colors its odors and its sounds had formed our mind, and our mind, along with our mandibles—frail but numerous and patient instruments— had transformed it. Was not leaving the familiar places to which we were adapted, and which we had adapted to us, in a sense, losing light itself, and the voluptuousness of smell and hearing, and the quivering joy of touch, since everything that we would encounter from now on would be strange, as injuriously unknown, hostile and frightening, like vague forms glimpsed in darkness?

Reason held sway, though. The retreat was organized cleverly. Hannibal, who knew the surroundings best, marched in the lead, without any burden that might trouble her sense of direction. A few soldiers accompanied her, mandibles ready for combat. The long column of laden workers followed, between two rows of soldiers. Aristotle marched in the middle of them, on one of the flanks. My recent exploit had led to my own military talent being recognized, and the troops forming the rearguard had asked me to remain with them.

We were going into the night and into the unknown, not knowing whether we were marching to the creation of a new homeland or to death. We often paused, to await the return of scouts sent out in all directions. They always came back to announce that there were ant-hills in the vicinity, and we resumed our anguished march, making prudent detours. Alas, our dread gradually became certainty: daylight would come before we found a propitious location for the new city. Daybreak would come, brutally, to reveal our misery to others, to disclose to avid enemy eyes the flight of the poor prey that we were and change our anxious fearful march into a horrible ordeal leading who knew where, through battles.

The evil day does in fact, arrive. Dawn, a hesitant ironic smile that gradually broadened into deafening, thunderous cruel laughter, surprises us as we are descending a steep slope where, from time to time, an exhausted carrier lets an impotent and dolorous larvae fall bruisingly to the ground.

The sounds of the morning rise up. We sense the excessive imprudence of that course through awakening hostilities. We camp as best we can, in a narrow clearing, surrounded by long dry grass. We deposit the eggs, larvae and nymphs in the center, a present burden, an entire future. The smallest workers remain close to those future living individuals, the prevention of whose death is as demanding as the life of an invalid. Soldiers remain too, ready to repel attacks. A cordon of sentinels keeps watch on all the edges of the clearing. The rest of the ants disperse, in numerous bands, into the forest of long grass, searching for something to eat, and for food to bring back to those who have stayed behind.

A few hours pass without anything amiss except the distress caused by the expectation of all evils. Gradually, we recover confidence. Already, we are wondering whether we ought not to proceed, in spite of the disquieting proximity of two nests, with hollowing out a new city in that location.

Suddenly, however, sentinels come running, announcing the approach of amazons.

Then the workers pick up their burdens and hasten their flight at hazard. Allowing themselves to be carried away by the invitation of the slope, they hasten toward the distant valley. The soldiers stay to fight.

A rapid and frightful combat! Thus far, I had only seen battles against bodies weaker than ours of equal in strength. The amazons were truly too superior. Our mandibles slid impotently over their chitinous armor, while their curved blades entered with sure thrusts into heads, killing at every stroke, and disengaging with astonishing skill in order to recommenced their murderous work, indefatigably.

We were very brave. No one recoiled. Heroisms amazed me. One of my sisters, cut in two, deprived of her abdomen and half her thorax, rose up obstinately on the two or three feet that remained to her and continued striking with her feeble mandibles. Futile valor, alas! In no time at all our center was forced and the irresistible red column reached our carriers.

Then there was frightful confusion. Every amazon killed a worker, picked up the dead ant's burden and fled. We hurled ourselves at the despoilers, trying to snatch their prey, and sometimes succeeding. We also contrived, sometimes, to leap upon the back of one of the huge barbarians and sever her horrible red head. I believe that if we had known where to seek refuge, we would have saved a good part of our future generation—but we did not have any goal. We were fighting against one danger, knowing only too well that if we escaped it, it would be to flee toward other dangers, less brutal by virtue of being not yet present, but more frightening in being unknown.

Heavy rain arrived, which put an end to the battle, hastening our flight toward the valley and the brigands' flight toward the heights.

It was only at the bottom, on the bank of the steam, that we stopped. We tried, under the downpour, to calculate our losses. Soon, however, it was necessary for us to contend with a new enemy.

We were no longer besieged by living beings but by an element. Water was still falling heavily upon us from the sky, inflicting countless injuries, and now the stream was rising menacingly. The entire slope was now streaming, becoming a torrent that would doubtless carry us away before long.

Several ants began moving as if they had drunk too much aphid honey. Their drunken gestures revealed, with a desperate eloquence, that their reason had been unable to withstand the excessively repetitive blows of misfortune and the excessively urgent threats of danger.

We picked up these stricken individuals, and the one female that remained to us, and the few nymphs, larvae and eggs that we had saved. We made a kind of nucleus of those poor beings, around which we formed a ball. As if caulking a vessel, each of us secreted as much formic acid as possible. Then, a living and anguished raft—but a raft devoid of cracks, into which no water could penetrate—we allowed ourselves to be dragged away by the current.

XXX

The rain stopped. We arrived at a confluence. The contest of the two swollen streams threw us toward the bank. We felt a shock. Immediately, in less than a second, the ball disintegrated. Each of us stretched out numbed limbs, shook antennae weary of immobility, and got as far away as possible from the water.

Then we tried to take stock of the resources and dangers of the place where we were.

Alas, we were not on land. We were on a tree that must normally have stood on the bank, but which the water had now surrounded. Its lower branches were inclined, heavy with mud, and foreign grass and branches. We gazed, stupidly, and the water, which was not going down, and thought that we were doubtless going to die of starvation.

The sun set. Few of us went to sleep. Several remained at the water's edge, the tips of their forefeet brushing the water, in order to sense any decrease, to seek, by means of small repeated thrusts, the hope of deliverance. They barely had to move in order to follow the gradual lowering.

The sun rose. We started searching the corners of our tree, looking for a few insects to devour. It was a meager hunt, which exhausted up all our resources for one inadequate meal.

There was nothing more we could do but wait until circumstances finally consented to deliver us, or their obstinacy killed us.

Days passed. Individuals began to die, while gazing at the water that was going down so slowly. A few comrades devoured the first cadavers, and were universally criticized. The cadavers of the second day of death were shared between the entire population. We also ate the eggs, larvae and nymphs. On the third day, cadavers were too rare, and we fought over them in order to obtain our morsels. On the fourth day, we killed one another in order to eat.

Closer to the bank, islets of muddy grass emerged, increasingly more numerous and closer together, trampolines on which our obstinate hopes bounced all the way to firm ground. Another two interminable days—two days of hunger and crimes—passed before it became possible to reach the shore, amid a thousand sticky traps.

The danger having passed, there was a general outburst of affection. All the individuals who had been thinking about devouring one another the day before, lying in wait for a moment of inattention or weakness in which they could hurl themselves upon their neighbor, to kill her, open up her chitinous envelope and eat her flesh, were now loving, caressing one another, singing tender and melancholy tunes.

After the first surge of joy, our anxieties returned. How few in number we were! How many had died in the battle against the amazons! How many had gone astray in the flight, probably drowned—and, if some miracle had reserved them for another death, were dispersed, prey that could not be rescued, separated from our aid by the immensity of the stream! How many had died of hunger on the tree, and how many, to our shame, had succumbed under the thrusts of their famished sisters...

Irremediable losses. No children would come, as uncertain and charming as hope, to replace those disappeared. We had devoured our own eggs, larvae and nymphs. Our last egg-layer had died of hunger on the tree. We were a people devoid of strength, with no future. We were no more than the death-throes of a people.

The irreducible Aristotle affirmed that our nation would live. It was merely a matter of not being discouraged, choosing the location of a new nest prudently, and waiting, obstinately alive. In the epoch of fecundation, we would keep a careful lookout, and would collect a few stray females.

Yes, but how could we wait? How could we survive the poverty of winter without provisions? When the belated smile of spring returned, would hunger have spared a single one of us?

Aristotle scolded our weakness. Certainly, she admitted, disdainfully, we would be poor; certainly, we would suffer; but by dint of hard labor and ingenuity, we would find what was necessary. First, it was necessary to sketch out the city, which would be finished later, and then, before the first chill came, to search, to glean, to store. Even during winter, fruitful subterranean expeditions would be mounted; sleeping insects would be tracked to their lairs. Finally, she affirmed, the obstacles that seemed to be the most invincible during the initial stupor, would collapse as if of their own accord under active, persistent, unfailing effort, and the courageous will to live. And she praised the hard life boastfully, declaring it as beautiful as a battle without truce, continually victorious.

Hannibal said the same valiant things. One after another, without conviction and without pleasure, uniquely because, in our stupor, and our exhaustion, as if we were asleep, their speeches reawakened old mechanically active habits, and we set to work. The location of the future homeland was chosen: poor, lost in a land of famine, but, for that very reason, distant from any ant-hill and depopulated of any carnivorous prowlers, where our weakness would be sheltered from attacks.

We were about to begin digging when a human came to lean over us. There was no nest in which to dive, and little grass, lying on the ground like a few damp hairs on a man's head. The horrible walking mountain picked us up one after another, and enclosed us in a prison of glass.

We were too weak, too tired and too discouraged to be overly distressed by a further misfortune. Under the repeated blows of destiny we had become indifferent and immobile prey. Only Aristotle and Hannibal appeared, from the first moment of captivity, to experience a keen anguish.

My left-side mind tried to divine what the human wanted with us. I don't know why, but I supposed that he wanted to feed us to chickens—and I almost rejoiced, like a ruined man who finds an opportunity to gamble. If I escaped the murderous beaks, I would easy find my sustenance in the poultry-yard.

My supposition was false. The human transported us into a large closed and almost empty room. There was nothing in it but a chair and a round table—I took account of these details subsequently, especially after resuming human form. On the table there was a strange item of furniture: a flat box composed of a wooden framework hermetically sealed by two plates of glass.

The human sat down. He opened the frame, and then the prison into which he put us initially, which was a large test tube. He tipped us into the frame, which he closed again.

Anxious and curious, we ran around our new prison. In the middle of one side, a little opening permitted me to get out, and almost everyone followed me. We found ourselves on the wooden table-top.

There was food there. We went past without touching it. Curiosity and the desire for liberty held sway over hunger, which was beginning to be felt keenly.

The edge of the table was not far away.

Soon, I would pass underneath it, flee down the leg and hide myself in some interstice in the floor or hole in the wall.

The human has just gone out; by the time he returns, I'll be invisible.

Still on the tabletop I encounter an inexplicable ditch full of water. For a long time I move along it...

I'm not mistaken, though; I've passed this spot before. Have I gone astray and retraced my steps without realizing it? It's very improbable, since I'm not carrying anything. But then...

I shiver, and dare not think precisely about what has made me shiver.

I continue my journey, always in the same direction. Here I am again, back at the point I've already recognized. Yes, the stream is circular. I climb on to the frame, stand on my hind legs, and observe at a glance the exactitude of the horrible conclusion. And while my right-side mind is desolate, my left-side mind is amused, and compares me—the pedant!—to the humans of Homer's time, enclosed on the earth by the circle of the River Ocean.

Aristotle and Hannibal arrive beside me. They too have understood. They gaze with terror at what I'm gazing at.

Others follow, then others, and yet others. Soon we all know that there is no hope of escaping the cruel mountain that walks on two feet.

XXXI

"I don't understand any of this," Aristotle says to me. "What does the mountain that walks on two feet want with us? Why is it[16] imprisoning us on this table and furnishing us with nourishment? Is formic acid as precious to it as aphid liquid is to us?"

"I don't think that formic acid is agreeable to him," I replied. "In any case, we scorn certain species of aphids as too small. We'd be a very minuscule herd for that giant."

"In that case," she said, despairingly, "it wants to eat us?"

"Not that either. His odor is unbearable to us; ours must displease him."

"Get away! It smells bad, while we smell good."

"We smell bad according to the antennae of a strange ant, which smells bad to us. In the same way, I believe that being, whose odor offends us, doesn't like our odor."

Aristotle reflected momentarily, as if impressed by my reasoning. Soon, however, her antennae trembled in a fashion analogous to your laughter, and she affirmed, with conviction: "What you're saying is too subtle to be true."

"I think I know what that man wants with us," I said. "This science reassures me. We'll suffer from being captives, but he won't do us any other harm. He'll give us food and care for us as best he can, without thinking about eating our flesh or stealing our formic acid."

"Lunatic!" she protested. "If it were as friendly to ants as that, it wouldn't imprison us. It wouldn't have captured us, but

---

[16] Aristotle uses a feminine pronoun at this point—because *montagne* is a feminine noun, not because she is attributing a sex to the human—but English pronouns work differently. I have taken the view that Aristotle would think of the bipedal mountain as "it," whereas the narrator, whose human component knows better, would naturally use "he."

would have brought us food while leaving us free to enjoy the grass and the sky."

"I'm not saying that he's a friend of ants," I replied. "I only said that he'd do his best to care for us."

"But why? Why? What can it want from us?"

"He wants to see how we live, to study our actions, deduce our intelligence, try to get to know another life than his."

Aristotle made a proud gesture. "You're attributing a very powerful thought to it," she said. "Ants are the only intelligent animals, and they've never devoted themselves to such studies."

I shook my antennae mockingly. "All animals think that they're the only intelligent species."

"Get away! Except for ants, no animals have any idea of intelligence. Are your humans capable of digging a nest?"

"Their poor eyes like the light and they wouldn't voluntarily live underground, but just as we construct shelters along our roads, they build houses proportionate to their size. The one that has captured us has been able put the prison in which he's enclosed all our people in a corner of a room in his house, less cumbersome than a grain of wheat in one of our granaries."

Aristotle avoided that dolorous point. "I know that they cut wheat," she said, "And pile it up in mountains that disappear thereafter. Since we don't know what becomes of those provisions, you can argue, without too much implausibility, that they collect it in stores, but when the country isn't spontaneously rich. Do they sow as we do?"

"The lands that seem spontaneously fertile to us are fecundated by them. And if we can usually be content with our harvest, it's because they sow them every year."

"You're making fun of me. Do they have aphids, as we have, that provide them with fluid, and do they construct stables to protect them?"

"Yes, except that their aphids are enormous and have no wings."

"Do humans, like us, have military genius? Can they march against the enemy in serried columns? Do they have the science of flanking movements and the cunning of diversions? Would they ever have thought, as I did, of opening the caterpillar tunnel in order to take the invaders by surprise? Would they have caused the crater to collapse in order to frustrate the amazons as you did?"

"Some humans have military genius."

"Would they, like us, have attracted the attention of the aphid-owners to a distant attack while a party of ours took possession of the livestock?"

"Many humans are skillful in taking possession of the property of others."

"But are humans capable of a collective endeavor in which several collaborate willingly, without anyone forcing or being forced?"

"On that point they're inferior to us. Among them, as among the amazon ants, there are individuals who work and others who do nothing, and those who do nothing command those who work. The fact is all the more despicable because the masters and slaves, in this instance, belong to the same species, and often to the same people. But several humans can, like several ants, collaborate. I recognize another human inferiority, however: the idea of the whole endeavor does not always exist in the mind of every worker, but is often only conceived by a leader who directs subordinate and uncoordinated movements from without."

"You're saying, then, that there are a small number of intelligent humans—but you must confess that all of them are not capable of affection for their fellows."

"They too are animals that mingle good and evil, and it does happen that a man can have a friendship with another."

"That affection sure cannot, like ours, surpass the limit of death. Only ants have pious cemeteries near their dwellings, where cadavers can be protected against flesh-eaters and allowed to dry peacefully in the sun."

"Human flesh, being too abundant, doesn't desiccate after death, but becomes a noxious mud. However, the survivors carefully bury the fresh cadaver in a box in a kind of vast subterranean ant-hill."

"Ants have a language."

"Humans also speak."

"Imbecile! Show me their antennae."

I tried to explain that human express themselves primarily by means of sound, but Aristotle mocked the notion. "Get away! They're silent beings. I've never heard any music coming from them."

"Their music is too forceful for our tibia."

"Too forceful! What is this absurdity? When we hear a sound, if that sound is doubled, we hear it twice as loud."

"Not always. You hear the sound of your teeth cutting an ear of wheat. When a human, with the great artificial mandible with which he extends his limbs, cuts a hundred ears, you don't hear anything. You can hear the footfall of an ant, but you don't hear the heavy tread of a human."

My friend reflected briefly. Then she admitted: "You have singular ideas, some of which might well be true, but you depart from plausible observation to dream up unhealthy follies. It's not absolutely impossible that those beings emit sounds unheard by our tibias, but how implausible it remains! In any case, we know the poverty of the language of sounds, and that they can't articulate them. Then again, truly, what suggests that those heavy and deformed masses speak, think and have a soul?"

"They have one, though. And while they would marvel at some the things we do, you'd be astonished by some of their actions."

"Yes," she said, thoughtfully, "inferior beings sometimes have extraordinary flashes. Thus, the other day, an aphid..."

But the human came back. Our philosophical conversation ceased, and we watched.

XXXII

The human opened our prison and deposited it on the floor. Then he sat down and considered us.

"He wants us to make our nest in front of him," I said to Aristotle.

"Perhaps. Its intelligence is awakening, and it wants to learn the art of building from us. But it won't see anything. First we're going to cover that strange transparent wall with a layer of earth."

"He's cleverer than you think. Our prison is narrow; if we do as you say, we won't have enough space left. We're obliged to accept as the partitions of some of our chambers the unbreachable transparent wall. He'll be able to see us working."

My friend's antennae initially brushed lightly, like a murmur: "There are astonishing hazards that resemble planning..." She soon started again, however, disdainfully affirmative: "I'm not one of those naïve individuals deceived by the strangeness of such occurrences. I know full well that that creature isn't intelligent, that it isn't an ant..."

Before the eyes of the observer, we reconstructed our nest. When the human went away, he was careful to cover the glass with an opaque screen.

"You see," I said to Aristotle, "he knows that we like darkness in our home, and procures it for us as soon as he has no need to watch us. He isn't malevolent."

"You explain all these fortunate coincidences as evidence of intelligence," she replied. Then she became triumphant. "If he was an intelligent as you say and he had the plan to study us that you impute to him, he'd understand that he's putting us in an abnormal situation and that we won't act as we would in ordinary life, wouldn't he? He'd understand that his manner of study is distorting the object of his study."

The objection was sound. I tried to reply to it, but Aristotle didn't let me finish. "How, for example, could he appreciate our ingenuity and activity in finding nourishment, since we find it without difficulty in the vicinity of our nest?"

"He'll see us storing the wheat. Who can tell whether, eventually, he won't make us earn it?"

"Why has he chosen an incomplete nation, without females, without nymphs, without larva and without eggs? He'll remain ignorant of the most interesting of our mores, will never know what a united family we are in normal existence, what future-orientated people we are..."

The human reappeared. He tipped a heap of earth on to the table, in which eggs, larvae and nymphs were mingled.

"Imbecile!" said Aristotle. "That future doesn't even belong to our species. Does he imagine that we're going to hatch out strangers?"

We transported the earth into our nest but initially disdained the rest. But Hannibal, passing that way, said: "That future stinks!"

Rapidly, we threw those beings that were yet to be but already smelled bad into the surrounding river. For a moment, at one point, the river was filled in. We tried to cross over, but the human seized us with brutal fingers and threw us back into the courtyard of our prison. Then, with a single gesture, he cleared the broad ditch and threw away the unfortunate nymphs that we had refused to adopt.

The human turns away, picks something up and places it on the table. There are *Aphoenogaster barbara* females and two amazon females. Aristotle introduces the egg-layers of our race into the nest, while Hannibal leads the assault against the two giants.

The first attacks, naively directed, do not succeed; several of us fall, their heads crushed between the powerful jaws.

While staying out of range of the murderous fangs, I throw myself upon the antenna of the stronger giant. I seize the tip solidly between my mandibles. I follow the enemy's movements, retreating when it advances toward me, advancing when it recoils in an attempt to free itself. A comrade has seized the second antenna. Others grasp the feet and pull them out. Now the amazon is lying on her belly, immobilized. Now Hannibal is astride her back. Like scissors biting into a resistant object, Hannibal's mandibles open and close several times around the neck. Finally, my effort against a dead resistance makes me take two steps backwards; the neck is severed.

I look at the other amazon; she has just suffered the same fate as her companion.

The human is there, sitting down, nodding his head in approving manner, astonished by our skill or rejoicing in an anticipated result.

XXXIII

"I'm observing the mountain that walks on two legs very carefully," Aristotle said to me, "and although, strictly speaking, all its actions are explicable in terms of simple instinct, I think I can recognize a few glimmers of intelligence therein. But too many things are lacking for it to be considered the equal of an ant."

I interrupted her. "I've never claimed that human are the equals of ants, but you're too scornful, and you're denying the greater part of their riches."

She pointed out to me that you lack the majority of senses. I was obliged to admit that the observation was accurate, but her enumeration of your poverties soon surpassed the limits of the truth.

"That being is deaf," she affirmed.

"How do you know?"

"I've submitted it to absolutely conclusive experiments. I've played the strangest music in front of it. My feet have beaten the ground in such a way as to produce disturbing sounds, but its forefeet have never tensed in the manner of a being that is listening."

"The sounds that we produce, and all those that we can hear, are too weak to reach him."

"That's plausible," Aristotle admitted, "but never, in any circumstances, have its forefeet made the gesture of listening."

"Look how singularly he's tilting his head at this moment," I said. "I believe that he's listening to some sound that's very faint for him but too enormous for us to be able to suspect it."

"You think so?"

"The organs that permit him to hear aren't in his legs. They form two heavy and barbaric ornaments to either side of his head. Do you see those enormous excrescences so grossly shaped?"

Aristotle interrupted me furiously. "You can't say two sentences seriously. Your love of paradox is tempting you to the most inconceivable absurdities."

And she recommenced enumerating the poverties of that vast and wretched being, so ponderous, so badly designed, and blind in every direction but forwards.

XXXIV

"Would you please silence your ant pride for a moment, Aristotle? I'll tell you true and marvelous things about humans—their veritable poverties and their unsuspected richness."

"Speak."

"At this moment, that creature is committing the same injustices toward us that you're committing toward him. He too is scornful of us..."

"The presumptuous imbecile!"

"Or rather, which is more insulting, he's admiring those faculties of ours that he also possesses, astonished that we, who aren't human, can show some glimmer of intelligence."

"You're assuming a very excessive stupidity on his part."

"I believe him, primarily, to be blinded by the same pride that prevents you from seeing very well."

With a start, though, she said: "It isn't pride to know that ants are the only beings endowed with reason."

"Look. The door's opening. Another human is coming in. They're making gestures. They're surely talking about us. And, recalling your words, I believe I know what they're saying. The observer is saying: 'It's astonishing how intelligent these little creatures are. Would you believe it? They do this, they do that!' The comrade is replying: 'Instinct is sufficient to explain all those action.' 'No,' says the observer, 'I assure you that they have some intelligence.' But he immediately adds, prudently: 'Nothing comparable, of course, to the human mind, Humans are the only animals endowed with reason.'"

"You have a very disturbing way of thinking."

"Watch them for a moment," I said. "I'll prepare something. Perhaps I've found a way of helping you understand my eminent regarding humans and us."

There were grains of wheat nearby. I arranged a certain number of them in such a way as to design two overlapping circles.

I went back to Aristotle and showed him my work.

"What does that mean?" he asked.

"The circle on the left," I said, represents human thought; the circle on the right ant thought. You can see the small part that is common to the two domains. The human only thinks that we have the intelligence that he shares with us, which is that contained within both his circle and ours—that poor section that I'll fill with wheat."

After shading the common sector to render the figure clearly, I went on: "But how can we divine what is in the original part of his circle? We know that he doesn't have this or that, but almost everything he possesses is inconceivable to us. Everyone knows the poverties of his neighbor, but is ignorant of all the riches of that neighbor."[17]

"I know that you're delirious," Aristotle declared, "but your follies will end up troubling me. Then again, the universe

_____

[17] The narrator has, of course, drawn a Venn diagram; the illustrative device in question was first contrived and popularized in the 1880s.

and thought must have marvels that our eyes are incapable of seeing and our minds impotent to conceive. That idea, I know, is crazy, but it irritates me that it can be imagined, can be expressed. Now I'm tormented and anguished for hours on end. I don't know whether I'll be able to sleep tonight." And she begged: "Oh, my friend, tell me quickly that you're joking, that you've never believed what you've just said."

XXXV

I had said to Aristotle: "Humans are fortunate beings. Among them, no one has visible wings, but everyone is able to love; there are only males and females, no poor neuters who..."

She had interrupted me. "See what contradictions your love of the strange is pushing you! You claimed that these beings are intelligent!"

I strove in vain to explain that sex is not necessarily a badge of mental inferiority in all circumstances. One finds it so difficult to understand things that are very different from those with which one is familiar. Aristotle repeated, obstinately, that a sexual individual is entirely given over to the folly of wings, incapable of any practical endeavor or any precise meditation.

Without being stopped by her objections. I caused her further amazements.

"In that species," I affirmed, "the males are bigger and stronger than the females. I will even dare to say that they are more beautiful when they are beautiful, which often happens in scantly populated ant-hills, for that beauty is, if I can permit myself the repetition, made of beauty, while that of females is made of grace and..."

I hesitated momentarily. My left-side thought said: "Her beauty is made of smiles." But a smile is something exclusively human...

My antennae did not know how to translate that; they finally resumed: "The beauty of the females is made of grace and music."

Aristotle multiplied her mockery of those wingless females, weighed down by eggs, whom I affirmed to be graceful and musical.

I could not succeed in making her understand that a woman is not a wretched egg-layer fecundated for life by a single amorous act, that her allure can be animated and her face radiant with the hope of other kisses, that she does not drop an egg at every step and that, if it happens that an infant is made, the accident is quite rare.

XXXVI

I shall not try to repeat my other difficult dialogues with Aristotle—as, for instance, when I tried to explain to her that humans distinguish three colors in our black, while certain rays that are colored for us do not speak at all to their organs, and that the vibrations that convey sensations to the ant and to the mountain that walks on two legs offer the two spectators utterly dissimilar spectacles.

The only thing that I could get her to admit is that the enormous difference in stature had to modify all forms and contours.

"Yes," she said, "impoverished by their height and mass, the rare objects that don't escape their distant sight must seem very small."

"They see as small things that you see as large. But they see their companions as normal, which we cannot embrace with a single glance, and their eyes can embrace the territory of several ant-hills from a single position."

"Perhaps," she said, "but what interest can those immensities offer, which the ignorance of detail transforms for them into monotonous deserts?"

Our conversations always finished the same way, with Aristotle, impatiently, almost abusing me. Her hostile antennae said, with rapid thrusts: "You're affirming the craziest hypotheses as certainties. If you offered them as ingenious games, one might, while wishing that they were less implausible, be amused by their unsteady boldness, which crumbles at the first impact of reason. But you, presumptuous lunatic, speak like someone who knows."

I lacked courage. I answered, truthfully, but with an amiable skeptical quiver that transformed it into cheerful banter: "You know very well that I've been a human."

She became increasingly irritated. "That bad joke authorizes excessive absurdities, even for an ant amusing herself and dispensing with all observation. I'm truly too kind in lending attentive antennae to the incoherent babble of a trickster like you!"

I shall not say any more, either, about the puerile absurdity of the experiments carried out on us by the human, or the ridiculous conclusions that he must have drawn from them. You can find those poor vanities, or similar ones, in any book about ants.

XXXVII

Our captivity was aggravated.

Did the human need the table that supported our city, or did he find it interesting to imprison us more? I don't know, but the table disappeared. The frame that contained our nest was placed on top of a large drinking-glass whose foot plunged into a plate filled with water. We could only get out underneath the cage and along the rim of the glass—not a very interesting walk, which one was scarcely tempted to repeat. For a brief interval every day, however, the entrance to the box was extended by a glass tunnel, which opened into a sheet-metal cage where we found sugar, honey and other provisions of food.

Winter must have arrived, but the human, sensitive to the cold, maintained a high temperature in the room where he spent a part of his life sitting, leaning toward our prison, watching us.

Our overly narrow city did not permit us to flee the heat, and we suffered a great deal from it. On the other hand, the air in the apartment was unbreathable, infected by the violent human odor. We felt weak, almost ill, and were no longer philosophizing. Aristotle was so furious that she would have beaten me if I had persisted in pleading the cause of the mountain that walks on two legs. We spent long days inactive and interminable sleepless nights suffocating, cursing our torturer's cruelty or lack of awareness.

A disease began to spread, disagreeable and disgusting to begin with, which soon became dangerous as well. Among the animals that live in ant-hills are parasites tolerated because it would take too long to get rid of them and they don't cause any appreciable damage. Acarians—it displeases me to write the vulgar name and to admit that I had ever had, even outside human life, *lice*—of various species roamed freely in our tunnels and attached themselves to one of us from time to time in order to drink a drop of blood. The little creatures do not live long and scarcely caused us any inconvenience. Their light bite is an almost agreeable tickle, provided that it is not repeated too frequently.

In the abnormal conditions in which we were now living, however, the acarians multiplied until they became a nuisance, and a danger. The mouths, especially, and the antennae of the majority of our comrades were covered with them, and I dared not talk to them, for fear of being invaded during the dialogue.

It is almost impossible to grasp the little acarians that one is carrying on ones person. One can, it is true, request the services of a friend, but almost all the ants, as if numbed by captivity, lived in a stupid indifference. Apart from me, only Aristotle, Hannibal and two or three others battled against the ignoble invasion.

While Aristotle cleaned my antennae, my left-side thought pictured a little peasant girl and her mother, in the frame of an open door, on a perron horned at the corners and eroded by rain. The mother was sitting on the upper step; the child, lower down, had her back turned to her and was leaning backwards toward the maternal skirt. The old hands, the color of earthenware, were actively searching the blonde hair. The image, very precise in streaming sunlight against a background of warm shadow, had a certain beauty, and the air was charged with the odors of new-mown hay. To the left, however, I experienced a certain disgust while my right-side mind enjoyed a progressive deliverance.

When it was necessary for me to render Aristotle the same service, I strove to extinguish my left-side mind, to expel all human thought. I did not always succeed, and I suffered from the need that I could not refuse.

XXXVIII

One day, the sheet-metal cage contained provisions in considerable quantity. Perhaps our jailer was going to be absent for some time. As soon as we had transported all those riches to our home, the man, after having taken away the food-depository and the tube that connected it to our home, closed the entrance to the city hermetically and covered us with the black screen.

For a long time, we did not go out again, scorning the deceptive promenade that led so quickly, by such a monotonous path, to an uncrossable sea. However, it was furiously that we lived enclosed. In any case, the hole was necessary in order to dispose of rubbish. Would it be necessary to let ourselves be invaded by ordure of every sort?

Aristotle said to me: "That being you praise so much is a very cruel lunatic."

I shared Aristotle's opinion. My left-side mind reminded me of the monstrous inhumanity of certain masters of the world, and the sanguinary caprices to which children subject animals. Was our master a Nero without an empire, who, rendered puerile by his impotence toward his peers, was sating his hunger for torture on poor insects?

Now, in the sealed city, individuals began to die. First there was one cadaver, then two, and then, that same evening, perhaps ten. The presence of corpses in a habitation is unbearable for an ant. We became irritated in thinking that we could not free ourselves of those immobilities creative of phantoms. Not only could we not carry them, piously, to a well-kept cemetery, but we could not throw them out of the city.

Certain anxieties, growing rapidly to the point of madness, produce crazy gestures. We took hold of those bodies, of which we knew only too well that we could not rid ourselves, and paraded them interminably around our prison. When fatigue forced us to abandon them, others immediately picked them up and continued the funereal promenade. A strange force prevented us from leaving them lying on the ground. That would have been, it seemed to us, a definitive acceptance of the frightful presences; at the mere idea of that consent, fury and terror rose up within us. Charged with the macabre burdens, we ran aimlessly. The funeral voyage would doubtless have lasted until the death of the carriers, but we could not live in the presence of motionless corpses.

That folly lasted for several days, harassing us all, depriving us of sleep, agitating us with fear. When we were carrying a cadaver we fled precipitately, pursued by vague and grim images. When we rested, we followed the carriers at a distance, in spite of a violent desire to avoid them, as if we were attached to them by an unbreakable cord and drawn along by their irresistible march.

The deaths became countless. The time came when every living being had a cadaver to carry. When fatigue parted our mandibles, letting the funereal burden fall, we stayed with it, breathless, breathing until the moment when our dolorous limbs could drag us along again, weighed down by the murderous load.

The dying continued. Now the carriers were less numerous than the burdens. We carried one cadaver and stepped over cadavers, and stumbled, terrified, over other cadavers. The city was a city of the dead.

Cadavers, cadavers, cadavers everywhere; in the chambers, in the tunnels, in our provisions: thousands of cadavers. And among the cadavers that are cluttering the entire city, five or six living individuals who are running, each laden with a cadaver, and bounding, madly, trying to avoid the inevitable cadavers, and who, whenever they encounter another living being, gaze at her with haggard, bloodshot eyes, hostile by virtue of pain.

And now, all the living individuals have come together at a single point, near the closed door. Each one abandons the corpse she is carrying, and, in a madness made of horror, they throw themselves upon one another, striking out furiously, tearing one another apart, killing one another.

Another minute, and the city, so vibrant with life a few days ago, will be no more than a vast tomb sealed upon the dead.

XXXIX

The mad combat ceases. A light, brutal in its suddenness, blinds us. The lifted screen allows daylight to traverse the sheet of glass; and the human, the horrible torturer, gazes avidly at all our evils.

He takes our cage, and opens the frame in the middle, like a giant separating an immense palace into two halves. His devastating action has demolished the city, ripping open chambers and tunnels, and now, before his fingers, which try to seize us amid the crumbling debris, we flee recklessly.

One after another, he grasps us. He puts us into a box exactly similar to the first prior to our constructions; it's empty, bare, devoid of shelter and devoid of provisions, but it is also brand new, utterly fresh. After leaving the noxious city, it scarcely seems malodorous to us; it only bears the odor of human fingers, so suffocating to our healthy organs, but almost unperceived by our sense of smell overloaded by the charnel house. And the box is placed, with its entrance open, on the table where we already had a place to walk.

Only six of us have survived. But into our new domain the human introduces an equal number of strangers, six of the little *Lasius* from which we once stole the aphids. Undoubtedly the human wants to give himself the spectacle of a combat.

The *Lasius* are weak and cowardly. We could kill them easily. But what's the point? Are there still homelands, are there still instincts of hatred, after so many horrors traversed and before the horrible future that we foresee, a bleak desert in which no oasis of hope is smiling?

The little *Lasius* are trembling in a corner, ready to put up a paltry defense, ready to accept imminent death with a grim indifference. What tortures have been imposed upon them too, under the pretext of experiments?

When they see that we are not seeking to do them any harm, they dare to move. Gradually, they come closer, timidly, coming to place their mouths against ours, offering us nourishment. We speak to them; they reply—but the two languages are too different; we don't understand the responses they make to our uncomprehended questions.

They look at us continually, watching out for our needs and desires, running obligingly as soon as they think they have divined one.

Days pass, and nights, mortally monotonous, with no future, with no objective, without fatigue. The servants spare us any effort, immobilizing us in an increasingly narrow ennui.

Outside, the weather changes. We sense, vaguely, that vegetation must be extending its slow, silky blackness toward the sky, that the earth must be singing the vast song of renewal, for the sight and the hearing of all free creatures.

So many things separate us from that distant joy, but we nevertheless receive an excitement, an unquiet desire to live. We walk a little more, always to the limit of our domain. We walk, melancholy, along the circular river.

Alas, our torturer arrives. Let's go back in until he leaves.

Between us and the city, he places six amazons, and he waits.

The great red barbarians, astonished at first to be in exile, look round. The *Lasius* forget us, running to serve the new-comers. I understand the servile behavior of the little creatures now; they have been slaves of the amazons for a long time.

The amazons are hungry; they eat.

I say to Hannibal: "Once sated, they'll kill us."

"No," she says. "We have no children to steal. They won't attack us. Perhaps we'll be obliged to serve the stupid giants, but it's us who'll kill them, one by one, while they sleep.

Fear makes me shiver, and also the hope of the murder. And my left-side mind sees a little lost Ulysses, trembling and smiling, amid six Polyphemuses.

XL

I felt an abrupt strange pain, which occupied the whole of my suddenly immense body: the pain of a crazy dilatation, of an outburst.

And, suddenly human, I found myself standing on the ta-ble, which was a side-table, and which my weight caused to fall over.

An unfortunate gesture plunged my hand into the pane of glass covering the artificial ant-hill. I pull it back bloody, with shards embedded in the flesh.

As I got up, a woman came in: my wife.

"What's that noise, Octave?" she said. "You frightened me." Then, seeing my hand: "You've hurt yourself!"

With water that was in a pitcher—doubtless to renew the circular river, to prevent evaporation liberating the ants—she set about washing the cuts.

I wasn't badly injured. I was soon able to escape the cares of Madame Octave Péditant and remain alone in that room where I had been imprisoned as an ant for several months, and where I had become a man again.

By dint of searching, I found all the ants: the six ama-zons—I hastened to kill those vile slavers; the six *Lasius*; and, which astonished me at first, the six *Aphoenogasters*. How had the number remained complete after my involuntary desertion?

A moment's reflection enabled me to understand. At the same moment that I had become Octave Péditant again, the ant that had replaced me in human life had resumed her primitive form.

It's probable that she had not conserved her ordinary thought during her year-long exile, and I've often thought about the nostalgic sentiments that drove that ant, having become a human, to study ants.

XLI

I examined my former companions at length, trying to recognize them, but could not succeed in doing so. Which one was Hannibal, so prudent in advice, so skillful and brave in combat? Which one was Aristotle, the benevolent genius, who had rendered me so many services, who had saved my life one day, under the funereal strawberry-plant?

I put the poor insects in a test tube. I carried them to Chambrançon, to an abandoned nest. I took both the *Aphoenogasters* and the *Lasius*, since they were living on good terms, and because the community was very poor in mandibles for the maintenance of a city and other necessary tasks.

I conserved for that ant-hill a patriotic love that has caused me to commit crimes against other ant-hills. I searched for the nest of the amazons that forced us to flee, precipitating us into too many misfortunes; I destroyed the lair and killed all the warriors.

After having rendered security to my friends by the massacre of the amazons, I searched for another *Aphoengaster* nest. I stole eggs, nymphs, larvae and two egg-layers from it. I took them all to Hannibal and Aristotle. To give my dozen protégées time to raise that numerous family, I take grains to their crater, which dispenses them from any harvesting. I'm proud to repopulate my city.

I spend hours contemplating my compatriots, desolate at being exiled by my size. Sometimes, I pick up an ant; I study her quivering antennae, her eyes, radiating intelligence in all directions, and the rapid power of her movements. And, as absurd as if I were bending down to enter her home, I lower my voice, my gross voice that can no more penetrate her hearing than the camel of the gospel can pass through the eye of a needle, and I interrogate her:

"Who are you? Are you my friend Aristotle? Do you understand what I'm doing for you, and are you grateful to me?"

She can't distinguish me from any other mountain that walks on two legs. She agitates, distressed not to be free, trembling in fear of being crushed. I let her go; I follow her with a long nostalgic gaze.

I cannot make my thoughts known to her, nor know hers. She will never hear my voice, and the movement of her antennae is as obscure to me as the Chinese characters that the finger of a Mandarin might design in the air before my ignorant eyes.

And the ant that is fleeing from me in terror sees, in colors other than my colors, a universe other than my universe, an entire fairyland that I can no longer recover in my memories, of which I can no longer dream.

I have lost my rich ant thought, alas, my rich ant memory, and my rich ant organs! And you, fleeing Aristotle, enjoy many senses of which I no longer have any idea, in my singular impoverishment.

But a sound of footfalls troubles my meditations. I turn round and I straighten up, impelled by the spring of a crazy hope.

If the enchantress returned…oh, how I would beg her to make me an ant again, thus time forever, freeing me from the trouble of all human thought, all human memory.

Yes, I would beg her avidly, for I have only found utterly insufficient compensations for the rich lost universe. Sexual intercourse is a poor paradise; a wife is such an irritating fe-male.

I console myself slightly, thinking about the length of my life. An ant dies after eight or nine years. But an anxiety grips me: will destiny count my year as an ant as one year, or as a eighth of my existence? The anxiety grows; I recall Madame Péditant's first words.

"What's the matter with you? You seem to have age ten years since yesterday!"

XLII

I'm rich. I've become the heir of a relative that I didn't even know. The enchantress has kept her word.

I've fled administrative stupidity; I've handed in my res-ignation.

I've had a house built at Chambrançon, in order to live near my ant-hill, to spend as much time as possible gazing at my friends, whom I no longer recognize among the innumerable new population.

That is my only joy.

My human life is very unhappy. I love my wife as hate-fully as I loved the ant Marie. I have furious jealousies of which I cannot speak. She often says to me: "You were perfect for a year, but since the day when you cut your hand and when you suddenly had, for no reason I can guess, so many white hairs, you're worse than before."

And with caresses that irritate me, she begs: "Become once again the delightful Oscar of that year when we were so happy."

When she talks like that, praising my replacement and criticizing me, I have a mad desire to kill her as I killed Marie. At other times, I'm tempted to destroy the restored ant-hill and massacre all its inhabitants, in order to kill my rival.

No, I shan't kill my dear Aristotle.

I avoid humans. Every time I encounter one, his stupidity appears to me to ne enormous, to the point of making me suffer.

My sole distraction has been writing this book, and thinking, maliciously: *No one will believe me, and will praise the power of my imagination, when they ought to criticize the discolored mediocrity of my memory.*

But now that the book is finished, what will become of me?

THE PROPHET'S BRIDE

To Gabriel de la Salle[18]

The prophet who is still unknown here, but who will emerge in our midst—perhaps tomorrow—tragic and consolatory, fell silent. He had just announced the necessary and reasoned furies of the next Revolution and the joys of Equal Love that would follow. His soft and ardent words had been applauded by a few literate men indifferent to spoken words and charmed by what they called his genius. The rich, however, to whom he preached Sacrifice, drew away laughing—and the poor, whom he exhorted to Revolt without hatred, became irritated with him, the old fearful of Revolt by reason of hatred, and the young for want of hate.

Through all the streets, as if in swollen canals, the noisy crowd circulated slowly, and the great plaza was a basin gradually hushed and emptied, where only four or five men soon remained. These approached the Prophet, who looked at them, smiling, and one of them, speaking for them all, said: "Master, would you like half of our wealth and half of our time to help in your work?"

Immobile, without ceasing to smile, he replied: "No." As their eyes clouded with astonishment, however, he explained: "What you call my work is *the* Work; there is no compromise with the Unique Affair. Whoever does not give all that he has and all that he is gives nothing, and can do nothing for himself or for the Work. Goodbye."

---

[18] This Gabriel de la Salle (there have been others) was co-editor of the literary/political periodical *L'Art Social* in the 1890s.

He made as if to leave—but seeing them saddened, in a discouraged fashion, he added, for pity's sake, an encouragement he knew to be futile: "Don't let the semi-generosity that is within you be extinguished. When I pass this way again, one of you might be ready."

The men withdrew, their heads bowed at first, but soon with insolent and mocking expressions.

As the Prophet drew away, turning his back on their flight, a handsome adolescent who had been hiding behind a tree emerged. He was scarcely sixteen years of age, with a slim, almost feminine build and a soft fresh face around which blond curls fell in waves.

Timidly, he approached. Tremulously, he took the Prophet's hand and kissed it. Then, looking at him with his naïve and enthusiastic eyes, he said: "Master, I heard everything; the duty of which you speak, and the ignominy of men who shirk that duty, and the cowardice of men who trade in duty—and I am entirely yours."

In an impersonal voice, the Apostle replied: "I'm leaving for the East. Go west, and everywhere you encounter men try to sow the divine seed in their hearts."

The innocent's blue eyes grew sad, and tears ran down his gentle face. His voice wept too. "Master, repeat your order and I shall die, for my heart has passed into you, and as soon as I can no longer see you, I shall fall, never to rise again, into the ditch at the edge of the road.

The Prophet gazed at the child who spoke thus, and he understood. Then, authoritatively, he said: "In a body that is scarcely that of a man, you bear a woman's soul. Woman, be what you ought to be."

The child felt a strange disturbance throughout his being. It seemed to him that a wound opened up in his body. Weak, in search of some support, he put his head on the Prophet's breast, smiling and dolorous. And the Prophet, bowing his head, betrothed himself with a kiss on the forehead to the loving and anxious woman, who immediately became—oh, how clearly her smile manifested the fact!—a triumphant woman. And the groom wrapped his powerful and supple arms around the neck of the Bride he had just created. The austere face was lowered further, and with a kiss on the lips they were doubtless about to espouse one another when the stones fell upon them, accompanied by jeers.

"Let us flee," said the Apostle, "out of pity for these men, who will be rendered more wicked by the accomplishment of their crime."

And they fled, hand in hand.

They walked until dusk. Without looking at her, the Man sensed the eyes of the Woman upon him, heavier, warmer and more anxious than the little hand he felt in his own strong hand.

In the twilight, they ate fruit picked from the trees on which the sun than shines for everyone ripens the fruit for everyone.

Without looking at his bride, the Prophet, who still felt her amorous and dolorous gaze weighing upon him, asked: "Why are you sad?"

"I will tell you my sadness," she replied, "when you espouse me with a kiss on the lips."

The Prophet frowned because, already too womanly, she wanted to impose conditions. Severely, he ordered: "In the name of Truth, tell the truth."

Then, tearfully, she explained. She had reflected deeply since a kiss on the forehead had specified and sanctified all her victorious emotion. She had sensed how wicked the men were who would laugh at the Prophet and would want to stone holy love because he did not hide it. The regeneration of these wicked souls was impossible. The work to be done—the only work—was to give rise to the good people who would multiply and, later on, destroy the wicked. To do that the two of them ought to retire to a lonely place and adore one another, secretly, quietly, happily and jealously. Let him be hers alone, as she would be his alone, and the happiness of the universe would be theirs in superabundance.

As she sensed that these words would not convince him, she raised herself up on the tips of her weary little toes and wrapped her arms around her beloved's neck, in order to persuade him to incline his head and kiss her repeatedly.

The Prophet remained upright and tall. Pushing her away with implacable gentleness, he said: "So, poor Woman, you will always be Jealousy, never Love!"

Coaxingly, she protested: "You know full well that Love never comes without Jealousy, you who send away those who would give half of themselves!"

"O Woman!" he cried. "O Sophist of Egoism! One must give oneself entire to Good and the Future, not to that fragment of the defective Present, a person. What you call love is hatred veiled with kisses, but which jealousy denounces!"

"Oh, I am suffering" she implored. "With a kiss on the mouth, espouse me, and I shall be your slave."

Seizing his frail and powerful arms, she suddenly threw herself backward, trying to draw him into a fall—but he remained standing, and said: "The clear night forbids me the lie of such a love. I can no longer espouse you—you who already believe that you have rights over me that are superior to my Mission; you who desire to enchain the truth in your narrow arms and jealously make it your truth!"

As she wept and uttered exclamations of love mingled with jealous insults, he went on, compassionately: "Poor child, it would be better for you to go."

"No," she said. "My heart still hopes—and when it ceases to hope, I shall cling to you, in order to die pressed against my wicked beloved."

The Prophet said to the Night: "Forgive me, Infinite. I have created suffering because I wanted to correct the errors of nature before which the false Laws of man stood up. So long as justice is not the queen of the human realm, our triumphs over the empire of things will increase the weight of evil." He bowed his head like a guilty man, sighing: "I have failed in my duty; I am punished."

He raised his head again, however. "I must pardon myself, for I have work to do that regret would disturb. Depart, remorse, the final egoism."

On the roads where her feet grew weary and bloody, through the crowds in which she wept at the insults hurled against him and in which the stones thrown at him wounded her, she followed him everywhere,

Sometimes she repeated all her sacrifices, all her love, and asked: "Will you never be touched by my constancy?"

He did not reply. He did not even deign to say to her: *Your constancy is made of pride, of jealousy, of the need to conquer the man who refuses you.*

Once, however, his silence incensed her, and she cried: "I hate you!"

He remarked, simply: "You say the same thing when you declare: *I love you.*"

One day, after one of his sublime but futile speeches, when the jeering crowd had gone away, a dark-haired young man, scarcely twenty years old, with a black and proud gaze and a courageous manner marched straight up to the Prophet and said: "Master, I belong to the Work with all that I possess. Lead me, or tell me where I must go and what I must do."

The Apostle rejoiced on hearing these words—but the hateful amorous woman had seen his joy. She came to the young man, her imperious fingers seizing his astonished hand, and she said: "Friend, he will take everything from you and pay your salary in misery. Give your heart to me instead, and I will give you mine, and we shall isolate ourselves in ineffable happiness."

The young man looked at her. He saw that she was beautiful and that her eyes were two flames of passion. He shivered from head to toe. He turned to the Prophet, and tried to go toward him—but his feet would not move and his gaze, so valiant a little while before, detached itself from the woman slowly, with regret.

The Prophet saw that hesitation, and that the young man was not ready. He said, softly: "Listen to her, my son. This is my daughter, who I created for you, and in whom I placed that words that she has just pronounced. Kiss her on the forehead, to betroth yourself to her.

The young man sensed a sudden surge of joy through his entire being when his lips touched the forehead of his bride.

The Apostle continued: "Lean forward slightly, that I may place my hands upon you."

Leaning forward, they looked at one another, smiling—and they heard the Prophet's words like a very soft and meaningless noise, like the song of a bird.

His hands extended, he said: "Go, love and suffer, you who are not yet Generosity, you who are already Aspiration. Be fruitful and multiply. Your children will suffer as you do. Some, alas, in order to escape pain, will kill the aspiration within them and will become the satisfied brutes of old—but others will strive nobly, like their father and their mother, and perhaps one of them will kill the egotistical brute within himself and become the divine Bounty that no longer suffers.

When they no longer felt the extended hands upon their heads, and no longer heard the grave words that reached them in the guise of a joyous chirping, they straightened up, made a slight silent bow and drew away.

He watched them go, but they rounded a bend in the road and he could no longer see them. Unconscious and motionless, he listened to the sound of their footsteps. Then it seemed to him that they stopped, and that, with a kiss on the mouth, they espoused one another. And he had a vague sentiment of sadness, which became less vague, and finally became almost precise:

"I am so very alone!"

But he shook his head. "In truth," he said, aloud, "I believe that I shall always think of myself!"

And, leaning on his staff, he resumed his forward march, toward people who would doubtless jeer him or stone him, but one of whom might feel good after having heard him speak, or having seen him expire beneath the stones.

A TRANSITION

All the accounts of the conversation between Don Juan and the Commander are inexact, and none of the puerile speeches credited to them by various authors were pronounced. The veritable dialogue expressed profound and singular things, which it is perhaps my duty to make known.

It is quite true that the statue invited Don Juan to supper and that he accepted. Then the man of stone admired the valor of the man of flesh, and the latter, with a smile that was sadder than it was haughty, said: "I have no need of courage. I am a man for whom no danger exists."

"Do you believe yourself to be immortal?" the Commander asked, ironically.

"No," the Seducer replied. "And yet, I cannot die—because I am not alive."

Astonished, the statue took a step back, and it exclaimed: "You know that! Already!"

"Yes, I found out yesterday, while walking in the forest."

"What did you find out?" the Commander objected. "Words are capricious and vain. Each of them has numerous significations, and in the majority of those significations, is very poor in meaning. Perhaps you don't know anything, and haven't said anything."

Very precisely, Don Juan affirmed: "I know myself, and what I am saying." And he explained: "Every living thing is eternal. It is an infinite poem, each of whose successive existences speaks a line. *One* line, you understand? One single statement and one item of music, the astonishing and unique flower of a new sentiment on the stem of a new thought. Personally, this time, I have been a miserable and painful transition, creative of unity but devoid of unity and personality in itself—dispersed by its effort to embrace too much past and too much future. I have no present."

He paused for thought, and spoke slowly:

"Sometimes, in passing by certain places unknown to our present memory, we have a vague desire to install ourselves there; we dream of living and dying in that frame, which seems cheerful to us. Hooked by their current destiny, by the necessity of accomplishing all the day's work, others pass by. That false need, to which they cannot yield, is the reminiscence of a former sojourn, or sometimes, if I may put it thus, the blind prevision of a future life. I, who had nothing to do, who was not a being and a determined act, have stopped everywhere; I have transformed into reality all my indifferent desires and have yielded to all deceptions. At the end of a day of idleness, I yawn, or I lie down bored, on any lawn that beckons to me."

More bitterly, he continued:

"The noblest expression of unity is unique and veritable love. Certainly, the most faithful man abandons himself to other desires, and even to other possessions, which are beautiful memories or adorable presentiments. Every line of the poem is clarified by the reflection of all the preceding lines, quivering in anticipation of the lines to come. I, alas, am not a new idea, a new love, an augmentation. I have not loved anyone. I have added no wealth to my treasure; I have only taken inventory of my possessions. My lips, in hasty kisses, have tasted the amours of my previous existences and the amours of my existences to come. I yearn to escape this cluttered and painful transition, to rest in the long-felt beauty of a genuinely conceived idea, a genuinely experienced amour. For pity's sake, help my dispersion in death. Kill the dead thing that I am, in order that, after the necessary proofs, I can attain the unity of life again."

Lowering his head, heavily, he asked:

"Has the beloved of my current life not come to this earth? Or was I unable to recognize her? Speak, you who must know better than I."

The Commander did not say a word. And, as Don Juan repeated his question, he sniggered cruelly—but Don Juan raised his head again, and said, with a resigned smile: "That's not it. Destinies are not deceived, and, undoubtedly, abridgement is necessary to the good order of the whole. But I thank you, my Lord, for the fact that this fatiguing and tedious transition is finally to be terminated."

And without the earth opening, without the thunder rumbling, without the statue lifting a finger, Don Juan fell, seemingly killed by an overly exact consciousness of his own non-existence.

SACRIFICES

God thought: *I am powerful*—and the souls of kings were irradiated.

Then he asked himself: *Over what does my power extend?*—and universes were sown in space, in which the kings carved out kingdoms.

God affirmed: *I am all-powerful*—and from the glorious Center sprang haughty souls: Caesars, Alexanders and Napoleons.

But the Being asked himself: *Am I really all-powerful?* And he replied: *Yes, in the sense that no power exists outside of me and my creatures...but am I all-powerful to the point that nothing is impossible? How can I know that, any thought of mine being creative and the impossible being for me the indispensable?* And he continued: *I cannot know what my limitations are, nor whether I am limited. O weakness!*

Now, during this reactive meditation, shadows of negation were projected over the worlds, beside the powers irradiated earlier. Next to each Caesar a Brutus stood up, next to each Napoleon a Wellington, next to each Alexander an impotent Porus and a great mysterious cup overflowing with so much life that it delivered death.

The Creator gazed at the worlds delivered from tyrants and the heroic murderers of tyrants. The conflict between those who wanted to have everything and those who did not want another to have everything seemed somber to him.

He regretted: *The earths that I have created are evil*—and that repentance was translated into deluges of water and fire, into terrible disasters.

God wept to have had this maleficent remorse—and gentle and weak individuals, long processions of tearful victims, wandered about the worlds.

I am, however, good, the Being said to himself. *Bounty must act, and be strong*—and admirable men, of active devotion, came forth. And God smiled at Vincents de Paul.

Now, the Spirit had many other dreams and many other thoughts.

The Unique had affirmed: *I am the Evidence*—and there had been the Theresas and the Bonaventures, the Platos and the Plotinuses, all the mystics, ecstatics and seers of the ineffable.

The Immense had thought: *I am infinite in detail, impossible to embrace in entirety*—and the scientists who searched painfully and found a few particular verities of their universe, but who did not see God, had appeared, bent over their flasks and alembics.

The creative Thought had mused: *I am Beauty*—and the Homers had sung to the accompaniment of the lyre, the Phidiases had given harmonious life to marble, the Raphaels had made serene canvases smile.

When God had thought a great deal, he compared the creations of his thought to himself, and he said, astonished: "The ensemble of worlds is now greater than I am!" And this astonishment created throughout the universe the stupid souls of atheists and deniers.

Now, the Generous perceived that his diminished power no longer produced any but incomplete beings, miserable and malevolent. Then he pronounced the word SACRIFICE!

The Word made the worlds tremble, for now the creator was no longer outside creation. The waters, matrices of living beings, quivered, saddened, no longer feeling the fecund breath of the Spirit over them, and broadcasting in sinister voices: "Great Pan is dead!"

But the Word was made flesh—and the souls of infants smiled in cribs, while the gleams in their eyes were reflected in the sky in guiding stars and their wailing rebounded as echoes, singing in the heights: "Peace and good will to men."

Each Jesus went through life in his own world doing good, understood and beloved by some, persecuted and finally put to death by the powerful.

Each dead Jesus descended, weighed down by pity, to the earth immediately inferior to his own, which his compatriots, vaguely aware of it, called Hell. He spoke words of hope to the inhabitants of that more dolorous world. Returned to their homelands, the Christs were reincarnated, and appeared to some of those who had loved them, affirming the power of life and the resurrection of good. And each one promised that, once reconciled with the Father, he would send them the Holy Spirit.

Each Jesus then rose up to the immediately superior earth, which his compatriots, vaguely aware of it, called Heaven or Paradise. And the one that belonged to the most perfect world returned to the Center, to recommence God.

And the sublime procession of worlds rose up, suffering but buoyed up by hope, toward God, to remake him in entirety. And everywhere the Idea of Love was fought by the Forced of Hatred. A few clever powerful individuals even tried to take possession of the martyr Idea and crown themselves with it; as Pauls had begun to give Gentiles a common soul, Constantines hoped to reign over all nations. But everywhere the bloody idea, changing its name, sometimes nameless, continued its terrible and smiling march through the forces that tore it apart, but which it dragged slowly in its wake, unperceived by almost everyone.

When time came to an end, when God was reconstituted in entirely by the voluntary death of the universes, he thought, in an initial fit of miserly joy, of rediscovering himself: "Every cycle resembles the preceding cycles. What good does it do to recommence my dilatation, the rewards of which involve nothing unexpected, and which is answered, century after century, by a concentration of worlds ever as dolorous?

But God perceived that this egotistical thought was transformed into evil beings.

Conscious of his inexorable power, which forced every one of his thoughts to take on concrete form, he said to himself: *I am too great not to create*—and resigned individuals, already great, Socrates accepted death and Zenos accepted the world, radiantly.

God's thought continued: *Besides, that necessity is sublime. Not only do I consent to it, but I desire it and I love it—for the double movement, always the same in appearance, is more beautiful with every cycle, since every time, the sacrifice of God dying for the life of worlds, and the sacrifice of worlds dying for the life of God becomes more conscious and voluntary.*

And God, smiling, continued to extinguish himself in luminous universes and radiant souls.

THE SON OF GOD

Before assembled Greece, the athletes competed for prizes and glory. The elegant games of running and fighting were over. The brutal pugilism was about to begin. Four pairs, selected by lot, had just been introduced into the stadium. Gazes, gestures, whispers, spoken words and exclamations were all directed at one of the eight combatants, the tallest of them all. And the words were exchanged between the spectators:

"There he is! There he is!"

"That's him: that's the son of the god!"

A bizarre mixture of emotion and skeptical curiosity surrounded the gigantic and redoubtable athlete with its warm and heady atmosphere. He was certainly more vigorous than the others, but perhaps less supple and less skillful, ponderously slow in mind and body.

He was a barbarian from Troad.[19] When the judges of the games had asked his name and that of his father, he had declared: "My father is a god, for I am Attalus, the son of the river Scamander."

In one group of Athenians the conversation was particularly animated, but also particularly cheerful. Curious young people were surrounding an old man with venerable hair and beard, malicious eyes and ironic lips. His features, both noble and fine, retained a singular beauty. His name, Cimon, was surrounded by the same aureole as that of Alcibiades. It only had to be pronounced to give rise to thoughts of the most moving adolescent beauty, the most singular spirit of adventure, famous voyages, a thousand heroic dangers and innumerable successes with the women of every land.

---

[19] The region once ruled by the city of Troy.

The old man with the noble expression and the penetrating smile said: "Enough poets have put the Scamander into tragedies. I remember, with laughter on my lips and laughter in my heart, that I once had the juvenile audacity to put it into a comedy."

The young people begged him to tell the story to which he was alluding. And he, directing glances toward Attalus, the son of the god Scamander, in which malice struggled against a mysterious tenderness, began in this fashion:

"Adolescents as dear as sons, you have asked me to tell you about one of the prodigies that are the glory of the gods. My well-known piety does not permit me to refuse.

"The desire to see the world and the restlessness of youth had led me to the glorious and melancholy region where the ruins of Troy lie dormant, corroded by the sun. As a man desirous of learning, I informed myself of the customs of the land. Among other interesting details, I learned of one practice that touched my religious heart. Before marrying, the young women bathe in the waters of the Scamander, and offer their first favors, without fail, to the river. The god, I was told, disdains almost all their insufficient beauties. There had, however, been one example to the contrary.

"Among the brides-to-be of that time, I had noticed one, in spite of her slightly sly candor, for her supple and charming grace. Callirhoë attracted me like a paradox, for she bore the mind of the most ponderous barbarian within the most prefect Greek body.

"On the appointed day, she went with her companions to the pious ceremony. The crowd stood respectfully on the bank, some distance away, while the young women, dispersed by the bends and caprices of the river, pronounced in tremulous voices the ritual words: 'O Scamander, accept the homage which I owe to thee!'

"Callirhoë's heart almost ceased beating, gripped by an overly glorious expectation and the hope of an excessively powerful joy. The rushes quivered around her; the god rose up with a harmonious slowness. He had the form of a young man

164

and his head bore a crown in which the dazzling whiteness of the narcissus was interwoven with the shining green of reeds. In a voice that was both proud and soft, he replied; 'I accept your offering, O most beautiful of Trojan women.'

"He led the young woman into the grass on the shore. From a distance, the enthusiastic people sang of the glory of Callirhoë and the generosity of the god.

"A few days later, the newlyweds appeared with all their ornaments in a procession in honor of Venus. Lost amid the innumerable spectators, I watched with a joy compounded out of memory and laughter. But then, all of a sudden, Callirhoë quit her place, ran to me, threw herself at my feet, and these words fell from her overflowing heart: 'O Scamander! O my first husband!'

"The crowd was astonished, then became annoyed and cried sacrilege. It rushed forward to capture me. I don't know, in truth, by what prodigy I succeeded in escaping it.

"Callirhoë, her husband and a fraction of the people would not renounce their pious certainty for so little. Several of them had even seen the god, when they tried to take hold of him, rise into the air and transform himself, among the sun's rays, into a light and luminous cloud.

"Nine months later, Callirhoë gave birth to a son, whom I love paternally, as we all ought to love the children of the gods. I wish, with all the ardor of my piety, for Attalus to be victorious. I declare, moreover, that it is certain, for his divine father could not do any less for him."

Cimon fell silent, and, with everyone else, watched the combat that had begun. The fight did not last long. With an awkward and roaring fury, Attalus threw himself upon his adversary. The latter, a Greek almost fragile in appearance, was quick to evade the attack. The son of the god, who had no obstacle in front of him, fell heavily on to the ground, uttering cries of fury and pain. Already, the supple Hellene had leapt upon him. With one hand squeezing his neck and two knees pressed down upon his hips, he held him against the ground.

Meanwhile, he struck precise and cruel blows, until Attalus finally cried for mercy and confessed himself defeated.

Amused by the triumph of cunning over brute force, and joyful at the victory of a Greek over a barbarian, the people burst out in long and interminable acclamations.

Old Cimon shook his venerable and mocking head. He prevented a tear from running from his eye, and tried to smile. And he said to the young people surrounding him: "If piety is diminishing in the hearts of men, you'll admit that it is the gods' own fault."

THE PROMISE

A mortuary chamber. On the bed, a dying woman, very young and very beautiful, in her final costume. The stage is only lit by a single candle.

The curtain rises.

THE SURVIVOR

is sitting beside the bed, his head in his hands. His entire attitude is expressive of grief and meditation.

He raises his head and looks at the dead woman for a long time. Then he says:

Alba, Alba, you have abandoned me, then! Your form is there, and your beauty, more beautiful still if my eyes do not deceive me—but where is that which was profoundly mine, the person that I loved, and who loved me?

Has this long dolorous vigil not made a madman of me? At times, it seems to me that you're still here—you, and not your cadaver. And it seems to me that you're trying to keep old promises...to keep THE PROMISE.

(*He passes his hand over his forehead.*)

Do those who watch over the dead have the sentiment of an inexpressible presence? From where, full of life and without anything enabling the stupid accident to be foreseen, do your words come...like the waters of a river flowing toward the sea...all flowing toward death, toward the problems of death, toward—oh, the words that astonished me for a long time, but which you succeeded, afterwards, in rendering familiar to me—the expansions and beauties of death?

Do you remember, Alba, how all those mysterious speeches ended?

"The one who goes first must return to tell the other what happens on the other side."

Then you made the mad promise, and demanded the implausible promise from me.

And now, here we are...my eyes, fatigued by tears, fatigued by the vigil, deceived by the pain, that rebellious madness which ignores the impossible and its frontiers, sometimes, yes, my eyes believe that they see something floating in your sealed face...something like THE PROMISE making an effort to fulfill itself.

I know full well, however, that you are no longer there, you, my only love. I know full well that the two worlds are irredeemably separate. Your body alone remains before my eyes, for a few more hours. Alba, dolorous seed, the heavy fraction of that which was you will plunge into the earth like a root—but your soul, doubtless, is already a branch, which, amid an azure inaccessible to the living, displays itself lightly and happily.

A DISTANT VOICE
Lightly and happily.

THE SURVIVOR, *shuddering*.
Who spoke? Is that you, Alba?

THE VOICE
Alba.

THE SURVIVOR, *leaning over the dead woman*.
It's you! Here with me, there's no one but you. Oh, what is it that I see? On your dead face, but a little above, what is it, then, that quivering...that light? Is it your life? Is that you, Alba?

THE VOICE
Alba.

THE SURVIVOR
Oh, I'm mad! It's not possible that I can really hear...

...And that I can see... And yet, if I can really see, slightly above the face weighed down by abandonment, that floating light, so light, which is inexpressibly reminiscent of the vanished gaze and smile...and which, perhaps, has twice said: Alba...

THE VOICE

Alba.

THE SURVIVOR

My Alba, if that's you, what are you doing? What do you want? Oh, I feel my heart breaking, for one would think that the light, which is perhaps you, is striving and suffering.

THE VOICE

Striving and suffering.

THE SURVIVOR

Who are you, voice that I hear? Are you an echo of my thought? Are you Alba's thought?

THE VOICE

Alba's thought.

THE SURVIVOR

Why are you suffering? Toward what are you striving? Are you trying, for one more moment, to animate that body?

THE VOICE

Animate that body.

THE SURVIVOR

How did you come by that desire? Are you trying to make a visible movement, in order that I might be certain that you are here?

THE VOICE
Here.

THE SURVIVOR
Tell me, will you come back to the life I knew? Answer me: do the periods of free life and the periods when existence is weighed down by a body alternate regularly, like wakefulness and sleep?

THE VOICE
Wakefulness and sleep.

THE SURVIVOR
Doubtless, then, my Alba, you have recovered a series of memories, a tradition, a continuity, the eternal identity of your being. Your free life is fusing with all free lives—but your corporeal existences are drawing away and fading away, disappearing like a choir of dreams. Doubtless, Alba, you will soon forget me—for you, I was a dream during a sleep.

THE VOICE
A dream during a sleep.

THE SURVIVOR
At least, my Alba, while you are still close to me, speak to me softly, at length, with love and with light.

THE VOICE
With light.

THE SURVIVOR
Yes, what you say must suffice to enlighten me. One remark, however, afflicts me with anxiety. You have not pronounced a single new word. Independent voice or echo of mine, you always repeat the lasts words to emerge from my mouth. That is not sufficient.

THE VOICE

That is not sufficient.

THE SURVIVOR

Oh, give me more. Let my ear hear a word that I have not yet said, that I have not yet thought. Grant me that clear, complete proof, if I am not asking for the impossible.

THE VOICE

The impossible.

THE SURVIVOR

Ah! I understand. Already, no doubt, you have forgotten our language of sleep. The dead can only—rarely, and with so much difficulty!—repeat to a living person thoughts emerging from a living brain, words emerging from a living mouth.

THE VOICE, *getting weaker*.

Words emerging from a living mouth.

THE SURVIVOR

Oh! Voice, how weak you are becoming.

(*Leaning over the dead woman*.)

And you too, light.

(*The first light of dawn enters the room*.)

Nothing more. On the dead face, no light, no flotation...speak, Alba—are you still there?

(*He waits. He listens. Nothing*.)

Answer, answer me! Once again. One more time, I beg you.

(*Nothing*.)

Was I dreaming? Or did I make momentary contact with the true life, the true vigil?

Alba, Alba, if you have departed forever, I want to die, I want to join you.

(*He throws himself recklessly on to the dead woman, while the curtain falls*.)

THE LIVING CORPSE

There was once a queen of a northern country who was the most beautiful in the world, but evil demons possessed her. The son of the king of Arles, having heard of her renowned beauty and misfortune, took a large sum of money and set forth, without telling anyone about his project, in the hope of liberating her and marrying her.

On the evening of the first day of his journey, he arrived in a foreign village. All of its people, gathered in the central square, were crying, agitating and quarrelling around a coffin. The prince asked what had caused such great disorder.

"The dead man," they told him, "has left considerable debts, and his creditors are opposing his burial."

"Are they men devoid of faith, then?"

"They are excellent Christians, but they are no less fond of their money. They need it for good works that genuinely please God, which their confessor has recommended to them, and they need it to buy indulgences."

"Let the dead man be buried," said the indignant prince. "I will pay all that he owes."

When the Generous Prince had finished paying out, he no longer had a penny of the money he had brought for the voyage. He sat down to one side, glad of his good conscience, but slightly embarrassed for the continuation of the plan with which he had set out. People are always a trifle embarrassed to find themselves penniless, when it is the first time that it has happened to them. Poverty is a trade like any other, which requires an apprenticeship.

A man tapped the Generous Prince on the shoulder, however, and said to him: "God has sent me to get you out of trouble, milord."

"Who told you to call me milord, and who are you?"

"I'm the dead man who was buried thanks to you."

"You seem very much alive for a dead man," said the Generous Prince. Having looked harder at his interlocutor though, he saw that a strange light was emerging from his eyes, which was not of this world. The man's pupils had the form of a cross, and a flaming Jesus was extended on that cross.

Besides, the Living Corpse added: "The Lord said to me: 'Go and do the work of the living until the son of the king of Arles has liberated the most beautiful queen in the world from demons. Go; it is me who lives within you, with all my prudence'."

As the Generous Prince had not confided his project to anyone, he was forced to recognize that God had performed a miracle to reward him for his good deed. "What shall we do and where shall we go?" said the Generous Prince, confidently. "The prudence of the Lord, which lives within you, must have told you that I haven't a penny in my pocket."

"We shall draw upon my uncle's treasures."

"Who is your uncle?"

"A giant rich in money, rich in magic objects, rich in three enormous heads, and rich in a strength that permits him to fight alone against five hundred armed men and vanquish them."

"Alas, if we try to lay a finger on his treasures, he'll make a mouthful of the two of us, scarcely enough to fill his hollow tooth."

"Man of little faith, have you forgotten that the prudence of the Lord is within me? Man of little memory, have you forgotten that in stories, all giants are very stupid? Let's just mount up."

Half a league from the castle, the Living Corpse hid the Generous Prince in a cave. Then he rode on alone, at full tilt, and went to knock on the door with all his might. The giant, furious at been woken up when he had only just gone to sleep, shouted: "Who's there?"

"It's me."

"Who's *me*? Everyone calls himself *me*."

"Me, your nephew."

"How is that possible? I was told that you were dead."

"People say many things. I've come to bring you some urgent and very bad news, my poor uncle."

The giant's three heads, however, emitted three bursts of laughter so loud that they made three distant mountains tremble, whipped up three storms on three oceans and caused three rivers to flood in three valleys. And the three monstrous heads said: "How can news be bad for us? We are three heads, and we can beat five hundred armed men and make them flee like wisps of straw in the wind."

"Without doubt," said the Living Corpse, "but the king has sworn to kill you, and he is drawing near with twenty thousand armed men."

"We're doomed, we're doomed!" moaned the three heads. And in three distant churches, three bells began to toll the knell all by themselves.

"I shall save you," said the Living Corpse, "but swear first that you will give me, as a reward, the four things that I ask of you."

The giant having sworn, his nephew locked him in the cellar. "Don't move, whatever happens. I'll keep the key until the king has gone. Not finding you anywhere, he'll think you've gone away and disband his army. Then I'll come and let you out."

The Living Corpse and the Generous Prince spent the night in the castle. They made a lot of noise, as if they were an entire army. In the morning, the prince drew extensively on the giant's treasures and left in advance. When he was far enough away the Living Corpse released his uncle, who was still trembling with fear.

"Well," said the Living Corpse, I have to go now. Give me the four items you owe me, quickly. I choose that bashed in old hat, that tattered old cloak, that chipped old sword and that worn-out old slipper."

"Who told you what those old things are worth?"

"What does it matter? Besides, they're all worthless to you, who are in a state of mortal sin."

"That's true," said the giant, giving the objects to his nephew.

"Because I'm in a state of grace," the Living Corpse added, "this hat will procure me all knowledge, this cloak will render me invisible, and this slipper, worn on my left foot, will give me lightning speed. As for this sword, it will cut through everything I strike with it, whether it is a wall of diamond, the hide of a rhinoceros or a demon's skin."

Guided by the Living Corpse, the Generous Prince soon arrived as the castle of the Possessed Beauty. That same evening, the queen offered a magnificent feast to the suitor. When the meal was finished, though, she wiped her mouth with a handkerchief. Then, hiding the handkerchief in her dress, she said to the son of the king of Arles: "If you don't show me that handkerchief tomorrow morning, I'll have your head cut off."

In the middle of the night, her demons transported the Possessed Beauty to the infernal regions, and she gave her handkerchief to one of the most terrible demons. Through the hat of science, however, the Living Corpse had found out what he had to do. Clad in the mantle of invisibility and the sandal of rapidity, he had followed the lady. No one suspected the presence of a stranger, and he had no trouble taking possession of the handkerchief.

One can imagine the astonishment and anger of the queen when the Generous Prince showed her the handkerchief—but she did not let her sentiments show and invited the prince to supper again. At the end of the meal, she said: "To-night, I shall kiss someone. Tomorrow, if you don't show me the head that I kissed, I shall have yours cut off."

At midnight she went down to Hell and quarreled with the demon that had let the handkerchief be stolen. Then she calmed down, explained how she had repaired his negligence, and kissed him on the lips.

The Living Corpse was there, of course, invisible and attentive. As soon as the lady had gone, he took the sword that cuts everything it strikes, sliced through the demon's neck and took its head to the prince. He said to him: "You paid my debts; I'm giving you what you need to pay yours. Adieu." And he disappeared, along with the magical objects given to him by the giant.

When the Generous Prince showed the Possessed Beauty the head that she had kissed, she cried: "These demons are too stupid. They finally disgust me."

She burst into laughter, and was liberated—for the parish priest perhaps does not know that laughter is the best exorcism, which gets rid of the most obstinate demons.

The marriage of the queen and the son of the king of Arles took place that very evening. They were happy, lived for a long time, and had many children.

APOLOGISTES' DREAM

Canon Apologistes, the former professor of mathematics at the Minor Seminary of Platanopolis, had promised the *Christian Philosophical Review* an article on the mystery of the Most Holy Trinity.

As yet, he only had the key idea of the article, but he was greatly intoxicated by it. He went to sleep telling himself that he was possessed of genius—a genius unique by virtue of its composition: mathematico-theological genius.

Let us try to render the brilliant canon's idea intelligible, even to the profane and those devoid of genius.

Why does one ordinarily experience some difficulty in reconciling the unity of God with the Trinity of persons who are not mere aspects or mere powers, and who are not only divine, but each of whom is God? It is because we think in accordance with the lowliest of human methods, that which emerges from naïve addition. If we want to understand Him, God deserves that we forsake such slothfulness; let us therefore make the effort to climb to our highest level and apply to the All-Powerful our least impotent methods.

Does He ever proceed by simple addition? Is it the case that, for a grain of wheat confided to the earth and Providence, He only renders two grains of wheat? Far from it. He *multiplies* seeds. His fecundity *multiplies* inexhaustibly each of His thoughts. Can anyone count the number of individuals comprising any species you care to name, or any one of His divine dreams?

So far as our feebleness permits, let us think as He thinks, according to the fertile and soaring method of *multiplication*.

Let us no longer add up the three persons. Let us no longer represent them by the meager signs $1 + 1 + 1$. Let us express them in a richer symbolism: $1 \times 1 \times 1$. Father, Son and

Holy Spirit, God manifests thus a power all the greater for being triple. He is, triumphantly, Unity to the third power, 1^3. Eternally multiplying himself, eternally multiplying that eternal multiplication, he is, in all his glory,

THE CUBE OF UNITY

It was also in glory and in light that seemed to repeat and multiply itself that Canon Apologistes fell asleep. His lips were parted in joy, but they became pursed during the dream by which he was visited.

The Devil appeared to him, horned, hairy and hilarious. Not only was he laughing with his open lips and his sonorous throat, but he was laughing with his tail, which was shaking like a hand-bell, and with his entire twisting and swaying body. In the midst of his loud and active gaiety, he said: "At the Council of Soissons,[20] Abelard was condemned for having compared the Father, the Son and the Holy Spirit, who formed but a single essence, to the three propositions that form a mere syllogism."

"But my proposition," the canon protested, "Is not concerned with logic."

"Nor with mathematics, as I shall demonstrate to you shortly."

At this point, the canon was too sure of himself, and his laughter was equal to the Devil's.

But Satan continued: "Wallis, a professor at the University of Oxford, was ridiculed, so far as he is remembered at all, for an ingenious and stupid, savant and puerile parallel between the three divine persons and the three dimensions of

---

[20] A Synod held in Soissons in 1121 ordered the burning of Peter Abelard's *Theologia* because of this and other supposedly-heretical suggestions.

matter.[21] I had, however, warned Wallis as well as Abelard. Alas, Luther is the only churchman who has ever listened to me profitably."

"What did you warn them about?"

"I warned them, as I am warning you, that they were emptying God of any concrete existence. You are the one most guilty of that impiety. More than that of either of the other two, your God becomes abstract, flaccid and impotent. Only abstract unity can multiply itself without increasing."

"*Vade retro, Satanas.*"

Milord Satan would not consent to go away. He asked: "Do you believe in a concrete and powerful God, and a God who is real and, if I might put it thus, efficacious?"

"Assuredly."

"From which it follows that, in multiplying himself, he increases."

"The infinite is incapable of increase."

"I shall not challenge you to distinguish the infinite from the inexhaustible, for, in that controversy, we would both have to admit infinity, however contradictory the concept might be. If we agree on principles, we can have a discussion. Now, in as solemn a fashion as possible, I declare by my horns and my tail, and I declare by my infinity—for the lining must be the same size as the garment—I declare, I say, that as soon as one multiples something concrete, it equals, for your feeble gaze, a hundred or a thousand. For the force of my thought and my sly adoration, it gives much more, and more than I can say in your language. Unlike you, I am not impious enough to limit the divine powers to three. How wretched your cubic trinity is! Imagination of your weakness, poor sensible being akin to Wallis, has only three dimensions. Know that, beyond your

---

[21] John Wallis (1616-1703), the Savilian Professor of Geometry at Oxford, was the second most prominent English mathematician of his era, after Isaac Newton, with whom he shared an interest in esoteric theology; the analogy in question was proposed in various letters and sermons written *circa* 1690.

distorted forms, the actual dimensions are much more numerous. Does not a little good will inform you that the three dimensions are miserable abstractions? The rich complexity of the slightest concrete object contains dimensions and directions as infinite in number as its points, its lines or its planes. The human being who has understood God most profoundly, Spinoza, could only name two divine attributes, but he did not hesitate to affirm that the attributes inaccessible to human thought are infinite in number."

"What do Abelard, Spinoza and this Wallis whose name you have taught me matter to me? You haven't proven anything against my explanatory comparison. It shocks you precisely because it grasps the divine essence in its enlightenment."

"Like the Gascon philosopher's blasphemy, your blind comparison creates, at a single stroke, a thousand gods."[22]

"O Father of Lies!"

"Since you honor me with one of the names I love, I will make you a concession: you have no more than a hundred gods."

"I confess one sole God."

"Ah! Ah! Ah! Your unity-cubed God, which belief will give me a laugh for the rest of eternity. Is a cubic meter only a meter and only has ten decimeters?"

"It has a thousand cubic decimeters," murmured the former professor of mathematics, anxiously.

"A hundred times more decimeters than the meter not yet multiplied by itself. A God in one person is ten times a tenth of a God. Your God in three persons, your God cubed is worth a thousand cubic decimeters. A thousand tenth-Gods makes a good hundred Gods.

---

[22] "The Gascon philosopher" was an appellation commonly applied to Michel de Montaigne (1533-1592), whose mild and inquisitive skepticism made him a important figure in the history of French freethought.

The canon thought that he had found a decisive insult. "Shut up," he cried, "you cubic lie!"

Satan, delighted, replied in a fond and gentle tone: "Dear cube of stupidity and nothingness, we both share a belief in zeroes with the exponent 3, impotence to the third power. Let's be serious and piously adore in me the fourth person of the Most Holy Complexity, which you so meanly call a Trinity. Some people suspect the fourth dimension; be the man who will henceforth know that the Devil is a part of God."

The unhappy canon made the sign of the cross. If he expected to put the Adversary to flight, he was mistaken.

Satan took hold of Apologistes' hands and separated them, giving the priest's body the poignant form of the cross. Meanwhile, he laughed, as an entire class of children laughs around a humiliated schoolmaster.

And during the little leaps of his laughter he instructed: "Adore in me the creator of God, or, at least, the creator of the unity, such as it is, of your God. Before me, before I became manifest, the Father, Son and Spirit were three gods. I raised the Adversary before them; against me, they were one. Adore the one who has created the most sacred of sacred unions." He paused, and then continued: "Some years ago, you delivered a beautiful sermon on war, every word of which I breathed into you. You said then: 'Thanks to German aggression, all Frenchmen now have but one heart.' And you cursed the era of peace 'in which Frenchmen did not love one another.' Before me, if you can imagine a time before me, your gods did not love one another. Against me, they are one sole God. If I disappear, the cluster falls apart."

Apologistes woke up with an atrocious migraine.

"Oh," he said, "my article! Shall I find the strength to write my article?"

He took a double dose of sedative and, without any other breakfast, sat down at his work-desk. He began to write: "God is the cube of unity."

The formula delighted him, like a cascade of pure and vivid light in places that had lately been dark. He repeated it, like a powerful ejaculatory prayer. It filled him with joy and pride. He mingled it with other, inconsistent words. In a whisper, he let slip the utterance: "Poor St. Augustine, a genius in other ways, despaired of explaining the facile mystery because of his utter lack of mathematical genius."

THE PACIFISTS

I

This, voluntarily incomplete, imprecise and dishonest, is the account of a voyage. I shall not strive deceptively, like a banal voyager, to astonish, to interest, or to create nostalgia for a crazy country into which singular circumstances threw me. I hope to avoid any crime against my homeland and modern civilization; I hope that I do not inspire in anyone a desire to find the lost island. The strange life that people lead there frightened me at first, but afterwards took possession of me like a vertigo. I can no longer succeed, except with great effort, in understanding its distant seductions, but when I was plunged into them, I smiled at them for a while, and, from the most intellectual to the crudest, all my companions, almost without exception, were definitively stuck therein.

No sailor will read this book—that is a point on which I an entirely tranquil—but it risks falling into the hands of a few dreamers. Those unbalanced individuals will see herein—and I would not want them to emerge from the vision dazzled—an immense paradox lived for centuries by countless human beings; they will see a utopia that has found its place, which has established itself in an immense territory and is developing harmoniously and logically there like a monomaniac obsession. May the clever mixture of truth and lies, naïve expositions and skillful restrictions, that I am presenting cure those anxious readers rather than making their condition worse!

But it is not for those miserable souls maddened by liberty or fraternity, those lamentable sufferers of the gangrene of the infinite, that I am writing. If I did not have more interesting people in mind, I would certainly have abstained. My book will indicate to a few physicists and a few horticulturalists

183

useful directions for their research. That is my goal, my hope and my excuse.

The name of our vessel, its port of attachment, the destination for which we were heading and the place where we found ourselves are as many items of information that I have to withhold. I am not one of those gossips who, under the pretext of exactitude, vulgarize the formulae of poisons and indicate routes of death. I am tempted to begin, with the casual negligence of popular tales: *Once upon a time there was a ship at sea...*

You shall not know my name, nor those of any of my companions. The Captain will be called "the Captain," as the ship will be called "the ship." I shall call myself Jacques. The only comrade, doubtless, about whom I shall speak particularly will be named Charles. Needless to say, those two names are made up.

Under the intense sunlight, the sea had a noble beauty. The waves were flowing with a robust movement, playfully. Charles, the Hellenist, and I had been gazing silently for some time at the soothing rhythm, compounded of force and idleness. But my friend broke the charmed silence and on an even and imprecise ocean of reverie, as sudden wave of thought sprang forth, almost brutally, rearing up and falling back.

"A beautiful country," he said.

An absurd thing to say, for a start, as black as stupidity and without apparent significance, but through which he seemed to me to divine the glimmer of I don't know what mysterious meaning, which appealed and fled, irritatingly.

I looked at Charles suspiciously, and very stupidly—I knew that I was being stupid but couldn't help saying it. I asked that grave, austere fellow, ignorant of laughter and fantasy: "Are you making fun of me?"

Wounded by that supposition, and by the vulgarity with which I expressed it, he drew away and said, disdainfully:

"You're decidedly one of those in whose company it's best to keep quiet."

I was on the point of insulting my friend, or insulting myself. I felt a surge of anger. Against whom? Against him? Against me? Against the rhythm of the water in the light, which now seemed monotonous and annoying? Against all of them at the same time? For lack of the ability to choose a target, my sarcasm remained still, enclosed like a bullet in a cartridge.

Leaning on the bulwark, I gazed at the movement of the sea, still calm and equitable. Its aimless, limitless uniformity, untiringly repetitive, wearied my eyes and my consciousness. In my inundated mind, the waves affirmed, in duration as in space, I don't know what constant and nauseating monotony. I finally murmured, in a yawn: "Tedious eternity!"

A contradictory and mocking echo, Charles replied: "Admirable change!"

He was sitting on a bench and holding an open book in his hand.

"You're very banal," I exclaimed, "if you can admire a pedestrian agitation that's always the same. It seems to me that it's necessary to be younger than us still to marvel at the cycle of the seasons or to be amazed by the fact that the waves that rise up fall back, and that every summit has a valley for its necessary companion. Oh, day and night, the rhythm of a broad yawn that only closes to reopen again!"

The serious fellow laughed. "You have lovely teeth, and I like it when you yawn."

I was about to reply...what? What stupidity? He did not give me time.

"Do you know where we are?" he asked.

"No—and it's all the same to me. Can you see a difference between forty-five and forty-six degrees of latitude, or fifty degrees of east longitude and fifty degrees of west longitude? You're very lucky!"

"It's not a matter of that," he said. "I think that at this very moment, we're over Atlantis."

"Atlantis is a name I've heard or read somewhere," I remarked, negligently, "but for me, it's just a name."

I looked, with a vague, somnolent curiosity at the sea, whose aspect rapidly changed. The waves, like happy children a little while before, were now toiling laborers. Innumerable monstrously strong clumps of weeds were impeding their thrust. With millions of arms, hardly quivering, the heavy algae were holding the ocean back, like a obstinate population of women slowing down the march of an army. The sea, paled by its increasingly futile effort, lost the beauty of its color along with the free grace of its gestures. Among all those tangles, with whose shiny, sticky, yellow and flat ugliness it mingled, the water dragged along, muddy, harassed and livid.

Charles had sought out a passage in his book. He read the Greek with a painfully contrived emphasis; then he translated the frightful text.

"*A powerful army, departing from the Atlantic Ocean, insolently invaded Europe and Asia. For one could cross that Ocean then. There was an island situated opposite the strait that you call the Pillars of Hercules. That island was larger than Libya and Asia combined.*"

"Yes," I sniggered, "I remember now. Atlantis, a huge island, indeed, lost by the ancients. But Christopher Columbus found it again. A scientist explained to me that his Atlantis is now called America."

"Your scientist was mistaken," he said.

"How do you know?"

"The ancients knew both Atlantis and America."

People who praise the knowledge of antiquity excessively wound me, like those who praise foreigners too much. A good man considers his century as a homeland and accepts with enthusiasm the duty of excluding from his affection the dead epochs for which he can do nothing. To declare another century superior to ours, or to proclaim another land superior to ours, are hostilities against us, and the damnable behavior of a misanthrope. The person who knows how to love human beings prefers those nearest to him. I shrugged my shoulders at Charles' insulting affirmation, and murmured a vague formula of criticism: "Get away!"

The enemies of Reason, France and Progress are masters of the art of interpreting texts. The Hellenist, once again, read a Greek sentence vaingloriously. Then he translated it.

"*Navigators passed from Atlantis to the other islands, and from them to the continent bordering that sea.*" He concluded, without a second of hesitation: "The *continent bordering that sea* is America."

"How come your ancients, if they knew about America, never went there?"

But a systematic sophist has an answer for everything.

"After the disappearance of Atlantis," Charles claimed, "the ocean was no longer navigable. Listen to Plato again: '*Great earthquakes and inundations occurred. In a single day and one fatal night, the island of Atlantis disappeared beneath the sea, and that is why, to this day, one still cannot travel or explore that sea, navigation finding an insurmountable obstacle in the quantity of mud that the island deposited as it sank.*'"

He continued explaining. All the ancients observed the impossibility of navigating in an ocean of mud that as still defended by gigantic hostile seaweeds, as obstinate and inextricable as an immense dense herd of cephalopods. Covered in a few hours by a thin layer of water, Atlantis continued for a long time, and is perhaps still continuing, to sink slowly. For thousands of years, it was not so much a sea as a thinned out and miry land, an infinite prairie of weed floating in the mud, and which the low tide still uncovered in Aristotle's time. Those who attempted the adventure only spoke with terror of that crazy expanse, ground that yielded beneath the slightest weight and sea that would not yield to any effort. Christopher Columbus could not come before his time. It was necessary to wait, in order to traverse the Ocean, for the uncrossable Sargasso Sea no longer to fill it entirely.

I made Charles stand up. I showed him the singular environment in which we were sailing, the increasingly dense network of weed, and mud that was becoming steadily less liquid.

"We're entering into what remains of the Sargasso Sea," he said. "I think it's impossible to get through."

"So," I asked, with an ill-defined anxiety, "you really imagine that we're over ancient Atlantis?"

"I'm sure of it," he affirmed.

And he summarized what is known about the island, lost eleven thousand years ago. Not much, in sum. No other source than Plato's two dialogues: the *Timaeus*, which contains a few incidental and meager lines about Atlantis, and the *Critias*, of which we only posses a short fragment. In the latter work, the author wanted to tell the story, in accordance with a tradition collected in Egypt by Solon, of a glorious victory won by the ancient Athenians over the Atlanteans. He begins with scarcely credible information about the noble morality and generous politics of the prehistoric Athenians. Then he passes on to their adversaries. He reveals to us, after the mythic origin of those children of Neptune, their great agricultural and martial endeavors, the canals that they dug, the ramparts that they built, and an entire enormous and harmonious way of life.

Charles reiterated enthusiastically, in Greek and in French, the fertility of the land, the ingenuity of its inhabitants, and the power of their empire. His description droned on, about wars, the political constitution, the times of virtue and prosperity. Then he lamented the moral decadence and the anger of the gods. Finally, in a voice that wept as if over a noble destiny interrupted too soon by death, the grotesque scholar deplored: "There, alas, the incomplete dialogue stops, three-quarters of which is lost..."

In the whole of that absurd and uncertain narrative, one detail had struck me by its precise bizarrerie. The Atlanteans possessed in abundance a metal that is not found among us, and which disappeared with their island. It was, with the exception of gold, the most precious of metals. Plato refers to it by a name that no longer corresponds to anything and a Ho-

188

meric epithet. He calls that vanished wealth "orichalcum of the fiery gleams." It was so common in the land that many monuments were lined with it, including ramparts.

I interrupted my friend in order to point out to him the increasingly frightful aspect of the sea. It was now heavily thick and motionless: a prairie, seemingly devoid of a single drop of water—merely a vast, almost solid, expanse of sticky mud, agglutinating an entire immense and dense population of gulf-weed. The ship had slowed down, and was laboring, a fatigued coulter opening a difficult furrow. Against the sides, scarcely quivering, eddies of mud and weed rose up. Behind the plow, the furrow fell back like a pair of door-curtains, and the sea closed up, becoming once again I don't know what heavy ugliness, equally sad, obstinate and immobile.

At that moment, the Captain went past us.

"It seems to me, Captain," I said, "that we're not going very quickly."

"In God's name, no!" said the mariner, laughing. "The ship is like a blunt scythe deprived of a handle, which is caught and held in the middle of an overly dense meadow."

"The Sargasso Sea," said Charles.

"Yes, I've strayed a little from the usual route. I'll give new orders. The short cut I imagined is slowing us down too much."

"Is it still very large, Captain—the Sargasso Sea?"

"Pooh! Ten times the size of France, at the most."

"And no ship ever goes through it?"

"For sure! I was far from having that pretention myself. It seemed to me that a little secant of fifty leagues was possible. I was wrong; I'll give it up."

He drew away.

"Damn!" he cursed. "We'll have bad weather tonight—but I don't want the squall to catch us over these blessed depths!"

He had not taken three steps before a frightful phenomenon occurred. The ship began creaking, leaned forwards and then backwards, swayed by a mysterious force.

189

"What's that?" said the captain.

"A seaquake," Charles replied.

The same strange shock was repeated twice more; then there was a formidable seething all around us. The water, with loud gurgling sounds, rose up and fell back, not with the rhythm of the waves, but with enormous vertical leaps. As far as the eye could see, the mud was boiling, and the gulf-weed, alive and green a short while ago, now faded and baked, was agitating in the vast confusion. It was as if we were lost in a vast cooking-pot full of herbs, and no heat had ever made me suffer such anxiety.

Negligently, Charles said: "The Sargasso Sea is still a volcanic region."

II

While the Captain ran to give orders that had become urgent, in the midst of waters, so calm a little while ago but now boiling, an immense jet of water and vegetation sprang forth like a bouquet, an improvised geyser of prodigious height and mass. Suffocating in the increased heat, we saw the enormous weight falling back in our direction. It struck the ship like a rock shattering into a thousand pieces on impact. Fortunately, I was as far away as possible from the blow, which would have crushed me—but the shards burned me cruelly.

Under the formidable shock, the vessel screeched a thousand splintering creaks; one might have thought it the cries of an army taken by surprise and overwhelmed. The wave fell back into the sea, dragging wood and rigging with it, perhaps a quarter of the vessel. The ruin that remained began to sink slowly into the mud. With a bleak terror, we looked down at the fragile support at our feet, which was bogged down. Suddenly, amid a terrible commotion, there was a loud rumble: the boiler had just exploded.

Charles and I were at the least exposed point. The captain and the other survivors fled toward us. The fragment of the ship that carried us was sinking, no longer with a slow and regular swaying, but in abrupt, repeated, rending shocks. No order had been given; there was no regulation maneuver. We all precipitated ourselves into the lifeboats, and, with a unanimous effort, hurled them into the sea.

The intolerable heat diminished slightly, and the vast seething calmed down. Risking their lives, brave and dexterous sailors succeeded in saving weapons and a little food. The Captain was not encouraging their efforts. He was repeating, with demented persistence: "Do what you like, lads, we're doomed!"

But Charles affirmed: "Where there's life there's hope."

"Hope for what?" someone demanded. "We'll never get out of this mud. Even if we do get out, we're so far from any land, so far from any shipping route, so far from any possible rescue! And we only have food for two days."

"I think that we're quite close to an unknown land."

Most of them looked at Charles as if he were mad; two or three turned pleading and confident eyes toward him.

Darkness surrounded us, compounded of night and fog.

And there were long, tragic hours of immobility and silence.

III

Dawn broke, cruelly radiant. No breeze was blowing. Around our agony, the vast peace of death extended. Impassively, Charles indicated the direction of our hope. Then he seized an oar and, setting the example, vigorously stroked the heavy mud.

A few others imitated him, without vigor. I could not help sniggering, and said: "Cadavers trying to move their coffin!"

"So long as effort remains possible," Charles cried, "resignation is called cowardice." When I shrugged my shoulders, he added: "The cadaver is you!"

His words did not trouble me. I was not naïve enough to stop at their insulting appearance. By a strange transposition

191

of the senses, I seemed to see the words instead of hearing them, and what I saw were violent gestures that were trying to rouse nearby courage. What did words or gestures matter, in any case, to people who were going to die? I let a gaze of indulgent superiority fall upon that vain agitation, that insane effort—and cowardly, in sum!—to escape the inevitable. Then I looked up at the sky, with proudly indifferent eyes. I thought: *Your thoughtless azure is no calmer than my thoughts*.

But I uttered a cry of astonishment. Two strange birds—truly, one might have thought that they were human beings—were gliding in the blue. They were heading toward us.

At the same time as I had cried out, Charles had cried out. I followed the direction of his gaze. He had not seen the same thing as me. Standing up, his arms thrown forward like enthusiasm incarnate, he was pointing at bright lights, at some distant blaze. An immense curve was flaming in the distance, of which we could only see a convex fragment, and which seemed to be infinitely prolonged in either direction. And Charles shouted words that only I understood: "Orichalcum of the fiery gleams! We're saved! Orichalcum of the fiery gleams!"

Everyone looked in the direction in which Charles was pointing, but they looked with a bleak astonishment. What connection could there be between salvation and the menace of that sea in flames?

The flight of the two beings that I had perceived brought them closer. I went to Charles, tapped him on the shoulder and said: "Bizarre birds!"

After a single glance, however, he retorted: "Birds? You can see quite clearly that they're human."

Turning to our companions, stupefied by the unexpected and capriciously changing novelty of the spectacles, he resumed his wearing cantilena of hope: "Rejoice! Rejoice! Look, the Atlanteans are coming to our rescue!"

Then, armed with a white rag, he started making signals of appeal. As if the strange airborne beings might be able to understand French, he shouted: "Generous Atlanteans, save us!"

The frightful beings were only too distinct now. In spite of the negations of the mind, the eye was forced to recognize them as human. Upright, their limbs immobile, they were soaring through the air. As harmonious and incredible as apparitions, they came on, borne by I don't know what breath of mystery or will. Their bodies were naked, except for a girdle around their waists. In vain I searched for the apparatus that permitted them to sustain themselves in mid-air; I could not see any.

They descended almost to the level of the water, and stopped three paces from the lifeboats. Charles spoke to them and one of them replied.

"Have no fear," he recommended. "I'll go to warn friends, and you'll be rescued in less than an hour."

I burst into laughter, triggered by alarm—mad laughter—and shouted at Charles: "See! Your Atlantean birds speak French!"

As resistant to astonishment as a brute, he conceded, vaguely: "That's singular, indeed. We'll know in time…for the moment, let's welcome helpful destiny without worrying about its name."

One of the flying men had departed at a rapid velocity. The other was hovering in mid-air, moving around us, and spoke to us amicably.

"We are indeed Atlanteans," he declared to Charles. Then, addressing me, he added: "Don't be astonished that we know French. I know fifteen cruel languages."

I was scarcely in any state to ask for explanations. But Charles, half affirmatively and half interrogatively, said: "You say *cruel* as the Greeks said *barbarian*?"

"Yes," the Atlantean admitted. "But you'll have time to understand these things."

His companion had thrown himself into the distant furnace that was still setting the entire horizon ablaze in front of us. Soon, canoes appeared, surging from the conflagration.

Their curved extremities rendered them similar to the funeral barges of the ancient Egyptians, but we realized that they were flat-bottomed. They came toward us, rapid and disquieting, in vertiginous fashion. They flew toward us...were they really flying? Sometimes, I thought I could see that they were not touching the water, that they were gliding through the air, like the humans just now.

I remarked on that to Charles. He shrugged his shoulders and said: "You're still astonished by everything..."

IV

Singular, the boats that picked us up: with no sails, no oars and no boiler, they had no means of propulsion that I knew. Each of them was manned by a single individual, and maneuvered very oddly.

Sitting in the prow, the mariner placed his hands on a kind of keyboard. Depending on the touch he applied, a long metal spike, a bizarre bowsprit, turned to the right or the left, drawing the docile craft behind it.

I could vaguely imagine what was happening. It was something unknown, an invention that the Cruels—as the Atlanteans must call us—might perhaps make tomorrow. The greater or lesser rapidity of our progress also seemed to depend on the pilot's gestures.

The ten boats that were carrying us moved in two lines. On examining the nearest ones, I saw that they were surrounded by a band of fabric. *They're dressed in Atlantean girdles*, I thought.

In the crumbling heap of stupors that comprised that day, many details, even among the most frightful, remained unperceived, silent units lost in a crowd until the moment when the impact of another detail rendered them sonorous, as it were. A comparison immediately imposed itself here. The humans' belts, I suddenly remembered—and my eyes confirmed it— were fitted with the same mobile spike, albeit much smaller, as the girdles of the vessel. I thought I remembered that, in their flight, the Atlanteans sometimes extended a directive finger toward that metallic spike.

It seemed to me that the fabric sometimes pressed the boat narrowly, and sometimes drew slightly away from it. My observations still retained some uncertainty, as if floating in a dream, but I would almost have affirmed that when tightly, the vessel was flying at top speed; it was necessary, at those times, to turn away in order not to be suffocated. When the fabric was slightly apart from the wood, the progress slowed down.

I studied the belt of the mariner maneuvering the craft behind us, a few meters away. It bore eleven buttons. The bottom button opened in the same fabric. The others hung down at the end of ribbons of varying length. At that moment, only the top button was being used, and the apparatus seemed very slack, hardly maintained in place. The man was like a hovering bird, stable, but very free in his movements, buoyed up by lightness and ease. I thought I remembered that, in order to stop, the flying Atlanteans had unfastened several buttons. Had not the one who had remained immobile for some time a few centimeters above the water undone all the buttons with the exception of the top two?

I was completely absorbed in these observations, comparisons and inductions when I felt myself lifted up, as if in a nightmare. The first line of boats, it seemed to me, as my heart skipped a beat, was taking off. Soon, the second line was also in the air, a flock of rapid and tremulous birds.

"What's happening?" I asked.

My companions, hanging on to the sides and clutching their neighbors, were tottering, and crying out.

"Have no fear," said our pilot, while the boat came back down to skim the surface of the water. "We've just doubled a reef."

The sea was now a cheerful blue, like the Mediterranean on a fine day. Son, however, we entered into the glare of the blaze that closed the approaching horizon before us.

We arrived in that ocean of fire. A few meters away, without a breach, a crown of rocks curved away, uncrossable by ordinary vessels. Ardent red florets ornamented it, advertising the dangerous crown throughout its extent.

"The orichalcum with fiery gleams serves them as a lighthouse," said Charles.

Instinctively, I gripped the side of the boat. In order to double the "orichalcum rocks"—as Charles called them, experiencing a need to impose the familiarity of a name upon everything, no matter how provisional or inharmonious—we were flying at a height of some thirty or forty meters.

And land appeared, close by. The first glance revealed its astonishing fertility. Above the gigantic trees, however, once could distinguish outcrops of white stone here and there, which traversed the tangled verdure: the tips of tall pyramids.

Charles diverted my attention. "Have you noticed," he asked, "that our pilot is a woman?"

"Yes. And there are several women among the mariners guiding the other boats." I added, disdainfully: "These idle savages make their women do men's work."

My friend looked at me with a shock that made me burst out laughing.

"You call them savages!" he exclaimed.

"Well, if you know another name for people who go around naked...their belt isn't a vestment—not even the fig-leaf of civilized statues. It's an apparatus, an organ of flight, and they're immodest enough to set it too high..."

"You don't sense the overwhelming superiority of these people, who...?"

I turned round, irritated. Half in jest, as when one wants to avoid an argument with a stubborn individual, I said: "Personally, for a start, I call any man a savage who doesn't resemble me."

The pilot had heard. She turned her had, smiling, and remarked: "We say *cruel*—but we have reasons."

I responded with a vague ironic salute. Could I argue with that individual, who seemed to know us, and about whom I knew nothing? Then again, when pilots chat, it can be dangerous for their passengers. My bad mood was expressed internally, in the approximate terms: *What right does she have to speak French?*

Everything irritated me. I felt resentful toward the Atlanteans who had saved us. I begrudged the fact that they were so knowledgeable, that they were manifestly such skillful navigators as to have conquered the air. I begrudged them their astonishing beauty. Their ruddy brown skin had the heroic color of lions. Shaking my head, I affirmed: *Men ought to be white.* Their long dark hair formed a warm and bold harmony with their skin color. *My God, how garish it is, that fawn and black!* I laughed, mentally, at those beardless men: *They resemble their women so much that they have to remain naked to tell the sexes apart.* I called their slender and supple grace weakness. Their features were symmetrical, but their noses, aquiline toward the summit, descended in a straight line only to part in the middle. *Oh, those convex Jewish noses!* And I insulted the delicate smallness of their extremities: *Truly the hands of sickly apes!*

When Charles, emerging from a long contemplation, said in a low voice: "More beautiful, yes, more beautiful, than the Greeks," I shrugged my shoulders.

After a disdainful silence, I remarked: "How tedious these people are to look at. They're all alike."

"So are we," affirmed the Hellenist. "We must all resemble one another in their eyes, unaccustomed to our race."

If the overly narrow boat had permitted it, I would have moved away from that enervating stupidity. At least I could turn my back and enclose myself in the refuge of silence.

V

With its abundant crown of trees, surpassed here and there by the tip of a pyramid, like a protruding jewel, the coast seemed from afar to be an appeal and a promise. Seen at closer range, it offered a tormented and grimacing cliff, a vertical vertiginously sheer wall, bristling with threatening angles, hollowed out by grottoes in which shadows and terror lurked.

The boats, one behind another, glided straight ahead, rapidly and blindly, as if to hurtle into that unshakable hostility. I was in the first canoe and I imagined that it would rise up abruptly at the foot of the wall, like an enormous bird. The cliff was more than two hundred meters high, and I was not without apprehension at the prospect of that enormous vertical leap.

A sudden change of direction threw us into the midst of rocks, into a channel that was still invisible at a distance of a few paces. The narrow pass extended through a thousand meanders to end at a port.

A crowd was waiting whose members saluted our arrival strangely, blowing kisses with their hands. The men and women were naked, like our rescuers. A few of them—they doubtless lived in the vicinity—did not even have belts.

All the gazes were amicably curious. From time to time, an indigene, as if attracted by a particular sympathy, took the hand of one of us and said: "Come with me, friend," or, more bizarrely: "Brother-friend-man, come with me."

As I watched my companions draw away in the most various directions, I felt an increasing anxiety. Why were they separating us like that? What treason was hidden beneath the smiling manners and fraternal speeches?

Those reflections must have rendered my expression surly. I was the last that anyone selected and approached. I became the "prey"—that was the frightful word I thought—of an old man without a girdle.

My host's age did not reassure me. Only the whiteness of his hair and, when the mouth ceased smiling, some indefinable air of venerability, communicated the idea of antiquity. The beardless face did not have a single wrinkle, and the muscular and replete body showed no sign of decrepitude.

He took me by the hand and said in a soft voice: "Would you like to come to my home, young man?"

I could not find any amiable reply. I contented myself with expressing my astonishment aloud: "Does everyone here speak French, then?"

Without appearing to notice my bad mood, the old man explained: "Those who don't know French have naturally left the joy of receiving you to us." He added: "I live close by, a hundred paces away over there, in the tall trees that crown that mound, but if you're too tired, I'll obtain some flying belts."

"In truth, I'd rather walk."

The path we followed was shaded by bushy trees. They were most orange and lemon trees—but how much larger than the ones with which I was familiar! Amid the varnished verdure of the foliage, the granular greenness of unripe fruits was rounded out. Meanwhile, the white flowers broadened out like promises, and the heavy realizations of golden fruit inclined the noble effort of the higher branches. Everywhere, among those colors of an almost wounding brightness, gray pyramids, which were houses, introduced a kind of discreet smile.

"Are you hungry?" asked the old man. "Are you thirsty?"

From a hanging branch that suddenly straightened, he plucked an enormous orange, as if made to inundate the throat of a Hercules. As we went past a clump of banana trees, he also offered me a banana, alarming in its gigantic proportions.

Increasingly, I suspected his amiability of hiding some malevolent design. I sensed that I ought to put on a similar act, but fatigue and so many dangers had worn me out and had rendered me incapable of constraining myself.

"No, thank you," I said, refusing the fruit. "I'd rather have something more substantial."

"You'll find cakes in my home, honey, eggs, milk and cheese."

"Not the smallest beefsteak?" I protested.

The smile disappeared from the old man's lips, and he declared, with an absurd energy: "We're not murderers."

I was astonished. "Murderers? I'm not asking to eat a man; I'm asking to eat beef."

The paradoxical old man countered: "Does the existence of an ox not seem to be life to you, then? Does its death not seem to you to be a death, or its pain dolorous?"

199

I made no reply. My suspicion swelled, tortuously. That apparently gentle dementia had to conceal truly terrible mores. Perhaps the people respected the cattle in their meadows because their mouths only liked the taste of human flesh. My host would doubtless wait for my first slumber to kill me and devour my poor body.

The view was, however, nobly placid. The earth set forth and displayed its fecundity like an unusual mixture of confidence and glory. Behind the shiny verdure of orange trees and the immense leaves of banana trees, coconut palms and date palms were agitating their plumes high in the sunlight. Further away, among all kinds of trees that raised leaves as large as tablecloths and fruits as buxom as food-baskets to vertiginous heights, among ferns twenty meters high, unknown giants extending their animated branches like arms in the wind, where they writhed like serpents. Lianas ran from one to another like light gangways or hung down, swinging, like some kind of heavy tapestries.

Everywhere, birds were singing and monkeys gamboling. Macaws with colors as vivid as trumpet-shells, birds of paradise, peacocks and lyre-birds put the living beauty of their plumage into the verdure, alongside the red and gold of the fruits, and hummingbirds made the air quiver with colors and harmonious curves. But the innumerable pyramids, which one sensed to be inhabited by humans, and the humans who were swimming in the sky at all heights as if in an ocean of light, or floating a few meters from the ground, eating fruits, chatting and laughing—especially those who were saluting us by applying their small hands to the pure lines of their lips and then directing them towards us with a movement of ineffable grace—completed the opulent beauty of nature with a touching and fraternal human beauty.

Those humans liberated from the ball-and-chain of weight seemed to be compounded out of love, joy and freedom. Like smiles that uncovered and veiled the thoughts of the universe, their movements, of a beauty beyond words, floated over the marvelous and pacific face of the earth.

Like the rest of the landscape, the path was populated by birds and monkeys. No animal fled at our approach. Songs and cries were often directed toward us, like salutations; with his lips and his gaze, my companion smiled at the animals we encountered.

A large blond monkey, letting itself fall close to us, wearing a serious expression, started mimicking my fatigued and irritated gait. The old man caressed the indiscreet individual, which allowed him to do it.

"Is it domesticated?" I asked.

"We don't do any harm to any person, and have no need to domesticate any person."

I was astonished by the word "person." Was it the mistake of a man speaking a language with which he was insufficiently familiar? Or was the old man mocking me, comparing me to a tame monkey?

With an equivocal laugh, the old man added: "He has no more need to domesticate me. We're two innocent animals, and my grimaces amuse him, just as his amuse me." Then, addressing himself ridiculously to the monkey: "You are, like me, a gesture and a conscious wave of the earth, is it not so, cousin?"

I bit my lip in order not to laugh, and in a grave voice expressed a wish: "I'd be glad to hear your cousin reply."

The old man laughed loudly. "Unfortunately," he said, "the cousin hasn't learned French."

He turned to the animal and pronounced a few strange syllables. The monkey drew away in a zealous fashion.

"Do you speak his language?"

"No, I'm more ignorant than he is. He's the one who understands a little of mine."

"Would it be indiscreet to ask what you said to him?"

"I said to him: 'I'm a poor human without a belt; fetch me a few dates.'"

The monkey came back caring a branch from which dates hung down, trembling, as heavily massive as pears.

"He's a servant," I remarked, scornfully.

But the old man defended the monkey's honor: "Not in the least. He knows that I'd go to some trouble for him as he does for me. Take note, as well, that I explained to him that I could not do for myself what I was asking him to do for me."

I approved, in an earnest fashion: "What you did was just and natural. You've paid the monkey in the monkey's currency."

I laughed, content with my wit and reassured, without knowing why. The old man laughed too. I sensed that there was more malice in his laughter than in mine, when he replied: "You'll excuse me, brother, if I don't understand all the subtleties of your language."

VI

The beauty of the spectacle occupied my consciousness more and more, chasing away my mistrust and ill humor. Reassured and smiling, I arrived at the small pyramid that served the old man as a dwelling. A corridor divided the ground floor. My companion ushered me into a large room on the right.

"You're at home," he told me.

Everything seemed prepared to receive me. Laden with all sorts of fruits, cheeses and cakes of singular form, a large table was waiting. It also bore a large jug full of water and another full of milk. A few simple chairs, a set of bookshelves and a bed completed the furniture.

My host continued: "You doubtless desire to be alone. If you need me or desire to see me, you only have to call to me through that window. I'll be in the orchard that you can see. My name is Makima." Through a gap in the door, he asked: "And what should I call you?"

"My friends call me Jacques."

The old man went out, and I did justice to his meal.

I didn't touch the cheese or the cakes, nor the not-every-seductive liquids. I allowed myself to be attracted by preference to the unknown fruit. A few of them delighted me. I found out later that they were the soft *savinte* and the exquisite *palta*. I discovered one that was even more precious; it was called by a composite term that might be translated as "the blancmanger." Its melting delicacy perfumed and refreshed the mouth better than the finest of our ice-creams, but it caused a joyful energy to circulate through the entire body.

"You," I said, gratefully, "are almost as good as a beef-steak."

Sated, I lay down on the bed. But too many novelties were agitating my mind, which felt, since I had bitten into the blancmanger, as vibrant and joyful as light itself. I soon got up, shrugging my shoulders, and headed for the bookshelves. Surely, in this country without any relationship with the civilized world, there would be no book that I could understand. *And yet*, I objected to myself with a kind of anxious hope, *how do so many of these islanders know French?*

I was lost in a dream that the unknown fruit had rendered pleasant and which was unaware of impossibility. For a moment, I turned my back to the books and my heart beat rapidly. I hesitated before the probably disappointment, perhaps tremulous at the idea of an alarming, impossible satisfaction. I think that the abrupt movement that brought me in front of the bookshelves was a veritable act of courage.

That astonishing bookcase only contained French books: all the great works of the last three centuries, from the *Essais* to the *Destinées* and the *Contes cruels*,[23] and also the rare works interesting to our generation.

Here, marrying in a sublime quiver of eternity the saps of yesteryear with the forces of today, ancient forms with the present aspects of human aspiration and servitude, is the latest novel by J.-H. Rosny. Perfect in form and charged with all our

---

[23] The *Essais* in question must be Michel de Montaigne's; *Les Destinées: poëmes philosophiques* (1864) is a classic of the Romantic Movement by Alfred de Vigny; *Contes cruels* (1883) is a generically definitive collection of short stories by Villiers de l'Isle-Adam

hopes and all our discouragements, at the foot of the heroic Caucasus, is *La Nef* by Élémir Bourges.[24]

Then I discover titles of books and names of authors that I don't know. The limpid verses of Émile Boissier reflect, along the *Chemin de l'Irréel*, amid moving misty forests, the stooping and whispering figures of the Night, Voluptuousness and Death.[25] Jacques Fréhel's *Cabaret des larmes* at *Le Précurseur* raise before my eyes a Brittany of mystery and passion, a bitter and delightful marriage of the gilded perfumes of the heath and the glaucous odor of the sea.

With a scornful smile, in the presence of those ignored and admirable books, I thought about the success of publicity, the fuddy-duddy writings that the sheep-like public proclaim as masterpieces for a season, following the mercenary newspapers and the imbeciles who call themselves critics.

Night exiled me from those freshly-discovered beauties. I observed with a mixture of resentment and patriotic pride: "These Atlanteans know how to steal like birds; but they haven't been able to give me a candle or a match, any more than birds could."

----

[24] Ryner was a great admirer and close friend of the elder Rosny, who tried on three occasions to have him admitted to the Goncourt Academy, presumably with the support of fellow member Élémir Bourges, a key figure in the Decadent/Symbolist Movement. Only the first part of Bourges' *La Nef* (1904) had been published when this line as written; the second did not appear until 1922.

[25] Émile Boissier, another good friend of Ryner's, was another poet closely associated with the Decadent Movement; *Le Chemin de l'Irréal* was published in 1895. He was also a prolific ghost-writer, for "Willy" (Henri Gauthier-Villars) among many others, and the extent of his prose and dramatic works is unknown. It is surprising that the narrator, otherwise depicted in such hostile terms, has such avantgardist literary tastes, but the author presumably thought of the passage as an advertisement.

VII

I emerged from a sleep populated with dreams. In a fearful immobility, I wondered: "Have I dreamed *all* of it?"

Beside me, on the bed, I found books: French books, one of which was dated the present year. I also affirmed to myself that I was in France. I was surprised that there was no enthusiasm in the affirmation. *Am I regretting the nightmare in which the old cannibal respected the ox because of the exclusive love of meat that I have?* I could not help laughing. *My God, how stupid one is in dreams! He was certainly the gentlest of men, that naked old man who couldn't fly, for lack of a belt, and had a monkey for a domestic!*

In my memories, filtered by sleep, the strange country appeared to me to be beautiful and desirable. *That wouldn't be a banal holiday. I'd be able to borrow a flying belt and think I was a bird. I could peck the delicious-seeming and refreshing fruit in the branches of the trees. I could live in a new landscape, in terms of colors, forms and proportions, which flight undoubtedly multiplies and renews continually. The old man could tell me, I suppose, beautiful and calm stories. But it will be necessary to find Charles and talk about these things with someone who could assume almost the same viewpoint as me.*

Now the aquiline features and supple bodies of the race interested me. A youthful emotion lifted up my sense, and I said, with a laugh: "If I have the same dream again. I'll ask the pilot to take off her belt for me."

I got up. My gaze searched with increasing anxiety for the most elementary toilet apparatus. I went to the table; I tasted the fruit that had left me the best memory. The sensation was renewed, profoundly and broadly delicious.

What luck! I can live the beautiful dream!

I ran to the window. I called out, almost more incredulously: "Makima!"

The old man appeared, airborne. He asked me how I was. I was slightly shocked that he kept addressing me as *tu*. Soon,

I accepted it indifferently. *It's a general habit among savages, and they're no more wicked for it.*

"Where's the bathroom?" I asked.

Makima smiled—he smiled a great deal, did Makima—and showed me a stream running ten paces from the pyramidal house...yes, pyramidal, my old Maspero.[26]

"There, my friend.

"There's a slight dearth of towels..."

But the old man, indicating an admirably low tree whose large pale and supple leaves hung down like napkins, said: "You don't say...!"

That idiomatic expression amused me. *You, old chap, when you claim to be ignorant of certain nuances of my language, are bragging. If I gave you a little push, I'd wager you can speak argot.*

When my toilet was concluded, I lay down on the grass and yawned.

"Are you bored?" Makima asked, sustaining himself in mid-air with the precious belt, eating enormous cherries. "You're bored, even in this European orchard?"

Trees, leaves, flowers and fruits—everything had frightful proportions. Once the initial astonishment was past, however, I did, indeed, recognize the magnified forms. Here, as big as our oaks, are peach-trees, a single leaf of which would cover my head, and a single fruit would nourish a man. Here, as tall as eucalypti, are pear-trees whose pears hang a heavily as calabashes capable of slaking the thirst of an entire day's journey. Those enormous green and red balloons that create an amusing gleam in the thick foliage are doubtless apples. Giant elms sustain, in the Virgilian mode, vines as thick as my body, and every grape in their long clusters is as large as a French peach. Close to me, strawberries scrape the ground, as heavy as ordinary pears. I think: *They're too big; they can't be any good.* I taste one, with a disdainful tooth; I eat ten avidly.

---

[26] Gaston Maspero (1846-1916) was the leading French Egyptologist of his era.

More perfumed than the little strawberries of our woods, they melt into my happy mouth. *They're not strawberries, they're fondants, sorbets, I don't know what ravishing synthesis of the known and the unknown.*

On the other side of the stream, flowers, swaying in the wind, send me the intoxication of their thousand perfumes. I look at them; in spite of their disconcerting enormity, I recognize the harmonious roses. The others worry me and attract me with I don't know what mixture of familiarity and strangeness. They seem to be smiling friends wearing masks. No, I'm not describing my impression accurately. It's more like: *I've lived away from my natal village for a long time, and now, young women that I doubtless knew as children are greeting me as they pass by, but I can't put names to their mature faces.* Oh, the emotion compounded out of sweetness and bitterness! *Until now, have I not been living as an exile?*

"Old man," I said, "if you've had enough of those excessively large cherries, which are perhaps only excessively red apples, tell me the names of these malicious flowers that seem to be mocking me, saying: *you know us, but you don't recognize us.*"

"They're all flowers from your homeland."

"Yes, as the roses are eglantines."

"You've said it, my son. In spite of the little time that your wars, your contests and your crazy struggles against other humans leave you, in spite of your bizarre preoccupations, your puerile industries, your tedious and invasive pleasures, you've created one of the flowers that nature requests of humans, and of which she furnishes the vague design. We, more fortunate, have a thousand flowers—we doubtless have all the flowers. Everywhere, we hear the appeal of the earth: 'I sketch,' she says to us, 'come and finish. I need your faithful collaboration to become myself. I am the one who aspires, and you are the great consciousness of my thousand desires, the sole divination possible of my millions of means. I am the block that wants to become the statue, and I have no other means of imploring than yours. Don't refuse me your aid. I

207

will reward you as a queen spoils a child. Eat this wild berry; do you not taste, in its fleshless and bitter dryness, the presentiment of a delicious fruit? Take this poor seed and cultivate it, in order that it might become rich wheat. Care for this eglantine, this violet, this forget-me-not, and make me flowers. Realize in me all the desires with which I penetrate you, all the dreams that I inspire in you. I only have you to aid my dreams—our dreams—to hatch out, to make my hesitant efforts precise, to make eloquence out of my babble, to deliver me of the thousand aspirations that are laboring within me, and to crown me with my thousand aspiration. Never draw away from me, O my beloved son, but perfect me constantly, in order that I might perfect you constantly.'"

"You're eloquent, Makima, even in French!"

"No, my child, it's the rose that is eloquent, the realized eglantine. It's that realized violet, that realized forget-me-not, and that realized lily." His fingers indicated the flowers, each of which raised up its form, color and perfume: a bouquet of harmonies; an opulence without heaviness.

Oh, the beautiful Greek vase that you are, realized lily! Your noble white curves, cradled by the caresses of the breeze, sow warm and voluptuous scents with the gold of your multiple heart. You create dreams, radiant calyx, of sensual communions. Your pulp, more delicate than a luscious fruit or a blonde skin, causes vague desires for light nourishment to quiver within me, and precise desires for kisses. But you, realized violet, you raise up a mauve plume into the sunlight, or allow loose tresses to float in the wind. Rich realized forget-me-not, you display before my glad eyes a flower-bed of stars.

Come back to cure my incurable exile, lived dream, dream of a Homeland, dream of a Place where everything is beautiful and generous, where humans have remained faithful to nature, where nature is penetrated by humanity! Render me your vanished perfumes; revive your colors faded by difference; restore your forms that forgetfulness has already degraded, your forms that are no longer for me, also, complete harmonies and reassuring equilibria, but ruins that are becoming imprecise, invaded by the sad grass of regret. Render me your fruits, more nourishing than our meat, more refreshing than our ice-creams, more fondant than the masterpieces of our confectioners. Render me your thousand flowers, of which our countryside only offers me a distant hope, your flowers that are ten centuries of evolution beyond the poor abortions to which we give their glorious names. And again, above my charmed idleness, which gazes, which aspires and which listens, suspend in your joyful light, among the dance of radiance and hummingbirds, render me the old man with the savant and enthusiastic speech.

VIII

In the preceding chapter, I abandoned myself to a surge of enthusiasm that would have shocked me on the part of someone else. I now owe good Frenchmen hasty apologies and brief explanations.

Of the forty castaways, I am the one—I declare it gloriously—who was most resistant to the Atlantean seduction. No one remained more faithful to civilized customs than me. A significant detail: I am the only one who did not, at any time, renounce clothing.

Alongside those proud observations, however, I have to make some painful but useful confessions.

The rich novelty of the landscapes, the penetrating succulence of the fruits, the sovereign beauty of the flowers, the gently charming mores and the absolute liberty that I enjoyed amid absolute liberties, and also certain aspects of material progress that I will mention in due course, sometimes excited joy and love in me.

I would not make the danger of the utopias of which some of our compatriots dream sufficiently sensible if I did not reveal all the perverse seduction of the utopia that I loved, all the delightful folly that invades the being in an environment like Atlantis, that paradox of five hundred thousand square leagues and eight hundred million inhabitants.

Am I not obliged, in any case, in order to express an epoch of my life, to reconstitute my thoughts in that epoch, to intoxicate myself with the memory of old intoxications?

It is probable that I shall utter other enthusiastic exclamations. The reader should know that those joyful echoes resonate in my present with sadness and shame, should sense that I am confessing my sins. It is in order better to deny it that I am revealing that past sacrilege. I have returned to reason and noble sentiments.

France, you are my mother and I love you, and I scorn as poverty any wealth that is not French. One does not choose one's mother or one's fatherland; one accepts with all one's love those that destiny has given you. One does not compare them with other mothers and other fatherlands with impious and impartial eyes. A good patriot and a good son repeat, in spite of all the things he sees, these certainties, which come from more profound depths than the eyes: My mother is the best of mothers; my France is the best and most beautiful of fatherlands."

Anyway the life of the Atlanteans, considered coldly, has nothing desirable about it. People will understand, in reading me, that social discipline is the ultimate good. Beings organized like us, minds formed by French traditions and French education, can enjoy liberty during short vacations, but everything in them soon protests against anarchy; everything in them demands the intoxicating joy of command and the reassuring joy of obedience.

Liberty is the dream and pleasure of children! The true virile happiness is the accomplishment of a fixed and determined social duty; it is the sentiment that one is a cog in a complicated machine, whose place cannot change and which moves because the other cogs make it move.

National solidarity, you are my only love, and when I think of you, I am, like Spinoza before the abyss of substance, drunk on divinity.

IX

I divagated thus:

"Makima, this garden is a paradise. But all calm joy desires to caress the knowledge of immediate proof. My delight remains diffuse; I would like to make it more precise by comparison. The land is more beautiful when the blue of the sea defines and outlines it; and the sea, which surrounds the mariner for long intervals with imprecision and ennui, becomes likeable again as soon as land is in view. I would like to outline my joy, do you see? I would like to sense its limits, to sense something other in order to sense it more clearly. As Lucretius put it, Makima, *Suave mari magno*...but perhaps you don't know Latin?"[27]

"No, my child. The science of flowers and fruits impassions my life too much. With the exception of French, I don't know any cruel languages."

"I've just said crazy things, Makima."

The old man smiled. "You only said that you'd like to read a newspaper."

"You understood me better than I did, subtle Makima, and your translation is clearer than my text. Are you a subscriber to the *Island Monitor*? For we're on an island, I believe."

"We're on an island where the making of newspapers is disdained."

Glad to discover a superiority, I shook my head. "At this moment, Makima, you resemble the fox in a fable that I'm too polite to recite to you. You disdain that which you can't attain. Doubtless you and your compatriots are ignorant of the sublime art of printing.

"Didn't you look at the bookshelves in your room?" the savage asked, mildly.

"In truth, I only saw French books there."

---

[27] "How sweet is a great sea [to behold]"—the quotation is from *De Rerum Natura*.

"And you assumed that they came by steamship?"

"You're right. How the devil did they get here?"

Instead of responding, the malicious old man said: "What newspaper do you desire?"

"The most recent you can offer me."

"O most suspicious of guests, do you think me capable, then, of making you read one of yesterday's newspapers? You haven't understood my question. Shall I give you the *Petit Journal*, the *Figaro*, or something else?"

"It doesn't matter. I'm no longer so naïve as to have a preference between similar lies and equal stupidities."

Makima fastened a button in his belt, rose upwards and went into the upper floor of the pyramid through a window.

Ten minutes later he reappeared, and handed me the *Petite République*, *Le Temps* and the *Libre Parole*.

Striving to hide my astonishment, I scanned the news of the war and accounts of the parliamentary report with a distracted eye. The Russian and Japanese armies, very close, were finally about to engage in a decisive battle. The skillful Kuropatkin had received sufficient reinforcements and was preparing to crush the Nipponese beneath the weight of the "Russian fist."[28] Jaurès had made a speech, singing a song that he might have thought new, about the "noble reflective discipline that a democracy ought to possess."[29]

---

[28] This sentence suggests that the events related in the story are taking place in the early months of 1905, when Alexei Kuropatkin, the Russian Minister of War, sent Russian land forces into the first of two crushing defeats, at the Battle of Mukden. It is possible the novel was written then but did not find a publisher for some time.

[29] Jean Jaurès was the leader of the French Socialist Party in parliament, after its formation in 1902; it initially adopted a social democratic stance, in opposition to Jules Guesde's rival Socialist Party of France, although the two parties merged in March 1905.

I had read all that on the morning of my embarkation. I smiled before bursting out laughing, for I was increasingly certain that Makima had given me old newspapers. The date, however...

Momentarily, I hesitated, wondering whether my eyes were deceiving me. I reread more attentively. I perceived that the Russian fist was no longer closing in the North, as it had been the other day. And Jaurès was supporting the same law as on my departure, but this time, it was coming back from the Senate. Those differences seemed to me to be significant.

I dropped the papers and my mouth opened in a yawn. "The papers are becoming more and more tedious, Makima."

"The newspapers remain the same, my son. It's you that is becoming more demanding."

"Do you read many newspapers, Makima?"

"That curiosity grips me once or twice a year."

"You're a sage, Makima."

"No, Jacques, I'm an Atlantean."

The word startled me. "An Atlantean. So it's really true? This is really is Atlantis? A friend told me the old history of your country, but he affirmed that the island had disappeared eleven thousand years ago. Oh, I understand: after centuries, it has emerged again, and people of the red race have come to repopulate it. Is it from Peru that you've come, Makima, or is it from Mexico?"

"We haven't come from anywhere. The Atlanteans are autochthonous."

"What!"

"The island never disappeared entirely. The last polar cataclysm submerged, along with Gadirique, the province nearest to Europe, the low-lying lands of the other coasts."

"How did the error of the Egyptian priests and Plato arise?"

"The Ocean having ceased to be navigable, and the diminished island being, as it were, distanced from your view, you thought that we had been annihilated."

"But since then?"

213

"The Sargasso Sea protects us against your dangerous curiosity."

"It's a fact that it isn't convenient, your Sargasso Sea. But how long has it been that you've been living in this frightful isolation, miserably separated from the rest of the world, sadly exiled from all commerce with other nations?"

"We are," said the old man—and his voice, becoming simultaneously joyful and grave, took on a profound and religious tone—"in the year eleven thousand five hundred and fifty seven of the Fortunate Separation."

X

A multiple and graceful shadow passed over my head, like a flock of large birds; then, amid youthful laughter and silvery babble, a crowd of children descended toward us. There were about thirty of them, of various sizes, girls and boys.

"What's this, Makima?"

"They're my pupils, Jacques."

"You're a teacher?"

"Like everyone else."

"What, everyone?"

"There are two joys, Jacques: giving and receiving."

"That's possible, but what connection..."

"Material things belong to everyone. Whoever is hungry can eat the fruits that are partly my work and mostly the work of the earth. If I need a new belt, I don't worry about who has woven it from cotton and rubber and who has impregnated it with force."

I asked you a precise question, Makima."

"Direct responses aren't always the best ones, Jacques."

"I believe you're making fun of me."

"I never make fun of anyone, my son. I sometimes make fun of someone's impatience."

"I'll be patient," I said, with a slightly tight-lipped smile. "Design the meanders of your response in accordance with your whim."

"You do well, my child, to let the stream follow its slope. Material things belong to whomever has need of them, so I have only one kind of wealth to give: myself; and only one to receive: others."

"How do you give yourself, and how do you receive them?"

"In childhood, I could scarcely do more than receive. Youth disperses itself in kisses and endeavors that sing. Today, my initial ardors diminished, I sow fewer kisses and the movement of my hands becomes a harmony that is slower every day, and which produces less. By way of compensation, the speech of old men is inexhaustible, and my science, which displays itself joyfully, bathes and fecundates those who surround me as the waters of a broad river refresh its shores."

"What science do you mean? Your knowledge of flowers and fruits?"

"Yes—and also the facile secrets that old men and life have taught me, and which children don't yet know."

"To whom do you give this wealth? Is it to all those who desire it?"

"Of course! Kisses and science are, like all joys, generosities—I was going to say intrusions. I give, gladly, to anyone who loves me enough to ask me."

"So all these children are horticulturalists?"

"All these children love the earth, but most of them listen internally to multiple appeals. Atlanteans like me, who are passionate for a single kind of work are not very numerous. I have a narrow mind, Jacques, but I have no regrets; the part that I have chosen, perhaps with too exclusive a love, is so beautiful! Imagine it, Jacques: there is a fruit that I have perfected, and, since the blancmanger is partly the work of Makima, my friends pretend that it's the finest of fruits!"

"You've attained glory, fortunate Makima, and the stomachs of future races will be grateful to you."

"Laugh as much as you like, my son. Laughter without malevolence is a fruit superior even to the blancmanger."

Makima began his lesson. He was sitting in a tree. In front of him, on a supple branch that curved and swayed under their airborne weight, the children formed a marvelous garland, more beautiful and livelier than all the rest. It was the supreme and moving smile of nature in fête.

Sometimes, the old man translated what he was saying for my benefit. Ordinarily, I gazed at the graceful troop and listened to the incomprehensible twittering as I would have looked at and listened to elegant russet birds singing cheerfully. Soon, however, I began to feel embarrassed; the children were turning to look at me too frequently with what seemed to me to be expressions of pity.

"Are you talking about me, Makima?"

"I'm taking advantage of your presence to tell them how poor in flowers and fruits your country is. I'm also explaining some of the reasons for your persistent poverty."

"And what are those reasons, in your opinion?"

"I'm making them sad—but there are salutary sadnesses—by telling them that you've fallen below the animals. I'd like to enable them to understand—although such follies are very difficult to explain—what a social organization is, what a nation is and what a government is. I'm telling them what war is, and that you spend certain seasons killing one another. I'm telling them what an army is, and that your years of pride, initiative and open-mindedness are wasted learning the art of killing your fellows and the art of obeying your equals. They can't understand what a soldier is.

"They can't understand, either, what a worker is. I'm searching in vain for the clearest terms to tell them how goods are distributed among you, not in accordance with need and the laws of love and civilization, and not even in accordance with the effort expended and the barbaric rule of justice, but following complicated prescriptions like fraud and dementia. They can't believe that the fruits of labor belong neither to those who need them nor to those who produce them, but to the enemies of the laborer, to various arrogant parasites and wastrels.

"They shake their heads as if I were making fun of them when I affirm that the people who grow the wheat sometimes lack bread, and that, after having spent his life building, a mason can find himself without shelter in his old age. I can't succeed in explaining to them how your insane avidity for wealth impoverishes you, and why, instead of struggling as brothers against hostile nature or assisting benign nature with a common joy, you only think about despoiling one another and fighting one another by a thousand means, one of which bears, in your own language, the name of pacifism...

"Look how these are shaking their heads; they understand French and my words are stupefying them. Answer Jacques—is what I'm saying true?"

Who can measure the maddening power of the present; who can say how the realities that surround us and the words that give them a voice trouble us with inebriation and deform our thoughts and sentiments? The environment was invading me through all my senses, making me an Atlantean of sort. Without any argument—oh, how I blush in making this confession!—without any dispute, I declared: "Everything that Makima says is true."

"Poor Jacques!" cried the children.

With a delightful movement, they all surrounded me, several coming to caress me. They seemed to want to make me forget an unhappy life.

One little girl let herself fall to her knees in front of me and said, almost weeping: "I'm sorry, Jacques, I'm sorry."

"What have you done, my child?"

She stood up, greatly emotional. There were tears in her eyes. She reflected for a moment, however, astonished by her own action. Finally, she explained, in a saddened, slightly hesitant voice.

"It seems to me that people can't be unhappy without it being everyone's fault."

"Yours too, Telo?" asked Makima.

"Of course! Why don't we go tell them the truth?"

"They wouldn't listen to us; they'd persecute us and put us to death."

"Those aren't reasons," said the child, shaking her head. "Duty doesn't stop being duty because it becomes dangerous."

"Alas, Telo, our words would be even more dangerous for them than for us. Some would pretend that they love them, and would repeat them without understanding them. They'd translate our pleas for peace and love into war cries. We'd only succeed in adding one more cause of discord to all their other causes of discord."

"You're too scornful of them, Makima. You talk about them as if they're insane."

"Oh, Telo!" I exclaimed. "Makima is right: we're poor lunatics."

She looked at me with a singular tenderness. She smiled through her tears and said: "If you were mad, you wouldn't know it."

"I know it here, generous Telo. I know it in your midst, when I allow myself to be penetrated by the simple wisdom that emanates from what you say and what you do. Back in my country, perhaps I'd know it sometimes, in the evening, in silence and in solitude, but by day, I'd do as others do, and it's their contagious folly that I'd call wisdom. If my heart re-membered you for an instant and cried your words to me, like remorse, I'd impose silence on it. 'Shut up, heart,' I'd say, insistently, 'to be good among the wicked is to want to perish. Shut up, heart; adaptation to the environment is the first necessity of life. Shut up, heart; let me remain a man like all the rest; don't transform me into an apostle talking in the desert to an inattentive, mocking or hostile crowd; don't transform me into one of those martyrs, who are unsociable, after all, and criminal, since their obstinacy only succeeds in imposing one crime more on their brothers. Shut up, heart; you're not in your own country here; you're in the country of my cold, cal-culating mind, of my cruel and wise hands, that don't recoil before the inevitable.'"

I agitated the gestures, doubtless incoherent, of a person who wants to express simultaneously the two people that are inside him. The children moved away, alarmed, and perhaps frightened. One of them shouted: "But they're utterly insane, the Cruels!"

Telo, also frightened by my words, was weeping to one side. Head lowered, her attitude was one of defeat. Soon, however, she raised her loving face, obstinately.

"Nevertheless," she said, "by telling them about goodness, over and over, and loving them a lot, a lot..."

IX

"My children will soon arrive, Jacques; I have something to prepare for them. I'll leave you for a quarter of an hour."

Makima disappeared through the upper widow of the pyramid, going into the room from which he had brought me the three newspapers. I stayed where I was, head raised, gazing at that opening as if I were looking at a door to Mystery.

When the old man came back, with a small book in his hand, I said: "The place from which you've emerged attracts me and troubles me. If I'm not being indiscreet, tell me what's up there and what you do there."

"In a harmonious country where people are no longer enemies, no question is indiscreet. There is nothing for you to know to my disadvantage; I have nothing to hide from you. The place from which I've emerged is called the pantoscope."

Astonished, I repeated: "The pantoscope? You too have words that come from the Greek? That one means *the place from which one sees everything*?"

"The room's name does, indeed, have that ambitious meaning."

"I'm amazed, Makima, by the mixture of savagery and civilization..."

"Perhaps that's because what you call savagery is our veritable and profound civilization."

"No matter. My mind is astounded by some of the marvels you realize. But am I to believe that you really can see everything?"

"I've admitted that the pantoscope's name is ambitious. The poor apparatus doesn't even tell us whether there are men on the moon and it doesn't see the subterranean life of your miners. On the other hand, it permits..."

The children arrived. The old man interrupted himself, perhaps not without malice. "But I'll explain all that another time—or rather, I'll show you. For the moment, I belong to my young friends.

With his girdle almost entirely undone, but elevated nevertheless, as if floating, Makima sat on a branch of a cherry-tree. The children did likewise, perching amid the foliage like birds at rest. The naked magister, similarly perched, opened his book and began the lesson.

Meanwhile, I bit into an enormous fig that a low branch allowed to hang down like a teat. A disrespectful monkey had settled on my shoulder and was also eating, imitating my mannerisms. Sometimes, I looked at it and laughed. It looked at me, and twisted a grimace that might well have been an attempted laugh. Various birds were pecking here and there. We were brothers suspended from the bosom of the universal Mother.

Above our heads, the deep voice of the old man and the shrill voices of the children often seemed, thanks to a bizarrerie of the Atlantean language, to be the prolonged noise of a drunken party. We were eating reality and strength; they were drinking truth and intelligence.

In all the high branches, the children formed a spontaneous chorus of laughter. It was something sudden and charming. The air seemed to be happy. The monkeys and the birds, immobile and delighted, gazed toward the soft multiple sound. I felt inundated by the fall of a cascade of joy.

"What's so amusing, Makima?"

"Children are amused by trivia, Jacques. I was explaining to them, with the aid of the *Manuel de morale*, what an election is in France."

A few months before, I had been elected as a general councilor. I expect—and this is one of the numerous reasons that prevent me from signing these pages—that I shall soon be serving my country usefully in the Chambre. Even if I set aside the particular duties that the confidence of my compatriots created for me, an election still appeared to me, as to every good citizen, to be a singularly serious matter. I find a marvelous beauty and something akin to a religious significance in those solemn peaceful manifestations of the will of a great people. Wounded in my most profound sentiments, I said, with a mixture of ill-humor and disdain: "Universal suffrage is too noble an institution for savages to be able to comprehend."

Little Telo let herself fall from her branch, and, floating in front of me with her pretty aerial sway, she spoke with the uncomprehending impertinence of a spoiled child.

"Truly, Jacques, you've fulfilled your 'civic duty' yourself? You've been to put the little piece of paper in the…what did he call it just now?…the electoral jug?"

"It's not a jug, Telo," I said, severely. "It's an urn."

"Explain the difference to me, Jacques."

But while I searched for the words, she flew back up and. Perching on her branch again, she remarked: "But Jacques doesn't look that stupid!"

After a few minutes of sulky strolling, the tenderness of my heart brought me back beneath the branches laden with children and joy. They were no longer laughing up there. The little faces were taut with the effort of understanding. Makima, sensing that the young minds were getting weary, closed the book. He said a few words in Atlantean and then, doubtless translating, in French: "I could show you these things in the pantoscope, but there would be emotions too violent for your age, and spectacles too confusing, Ask our friend Jacques instead."

The five or six French speakers let themselves fall almost to ground level. Floating like enormous down-feathers, they bobbed around me, but at a distance.

Little Telo, with an uncertain mixture of boldness and dread, advanced and then recoiled.

"Jacques," she said, first, "you ought to get rid of that nasty bark that hides almost all your body and smells so bad. Pooh! It smells of dead animals."

"It's necessary to be tolerant, Telo. Clothing is, for me, a very old habit, to which I'm attached. It seems to me that these poor garments still surround me with a little of the fatherland."

"Do as you wish, Jacques. But that's not what I wanted to ask you. Have you fulfilled what your book calls 'patriotic duty'? Have you, as it also says, 'paid the blood tax'?"

"Certainly, Telo. I don't see what right you have to suspect me of being a coward or a bad citizen."

"What is he saying, Makima?"

"I'll explain it to you later. Carry on talking to him."

"Jacques have you held in our hands things that are used to kill other people? Have you done an apprenticeship in killing?"

"Of course."

"Have you gone to war, Jacques?"

"Oh, only an unimportant war, a trivial war, against savages."

"What are savages, Makima? Are they a kind of tiger, like those in Tibabrin?"

"No, Telo. They're people weaker and less wicked than the French."

"They're killed, then, to punish them for being mild and weak?"

Slightly aggravated, I explained: "They're killed in order to civilize them."

"I don't understand at all."

"It's quite simple, though," I affirmed. "When children are naughty and unruly, it's necessary to correct them."

But Telo shook her head mutinously, and while her hair opened out and spread out like wings, she said: "First of all, there are no naughty children—and what does 'unruly' mean?"

"A child who doesn't want to obey."

No words could describe the astonishment of the little savage.

"Obey? In that case"—she stopped, as if suffocated—"someone has commanded them to do something?"

"You've deduced correctly, perspicacious Telo."

"But it's bad to command. And if a mad person commands, it's bad to obey. Explain to me why you think children and weak people ought to obey."

"You're annoying me, Telo. You don't understand anything. In France, I'd reply by boxing your ears."

"We're not in France, and it would be very kind of you to reply by giving me a reason."

"Because…because children aren't grown-ups."

"Ah!" sighed Telo, vaguely.

She flew away, surrounded by her comrades. And she said: "Yes, Jacques is very stupid. It will be necessary to educate him, Makima."

"If he wishes…"

"But everyone wants to learn, just as everyone wants to eat."

"I thought you had other questions to ask Jacques?"

"Yes, but he replies so badly!"

"Try again, my daughter."

The children did not come back down. Perched disdainfully, Telo, hardly turning to look at me, let fall from above: "When you were a soldier, Jacques, if there had been a…what is it called?…oh yes!…if there had been a 'riot,' would you have been commanded to shoot at your own people?"

"Perhaps."

"What would you have done?"

"I would have done my duty."

"You wouldn't have killed, then?"

223

"I think you're foolish, Telo. The duty of a soldier is to obey."

"And if your mother had been among the rebels, Jacques, answer, would you have killed your mother?"

"I don't know. You're asking me such questions! There would then have been a conflict between my duty and my conscience, and I don't know what I would have done."

"What does 'a conflict between duty and conscience' mean, Makima?"

Almost as embarrassed as me, Makima stammered: "It's difficult to make that comprehensible to a sound mind. It's also difficult to explain why Jacques' conscience doesn't forbid him to kill other people's mothers." He shook his head, and hesitated for a moment. Finally, he said: "I'll never be able to do it in French."

He started speaking Atlantean. I went away, stunned and relieved, as one emerges from a nightmare.

XII

The next day, there was another of what I called, with slight ill-humor, "perched classes." Makima no longer had the *Manuel de morale civique* in his hand; he was holding a catechism issued by the Diocese of Paris. The birds and monkeys looked at the "scholarly branches" in astonishment. They had never heard such loud and frequent laughter.

I am far from being devout. In Paris, where no one notices his neighbor, I sometimes consent to take my mother and sister to mass, and, during the ceremony, I behave like a well-brought-up individual—which is to say, as correctly as the best Christian. But I more willingly accompany my father to the Lodge and laugh like an intelligent man at the jokes, sometimes a trifle ribald, of the brother orator about the stupid things that priests say and the stupid things they do. In the country, of course, in my electoral constituency, where there is no restraint of courtesy, I do the same myself, brutally and without concession. I never set foot in a church at any price, and at public meeting, I repeat, sometimes wagging an indignant finger at my opponent: "Clericalism is the enemy!"

Here, the enemy had changed costume, but my French heart did not hesitate to recognize him. It was up to all of us, me as well as everyone else, to laugh at those ingenuous savages, as much metaphysicians as the birds. The wretches were laughing at the convictions and emotions of my mother. Oh, how profoundly I sensed the truth of that noble dictum: *anticlericalism is not an item of export.*

Abroad, a Frenchman must show solidarity with all Frenchmen. We're all accused of stupidity by some. And, just as the true devotee is forced by our attacks to defend Tartuffes, so the patriot is obliged, among distant hostilities, to praise, without choice or exclusion, everything that comes from France. Before the enemy armed with rifles and cannons, there are no more radicals, opportunists and nationalists, there are no more rich and poor; there are only French soldiers. Before the enemy armed with laughter and incomprehension, I forget whether I'm a freethinker or a Christian; I only remember that, in philosophy or religion, every doctrine that flowers and bears fruit on French soil is necessarily superior to foreign ideas. At those times, a patriot knows how to make an abstraction of his personal tastes and sacrifice indifferent preferences. The positivist melon ordinarily satisfied me more than the Catholic pear, but against the spitting of strangers, I can protect both the fruits of France.

To laugh with those naked and indelicate individuals at the same things at which I laughed myself would have been a veritable treason. I felt all of my duty toward the doubly glorious nation that is the eldest daughter of the Church and the mother of Descartes and Auguste Comte. Oh, how distance reestablishes true perspective! One perceives, as soon as one is abroad, that Monsieur Combes and Cardinal Richard,[30] far

---

[30] Émile Combes (1835-1921) was the French prime minister from June 1902-January 1905, at the head of a left-wing coalition, but in the present context it is more relevant that he was a

superior to all possible savages, are two equal summits, two equal lights, two equally noble and powerful beacons! My synthetic love for the elements that seemed hostile and contradictory at close range, but constituted harmony and the fatherland at a distance, did not take long to express itself.

"Makima," I said, "do you believe that what you're doing now is polite?"

"It's instructive."

"Politeness is not a negligible detail in well-regulated education, and you ought to teach these children to respect your guest."

"What you call politeness is, I believe, a series of petty lies, a certain number of benevolent grimaces made without benevolence."

"Lies that caress are better than truths that scratch."

"We're not scratching you, Jacques. Everyone here loves you, naturally. Come on, laugh in your turn. Our language is ridiculously poor. Can you imagine that it only possesses a single word to say 'person,' 'friend' and 'sibling'?—with the result that I can't express the fact that you're a human being in Atlantean without directing a loving gesture toward you, and without my speech becoming' like our ordinary greeting, a discreet kiss."

"All that's very nice, but it doesn't prevent you from mocking me and laughing at my expense."

"Only at the expense of your god."

"At the expense of that which I love and venerate above all else. You're aggravating your fault."

"Let's see, Jacques: if you said 'two and two make five,' ought I, out of friendship for you, nod my head and pretend to believe you?"

"I don't know."

---

leading Freemason, and hence locked in conflict with the Catholic Church, as represented by Cardinal François Richard (1819-1908), the Archbishop of Paris.

"What! You don't know. But I'd only have that scornful indulgence for a lunatic. I'd be offering you the worst of insults."

"Perhaps—so what?"

"I have the right to laugh at the partial follies of someone who isn't mad. If, while walking, I fall over without hurting myself, you laugh. But if a lame person fell over, I hope you wouldn't laugh."

"What does all that verbiage prove, most ingenious of savages?"

"It proves that I ought to laugh—and how could I help myself?—when your catechism affirms that there are three persons, each of whom is god, and yet there is only one single god."

"No, you shouldn't laugh; you ought to be respectfully reverent, since you've been informed that it's a mystery."

"You make me yawn, with your mystery! What if I put a date in your pocket and insist that there are three. If I only find one, I hit you, and I respond to your astonishment and your complaints: 'It's a mystery, my son!'"

"You're being stupid, Makima."

"I'm glad to be saying stupid things, my child. I'm glad that, among you, no one has ever struck or killed anyone over questions of religion. I'm glad that the words *persecution, war of religion, inquisition, auto-da-fé, torturer* and *martyr* are as empty of meaning as the mysteries themselves."

I shrugged my shoulders and smiled in a superior fashion. "You're recalling such ancient things, my poor Makima! The distinguished men of today to longer talk about those antiquities. By dwelling on them, you're putting yourself at the level of the most coarse and ignorant."

"On seeing what you're taught, I suspect that the most ignorant of your compatriots might be among the least insane. You appear to me to have as much right to be scornful of them as a Chinese woman with tortured and deformed feet has to be scornful of a woman whose limbs remain normal."

227

"Do you know, Makima, that if you lived in Europe you'd be locked up in a lunatic asylum?"

"Are you quite sure that the whole of your Europe, and Asia, along with Africa, America and Oceania into the bargain, doesn't constitute one vast lunatic asylum?"

"And you say that you love all men? Open your eyes, Makima, and recognize that you're scornful of everything that isn't Atlantean."

"Because I love all humans, I detest everything that deforms them and lessens their humanity. I detest false and intolerant ideas, the mothers of evil sentiments."

There was a long silence. Then little Telo asked me: "Seriously, Jacques, do you believe that a virgin had a son?"

A shook my head sadly. "A strange question in the mouth of a little girl of twelve!"

"Your children learn the catechism much later, no doubt?" said Makima.

"Our children learn the catechism when they're very young, but they don't understand what they're repeating."

"An admirable method of education! A few Atlanteans amuse themselves by educating parrots. Should they be sent to your great seminaries and normal schools?"

"You're very intolerant!"

"What do you call tolerance, then? We don't do any harm to those who proclaim the most absurd ideas, but we invite them amicably, without violence, to reflect. Are our physicians intolerant because their love of the feverish goes as far as to want to expel their fevers? But they limit themselves to advising, and don't administer quinine by force. Too bad for anyone who, confusing his disease with his body, becomes annoyed when someone indicates the remedy to him."

I made a decision—courageous or cowardly? I don't know.

"Fundamentally, I have no objection to you mocking the old religion. I don't believe in it myself. But I respect those who do believe it."

"We respect everyone. We don't burn or imprison any-one."

"I respect the beliefs..."

"We don't respect absurdities, and we laugh at things that are ridiculous."

"Oh, leave me alone. You're injustice personified. Reli-gions are all as absurd as one another; if I knew yours, I'd laugh at it with as much reason as you're laughing."

"We have no religion."

"No religion! But that's abominable! What is it, then, that commands you to love one another?"

"You need to be commanded to love one another?" said little Telo, astonished. And, with a laugh that was mocking, and yet so tender, she asked: "Do you also need your religion to tell you to eat when you're hungry?"

XIII

One morning I woke up feeling very youthful, desirous of making the acquaintance of Atlantean beauty. I had dreamed a great deal about the pilot I had glimpsed. With na-ked women who seemed to know at the age of twelve how babies are made, nuptial ceremony could not be very compli-cated. Still, it was necessary to know, in order to avoid any major gaffe.

I hesitated to interrogate Makima on that delicate subject, all the more so because I had been sulking and avoiding my host of several days. To be sure, I thought him as good a com-panion as the next man, and capable of understanding the joke. More than once, though, the old pedant had exaggerated. An-yway, I don't mind people taking a rise out of me—I know that I have my faults, like anyone else—but a patriot can't tolerate anyone mocking France. After all, it wasn't Messieurs the Atlanteans who won the battle of Austerlitz or built the Eiffel Tower, was it?

That morning, however, my heart was so tender, so uni-versally benevolent...

Having taken my bath in the stream and dried my body on the toilet tree, while I was putting on my clothes, I called Makima. When he appeared in the air, I greeted him in the Atlantean manner for the first time, by blowing him a kiss from my fingertips.

"How are you?" he asked, returning the distant kiss.

"Good—very good, better than ever. And you? But what a silly question—you always have health written all over your face."

"All Atlanteans are as healthy as I am. Half the diseases of Cruels come from their malevolence and their worries. The other half comes from their mania for eating flesh."

"I'm in a curious mood today, Makima, and I'd like to ask you..."

"Speak, my son. You know what an old pendant I am, and how generously you flatter my mania."

"Are you a widower or a bachelor, Makima?"

"There are words, Jacques, that lose their meaning when one pronounces them here."

"Does that evasive response mean that you're married?"

"In our country, where the word 'bachelor' has no meaning, the word 'married' can hardly have any more."

"I'm no further forward, you sly dog. Are there not Atlanteans who live with a woman, and others who, like you, live alone?"

"I go to the starry gathering every day."

"The starry gathering? What's that?"

"I'll take you there, and you can see for yourself."

I understood that I had obtained what I wanted. And I said, by way of flattery and thanks: "You're true poets here, you know—and you have charming ways of designating things. The starry gathering, indeed!"

"It's appropriate that matters touching amour should be designated poetically. If, this evening, a young woman pleases you and you want to get to know her, you say: 'Would you like to rise toward the stars with me?' or even 'To rise with you toward the stars is my one desire.' Or better still: 'One hour with you toward the stars would be more precious to me than a thousand nights in the oneirogene.'"

"What did you say?"

"The oneirogene. You haven't yet made its acquaintance, but I dare say that you soon will."

The old man's eyes were sparkling with malice.

"Oneirogene?" I murmured. "That bizarre name comes from the Greek again—but I know so little Greek. If only Charles were here..."

I thought hard. I was reluctant to interrogate Makima about the oneirogene with which he was threatening me while, laughing. Was it something redoubtable, or ridiculous? The formula that preferred one rise toward the stars to a thousand nights in the oneirogene seem to suggest that it was a very relative good."

The old man's obscure malice irritated me somewhat. I did not want to let him see that, so I said, joking in my turn: "I shan't repeat any of the declarations you suggest. I know a better one."

"What?"

"I'll say: 'To rise with you toward the stars would delight my heart more than the blancmanger delights my mouth.'"

"And the woman will reply to you: 'Your words tell me that you're Makima's guest. Go tell the old man to take you to the oneirogene.'"

"You think..."

"I'm laughing a little, as you are. The chosen woman will certainly grant you, this very evening, if not a rise toward the stars, at least a conversation in the treetops"

"You employ strange formulae..."

"For intercourse, one rises very high. Merely to talk about love, one stops...."

"And you think that I only want to talk?"

Instead of replying, the old man said: "Idler! You haven't learned yet to maneuver with the belt. Don't you fear being awkward tonight?"

"It's really in the air that it's necessary…?

"Of course. On the ground, does love seem to you to retain all is poetry?"

"I'd sacrifice a little poetry without regret, to have a little security."

"Consider the ants, my son. They spend the greater part of their lives underground, but they have wings for those occasions."[31]

"You're making me jealous of the ants. I'd rather have wings than your apparatus."

"You'd lose in the exchange."

Makima went to fetch a belt.

"You ought to take off your clothes," he said. "The fact is that in the air, clothing isn't very comfortable."

The idea that I might only be granted "a conversation in the treetops" annoyed me vaguely. If the stipend were to be thus restricted, it would be humiliating to consent to a special and uncivilized costume.

I made a decision. "I'll remain dressed. If I'm able to procure a lover, I'll ask her to come into a wood with me. A wood in the moonlight is also poetic."

"As you wish," said Makima, shrugging his shoulders.

He indicated the elementary controls to me and fastened a girdle round my waist. It was not completely similar to his; it was complicated by a long, flexible tube attached to the side, the extremity of which Makima held in his hand. Evidently, it was a safety device, something that must serve for the first trials of young children.

"An hour of practice," the old man promised, "And you won't need the tethers any longer. It's better this way, as you say."

---

[31] The reader might feel, in considering the ants' "folly of wings" as described in "The Human Ant," that this Atlantean echo of their mating habits is less poetic than mere phraseology makes it seem.

An hour later, in fact, I could move through the air as freely as and more rapidly than a bird. What a singular joy intoxicated me as I soared lightly, paused to hover, leapt light toward the sky, and descended slowly and smoothly. At one moment, in the folly created by speed, I burst out laughing.

"Oh, the miserable sports of Europe! The poor people in automobiles, who can't even steer their dirigible balloons!"

"Don't scorn anyone," Makima said, with a sudden harshness. "It wasn't you who invented the belt."

XIV

We were flying, intoxicated by speed and liberty. We sometimes played a game familiar to all Atlanteans and all the island's birds. We uttered the singular cry: *Mara*!"—which appears to mean: "Flee!"—and immediately, before us, around us, above our heads and down below, the birds hastened their wings. The tightened girdle, however, gave us such superiority! A few seconds' acceleration, and we could catch a fleeing bird in our hands. We planted a kiss on the fine feathers of its head and let it go. While it drew away with a rapid or slow bound, looking round like a child who wants to be pursued again, Makima shouted: *"Ricnac, nasca!"* which must have been translatable as "Hello, cousin!" Just as the word *nelti* means human, sibling and friend in the poor language of the Atlanteans, *nasca* is the only word that they possess to say "animal" or "cousin."

Sometimes we were gliding rapidly in a joyful silence; sometimes, as if slowly floating, we chatted. The old man helped me to admire the landscape, introducing me to the mores and geography of the region.

"What is that singular house, Makima, so long and squat, so un-Atlantean, it seems to me, and un-pyramidal."

"It's the paper fraternity."

"What?"

"You'd call it, I think, the paper factory."

"Oh! Here a factory becomes a fraternity?"

233

"The word *neltial*—perhaps it would be better to translate it as 'amity' or 'friendship' than 'fraternity'—has numerous meanings, but not very distant from one another. Thus, we use it for the ensemble of people who like the same occupation, and one might say, for example: 'Makima belongs to the *neltial* of horticulturalists.' However, the word more commonly designates a group of friends who work together—for certain tasks prefer to be accompanied by a chorus of voices than a solo song. The fabrication of paper is a tune that desires to be played by numerous hands. Finally, the same name of *neltial* is given to the place from which the songs and products emerge. Among you, if I'm not mistaken, the word 'church' is similarly used to designate both the ensemble of believers and the place where they meet in order to believe."

"So," I said, my irony still veiled, "there are paper-making brothers?"

"The woman with whom I rise toward the stars is part of that fraternity. If she had as much passion for gardening as for me, she'd live in the cherished pyramid."

"And they exchange their paper for your fruits?"

"How obstinate these Cruels are in not understanding the simplest things! I've already told you that we no longer need the barbarities of exchange and justice, and haven't for a long time. When a brother—a paper-maker, a belt-maker or a physician—wants fruits he takes them from the trees without worrying about which brother gardener has helped them to grow and ripen. Just as I leave the fruits and everyone's disposal, all of them deposit the paper in the great warehouse you can see to your right. When I want paper, I only have to go get some."

"And you always find it?"

"Of course! Just as they always find fruit. With considerable difficulty, the papermaking brothers have traced two parallel lines, along the walls of the hangar. When the paper covers the upper line, they suspend fabrication. When it falls to the bottom line, one hears the song of voices and machines again."

"But what reason do they have for working?"

"In order to understand your question, I need, as it were, to transport myself mentally into the thinking of the cruel lands. Among you, where workers, deprived of everything, do not work for themselves or for other workers, but for a few parasites who are everyone's enemies, it can happen that the instinct of virtue, independence of justice—all that is noble in them—takes the form of abstention and idleness. Here, no one has any reason to disobey nature. Do you not have alternating needs for activity and repose? Are there not fatiguing sports in your country that only differ from labor in being unproductive? But if we expended all the activity necessary to us on the production of material goods, the island would become disagreeably cluttered, and we wouldn't be able to squander so much unnecessary wealth. Fortunately, there are games, there's art, there's science, there are languages, there's the pantoscope, flight, navigation, amour, education and a thousand other active pleasures."

"I've often wondered, without being able to find a reasonable answer, why you learn our languages. Shipwrecks must be rare here..."

"There hasn't been one for a hundred and forty-three years."

"Well, then?"

"What about your books, your poems, your novels, your philosophies?"

"Are you deprived of all those bagatelles?"

"On the contrary—we produce a great many, of superior beauty."

"Why not scorn ours?"

"They're interesting, because they're different. What is more moving, in any case, than the actions and mores of nations? One can only understand such things by knowing the language. For whoever knows how to look, every language contains the history of the people who speak it. Then again, your languages are not indispensable to us..."

"Ah!"

"A few archaic formulae which seem to be translated compose the language of politeness here, such as the '*Ricmac, nasca,*' that I address to animals I meet, or the "*Ricmac, nelti,*" that sometimes replaces the kiss sent from the fingertips. Those forms, the only ones that you've retained, are in reality foreign to the genius of our language. Atlantean is synthetic, an agglutinated language."

"Like the idioms of American savages!"

"Those savages are, indeed, of the red race, and their language resembles ours as an eglantine resembles a rose, or the poor flower of the lily of the field resembles the glorious realized lily."

"If your language is so admirable in its beauty, how can others serve you?"

"I was about to tell you. The heart has two movements, which you call, I believe, systole and diastole. You breathe in and breathe out. The earth has alternations of day and night. Do you think that your heart could be satisfied with one of those movements? Do you believed that breathing in or out would be sufficient to your life? Would the earth not become arid beneath an eternal daylight, and would it not become sad and sterile in endless night?"

"What are you getting at?"

"In the same way, intelligence demands the alternative movements of analysis and synthesis. So we all know, in addition to Atlantean, marvelous in its synthesis, at least one analytical language. Every time a thought appears to us to be worthy of expression, we express it in two forms. It emerges from the proof enriched and fortified. A thought that imperiously demands one form and refuses the other obstinately, is only of local or historical interest and remains far from depths, but one that is always beautiful and balanced passes joyfully from analysis to synthesis and from synthesis to analysis, is a truly human thought."

I was trying to follow that disquieting dissertation. The old man became enthusiastic. "Oh, I ought not to belittle the thought that satisfies our double desire, which remains harmo-

236

nious throughout its enlargement toward the circumference and its return to the center by calling it human thought. It's *natural* thought. It sings not only the profundity of humans but that of nature. It's the only one that our scientists verify objectively, the only one that our inventors..."

Annoyed by the sibylline hymn, I interrupted; "I don't quite understand. Explain to me how an Atlantean writer goes and getting a book published."

"Can you see those large fiery letters trembling above that distant pyramid?"

"Yes."

"They're announcing that the poet Marquina has just completed a collection of lyrics. Marquina is one of our favorite poets. Let's return to the most amicable of pyramids.[32] Let's go into the pantoscope. In ten minutes I'll have a photograph of the new poems, just as I've obtained, in recent days, copies of three newspapers, the *Manuel de morale civique* and the *Catechism*."

We scarcely spoke during the rapid return. As we passed over the "Paper fraternity" again, however, I suddenly burst out laughing and said: "Paper-making brother and paper-making sister: that really is too funny."

"I've read somewhere," said Makima, "that you have masonic brothers where you come from."

I blushed slightly, but soon objected triumphantly: "Undoubtedly, but they're not the ones who build houses!"

Makima nodded his head with an expression of approval, and in an amiably ingenuous voice, he said: "You're right, Jacques; that's what prevents their title from being ridiculous."

---

[32] The narrator inserts a footnote: "Makima is translating literally the expression by which an Atlantean ordinarily refers to the house he inhabits."

XV

As two pigeons fly blithely into a dovecot, we entered the pantoscope. The old man advised: "Don't go down. Don't set your feet on the vitreous parquet."

"Are you going to print a book in mid-air, lifted up by your belt?"

"I could, but perhaps you've noticed that our calmest pauses are not complete immobility. The Atlantean language refers to them as *floating*."

"That's the word I've thought several times."

I looked, curiously, at the place where we were. It was an irregular polyhedron. Over the numerous wall-panels, entirely covered in glass, a mysterious, soft and even light flowed. Beings and things, multiplied and deformed, took on fantastic aspects there. An apparatus stood on the "vitreous parquet" that was somewhat akin to our photographic apparatus. Makima was holding an undefinable object, flat and round: something similar, safe for its greenish tint, to a five franc piece. He pressed lightly, and the object produced a kind of cord, springing forth to the right and the left, about three meters long. Still holding that changeable matter by the middle, he tugged with both hands, as if to enlarge it. It was, indeed, enlarged, and at the same time, the two hanging sides rose up. When the fabric was about a meter long it was horizontal and almost rigid. Makima stopped supporting it and, by virtue of some unknown magic, the object remained suspended in mid-air.

"Let's sit down on the aerial bench," said the old man.

I did so, not without mistrust. Under our weight, the legless bench remained motionless and unshaken, as firm as the ground itself.

"I said *aerial bench*," my host remarked. "Perhaps it would have been better to translate it as *aerial bed* or *sky bed*."

"Is this furniture used," I enquired, with an anxious giggle, "when one rises up to the stars?"

"Of course—and this evening, you'll be carrying a sky bed in the pocket to the left of your belt."

Makima pulled a screen over each of the four windows, which seemed, like all the walls, to be formed by a sheet of glass. The light, which had previously been streaming monotonously around us, became irritated and excited. It condensed in unexpected places, sprang forth in brilliant gleams or blazed up in rotating roseate formation. Our images were fiery, not in the mirrors but *on* them, and each of our gestures showered sparks or flames over fifty surfaces.

Indifferent to these phantasmagorias, Makima rotated the photographic apparatus, calculating favorable directions with the aid of the compass on top of it. He opened a kind of drawer in the middle and slid out a large stack of paper. Having closed the drawer again he pressed a button. There was an audible click.

I did not see any of these things as natural and unique precisions. I only saw movements of light, multiple and blinking, sometimes cold and almost imperceptible, sometimes flamboyant, menacing and dazzling.

"In five minutes," declared one of the fifty old men of flame that surrounded me—I couldn't tell which—"I'll have Marquina's book."

"Atlantis offers singular commodities," I remarked—and was frightened by the fear that I heard in my tone.

"Is there any distant object that you'd like to see?" Makima asked.

What I wanted most of all was to escape that proximate spectacle. I declared, in a loving tone: "I'd be glad to see my parents."

"Where do they live?"

"Paris—34 Rue des Deux-Ponts."

Makima threw a black veil over my face. I felt him quit the aerial bench. I heard he crackle of sparks, then the roar of flames—noises that paralyzed me with terror.

Suddenly, I was far from Atlantis. In a silence that was also frightening, I was in Paris, in our poor street, in front of our house. The lit gas-jets were illuminating the scene with the precision of reality, and the rare passers-by animated it. My anxiety, however, was stimulated by the silence that surrounded the most necessarily noisy actions like an infinite negation.

"A strange dream!" I murmured.

Without a sound, an omnibus rolled painfully along the causeway. My father got out of it.

"Father! Father!" I called to him.

"He can't hear you," said Makima's singularly distant voice.

"I think I'm going mad."

With a mechanical gesture, I tried to pass my hand over my forehead. I displaced the cloth slightly; the vision disappeared; I was in deep darkness.

"Don't touch the Veil of Isis!" Makima's voice recommended.

Nearby and as abrupt as a start, that speech was accompanied by a nervous laugh.

I felt a hand putting the veil back in place, and the vision reappeared. The voice, now stifled by distance, breathed: "Which floor? Which window?"

I stammered the information, and found myself amid the friendly light of lamps, in our drawing-room—the drawing-room in which I am writing at this very moment.

My father and my mother, sitting in two armchairs, had the attitudes of people who are listening. My sister, sitting on the rotating stool, was playing the piano. I could see the movement of her fingers; I could see the keys going down and up again; I could read the sheet-music—but my soul was entirely taut with the desire, the need, to hear. But the creative gestures remained to me as vain lips agitate for the deaf.

"I want to hear!" I exclaimed.

"You're too demanding, or, at least, too urgent!"" groaned a voice that seemed subterranean. "The physicist Urimarca has now been studying the problem for ten years, and he dare not promise anything for another seven or eight years."

My sister stopped playing. She turned on the stool to face the moving lips of my father, and moved her own lips. My mother's mouth also opened for I don't know what mute words. Anguish, strangling me with its clawed feet, emerged from the precision of things seen, from the mystery of spoken silence.

Then my soul formed a smile heavy with emotion.

"Makima, Makima, I'm sure that they have a vague impression of my strange presence. I'm sure of it, Makima: they're talking about me.

A tremor shook my entire body: a great tremor of hope and love. The distant voice replied, as cold as death: "It's possible, but I don't know."

"What time is it?" I asked.

"Where I am," the strange voice replied, strangely, "it's one o'clock in the afternoon. Where you are, it's eleven o'clock."[33]

I shouted loudly: "Father, Mother, Sister—I'm alive! I'm physically close by."

The inexpressible sentiment of my presence, I had just understood, caused them to believe that I was dead. The three people who loved me had just lowered the lights and had sat down, their faces sad, veiled by the chiaroscuro and funereal thoughts, around a light side-table. They placed their trembling hands, fingers splayed, on the tabletop. I saw the table rise up and fall back, a precise shadow in the vague shadow.

I counted three raps. They said: "Yes."

They said: "Jacques."

They said: "I'm nearby."

They said: "I'm drowned."

My gaze went to my mother's hand, and I saw a tear fall upon it.

I shouted: "A frightful nightmare! I want to wake up."

Advice reached me, scarcely heard: "Lift the veil."

---

[33] This time difference implies, enigmatically, that Atlantis is in the Pacific rather than the Atlantic.

I obeyed. Again I was sitting on the aerial bench, in the magical room, surrounded by mirrors over which flickers of flame flowed. All the flames formed a grotesque and frightful chorus, composed of dwarfish fidgetings and giant quiverings. With crazy deformations, long and deep here, short and ridiculously shrill there, their dance suggested a hand opening a door and removing a notepad covered in mysterious signs.

An entire minute passed by. I asked: "That was a dream that I just had, wasn't it?"

"It was a reality that you saw."

My arms slowly rose up like two despairs, and strange funereal flames loomed up in all the mirrors.

"My parents," I wept, "think I've drowned."

"I can't disabuse them, alas. The physicist Ircile is studying means of sending visions to the Cruels, but the last time I saw her, she was only expressing distant hopes."

My face was a huge burn, refreshed by tears. A red flame appeared in the mirrors, furrowed by showers of white sparks.

"I'm too sad, Makima," I said. "I don't want to go to the starry gathering this evening."

"You're good, my son."

And the old man hugged me paternally.

XVI

On foot, I wandered for some time among the various orchards that surrounded "the most amicable of pyramids." Slowly, the cool calm of the trees soothed me. I ended up smiling at my recent sadness—a sadness with cause, surely. Far from the insane spectacle, I refused those phantasmagorias any reality. I regretted the absurd decision to deprive myself of the starry gathering that evening. But the old man's accolade and eulogy prevented me from taking back my imprudent words.

I shouted as loudly as I could: "Makima!"

A sound of rustling leaves announced the aerial presence of my friend.

"Makima, I'd like to visit a city."

"Come and put on your traveling belt."

While we were flying toward the city, my multiply awakened curiosity gave the old man no rest.

"In the shipwreck, I lost the pictures of my parents. Could you photograph their faces as easily as a book?"

"More rapidly, if you only desire a superficial photograph. For the Marquina collection I had to reproduce nearly four hundred surfaces, superimposed and opposed. The action of such numerous X-rays, if one goes too fast, is not without danger of confusion. It's prudent to take at least five minutes. One second is sufficient to take a photograph of a room and the people occupying it."

"Even at that distance?"

"Distance only exists for the transport of heavy matter." After a momentary pause, the old man continued: "At this hour, your parents are doubtless asleep. You'd prefer to see them in more lively attitudes. I'll satisfy your affectionate desire tomorrow."

All the astonishing things that I had encountered on the island assailed me at the same time: vague memories, agitated powerfully, like a crowd. In a kind of drunkenness, I declared: "You are, Makima, the most glorious and the most admirable of peoples. I hope that you will relate to me one day the proofs that you underwent in order to reach the luminous and peaceful summit. Tell me now by means of what physical principles you triumph over so many laws that still seem ineluctable in other countries. Is it by means of one force or several that you succeed in flying through the air, more rapidly and more smoothly than swallows, seeing what is happening a thousand leagues away, beyond the opaque curve of the Earth, and capturing distant images in a second?"

"I'm quite ignorant of physics and energetics, Jacques."

"Me too, Makima. I confess, for instance, that all I know about electricity is its name and some of its more commonplace effects. Nevertheless, I experience some satisfaction when I learn that some machine is powered by electricity and not some other force. Thus, the people of old rejoiced in thinking that it's Jupiter who launches thunderbolts, but Venus who agitates our sap in spring."

My companion let these reflections pass with indifference. Pointing at an immense building in the vicinity, he said: "Let's go down into that big pyramid. It's the dwelling of Nakchatra, a historian and physicist. He has collected many ancient devices and obsolete machines and has arranged them in chronological order."

Unfortunately, Nakchatra was not at home; I had to content myself with awkward explanations, perhaps confused by "the ignorance of a gardener," as Makima said—with a modesty that was, alas, only too justified.

Near the entrance the ground floor offered prehistoric instruments: stone axes, arrows armed with sharp stones, bronze weapons and utensils. Brief captions that my companion translated gave the information that those objects were anterior to the Fortunate Separation. The stone instruments were trophies obtained from the Cruels; the bronze tools and weapons were indigenous. Makima pointed out to me that the latter objects were designed for smaller hands.

"It was us," he affirmed, "who gave bronze to the nations, and it was as if ten centuries had suddenly been added to your progress."

Then came objects of iron, gold, silver and orichalcum. They resembled the ancient utensils that can be seen in our museums, or even items of apparatus still in use among us.

"These strange instruments," said Makima, "which I believe you still use, served for cooking meat in the odious epoch when our ancestors ate their animal cousins." And the old speech-maker ostentatiously indicated the most vulgar of cooking-pots and the most banal of turnspits.

On the first floor I found bicycles and automobiles, often little different from those that run us over on our roads.

From the second floor onwards, the objects took on unexpected, as if mocking, forms that seemed to be making fun of my ignorance. The captions indicated, however, that in that epoch, four thousand years after the Fortunate Separation, the principal motive force was still electricity. It was only toward the year six thousand that electricity had been dethroned by radioactivity. That was the time of dirigible balloons; their nacelles generally had the form of ships. Most of them were as small and graceful as yachts, but some were elongated to the proportions of our large merchant ships.

Radioactivity had given way to a new energy-source, solar force. Makima attempted to explain to me how it was captured, stored and utilized, with the aid of the captions. His words were like clumsy groping in the dark, which discovers nothing and whose contacts are irritating. I did not understand any of it, and I was already suffering from an intense headache.

The machines I had just seen and those I was looking at became confused, dancing around me in a sickening conga. As they went, slight modifications transformed them into fantastic animals and frightful humans. Floating and spinning before my eyes, I saw grimacing forms, melting obesities, brittle emaciations. With incoherent gestures, limbs as round as wheels, as stout as boilers, as long as pistons, jointed like flails, touched me, grabbed me, dispersing my garments and my body, like a circle of children sharing out all the toys on the branches of a Christmas tree. And in my aching head, those entities of metal and mist grated, screeched, rubbed, vibrated and whistled. Oh, how I would have liked to flee that frightful scientific bric-à-brac!

I dared not. I feared creating too poor an impression of my intelligence and attention span.

Surrounded by the increasingly numerous and increasingly farandole, I followed Makima into the Hall of Syndynamics. The voice of my guide, a vague buzz, mingled with the noises that the folly of things multiplied around me, and the present spectacle complicated its unforeseen extravagances with the extravagances of the imaginary spectacle. Obedient to a disagreeable necessity or a grim fashion, the syndynamic apparatus really did affect the forms of fantastic and menacing animals. It seemed to me that one of them bit the extended hand of the old man, while, as in a dream, I heard a feeble voice day, amid a deafening clicking: "About the year eight thousand of the Fortunate Separation."

In my increasingly fatigued eyes, those monsters of the apocalypse took on a more intense and more aggressive life. They dispersed the unique round, shrieking orders at the anterior monsters or, seizing them with hands of dementia and metal, with fingers and fire and folly, dragging them around me in a thousand circles that rose and fell, were disjointed and renewed, shrank and broadened out, sometimes crushing me with a tighter and tighter friction, sometimes vaporizing me, after a fashion, carrying away in their discordant flight I don't know what dolorous streamers of mist, which were my dispersed shreds.

It was with relief that I arrived at the uppermost floor. There, in the midst of a thousand unfamiliar objects, flying belts, sky beds and scale models of the pantoscope welcomed me, like unexpected friends in hostile territory. My shipwrecked thoughts clung to the tenaciously. Everything unknown became mixed up, powerful and unified, like the waves of a sea, like the swell of a tempest. Heavy and menacing waves rose and fell, always similar—but in that indefinitely repeated brutality, you were, dear flying belts, dear sky beds, and you, minuscule pantoscopes, the fortunate planks to which one could hold on, on which one could rest, to recover one's breath and one's hope.

Finally, we emerged. Among the fading sounds, which were no longer anything but a ringing in the ears, the old man continued, implacable, to explain.

"The force that we now employ almost uniquely was initially—two thousand years ago—called pandynamic, which is to say, it appears, the universal force, or the force of universal application. Ten centuries ago, it rendered the other physical energies so unnecessary and obsolete that we no longer experienced the need to give it a distinctive name, and we simply call it "the Force."

XVII

"Here's the city; let's go down."

"I can only see a region devoid of habitations and covered with trees."

"Let's go down anyway."

The trees were growing on uneven ground. Here and there, stones were perceptible between their roots.

"This is what you call a city?"

"Be indulgent to poor savages, my son. I'm showing you the best we have in the genre."

"There isn't a single city in the entire island? Not one town, not one village or hamlet? Not a single agglomeration of houses?"

To each question, the old man shook his head negatively. Finally, he declared: "We're over the largest and most recent city. It was only abandoned four thousand years ago."

"You're saying singular things."

"No. When you're civilized, you'll allow your cities to fall too."

"I assure you that you astonish me."

"When you're civilized, you won't impose any task on anyone, by means of violence, hunger or deceit."

"You perform many tasks voluntarily. Why have you neglected the glorious work necessary to preserve the city?"

"The 'glorious work' that renders a city habitable appears to us to be particularly repugnant and harmful."

"Explain."

"When, after upheavals that I'll tell you about later, the Atlanteans were finally a free people, liberated from all government, all imposed hierarchy and all organization, they continued initially to live in cities. Just as there are fraternities of paper-makers, belt-makers and physicists today, there were once fraternities of voluntary sweepers, devoted waste-clearers and brave sewer workers. But a certain Abitanis, of the waste disposal fraternity, started one day to preach against the cities.

247

'By consenting to poison ourselves more than the others,' he said, 'we're ensuring the duration of the general poisoning, which it would be so easy to suppress. Let us flee the cities and their inevitable infection and take refuge in the healthy countryside.'

"A thousand stupid objections were raised. People went so far as to accuse Abitanis of wanting to eliminate the progress of science, to destroy art and suppress human fraternity. In that era, there were still imbeciles able to believe that plants grow stronger and flowers more glorious under the trampling of a herd. Those blind people insulted the pioneer, calling him 'antisocial' and 'egotistical.' He continued his apostolate valiantly.

"By the time he died, the urbicides—I'm translating the Atlantean word as best I can—were in the majority. Nevertheless, it was a long struggle. For more than a century, the question of the abandonment of the cities was the most controversial of all issues. Meanwhile, the cities were depopulated, for, while a few urbicides continued preaching to the city-dwellers, most were content to go and live in the country.

"It turned out that the obstinate city-dwellers were the least courageous of Atlanteans. It became increasingly difficult to recruit cleaning fraternities. The members of those associations were overworked and fell ill. The physicians ordered them to take atmospheric cures. At the same time as health, however, they acquired a love of the countryside and didn't come back. Three hundred years after Abitanis' death, however, a few people still persisted in living in Hassipi, the poisonous city covered by these noble trees. It's so difficult to abandon the most pernicious habits! So many mentalities take a long time to take on a veritably plasticity! Today, we proclaim that the death of the cities was probably the most important benefit of Non-Organization."

While we made our way back o the most amicable of pyramids, Makima began to tell me the story of the twelve-thousand-year history of his homeland. I shall summarize his narration, which was a trifle long-winded and rambling.

About the times preceding the Fortunate Separation information is scant and uncertain. In spite of its lacunae, its inexactitude of detail and its absurd mythological coloring, Plato's *Critias* contains almost everything that the Atlanteans know about that distant epoch. After a long indeterminate period of placid pastoral life, they had become an industrious, warrior and navigator people. They worked metals with superior artistry, and made use of them primarily to manufacture weapons. Agricultural labor was light and indolent on land that was so naturally fecund that it yields a crop every three months, in a warm and stable climate that makes every tree an eternal marriage of a spring crowned with flowers and an autumn crowned with fruits.

Unfortunately, as avid as all "cruels," they were unable to be content with their own country and the true wealth that it lavished upon them. They hastened to conquer inferior lands, advantages of opinion, infamous glory, futile and criminal riches. They were proud of exacting tributes from people poorer than themselves. They captured slaves and increasingly disburdened themselves of all labor. They became masters of all the islands of the Ocean, the continent that would later be called America, the whole of Africa except for Egypt, and of Europe as far as Tyrrhenia. Defeated by a coalition at the head of which were the inhabitants of the land that would later be called Greece, however, they lost their European possessions.

Atlantis then formed a confederation of ten kingdoms. Their disdain for foreign peoples and the immensity of the booty to conquer in a world that was expanding before the boldness of their sails, would doubtless have been sufficient, in a few more centuries, to unite those brigands tightly and prevent any civil discord between them. If the polar cataclysm had not separated them brutally from the rest of the world, perhaps they would have remained conquerors, warriors and merchants, wolves and foxes, incapable, like all the avid, of perceiving the most obvious moral verities. Their material prosperity might even have ended up crushing their intelligence. They would have become ennui-stricken sybarites.

Makima claimed to have discovered traces of that tendency in the remaining fragments of the most ancient Atlantean poems, but the language had changed a great deal over eleven thousand years, and he confessed that people produced contradictory translations of those fragments. What he affirmed without hesitation, however, is that the Atlanteans were right to consider the immersion of the island as a great boon and to commence the epoch of the Fortunate Separation in that era.

The benefits of the Separation were not immediate. The catastrophe was followed by a chaotically troubled and bloody era. The cataclysm that had cut the Atlanteans off from all their conquests by rendering all navigation impossible had also completely destroyed three of the ten kingdoms and submerged the greater part of three more. Only the four in the center remained secure.

By a fatal singularity, at the moment of the cataclysm, the kings had assembled for the annual federal ceremony in the temple that Plato calls the temple of Neptune and Clito, but which was actually dedicated to the Phallus of Fire and the Marine Matrix—which is to say, presumably, the sun and the sea; or, more abstractly, the male and female principles, which, in the form of a couple or an androgynous god, are found at the commencement of so many theogonies. There thus remained ten kings for approximately six kingdoms. The three sovereigns that the sea had despoiled completely and the two who had been most impoverished demanded a new division. Those who had lost nothing refused, arrogantly.

Diaprepida, the province in which Makima lived, so many centuries later, had been inundated over some two-fifths of its extent. It was left out of projects of reorganization, and its king was able to disinterest himself in the quarrels that led to long and terrible wars between the other nine. With various alternations, frequent modifications in alliances, long truces and very short intervals of peace, those wars lasted more than three centuries. Meanwhile, the peaceful people of Diaprepida developed their commerce and increased their population.

They ended up being equal in number and power to all of the other provinces put together.

The depopulated and weakened lands feared and were jealous of the Diaprepedans. They united against those excessively fortunate folk, and that was the occasion for new wars that lasted for centuries. The Diaprepedans, having killed their king without replacing him, were ruled by an elected assembly; that political forms seemed at first to be favorable to the multitude, and the Diaprepedans, enthusiastic for liberty and equality, won major victories. Aided by the poor people of two other regions, they deposed their kings and founded what they called, not without pretention, the Universal Republic. The sovereigns of the refractory regions tightened their alliance, killed their children and made a mutual donation of their kingdoms to the last survivor. For two thousand years the island was divided into two nations, the Diaprepedan Republic and the Azaid Empire.

In spite of initial appearances, the Azaids and the Diaprepedans suffered the same ills. In both of them, a few rich people owned everything. They made the poor work for their profit, and only left them a small share of the fruits of labor. The unfortunate individuals of whom they had no need formed what was termed, in the language of the time, "the excess population" or "the scum of the population." Many of these reputedly useless and cumbersome individuals died in infancy; the others dragged out a meager and harsh life through privations. They sometimes tried to revolt, but the Diaprepedans and Azaids were fervent patriots who maintained formidable armies. Those armies were used to crush the rebels.

"If the misery of the people became too hostile, or there was a risk of their becoming conscious of their cause, a beneficent war served as an outlet for the fury of the unfortunate, deflecting the blows that would have been directed at the rich and diminishing the excess population slightly. A political writer of that period, the famous Arvakova, began one chapter of his book *On the Art of Ruling*, with the bizarre formula:

"War is a lightning-conductor raised over the Temple inhabited by the Rich."

Some revolutions succeeded, however. Their results were precarious, and more apparent than real. Sometimes, twenty years of empire interrupted the republic of the Diaprepedana or thirty years of republic vegetated among the Azaids. Whatever the political form, the Rich remained the masters. The so-called heads of the government were the foremen of the true overlords, their principal housekeepers and most faithful servants.

Finally, a savior appeared, whose name is no longer known. He called himself Nelti, meaning "brother." It was after the success of the great Nelti that the two words signifying "man" and "brother" disappeared from the Atlantean language. They are still found occasionally, it seems, in certain poems and historical novels, but the author always tales the precaution of explaining them in a footnote. Nelti went into the towns and cities of the two peoples repeating the following speech and similar ones.

"How can violence destroy the principle of violence? By gentle and be indomitable. Don't kill anyone, don't injure anyone. Allow yourselves to be injured, allow yourselves to be killed, without a backward step or a cry of pain. Never command and never obey. Don't work for anyone who does nothing. Learn that there is only one kind of labor, and that it is done with the hands. When you're hungry, go take what you need to sate yourself from the nearest field. All fields belong to you, as well as to the birds of the air. All fruits belong to you, as well as to the monkeys that climb in the trees. Are you less than the monkeys of the forest or the birds of the air? No, you're more than the birds and the monkeys. The beasts flee when a cruel who says: 'This field is mine, this tree is mine,' wants to kill them. You shouldn't flee. You should oppose the human courage to your enemies that doesn't recoil and doesn't strike. One person struck for the sake of right, if he shows neither anger not fear, enlightens a hundred people, but one who is killed for the sake of right, if he hasn't resisted or tried to flee, will have enlightened a thousand of his brothers."

Soon, a numerous crowd followed the preacher of force and love. To begin with, the Rich unleashed their armies against that population of passively destructive fools who refused either to command or obey, to have slaves or to be slaves, to exploit or to be exploited. Many of them were killed, but Nelti's prophecies were increasingly realized. At the first encounter, soldiers threw away their weapons and joined the saintly crowd, and, instead of killing in their turn, asked to be killed. Not content with not fleeing, excited individuals ran toward the blows, crying: "I want to die in order that my brother might understand, and, after having killed me, might love me. Strike, and my blood will be the red light that illuminates his eyes and sets his heat ablaze."

Wisdom or dementia, the thought exalted in such sentiments, gestures and cries became a powerful contagion. Soldiers wept, soldiers fled. After two or three horrible butcheries, the most brutal stopped, paralyzed by astonishment and impotence. "We can't kill these madmen," they said. "We can't kill these people who don't defend themselves, who offer us their breasts, who fall, smiling and blessing us. What can we do, anyway? There are too many of them, and death multiplies them even more."

After twenty years, there were no more soldiers, no more slaves and no more wage-earners. There were, among the multitudes that ate the fruits of the earth, a few obstinate and miserable Rich, who worked in isolation, trying to produce the futilities that had become necessary to their poor servile hearts, and who saw with a discouraged rage the gentle individuals invading their gardens and their houses, to take, amid friendly words and laughter, everything useful and overabundant. The Rich rarely continued to try the murder that could not change things. Often, they fled into solitary corners to weep and wear away their hearts with the acid of memories and regrets.

Finally, there were no longer any rich people at all. Almost all of them had melted into the great human Fraternity. The most tenacious had died of anger or melancholy. Then the liberated humans set about working and playing on the purified land. The great Nelti did not live to see that day. He had died a long time before. If he had lived, perhaps he would have prevented the folly and miseries that continued to weigh upon the people, doubtless less and less burdensome, but so absurd and futile, for several centuries more. Perhaps he would have prevented those gentle and courageous people, equal and fraternal, from continuing to poison themselves for a further thousand years in fetid cities.

"Follow the example of the birds of the air," he might have said to them. "They refrain from building their nests so close together as to make dung-heaps of them; each of them places on a fortunate branch the dwelling in which their young will be born and raised."

Free love is a great conqueror. Even before the destruction of the cities, the fraternal Atlanteans had sensed the relationship that unites humans with innocent beasts. They had ceased to kill in order to live, and to eat flesh.

Those individuals, open to all love and refractory to any servility, had accomplished moral progress that we can only imagine. Enveloped by mildness and the enlightenment of equal happiness, while enriching and embellishing their minds, they enriched and embellished their vast abode. In an immense and paradisal garden, they lived amid the vast realized flowers, the largest and noblest realized fruits, of which the perfume bore two names: thought and love.

"O landscape," proclaimed Makima, while his broad and enthusiastic gesture embraced all of the visible terrain, "you are born and you live, since you have the island for your mother and Atlantis for your father."

He also said, with a glorious certitude:

"Now, no progress in science, no multiplication of wealth, and no material burden can crush us, or even do us the slightest harm. Now, we are, irreducibly and for all eternity, beings who prefer harmony to power, beauty to riches, rhythm to quantity. We are able to pass indifferently over everything that is not liberty and love. We have no need of anything external, or even what we have. We have no need of anything, not even to eat in order to live. Irreducibly, and for all eternity, we are the only rich, the poor in spirit."

XVIII

"Makima, when you make yourself the herald of the eternity of your good fortune, you're yielding to a common illusion. Everything is affirmed or extended to the point of invading and denying other things. The sentiment of being expands gloriously, suppressing the sentiment of limitation. Our great mobility in all the directions of space has instructed us. We're able to respond to the numerous voices that surround us: 'You're not the only interpreters of nature and the horizon is not the frontier of nothingness.' But Time carries us away into a mist that never clears ahead of us, and its voice is infinitely more deadening than that of Place. We sometimes repeat the crazy affirmation of the Instant that cries out: 'My name is Eternity!' Loves or enthusiasms, all our narrow joys of an hour intoxicate themselves and dare not proclaim themselves joys forever."

"I'm familiar, Jacques with that law of minds and things. Ordinarily, I'm wary of it. I was wrong to say to whatever fills the visible moment: 'You fill eternity.' I was wrong to forget, momentarily, that the clepsydra is bottomless. Nevertheless, on the summit of thought to which I rise, no matter how much my ascension enlarges the circle of the horizon, it seems to me that I still remain at a center from which happiness radiates."

"Makima, if a curious god, dragging Atlantis over the astonished sea, were to attach it to one of the three continents tomorrow, what do you imagine would happen? Would you be a leaven of happiness sufficient to make the heavy dough rise? Or, crushed by our folly, would you perish in a futile fashion? Or would you become insensate and cruel again yourself?"

"We would, as once around the great Nelti, die without recoiling or killing."

"Perhaps. But I don't believe that the country I come from is ripe for conversion. You'd be lamentable martyrs, who would all die, taking the truth to which they testify with them."

"For another seventy centuries, no curious god will bring us into proximity with the Cruels."

"How do you know? Do you know the date when...?"

"Our submerged lands are slowly rising again. In twenty-four centuries, Atlantis will have larger dimensions. In seventy centuries, the entire Sargasso Sea will be navigable to vessels that cannot fly, and our ports, still drowned today, will become accessible."

"What will happen then?"

"You're asking for more than I can tell you. Know, however, that that fatal settlement date is preoccupying our scientists and philosophers. Complicated as the problem seems, when one has seven thousand years to solve it and all the power of love, despair would be premature."

"Who has made these calculations, Makima?"

"Several of our scientists. And their conjectures seem probable, for the figures they give only differ by a few years. One of these days, I'll give you an oral translation of a beautiful book by the physicist Ircile, *Atlantis the Savior*.

"You've mentioned this Ircile before, I seem to remember."

"Yes. She's the one who is researching means of sending visions to the Cruels. If we can project clear and complete images of Atlantis into your skies, and partial scenes of our happiness on to the walls of your houses, do you not think that the spectacle of enlightenment, pursuing you for seventy centuries, might modify the thinking of generations? Meanwhile, Urimarca is trying to perfect our poor pantoscope, and is on the brink of making it an auditory apparatus as well as an optical one. The child is perhaps already born who will combine Ircile's invention and Urimarca's gift in one ingenious kiss, which will permit us to make benevolent guiding voices audible to our poor people, at the same time as our dazzled eyes admire and love the goal to be attained."

I smiled, and said: "You're considering time solely as your ally; but that god has two faces, and he's your enemy too. The Cruels might discover flying vessels tomorrow."

"Whoever plays a game always has a risk of losing."

"Do you not believe that you would be acting prudently by sending us apostles now?"

Makima shook his head.

"The apostle," he said, "is still a sterile flower in your lands. You killed Socrates, Jesus and many others without obtaining any profit from their teaching."

"You're mistaken. We repeat the words of Socrates respectfully, and the world has become Christian by virtue of the death of Jesus and the martyrs."

"You're proud of repeating words that have no meaning on your lips, since you don't make them the principles of your life. If Socrates returned among you, would you kill him again, or, even more insanely than the people of Athens, lock him up in some lunatic asylum?

"As for your clerical Christianity, in what respect does that dementia recall the wisdom of Jesus, the enemy of priests and organized religion? You know full well that the priests of today would kill Jesus, as the priests of old did. You know full well that your priests, like your official scientists and the pretended artists you proclaim, are merely the servants and the flatterers of the Rich. You know full well that, willfully or not, they falsify the words of the man who insulted their adorations, and poison the well from which the people drink. They don't touch anything without soiling it, transforming the words of life into dogmas of death, war and servitude.

"I was wrong, my son, when I said that apostles are no use to you; you know how to render them harmful. As the cadavers abandoned after a battle spread typhus and the plague around them, great Words, which you slay with interested commentaries, become for you the germs of all social maladies. You only know the art of destruction. In the intellectual and moral order, as in the material domain, you are warriors and merchants. With the ideas given to you by apostles, as with the generations given to you by mothers, you only know how to make cadavers and plagues."

"An apostle saved you, though."

"Not one apostle: a people of apostles. When Nelti rose up among us, Atlantis was full of quivering *neltis* who could not succeed in translating their noble inner voices into external actions. The great Brother was able to teach them the words of love because they already knew love. He was the first crystal that a saturated solution is awaiting, and which determines the entire host of crystals. Your countries are not saturated with love, the desire for justice, individual dignity and fraternal will. No matter how much the ignoble liquid is stirred, the only crystals that will ever form among you are those of martial conquest or commercial avidity."

I could not help smiling at the strange comparison. Decidedly, the most intelligent of barbarians always lack taste.

Makima was no longer addressing himself to me. He seemed to be thinking aloud. "The apostle who has over his environment not merely a superiority of speech but also a superiority of thought and sentiment, remains a voice crying in the wilderness. He is not the corypheus who gives a voice to the tremor of the choir; he is not saying what the others want and are able to hear. Those who think they are repeating his words betray him. The treason of Luke and Mark is worse than that of Judas, but it is involuntary and fatal. The disciples betray the apostle as the vocal cords of a monkey would betray the monkey if he wanted to repeat what I say."

There was a long silence. Then the old man mused: "What one apostle could not do, might a population of foreign apostles be able to do? Oh, what a beautiful attempt: a peaceful invasion of all the Atlanteans armed with nothing but light; an immense inundation of verity flooding and setting ablaze the long night!"

But he answered himself: "How uncertain the results would be, alas! One can't extinguish the sun, but one can extinguish a thousand human flames."

He shook his head, which his hair crowned with white light, and concluded: "One does not run toward proofs so hazardous. One cannot take responsibility for causing so many crimes to be committed. It is sufficient to our glory that, if the struggle comes to us, no one will be frightened to the extent of striking, and no one will recoil..."

I interrupted him. "Do you want me to indicate to you a sure means of converting us? A small number of envoys would suffice."

"Speak, my son."

"If a few of your physicists came to inform us about the Force and its applications, to give us the belt and the kingdom of the air, to bring us the pantoscope and..."

The old man smiled sadly.

I persisted: "I assure you that the moral truths subsequently proclaimed by such benefactors would..."

"Poor fool! One does not put sharp knives into the clumsy hands of children."

"Your words are insulting and obscure."

"All material progress in an evil among unjust people. It renders them more incapable of knowing moral verity. It multiplies the oppressive power of the few, and makes the servitude of the many heavier. It exasperates avidities and hostilities. No, my son, one does not throw the weight of gold into a sinking vessel."

XIX

The sun was descending into the sea, already half-drowned, and we were flying toward the starry gathering.

"So," I said, "love is entirely free here? No ceremonies? No solemn promises before witnesses? No contractual guarantees?"

"Your words are empty," the old man replied, smiling. "Avoid, unless you want to fly at that altitude, the crawling thoughts of humans devoid of hearts and belts."

"The family, however..."

"You've seen our children. Did you find them to be unhappy?"

"Unhappy, no. Overly precocious, yes."

"You know my little Telo. When her mother, my beloved Osai, was pregnant, I went to live with her in the pyramid of the future.[34] I stayed there until the child was three years old and could fly alone. Then I came back to my orchard. But every day, when I get up, I go to embrace Osai and Telo. My daughter spends her afternoons in the garden, with the trees that I have planted, and which she sometimes calls her brothers. Every evening, I find Osai at the starry gathering. Those encounters are not sufficient for our eyes and our hearts; if a book moves me, if my mind stirs a particularly bright illumination in moving from analysis to synthesis or from synthesis to analysis, if a flower seems more beautiful or a fruit more flavorsome, I run to Osai to read the page, to sing the thought, to take her the fruit or bring her to the flower. Often, she's the one who runs, saying: 'Share this joy that has fastened my belt.' How many morning, after a night spent in the stars, we find ourselves incapable of separating! We take Telo and spend our day, sometimes in the air populated by birds or colors, sometimes in a canoe that rocks us before a picnic; but she often perches in the generous trees, weighed down by joy, on the banks of singing streams or beside the sea, rising up toward the light in myriads of smiles."

"But what if a father and mother don't love their child?"

"What if honey became aloes or a bird swam mutely in the ocean depths...?"

---

[34] The narrator inserts a footnote: "Which simply means that a child was to be born in Osai's house. The Atlanteans are so solemn!"

"Your laughter is absurd. I've often seen..."

"Yes, in your homeland, where Organization makes every man the enemy of all the rest; yes, in your homeland, where a child is a burden and where, for love of money, a son desires the death of his father, and a brother the disappearance of his sister..."

"There are monsters everywhere."

"Money, inequality and the other matrices of monsters have been banished from Atlantis for a long time."

"If one were to appear..."

"Do you think that love is something that can be commanded? Do you think it sufficient, in order to create a living being, to say to a cadaver: 'Stand up and walk'?"

Among these broad declarations, however, the old man began to tell a puerile story.

"A hundred years ago, a mother slapped her daughter. The child disappeared. Long years went by, without the mother knowing what had become of the offended child."

"The wicked girl! For such a natural gesture!"

"Infantile cheeks, with their flavorsome and moving delicacy, doubtless seem to you to be made to be bruised by the violence of robust hands?"

"I don't say that. All the same..."

"That mother was the last example of an unhappy Atlantean of which we know. Her misfortune, however, was not perpetual. After five years, the little girl came back. Without a word, she threw herself, weeping, into her mother's arms. There was no explanation. As if after a nightmare, life resumed its quotidian mildness and grace. The point of departure of that adventure seems banal to you, but in the eyes of our writers, it's singular. More than twenty novels have been based on it, which, I fear, would seem insipid to you."

"The fact is, my dear Makima...you've already told me that one can't be indiscreet... Have you known other women than Osai, and has Osai known other men than you?"

"We loved one another at our first encounter. More than fifty years have gone by in which our love has flowed like a river of laughter between banks of joy. Almost every evening still—for, having grown old together, we remain young to one another—we bound toward the stars. Osai was very beautiful and aroused many desires; a few women have had less explicable whims in my direction. Ordinarily, we reject those importunates negligently, and only grant conversations in the treetops. Sometimes, desire refused becomes dolorous. Then I say to Osai: 'Rise toward the stars with him, then,' or Osai says to me: 'You're being too cruel not rising toward the stars with her.'"

"Dangerous generosity," I remarked, shaking my head in amusement. "What if your brother had tried to steal Osai's heart, or if her sister had attempted to displace Osai from your heart…?"

"Have you seen people attempt what they know to be impossible? Perhaps, elsewhere. Here, there are no lunatics. We are free, moreover, of any sentiment of envy or jealousy. We don't complicate love with stupid conquering vanities of any sort, nor with the grim hatreds of the vanquished and the bitter need for revenge."

"Are all your couples as faithful as the Osai-Makima household?"

"Love is not a flat and uniform domain. Many people attach themselves to the first body toward which a joyful sentiment draws them and causes them to know voluptuousness. The causes of discord that tear your households apart don't exist there, but many men and women like change! Many always think that they glimpse a greater joy elsewhere. Some Atlanteans scarcely leave the most amicable of pyramids and slake all their thirsts from the same stream. Others spent a large part of their life flying off in all directions, perching on all branches, tasting all fruits, drinking all waters, sleeping curled up on all lawns. Love also knows sedentary individuals and travelers."

"How scornful you must be of those inconstant beings?"

"Why would we scorn people who are obeying, as we are, an instinct as innocent as ours?"

"You think them innocent, those beings who sow dolor on all paths?"

"What dolor are you talking about? There are no liars in Atlantis. From the very first words, even a woman coming to the starry gathering for the first time knows the character of her interlocutor. She has already interrogated herself with regard to her own instincts and grants or refuses judiciously. In any case, what does an error matter?"

"An error of that sort sometimes has consequences..."

"What consequences?"

"How annoying you are! You refuse to understand by implication even the things that cannot be said."

"Anything can be said."

"If the inconstant causes the faithful to have a child, and then abandons her..."

"A child is a malady before birth, a joy thereafter. But no Atlantean ever makes a child without a woman's consent."

"What do you mean?"

"Do you think that there are men here rascally enough to impose on a female who does not want it nine months of hindrance in her movements and minutes, perhaps hours, of intense pain?"

"You astonish me."

"I've read in our books that sexual intercourse is a kind of wound that leaves some venom behind. If a woman made you ill against you will..."

I could not help busting out laughing. "It couldn't happen against my will!" I declared.

"What would you think of her? You're not answering? If you made a child with a woman who had not asked you for one, you ought, my son, to think the same thing."

XX

Around an immense clearing, invisible instrumentalists were making sounds dance in the dark quivering trees.

A strange thought passed through my mind: "A Venetian feast for the ears is being given here."

There was no other illumination than the vast calm light of the moon and the emotive scintillation of the stars. Divided into a thousand circles, an innumerable crowd was turning in the same slow rhythm. Sometimes the music became livelier, seemingly launching forth into the sky. Then the circles suddenly came apart, couples rose up in a waltzing movement, as in engulfed by a whirlwind whose spinning base was supported on a star. The majority let themselves drift down again, indolently; a few rose up vertically, like twin skylarks, while the music, as imperious and irritating as a rut, multiplied its bounds. The couples who had fallen back waited for a few moments, chatting, laughing as if tickled, their gazes phosphorescent. Soon, in a circle of melody, initially slow and whispering, scarcely perceptible, dreamed rather than heard, the circles formed again.

It was an intoxicating spectacle, all those harmonious and supple bodies, which seemed to be vaguely promising all their nudity to one another in the round, which would pair off in the rising waltz, and finally lose themselves, consummations hidden in the blue mantle of distance. Stars, you poured kisses down upon me along with your light. After each numerous flight, I sensed an immense cascade of caresses falling from the heights on to my face, my shoulders and my entire body, whose gliding dressed me in joy.

The emotion was too intense. I threw myself into a round, and the singular individual who dared to venture fully-clad into the festival of nudity received a fraternal welcome. When the circle dispersed, I felt embarrassed by not resembling my neighbors sufficiently, and abstained from seizing the waist of a young woman and bounding into the waltz, in which the tawny bodies became flames that rotated as they rose up. Numerous Atlanteans lingered too, more impassioned by dancing or less hurried than the others. I noticed one couple who ceased climbing, twenty meters from the ground and drifted horizontally, borne by a lazy and indifferent breeze.

They only wanted to chat in the treetops. The sight of them suddenly saddened me.

The second time the round disintegrated, I took a young woman by the hand. I did not draw her into the air charged with perfumes, melodies and caresses; at the idea of a possible refusal I had felt my face redden, as if in response to an insult, anger or folly. I drew the individual upon whom my desire had settled to one side, and said, whispering and enthusiastic: "Oh, to rise with you toward the stars…"

The woman made a sign that she did not understand my language. Then, her gesture having asked me to wait, she drew away. Meanwhile, the impetuous music, as if rigid, lifted me up by itself.

That imbecile has gone to look for an interpreter! My impatience was irritated. As if the fête, the dance, the tender or passionate tunes and the enlaced couples drinking in the sky and joy were not speaking with a sufficiently clear eloquence! As if my gestures were not sufficient to translate my words!

She's a simpleton or a coquette, I concluded. I also thought that a woman who understood French would be more agreeable to me, and I promised myself that if she had had the imprudence to obtain a pretty young woman for an interpreter, I would prefer the interpreter.

Two young women did, indeed, come back.

The one my eyes had not yet beheld appeared much the more beautiful. She was the one my smile welcomed and my desire enveloped. She started speaking, and at first her French seemed singular to me.

"Brother-friend-man," she said to me, "my sister-friend-woman Nekua has asked me to come to hear you, so repeat what you said so her just now."

"O my sister," I exclaimed, "I had perceived you at a distance and I asked Nekua to tell me your name, and I sang my admiration of your unique beauty to her. But there is something I wanted to say to you alone, and that I shall say: Since I perceived your harmonious body, I cannot conceive of any other happiness than my surge toward the stars in combination with your surge toward the stars."

She said something to Nekua, who drew away smiling and was lost in the reunited round dance. Then the one who had intoxicated my eyes turned toward me, amiable and grave,

"Brother-friend-man," she declared, "Meloe will be sad to disappoint you, but for a long time she will only be able to grant you conversations in the treetops."

"Let's go, Meloe! Take me anywhere you wish, to any destiny that you wish. Coming from you, cruelties would be more precious to me than enthusiastic kisses from another."

"Your words might afflict me, brother-friend-man, if I received all their contents. I only hear therein that you have a great deal to learn about Atlanteans."

"From you alone, it's from you alone that I want to learn."

"The fool, brother-friend-man, looks at the source from which knowledge flows; the sage only considers the quality of the information."

"The good tree only produces good fruits, and Meloe is the best and most beautiful of trees."

"Lost in dementia and caressant lies, there is a certain incoherent wisdom in you."

Exasperating my desire as the wind irritates a blaze, anger blew through me, with an impatience and hatred against the irritating pedant. It was not only physical pleasure that I wanted, it was the joy of domination and victory. The body toward which I had launched myself entirely seemed to be drawing away, escaping from me behind bushes of thorny words. Could I not trample the stupid spines, and could I not seize fleeting joy with the gesture that triumphs and stops? By virtue of her voluntary or involuntary coquetry, Meloe was becoming the only woman I desired. Oh, how I wanted to tenderize and humiliate her proud eyes, bite her flavorsome mouth, parted like a fruit, and kiss her breasts, pure cups that were crying out for lips! Ah, as in my youth, love and hatred launched forth toward the slender body, already swaying for the imminent flight.[35]

"Let's go to the treetops first, delightful Meloe. Let that hour be the hour of our betrothal. But if the morning surprises us before I have deployed the sky bed in the heights, know, too amiable friend, that my eyes will be weeping."

"Do you really want me to think that you're mad?"

"Who wouldn't go mad in gazing at you?"

Those words, so banal for me and for the reader, were astonishing for Meloe.

"Why are you insulting me?" she asked, in a dolorous tone.

"Me, insulting you? I don't understand that reproach."

"Have you not accused me of sowing harm and madness?"

"Oh, Meloe, forgive me! But I can only speak the truth, I can only proclaim my love and my suffering. You are the mirage that ignites the intolerable thirst, but retreats ungraspably before the bewildered course and becomes more and more despairing. Oh, become the water that appeases and renders life. You are the one who causes the fever and refuses..."

"To become quinine?"

"Jester! But please, let's fly to the treetops; my breathless heart will believe that it is closer to its desire."

"Let's go," she said.

And she took me by the hand and led me to a solitary wood. She sat me down on a branch, perched herself, like a wary bird, on a neighboring tree, and our conversation resumed, stranger than before.

---

[35] The reader might notice significant analogies between Jacques' confused sentiments in regard to Meloe and those of the narrator of "The Human Ant" toward Marie; Alice Télot presumably did, and doubtless took comfort in the fact that Ryner was doing his utmost to make his protagonists look bad.

XXI

"I'm searching my entire soul for the plea that will touch you, insensible Meloe."

"What! You would accept that someone would yield to the importunity of pleas! Love, brother-friend-man, is a mutual impulse, the encounter of a double desire. Is it the case, then, in your homeland, that one of two lovers thinks that they are granting the other a favor? Is it the case that one of the lovers is only the instrument of the other?"

"Alas, all that happens in my homeland."

"I hope that you have never known those kinds of crippled love, which must both engender dolor and repugnance."

"Alas, I've known many appearances of love."

"Those hours must have left you atrocious memories."

"Mixed memories. My body was sometimes joyful to the point of exasperation. Sensuality is a poem, perhaps less profound, but perhaps more eloquent, than love."

"Your words are obscure to me, and yet they sicken me. Like a beast that crawls invisibly in the undergrowth, but from which a vile odor rises."

I uttered a triumphant cry: "Atlanteans, proud Atlanteans, you too are slaves of prejudice! A beautiful woman's body is a perfumed fruit to a man; why should I not pluck the fruit without waiting for it to fall?"

"Madman! Cruel! You treat a living being, then, like a lifeless thing? You treat that which can feel joy and suffering like something insensible?"

"When I desire and the woman refuses, if I take her by force, it's the woman who is culpable of my violence."

"Why, if she has no desire?"

"Can she not show a little kindness, to avoid wounding her brother?"

"Your words are frightening. Would a disdainful concession not wound you? Would you not suffer if, under your emotion, the woman remained emotionless?"

"It's still better than nothing. 'Laïs doesn't love you,' someone said to a Greek. 'I don't ask the figs I eat whether they love me,' he replied. 'It's sufficient that I love the figs.'"[36]

"The encounter of two human activities bears no resemblance to the encounter of a human activity and a material passivity."

"I assure you..."

"No, I want to believe that you're populating this hour with ingeniously absurd words, which know what they are and are laughing."

"I've never been more serious."

"Then I pity you, because you're vile; you have the soul of a tyrant and a slave. You're saying: 'If I can't have an equal caress, at least I can give or receive a slap.'"

"Hold out your hand, that I might kiss it."

But with a movement of recoil that made the foliage rustle, she said: "Your lips shall not touch any part of my body tonight."

"Oh, wicked coquette!"

"Listen, brother-friend-man. If you continue to desire Meloe, Meloe will in the future be happy beneath your strange body. Meloe is Atlantean and sincere. She feels attracted to the strangeness of your body. Undoubtedly your form is heavy, but you are an unknown light, and on gazing at you, Meroe is stirred. Your bright golden hair, your pale hands and face, seems to promise a mysterious new joy. In spite of the awkwardness of your design, you are a pleasure to my eyes. But your kiss, presently, would be intolerable to me."

"Why, friend?"

"Brother-friend-man, you are, I hope, my heart to come, but you need a long bath."

"I've bathed three times today," I said, blushing.

---

[36] The reference is to the courtesan Laïs, who, according to Aristophanes in *The Birds*, was kept by Philonides. Other references to Philonides in Greek literature name her as Naïs.

"You need a long bath in Atlantis, a six-month bath, perhaps a year."

I did not understand. However, I bowed my head, ashamed and irritated.

The young woman continued: "A noxious odor emanates from you, the cruel odor, what poets calls archaically, 'the odor of the tiger.'"

Oh, how humiliated and hateful I felt!

Without noting my emotion, however, she continued: "First take off those garments that reek of beasts and death. Gradually, you'll cure your odor. Innocent nourishment and noble thoughts will slowly liberate you, and perfumes of humanity will flow into you."

I was too deeply wounded to reply.

"You have nothing to say to your future beloved?" she asked. Her voice was as gentle and warm as a caress.

"If you wish," she went on, "we can meet every evening at the starry gathering, and, from the first round, our belts will carry us, overflowing with the future, to the trees of remembrance, the amiable trees of the first conversation and the first solitude. Would you like that, my dear future heart?"

I shook all over, with I don't know what wild tremor, and between clenched teeth, I growled rather than said: "How do I know what I want?"

Her tone became exasperating in its condescending softness, as exasperating as a hypocrisy curbed under dolor, which expands in vain consolations. "You're hurt, *nelti*? I sense singular and malevolent things in you, a great inexplicable agitation. I'd like to find words to soothe your absurd seething. I'd like to know what word-smile would calm your present, what word-promise would dissipate your clouds and brighten your internal horizon."

"Nothing can any longer do me good."

"Listen, dear *nelti*, to a promise that would astonish an Atlantean and wound him, but responds, it seems to me, to the things that are in you; it might perhaps, ease the grip of whatever jealous claws are clutching and tearing your strange heart. Listen, *nelti*! Meloe promises you, for the duration of your bath, not to rise toward the stars with anyone. Meloe, insensible to starry words than emerge from other mouths, will wait until your body of white light is a joy for her all, as your face and hands of white light are a joy for her eyes."

My wound was too deep; any remedy would have become a poison for it.

"I'm not asking you for anything," I said, with an aggressive pride.

"Oh, *nelti*, you're scaring me, for your words are reasonable but your tone is mad."

"We no longer have anything to say to one another. I don't want to see you again. You arouse in me I don't know what crazy mixture of love and hate, and I don't know what monstrous desires, which make me suffer and which it's necessary that I flee. Oh, if I listened to what is bounding within me, I'd kill you, and it's our flesh, still warm but already insensible..."

I stopped, stammering, trembling, my throat dry...

Meloe smiled, inaccessible to fear. But her smile became a grimace of disgust, and she remarked: "Your words also reek of the tiger..."

Poor uncertain creatures that we are! How we need to be directed, even in our sentiments, by laws, customs and traditions—by the wisdom of our ancestors! How frightened and helpless we feel, as soon as we go astray beyond protective conventions! My momentary anger melted into tenderness. Tears ran from my eyes, and I cried, in a sob: "Oh, how unhappy I am!"

"You have no reason for sadness," the young woman affirmed, softly. "You are loved in the future, and for the present, you can ask your host to take you into the oneirogene."

Without knowing what it labeled, I hated that last word. I groaned, and shook my head in discouragement.

"Oh, the oneirogene...!"

271

"Why not, *nelti*? There you can, without tyranny, submit Meloe and her kiss to your whim. There, you can make reality with your dream and the present with the future."

Again my sadness stirred, trying to dissipate in anger. Exasperated, I cried: "I don't care about the future or the present! I feel capable of any folly, and I'm seeking bitterly an opportunity for active folly. Oh, if a man were here, what a relief I'd experience in fighting him, striking him, killing him..."

"Your thoughts decidedly reek worse than our body." And, after a moment of hesitant reflection: "Perhaps you're incurable? Perhaps you're one of those unfortunates that even Atlantis cannot wash?"

There was another silence, long, heavy and painful. Then, as if making an effort, Meloe asked, abruptly: "Have you killed?"

"Once, in battle."

"You're damned for life. The cruel odor will follow you forever. Go away, murderer!"

Those words were pronounced in a melancholy tone, but harshly. The young woman seemed to be exiling herself from a hope already dear and a dream already loved.

I protested: "I'm not a murderer. I was in danger, I was obedient to orders, noble and patriotic sentiments, and necessity."

"Coward!" said Meloe, in a decisive tone.

And she began to rise into the air.

In the distance, in the clearing, there was the last surge after the final round-dance. More and more imperious, the orchestra commanded the kiss, and, with increasing insistence, aroused lust. Meloe's movement displayed her completely in the intoxicated air. The bright night enveloped her tawny body with an infinite caress. A slender statuette, delicately formed, she drew away slowly, like an appeal of pleasure or folly. The rhythm and grace of her smooth curves combined its own ineffably gentle seduction with the violently seductive music.

I obeyed the order of the brutal music, the whispered order of the night, the moving order of beauty; I also obeyed the order of my shame and my fury. Could I allow the woman who had dared to offend me to depart untamed? An irresistible impulse precipitated me after her, and I howled: "I love you and I want you! I hate you and I want you!"

I don't understand what happened. My great leap did not raise me into the air at all. I was like a bird whose wings had withered. I only saw Meloe, through a kind of red cloud that enveloped me, smiling scornfully, touch her belt in an abnormal manner. Then I was as heavy as if my belt had been deprived of any power of flight. The branch on which I was sitting broke under my weight. I felt myself falling. Arms raised, my eyes full of terror and death, I fell heavily...

Two meters from the ground, my fall stopped. Above me, Meroe's flight described rapid circles. She was still touching her belt in an unfamiliar fashion. It was undoubtedly her who had caused me to fall, who had now suspended my fall and was making me dance on the end of an invisible elastic thread. The Force had properties of which I was still unaware.

In vain my fingers, trembling with hatred, buttoned up my belt; in vain I agitated the spike in the orientation of maximum power and a vertical direction. I descended gently. My feet finally touched the ground. I saw Meloe rise into the night. As beautiful and as luminous as an apparition, as ironic as the conclusion of a dream that is the recommencement of the eternal widowhood, she passed over the treetops and slowly vanished into the empty sky.

I cried, amid mad laughter: "Yes, rise alone toward the stars of Onan and Lesbos!"

My laughter continued, striving to be an insult; it persisted voluntarily, knowing that it was a lie; it was obstinate, even though I sensed that the innocent Atlantean could not understand the poor, absurd laughter, dolorous and false, that was pursuing her.

XXII

The morning found me in despair. Lost in a forest, perhaps twenty leagues from Makima's pyramid, I could not even succeed, poor crawling beast that I was, in orientating myself amid the obscure indifference of the underwood. I was being torn apart by contradictory thoughts. I would have liked to get back rapidly, to enclose my misery between familiar walls; without knowing whether I was heading in the right direction, I hurried; but I soon stopped, threw myself on the ground, and appealed for death with loud cries and stifled murmurs. I was a wounded animal whose suffering sometimes weakened it and sometimes irritated it to the point of madness, wanting succor and solitude at the same time, desperate to attain, via remedy or agony, the end of its troubles.

Sitting beneath a coconut palm, I cursed my useless belt. I examined it carefully, turning it over and over in my bare hands, searching carefully for whatever might have caused it to lose its efficacy. I could not see anything. The fabric seemed to me to be slightly slacker than the day before, but I was not even sure of that observation. For a long time I contemplated the dead or dormant apparatus stupidly.

Why, little by little, did the sight of it render the reality incredible?

Was it really true, I wondered: Atlantis, the flying men, myself flying through the air, as free as a bird, and the pantoscope, and the starry gathering, and the beauty of Meloe, her pedantic coquetries and her stinging refusal? Doubtless I was shipwrecked on some desert island. Charles' absurd chatter, fever, perhaps also a poisonous fruit imprudently bitten: that was what had created a strange delirium in me...

Shake off all those follies, Jacques, wake up and march courageously in the difficult struggle for existence!

A stream was singing its monotonous song nearby. Into its amiable coolness I plunged, after my hands—those two burns—the fire of my face. I drank long gulps of relief and valor. Lightened momentarily, I followed the direction of the flow. Perhaps it would lead me to an inhabited region...

My fatigue was like a weight that one thinks one can cast off, but is attached by a short chain, and soon makes itself felt again, now too heavy to be dragged and getting caught up on a thousand obstacles.

I ended up lying down in the grass and going to sleep.

The sentiment of a presence woke me up; I opened my eyes slightly. Yes, certainly, seen in a dream, all those phantasmagorias of Atlantis and knowledgeable, gentle savages! There was certainly a savage standing there, naked, looking at me, but he did not have the red skin that illuminated my dreams. He was as brown as the inhabitants of southern Europe and some Asiatics.

I waited, without budging, anxiously, preparing myself for any eventuality.

But the savage said: "My God, it's the dead spit of Jacques!"

I got up. "Is that you, Captain?" And I smiled. "Have you renounced European costume?"

"I should think so! The blessed females here think clothes smell bad."

"Ha ha! I've caught you, Captain. You've been to the starry gathering. Without wishing to be indiscreet, have you risen to the stars to deploy the sky bed?"

"Oh yeah! Go see if they're coming, Jean! The dirty little prudes! I've had to put my heart in my mouth and watch my language as in the Faubourg Saint-Germain. 'Later, later!' they told me, at first. But when I get carried away, at the first bold move, the first slightly virile or maritime word, the hussy, with an expression as if she's spitting down on you, says: 'You my old sailor, are an unscrubbable Cruel. Never, you hear, my good friend!' Oh, when they see me again at their starry gathering…!"

He paused, and then went on: "There's only one good thing in this pigsty of an island of savage poseurs, and that's their belt. That's amusing—to fly like a bird, navigate in the air like a rapid and supple boat that gets drunk on speed and flexibility. There's some god-damned French poet who made a machine called *Le Bateau ivre*.[37] I don't know what that is, but when I'm flying up there at a hundred knots a minute, I tell myself: 'I'm a drunken boat,' and I'm content—more content than with champagne."

His mouth moist with pleasure, he proposed: "How about a little flight, Jacques?"

I sighed. "I don't know what's happened to my apparatus. It's no longer working. Look…it's as sad as a deflated balloon."

The Captain took off his belt and buttoned on mine. He multiplied trials and manipulations. Finally, he said: "I'm damned, old man, if I'll be going up in the air again with this dirty gadget. It could just as easily let you go at a thousand meters of altitude. Imagine the crash!"

"Can you imagine," I said, pitifully, that I'm lost. Can you tell me where I am?"

"We're in a quarter they call Azaid."

"Is it far, this Azaid, from the coast of Diaprepida?"

"Forty leagues south-south-west."

"Damn! That's a long way to go on foot."

"Listen! If you still have any confidence in this belt sorcery, take mine, and in less than an hour, saving accidents…"

"If you're close to home, I won't refuse."

As I was getting ready to leave, my rediscovered compatriot stopped me abruptly.

"A few more words, Jacques!"

"Speak, Captain."

"Have you much sympathy for these god-damned Atlanteans?"

"Me? I detest them."

He took me by the hand and lowered his voice. "Then I have a plan in the making that'll give you pleasure. The day

---

[37] The poem by Arthur Rimbaud; the title of the Decadent classic translates as "The Drunken Boat."

after tomorrow, in the evening, while the swine are at the starry gathering, as they call it, come to our own gathering."

With gestures of discretion and in a mysterious tone, he gave me the necessary directions to the meeting place. It was an abandoned orichalcum mine.

"You understand," he murmured, "that with these swine, one's obliged to go underground. Otherwise their blessed pantoscope would find us in no time. Anyway, all in good time. Until the day after tomorrow!"

I rose into the air. I swiveled around, trying to get my bearings. On the distant horizon, letters of fire caught me gaze. The sky often blazed with such projections. Ordinarily, they spoke of unknown things in an indecipherable alphabet, but these said, in clear and amicable French: *Pyramid of Jacques and Makima.*

It was a precaution of the old man, to help me to get back, a radiant appeal cast over the entire realm to the lost child.

XXIII

I had not covered ten leagues in the direction of Makima's pyramid when the old man appeared, cleaving the sky like a thunderbolt. He fell upon me and embraced me emotionally.

"My dear son," he said, "What anxieties you caused me! All night I was tranquil. *The conversation in the treetops is lasting a long time,* I thought. *So much the better! My friend's heart and mind can only gain from it. Perhaps, too, my anticipations were mistaken and he has carried a joyful woman toward the stars!*"

Involuntarily, a sigh escaped me.

"In the morning, not seeing you return, I began to fear that there might have been an accident, and I experienced remorse—for, after all, instead of forgetting myself in the stars with Osai, I should have been watching over you, my dear son."

Between my teeth, I murmured: "Dirty voyeur!"

"I shut myself up in the pantoscope and, with the veil of optical force over my eyes, I started searching the entire island. The apparatus was trembling between my fearful and maladroit hands. I only had confused visions, in which you did not appear. Then I discovered you in a rarely-frequented woodland on the far side of the starry clearing, in the middle of Azaid. You were chatting with one of your compatriots, which explained why you had been delayed. Reassured, I was burning with thirst to press you to my bosom as soon as possible. I had already illuminated the appeal above the amicable pyramid. Tightening my most rapid belt around my waist, I left. I was obliged to turn back more than once, to fly backwards briefly. In spite of my long habit, my speed was truly— how can I put it?—unbreathable. At times, I believe I was traveling at five thousand paracas[38] an hour."

The old man's words fell dolorously and sonorously into my empty head.

"I'm hungry," I said.

"Absurd child! But there's food everywhere. Let's go down to the region of nourishment."

He chose the fruits that would reanimate me most effectively himself. In a nest of perfumed wood an enormous bird was watching, motionless. Makima addressed a few Atlantean words to it in an amiable tone; I only understood the two syllables of the word *nasca*, cousin.

The damnable fellow has family everywhere, I thought.

---

[38] The narrator inserts a footnote: "The Atlantean paraca is a millionth part of the terrestrial meridian. The Atlanteans claim that the calculations by which French scientists have defined the meter are false, but our error, or theirs, is practically insignificant, and one can count the paraca as forty meters." The meter had been actually defined in 1795 as one ten millionth of the distance from the equator to the North Pole (a quarter of the meridian) as measured by Jean-Baptiste Delambre and Pierre Mechain.

While speaking, the old man caressed the bird's back with his left hand; meanwhile, his right hand rummaged under the abdomen. He brought out an egg as big as a turkey's egg.

"Eat this, my son. The *nasca* would like to give you this egg, laid less than an hour ago. There's nothing finer for renewing vital energy."

The meal was delicious, and returned all my vigor, but my humor remained morose. On a proud man, insults weigh more obstinately than fatigue.

Sniggering, I asked: "What difference do you see between eating an egg and eating the meat that emerged from that egg?"

"What difference do you see between picking a fruit and felling a tree?"

"From the moral point of view, none. The future is as respectable as the present."

"And that which feels nothing as respectable as that which suffers?"

"Violence done to a child is more criminal than violence done to a man. What logical weakness stops you on that path? The egg is more respectable than the bird or the chick, more respectable than the tree."

"Ingenious trickster!"

"I'm addressing your sentiments of justice and equality. Let every seed play its part."

"You're suffering, poor child, and you're taking it out on the person who is present. It's not reason that is making you speak, but an unhealthy need for contradiction, some bellicose impulse. What makes you speak is, I fear, some vague commencement of hatred." With an amicable smile, he added: "Believe me, I don't accord any part of life to that seed."

"You have convenient ways of avoiding questions that embarrass you," I remarked.

The old man shook his head like a physician who hears delirium.

"Even if you're not culpable with regard to the egg," I went on, "you're culpable with regard to the bird that laid it." With a wry laugh, I concluded: "You've robbed your cousin."

But he addressed himself, ridiculously, to the absent bird. "O *nasca*," he said, "is it true that you would have refused that egg to Makima, who planted so many trees in which to build your nest and sate your hunger? Is it true that you would have refused that egg to Jacques who needed it? No, *nasca*, my unjust *nelti* is slandering you, and you have laid a little strength for him with the same pleasure that I have caused a great deal of strength to fructify for you."

We flew into the pantoscope. Makima flicked a switch, and above our heads, a large bay opened in the vitreous ceiling.

He took me be the hand. "Let's go up," he said.

Our flight took us into a pointed room that occupied the summit of the pyramid. The only apparent furniture was a bed.

"Lie down. I'll leave you alone with your thoughts. When you want to come out, press the button on the bedhead."

"What do I do here?"

"You express, in a whisper, in detail, the dream that you desire. It will come."

"Give me an example."

"Suppose you were to say: *I'm at the starry gathering, in a slow round, and I take Meloe's hand. Meroe's hand is trembling amorously in mine.* Then you would fall silent, and during your silence, that dream would be realized. Guided by your thought and guiding it, like two rivers combining into one, it would follow a fortunate slope. Sometimes, however, the vagabond mind deflects the dream away from your desire. If that accident occurs, you direct your thought by speech and you resume, for example: The music swells like a tempest of pleasure. *A turbulent leap carries me upwards, enlaced with Meroe.*"

You ply a fine trade, I thought, mechanically.

280

But the old man, smiling, said: "I don't need to go on, do I?"

He went out, closing the opening behind him. I was plunged into disagreeable darkness.

In a low voice, I said: "Soft moonlight inundates the room..."

Astonished, I saw a window suddenly appear in the thick wall. The moon was floating, white and full, in a clear sky.

"That's odd," I murmured. "It seems to be progressing, their ideal bordello."

The words had a strange effect! The room, increased in size, furnished with armchairs, divans and mirrors, was populated with phantasmal women, in whom I recognized the initiating courtesans of my adolescence. It really was, infinitely vaster, more luxurious, more comfortable and richer in venal flesh, the drawing-room of a tolerated house. The phantoms, increasingly precise and heavy, appealed to me by winking or making ignoble beckoning gestures. And like the multiple voices of the inundating flux, I heard a host of whispers: "Are you coming upstairs with me, pretty blond?"

XXIV

I had chased away the impure phantoms. I pronounced: "It's my mother's birthday and dinner time. My parents are sitting down, smiling but sad, at the family table, where one place—mine—remains empty."

As I spoke, the familiar décor came to live before my eyes. My mother, my father and my sister were, indeed, sitting there, smiling, and sometimes turning away to wipe away a tear. For a moment, I thought I was in the pantoscope, my eyes rendered penetrating by the veil of optical force. No, I was not in the pantoscope, once I could hear words and sounds: all of earthly life.

My mother plunged the ladle into the steaming soup-tureen, as my words directed and completed my dream: "I've arrived home from a voyage. I ring the doorbell. My mother hastens to open the door. She recognizes me…"

I did not think that there was any need to continue. The dream could no longer unfold, it seems to me, in any but a happy fashion.

My mother hugged me tightly, her joyful face bathed in tears of joy. She stammered, in a voice in which every word became weaker and more hesitant: "My son, my dear son! It's too much unexpected happiness. It seems to me that I'm going to die. Your mother isn't strong enough for the unexpected shock of such joy. The surprise is too great, my son. You should, you should have warned us."

In my trembling arms, the poor woman slid and collapsed, an inert parcel. My father, my sister and I hastened to help her, clumsy and anxious. My heart was a strange weight, which, through I don't know what thorny obstacles, fell and tore; then, suddenly, it lightened, swooned, melted. I reproached myself for the imprudence of my conduct.

"I'm a stupid…implausible!"

The last word was, in a night of dolorous affirmation, the lightning-flash of doubt that rips the horizon victoriously. It illuminated the fact that I was dreaming and that I could direct my dream. And a sentence was precipitated, determinedly, from my quivering lips:

"My mother is coming round."

She did, in fact, get up, slowly, waking up. And her hand passed over her brow and her eyes, chasing away the last vague drowsiness, the last floating clouds of obstinate stupor. Her cheeks, dull and bleak a moment ago, flourished once again with the colors of joy and the dimples of a smile.

I had no further need to appeal to my will. The dream unfolded by itself, a harmonious movement of four loves meeting up again. It enveloped me with I don't know what real and warm sweetness; it cradled me in soft pleasure; it finally lulled me to sleep like a child among fresh and paradisal visions. It enclosed me in several circles of dream and pleasure. I knew that I was dreaming such smiles and flowers, but I also knew that other smiles and other flowers surrounded my slumber, and that awakening would not cause me any loss.

How long that singular state lasted, in which I saw myself as a happy man who was asleep, while the precise joys of his life surrounded him with an atmosphere of dreamed-of happiness, I have no idea.

When I woke up, I felt at first that I was in a bath of love. But I sat up in my bed and a superficial anxiety slid over my happiness. A question posed itself within me: *How far does the dream extend?* Like a gust of wind that carries all perfumes away, that interrogation dispersed my joy.

Now I found myself alone in sepulchral darkness. I am not afraid of the dark, but the bravest man cries out in fear of too sudden a fall. My cry of astonishment was "Am I dead?"

O power of speech! I felt myself lying, rigid, in a narrow coffin; my arms were tight against my upper body, and along my naked limbs, and over the whole of my bare breast, and— hideous horrors!—over the whole of my face, there was a soft, viscous wriggling, searching and gnawing.

Oh! the grave-worms are despoiling my flesh! Oh, my eyes, my poor eyes!

The worms, slowly and inexorably, were devouring my eyelids and my irises. I screamed in horror, and clusters of worms fell into my open mouth. They disintegrated, numerously soft and active, invading my gums, my tongue and my palate.

On my tombstone, my mother, kneeling in prostration. All white and wrinkled so profoundly: old, oh, so old! I had never seen anything as old; oh, as old as despair!

I pronounced, in a whisper: "Death is a terrible nightmare."

Chased away by speech, the odious vision disappeared. Meloe, summoned, no doubt, by a memory and an unconscious desire, smiled at me, perched in a tree. And she spoke these strange words:

"Death is a terrible nightmare…yes…for the living."

"Meloe," I commanded, "I don't want you naked in that tree. It's monkeys and Atlanteans who perch in trees naked. Meloe, you're no longer an Atlantean: a woman belongs to her master's homeland. Clothe your body. Hide that body, which only belongs to me, from other eyes."

My thought covered Meloe in a silken dress, twisted and pinned up her hair in the Parisian fashion, and threw an elegant hat on to her head.

There! With Meloe on my arm, I walked along the boulevards, amid admiration and jealousy. The journalists of the terraces of the cafés were saying: "Good God! What a pretty woman! I'd give the proceeds of my last blackmail to sleep with her." The whores were saying: "A handsome fellow! If he wanted to be *mine* I'd give him all the cash I picked up, and how hard one would work to give pleasure to her little man!" The naive provincials were staring wide-eyed as we went past and nudging one another, whispering: "Oh, what a handsome couple! One only sees things like that in Paris."

"My carriage!" I said.

Harnessed to racehorses, a magnificent victoria pulled up by the sidewalk and I climbed into it with Meloe. I pressed myself against her and asked: "Are you happy, my sweet? Have you and regrets? Isn't it better to live here, rich, honored, inspiring jealousy, superior to others, than to be lost, poor indifferent units in the banal crowd of so many stupidly joyful bothers and so many four-handed or four-footed cousins?"

"Ah!" sighed Meloe. "I miss my belt and the power of flight; I miss the liberty of my naked limbs; I miss the opulent and mild beauty of the landscape, and the fondant flavor of the fruits, and my innocent meals, and the joy given to my eyes by the noble nudity of all my sisters and all my brothers. Oh, how I regret..."

I interrupted her brutally.

"You regret most of all, wretch, no longer being able to reject me; you regret no longer being able to manifest our hatred. Shut up and smile, slave!"

I had seized her wrists; I squeezed them hard enough to bruise them. But she escaped from me, abruptly, opened the door, leapt out on to the road and fled. I pursued her, in the breathlessness of a nightmare.

"Help!" she shouted. "Murder!"

And a purposive crowd, clamoring uncertainly, was running behind me, about to catch up with me.

"Oh no, not that! In ancient Rome...! I am the master, and Meloe the slave. Take off your garment, Meloe. Offer yourself naked to the whip of the Iorarius. The blows are going to tame you like a rebellious beast. I shall then possess your striped body. Since you don't quiver with joy at my kisses, your tremors of suffering, memory and apprehension will be more voluptuous than voluptuousness itself. Pleasure becomes insipid that is not sharpened by a proximal dolor. Be, simultaneously, the beauty that my body enjoys, the foreign dolor on which my mind feasts, and the humiliation that serves as the pedestal for my pride..."

I continued my games of amorous hatred for a long time. But the troubling idea crossed my mind too frequently that they were unreal games: the suffering with which I was giving myself pleasure, no one, alas, was suffering! My victory evaporated, a poor illusion, whenever I thought that there was no one to defeat.

In an enervated irritation, I finally pressed the button indicated by Makima. The opening that connected the oneirogene and the pantoscope let a beam of light through, again not natural, but which nevertheless put the phantoms to flight. And the old man was beside me, hovering in mid-air.

"Are you happy?" he asked, with an insipid smile.

Grimly, I replied: "More unhappy than ever." And, in reply to his gaze, which was stupidly astonished: "Real good fortune is victory and pride. Dreamed good fortune is defeat and humiliation."

"Ah!" he said, naively. "You're hostile, even in amour."

I burst out laughing at that infantile remark, and observed: "You may know today the mechanical secrets that we will know tomorrow, but your simplicity will always make you poor fearful savages in comparison with our rich complication."

He shrugged his shoulders. I feared that the preacher might be about to deliver a long sermon, but he only said: "You have very dolorous riches."

"Joy without suffering is scarcely felt, and a crown that does not bruise the head does not have the weight of gold."

"Are you trying to make me jealous of your bruises, and your rich domain of nettles and brambles?" In a pensive tone, he added the strange comment: "All is all; nothing is nothing. In a sage, everything takes the pacific form of wisdom and joy. In a madman, everything becomes mad; everything agitates the unappeasable and dolorous chaos."

That incomprehensible philosophy annoyed me. To put a stop to that vain chatter, I asked, while we were passing through the pantoscope: "Do you often enclose yourself in the oneirogene?"

"Very rarely. The island is such an orchard of objective joys! The oneirogene is primarily the refuge of those who die too late. If Osai quit the life we know before me, on returning from the obsequies, I would enclose myself in the oneirogene in order to die beside the evoked beloved. Do you see, over there, the large letters of fire on that pyramid? They say: 'Tacmar has entered the oneirogene.' Tacmar's friends understand that adieu. From time to time they look into the pantoscope to see whether the euthanasia is complete. Let me see, my son."

He stopped and I left.

Soon, he rejoined me in the large fig-tree.

"Tacmar is dead. Would you like to accompany me to his funeral?"

XXV

Through the highest window of Tacmar's pyramid a five-meter-long sky bed emerged. Narrow in the narrow passage, as soon as it was in the open air it widened of its own accord, becoming almost square. On the center of the airborne platform was the cadaver. Crouching, the legs drawn up beneath the thighs and the head inclined forward, he seemed to have departed on some motionless and pensive voyage. My astonishment expressed itself in bizarre terms that I had never thought.

(It sometimes happens that I say things unconsciously; scarcely pronounced, my words collide with me as if they had come from elsewhere, and then I try to understand them. That strange transposition was rare before my arrival in Atlantis; since then it has occurred with a frequency that frightens me when I think about it. Might it not be a precursory symptom of madness? I ought to consult a physician…am I stupid? As if physicians knew anything!)

So, I was alarmed by the strange speech that I had pronounced, for I had said, on looking at the cadaver:

"He seems to be in transition…"

I was still listening, in the stupor of my ears and my mind, to the unexpected vibrations produced by my lips, and I did not hear Makima, who was talking to me. It was only when he stopped speaking that I paid any heed to what he said. (Why, that day, did several of my perceptions arrive with disquieting delays?)

The strange and belated movement of my mind in pursuit of vanished words could only catch up with a few of them—the last. How mysterious they were!

"Our circular hope has given Tacmar the same attitude that nature gave him, a hundred and twenty-three years ago, in his mother's womb."

Perhaps I was about to ask for an explanation. A short distance away, I perceived Meloe. Impelled by some troubled sentiment, I headed toward the woman who had scorned me, and whom I hated. An anxious curiosity made me repeat, as I approached her, the remark that had appeared to evoke her in the oneirogene:

"Death, Meloe is a terrible nightmare."

Amazement! Her response murmured, as in the dream: "A terrible nightmare...? Yes...for the living." Fortunately for my reason, Meloe added new words: "For the living who do not know."

The first words, a sonorous echo of unreal words, had put upon me and around me I don't know what formidable oppressive shadow. The end of the sentence, abolishing the similitude of wakefulness and the dream, relaxed, if it did not dispel, the anguish. I tried, by the agitation of laughter, to throw it off completely.

"Do you know, then?" I asked—and my voice was a snigger that frightened me. "Tell me what you know."

And there was a vague tremor of hope in my anxiety.

But she enveloped herself in sinuous refusal. "If I told you what I know, you still wouldn't know it. What I know, the circular Word of life proclaims around you in billions of murmurs, voices and cries, but you don't hear anything, and what the universe tells you, you still don't know. If, one day, the profound and secret being that is You tells the appearance that you mistake for yourself what I know, then you'll know it."

And she laughed dolorously, and went on: "I forgot that you've killed, and, in consequence, have killed yourself. One thinks that one is killing outside—ha ha!—but one is killing inside. The profound You will no longer speak to that which you call your life. It is dead, until the awakening that you call death. In the poor animal in which there was human possibility, even the hope of knowing and being is crushed until tomorrow. Unfortunate is he who believes that he is seeking the light, but has put out his eyes beforehand!"

"Meloe," I said, irritated by those pompous and empty formulae, "I've possessed you in the oneirogene."

"What does it matter to me what happens in the oneirogene?"

"In the oneirogene, Meloe, I've beaten you. I've violated you, I've soiled you like a prostitute and whipped you like a slave. I've humiliated you in a thousand ways. I've..."

288

"In the pointed and multiform oneirogene, you were alone. You were only able humiliate and debase yourself. You have only been able to harm yourself."

Thus we contended, hatefully. In the meantime, we were flying behind the strange hearse, which was carrying through the upper atmosphere a cadaver adopting the semblance of an unborn child: an impoverished past stripped of its entire self, to which those lunatics had given the folded form of a future about to launch itself toward indeterminate hopes and riches.

"We're no longer in the oneirogene, Meloe, and here, in the face of the heavens, in the face of death, far above the life of the trees and the beasts, I'm proclaiming my hatred to you bitterly, I'm howling and roaring my desire to do you harm. Do you know that the only lust that you see arousing me is the lust to torture and kill?"

"In sleep as in wakefulness, in formless and limitless space as in the pointed oneirogene, all your ideas, your dreams and your desires take on the hideous form of your mind. I do not like the beasts and the thoughts that crawl; I do not like the beasts and the thoughts that stink; I do not like the beasts and the thoughts that hiss and dart venomous stings. Get away from me! Go toward my brothers, to whom you have revealed yourself less clearly, and who find your presence less disgusting."

"I like the scorn that I inspire in you, since it is dolorous to you. I like all the harm that I can cause you, and since my presence—oh joy!—has become painful to you, I shall impose my presence upon you."

"In that case, I'll go away," she said.

She rose up about a paraca above the crowd.

I followed her, declaring: "I'm obstinate, and my belt is as good as yours."

She turned angry eyes toward me, and I felt something akin to an outburst of laughter and voluptuousness throughout my being. But she almost screamed: "Go away, for I can no longer bear your madness and your stink! Go away, or my belt will disarm yours! Go away, or here and now, before these thousand of witnesses, blush with the humiliation of falling, a beast of the mire carried away in the claws of a bird and suddenly released!"

She put an irritated hand to her belt; I thought I could feel the air opening beneath my fall. I drew away, in hasty and tremulous flight, from that profoundly malevolent and dangerous woman.

XXVI

Tacmar's corpse, enclosed in an asbestos sack, had been placed on a pyre of odorous wood. A part of the cortege surrounded the pyre with three circles, strangely disposed. The first was about a paraca in diameter, and the Atlanteans who composed it, belt open, were touching the ground with their feet. The second caused to hover, at a height of half a paraca, a circumference of about six paracas. The third, a paraca higher up, extended a crown of at least twelve paracas. The inferior choir was rotating from east to west and chanting some kind of muted and lugubrious plainsong. The intermediate circle remained immobile and mute. The vast crown was rotating from west to east, singing a joyful song, a song as winged as hope.

The rest of the crowd continued its flight toward an unknown goal.

"Let us leave the low circle of appearance turning," Makima said. "Let us leave the hesitant circle of death. Let us leave the great and noble circle of higher reality spinning. And let us go, if you wish, to the cemetery."

While we glided with the crowd, he explained: "As soon as the body is consumed the statuary fraternity will collect the ashes and, kneading them with *multi* gum, will make them into a statuette in Tacmar's image, the size of a fetus."

The irregular rump of a mountain was soon winding beneath us. It gave the impression of an immense mound raised by human hands. Its sinuosities traced the form of a snake biting its tail. The head of the animal was represented by the summit; then the body coiled away, apparently some four hundred paracas long. The mountain progressively descended and shrank, diminishing into a hill. The snake's slender tail penetrated the wide open mouth from below. It was far from filling the strange rictus, but a large, unsteady ball seemed to be on the point of rolling out of the mouth or into the monstrous body.

"Eternity," said Makima, sententiously, "swallowing and ejecting the universe."

Between the symbolic globe and the walls, four passages remained. The Atlanteans all went in through the lower opening on the left, and it was only through the gap on the upper right that one emerged.

I went into the serpent's maw behind my guide. Inside, the chambers multiplied, forming a frightful labyrinth for the uninitiated. The walls were fitted with narrow shelves at various heights. Lined up there, in myriads, were statuettes, which were—Makima's words allowed me to deduce—as many dead people. Under each statuette there was a short inscription: perhaps a name and two dates.

What created the mystery of the place, however, was the lighting. It did not come from outside, nor was it spread by lamps, and no flame was burning in the immense crypt. It seemed to emanate, innumerably pale, from the statues themselves.

"Is it the dead that are illuminating us, Makima?" I asked, shivering.

"Yes, my son." And the incurable philosophical charlatan added: "Death alone illuminates the mystery."

XXVII

To begin with, the return was silent. Suddenly, my long reflections, heaped up, burst forth in triumphant peevishness.

"Only a few days ago, you affirmed that the Atlanteans were free of all religion, deceptive Makima!"

"That day, my son, we presumably meant by religion the artificial links that you claim to attach humans to one another

291

and with the unity of things. We call a closed system of dogmas a religion. If, to your better enlightened eyes, religion is now the immediate sentiment of human fraternity and no longer the crazy affirmation that we all descend from a unique couple sculpted by the hands of a worker devoid of hands, then we're the most religious of humans.

"Yes, if you call religion the unquiet and amorous dream that quivers around things and attempts to penetrate them like a subtle air, and which, knowing that everything is connected, does not know how it is connected, and imagines the unity in a thousand floating and emotional fashions, oh, how religious we are! But is it appropriate for the word that expresses life and its internal source also to indicate a crude mechanism and the key with which one winds it?

"Choose, Jacques. If you don't believe that your watch and your body are two similar machines, don't any longer confuse the mechanical religion that repeats with the living religion that speaks. Don't confuse the faithful follower, the mechanism that chimes the same festivals every year, the automaton that kneels and stands up in response to the distant gestures of a priest, with the religious man, the free spirit who meditates, loves and smiles. Should we call the worship docilely accepted from without religion, or the continuous and moving interior creation?"

I destroyed all that verbiage with the observation of a fact: "I've just seen at Tacmar's funeral that you have fixed rites that express a common doctrine."

"You're mistaken, my son. The fiery inscription that announced the imminent death of our brother also said that he would die in the circular dream. We have dreamed behind him dreams harmonious with his own. We have danced fraternally, to the rhythm of his final thought, a chorus of thoughts. But neither in him nor in us did any hope become a faith, or any imagination an affirmative fanaticism."

"How can you live in such uncertainty?"

"How can your thought tolerate the inconvenience and irritation of an attitude that doesn't change? Your body, while it's alive, sometimes needs to stand up, sometimes to sit down and sometimes to lie down, but your mind accepts the immobility and paralysis of the narrow coffin of a doctrine. In reality, it's you who don't have a metaphysical intelligence or a religious soul. That's because you live your elementary life without dreaming of the unity and without loving it. But why, then, pronounce words that are no use to you and whose fixity makes them into lies?"

It was on the tip of my tongue to say: *You're mad.* More politely, I said: "Your fleeting wisdom confuses me. But before me, Meloe affirmed the circle, and the multiplicity of existences, and I don't know what other mysteries, and she claimed insultingly that what she was saying, I couldn't hear."

"One only hears oneself, my son, and Meloe, causing the ungraspable flight of her thoughts to float in dreamlike words, doubtless sensed that she was not stirring one of your thoughts. She had observed that you're only capable, in respect of the fluid and formless mystery, of making two or three ridiculously solid and precise affirmations."

"You're mistaken. It was Meloe who was affirmative."

"Words, especially in your language are naiveties that always affirm. Those heavy and beltless things rest on the ground, and as soon as one tries to make them fly, they fall heavily. Someone who speaks about noble things speaks beyond words. Try to hear beyond words."

"Meloe claimed that because I've killed, I can no longer know."

"Meloe is right. A dead person is not alive. But I assume that she was only affirming her own life and the impulse of her soul."

"That's scarcely clear."

"I'm not a liar or a priest, to remain clear when I'm talking about mystery."

"Then you might as well not say anything."

"Do I know what love is? Even so, I have occasion to say: *I love.* In that word, to which my emotions give meanings so mysteriously individual, there is, as in every speech of sentiment of dream, the radiant center of a vast silence. Words are immobile appearances, but realities are living movements, As soon as my thought wants to follow a reality, it's not whatever word I pronounce that I hear, but my soul. The articulate word is as impotent before profound things as the cry of an animal before the most facile analyses. In the prison of words, all wisdom becomes folly. If you are not the Liberated-Liberator who can hear yourself and hear the neighboring soul, name the flowers, then name the fruits and the trees, rejoice in pretty appearances, be proud of being superior to an animal without language, but don't give the names of earth and mud to the limpid mystery. The mystery is like the air. Solidified by chemistry or definition, they become irrespirable to the body and the soul."

Amusing myself by taking on an irreverent tone. I asked: "Are you quite sure that you have one—a soul?"

Makima looked at me severely, and replied: "I've never killed."

There was no connection between the question and the response. I became irritated before those evasions of bad faith, but I did not let my annoyance show, and, sure of embarrassing my interlocutor, I said: "And how would you define it—the soul?"

Faithful to his evasive tactics, however, he said: "Haven't you understood yet? I'm not a priest, who pushes absurdity to the point of defining the indefinable."

Very softly, I observed: "There are procedures that facilitate discussion. In truth, without definite words, even my compatriot Monsieur de La Palice would no longer be able to see a means of speaking."

Makima continued beating around the bushes. "Language, even the most synthetic in appearance, is an instrument of analysis. In order to make material elements precise, language destroys that which is formal. In the domain of chemistry, we know how to recompose what we have decomposed, but it's not the same in the mental realm. The additions with which we think we're balancing our destructive analyses aren't real syntheses. You're the poor chemist impotent to remake what you have taken apart, and who says, naively: water is only oxygen and hydrogen; neither oxygen nor hydrogen is refreshing; it's therefore pointless to drink water when one is thirsty. You're the child who wants to know what beauty is, and disperses it into elements that could just as easily form ugliness. You're the lunatic who wants to penetrate the essence of a movement, and stops it in order to study it at his ease."

Here, as in other conversations, I'm repeating as best I can, but I can't guarantee an absolute exactitude. My memory is excellent, but these incomprehensible follies, these donkey-like stupidities of a barbaric catechism that seems to be braying yes and no in the same word, might—as the impartial reader will understand without difficulty—have been deformed in my memory.

XXVIII

In the ancient orichalcum mine, illuminated only by the gleam of the metal, all the castaways met up, with the exception of Charles, the Hellenist. That wretch had become a true Atlantean, an enthusiast of the puerile people, a renegade to our virile civilization and our valiant fatherland. With that exception, however—a glad observation!—all the civilized were there, brought together by a similar hatred of the savages.

The Captain took the floor. "We are," he began, "in a fabulously rich country of prodigious fertility. Alas, the spiteful determination of the indigenes renders its wealth and fertility futile. Abundant nourishment goes to waste here, and yet, elsewhere, in the lands we love, many people are dying of hunger. We owe it to humanity to return this great isle that has been stolen from it."

Everyone approved.

"We ought to bring to the common treasury the inventions these savages have made in optics and mechanics. We ought to plant and fructify on this land everything that it can produce. We ought to extract its inhabitants from idleness, the mother of vices. I've made the calculation, and I've found that on average, these indolent individuals only spend two hours a day in genuinely productive labor."

A murmur of indignation ran through the cavern.

"If you agree with my opinion, comrades, we ought to take possession of this land. We can divide it into provinces, each of which would be governed by one of us, and proclaim one of us as king."

There were a few protests: "No, no, no king! We don't want a king."

"You're right," the orator went on. "Kings have had their day. We'll provide a president to the republic formed by the federation of provinces."

"Yes, yes! That's it! A republic and a president."

"But we can't accord civic rights to the savages without danger. It's necessary, in their own interests, in order to bring them gradually closer to a nobly human life, to reduce them, under a name that remains to be determined, to a veritable slavery. A harsh necessity, perhaps, but unavoidable."

"Yes, yes, it's necessary!"

"Each survivor of the glorious enterprise will have his province. The one to whom your confidence accords the central province will be the president of the confederation. We'll leave our royal heritage to our sons, of course. For we'll establish, won't we, in this land of licentious mores, the European nobility of unique marriage and the closed family?"

"Bravo, Captain, bravo!"

"I believe we're in accord, my dear companions, with regard to the goal to pursue. We want to take possession of this country in order to save it. We want to take all this sparse dust of individuals devoid of laws and mores and cement them into a beautiful well-policed, well-regulated, well-disciplined society. We want to deliver from folly, anarchy and unproductivity the most admirable human domain that extends beneath the sky. As one guides a ship to port, we want to bring this island back to the concert of peoples and fix it, if I might put it thus, by means of the anchors of civilization and commerce. We'll valiantly realize all its power of production, and exchange its marvelous natural riches for the gold of the continents. Organized labor will produce twenty times the necessities of our regenerated people. Our gold mines will be more opulent than those of America or Oceania, and orichalcum, by virtue of its unique properties, will doubtless become precious to industry. Perhaps it's destined to replace debased silver in divisionary money. A few years of effort and, an infinitely richer and more populous England, we'll be the arbiters of the world."

The cavern resounded with long clamors of pride. "Glory, glory, wealth and long life to the kings of Atlantis!"

The Captain continued: "Perhaps you'll tell me, Comrades, that we're not very numerous for such a vast enterprise. Wrong, my friends. Every people has its internal divisions. In the human mind there's always a discontentment with what is, a noble aspiration toward the better. Those appeals of the future, one tries to stifle in oneself in periods of calm, but when troubles are produced, routinely, history shows us that force of novelty and hope raising nations up and soon ranging the multitude on the side of audacious innovators. A people is a latent revolution, which, as marble hopes for its sculptor, hopes for its revolutionary. Or rather, a tranquil people is a mass of dynamite patiently awaiting a shock."

He fell silent momentarily in order to let the noises of enthusiasm die down. Then he went on: "Take note, Comrades, that what you've just applauded isn't a supposition or a desire; it's a law of history. There are forty of us, hidden and as if folded in a corner of this darkness. Our war cry will deploy us, I dare say, a hundred thousand. The hundred thousand most vibrant, the hundred thousand bravest, will wake up at our first gesture, surrounding us with their powerful will. The irresistible wind of a hundred thousand initiatives will attract and carry away the increasing dust of neighboring passivities. Two days after our first proclamation, we'll be the majority."

He stopped for a few seconds, amid uncertain rumors. As they seemed inclined to last, he requested silence with an authoritarian gesture accompanied by an amiable smile. And he resumed: "It's sometimes said, Comrades, that Fernand Cortez took Mexico with five hundred men.[39] That glorious lie renders justice to Cortez, since the hero attempted the conquest of an empire with five hundred men, but the truth that conquerors ought to meditate is that the more valiant half of the Mexicans sided with the Spaniards against their vaguely obstinate compatriots. Comrades, our victory will be easy, for auxiliaries will come from all directions. Comrades, our victory will be glorious, because we'll have dared. Comrades, history will say: They were forty heroes who conquered an island five times as large as France and twenty times as populous."

The hurrahs were a tempest that rose and swelled, seeming to die down and recommence.

"My dear companions," the orator concluded, "We have all kept our revolvers, and I know of a sort of museum, the house of the historian Yupanghe, where innumerable weapons little different from those you know are lying dormant. I've observed this Yupanghe's habits, and I know a means of taking possession of a useful quantity of those arms without anyone noticing. We'll wake the noble sleepers up for a new life and glory. We'll be the princes awaited by all those sleeping beauties. On the other hand, the necessary powder and bullets are already prepared. In a week, as you know, the Atlanteans will gather in large numbers for the great theatrical festival given by the fraternity of the artistes of Azaid. We'll be armed in that vast unarmed crowd; we'll be the bold in that cowardly crowd. We'll offer them salvation, and, if necessary, impose it upon them."

"Long live the Captain!"

"Personally," said a voice emerging from some anfranctuosity or other, "I don't say 'Long live the Captain!' I cry: 'Long live the forty Kings and long live the Emperor!'"

---

[39] Cortés' first name was actually Hernán.

We were all—even the republicans of a little while before—as many echoes: "Long live the forty Kings and long live the Emperor!"

But as we went out, drunk on hope and glory, someone whispered to me: "Forty is really too many. Let's hope that thirty die in the enterprise. If not, we'll have to reconsider."

"Well," I replied, "some will depart laden with gold. Many of the new kings will ask no more than to sell their kingdoms."

"Shh!" said the Captain, who had joined us. "Come with me. We're going to find seven—the seven surest—and we'll solemnly swear to kill the others after the victory. I'll show you the means. Buy kingdoms—damn it! How you go on, my dear Jacques. They cost dear, kingdoms, and a good prince is thrifty."

XXIX

The Seven separated, saluting one another solemnly by the titles that they had just attributed to themselves.

"Goodbye, Emperor of Atlantis!"

"Goodbye, King of Ampheris!"

"Goodbye, King of Euemonia!"

"Goodbye. King of Mueseida!"

"Goodbye, King of Elasippa!"

"Goodbye, King of the Azaids!"

"Goodbye, King of the Diaprepedans!"

I'm ordinarily a placid fellow, indifferent to many things and devoid of revolutionary ambitions. In countries where there are laws, I obey the laws religiously, whatever they are, and I don't think of complaining about the reasonable limits that they impose on my appetites. But that day, in air refreshed and rejuvenated by the morning, I repeated to myself, as if with a furious joy, my companions' farewell.

"Goodbye, Jacques I, King of the Diaprepedans!"

The fact is, first of all, that where there are no defined roads, one can go anywhere; where there are no laws, everything is permissible and it becomes impossible to distinguish wisdom from folly, the accessible from the precipice, security from danger. The fact is, above all, that Meloe was a Diaprepedan. A few more days and the proud disdainful Meloe would be, relative to me, a slave trembling before her king. A king is always loved. Meloe would be the slave who trembles with fear, with admiration, and with love.

But what would I be? Would I be the amorous individual of the first starry gathering, and would I crown that haughty head with gold, glory and kisses? Or, remembering truly unpardonable outrages, would I make yesterday's disdainful child a rapidly-discarded plaything? Rather that. Among those Atlanteans, who were, properly speaking, true public women, yielding to all desires, I would doubtless be able to collect, cheerfully, a few temporary mistresses, but for the union that lasts a lifetime—or rather, the union that lasts eternally, since it creates the son and heir—for the noble union consecrated by law and solemnized by ceremony, I would wait for our relations with the old peoples of the continent to permit me to choose, from the royal families of Europe, a wife of my own race and my own rank.

I flew happily over the country that would devolve to me. Looking down, I said: "Land, produce, pyramids and inhabitants, all of this is mine."

I admired that strange land more than ever. Oh, how embellished a domain appears when it belongs to you!

Sometimes, enjoying the extent and the ensemble of my kingdom, I flew at a height, and it seemed to me that my eyes raised up and carried away that entire region, like the claws of an eagle lifting a prey. Sometimes I drew closer, avid for detail. Thus one steps back to possess with a single glance the entirety of the beloved, and then one approaches, in order to kiss her mouth or caress her breast.

Noble plains of Diaprepeda, you were as beautiful and intoxicating to me as Helen to Paris on the fleeing ship, or Eurydice recovered to Orpheus. Barley and wheat, fecund ocean enclosed by green cliffs of trees, you were agitating beneath the wind your broad and heavy waves of golden yellow, your broad and heavy waves of russet gold. Somber tresses of palm trees, you were in my emotional eyes, the very tresses of Meloe, and, between the lianas, a floating vestment that opens and closes, the modest tremor of your clusters made me dream of quivering breasts.

I let myself fall between the hedges of myrtles and drank the honeyed zephyrs. Then I walked for a while under a grove of cinnamons, which, weighed down by flowers, inclined in porches of shade and perfume. Further away, cherry-trees were swaying, living bouquets of green leaves, white flowers and red fruits. Murmuring streams continued my joy, while a thousand birds, with various songs, now ceasing, now resuming, proclaimed the intoxicating diversity of my delights and a river sang my glory broadly.

Among the grasses of the bank, birds of paradise were hopping, like a fête of colors, and peacocks were making the jewels of their rounded tails vibrate with an almost metallic sound, raised above them like dazzling awnings. Others, perched on low branches, allowed their beauty to display itself and descended calmly to the ground, like the brocades of a royal mantle. Hummingbirds were fluttering around my head, familiarly, a crowd continually dismantled and reassembled.

At the exit from the forest of cinnamons and cherry-trees, I meditated for a long time under gigantic orange trees. They extended above me a kind of emerald sky lit by stars as candid as promises, illuminated by golden suns as heavy and magnificent as realized glory.

XXX

The presence of an Atlantean was unbearable to me. In all of them, I hated Meloe's disdain, which wounded me, not as an individual sentiment but as the repugnance and scorn of an entire race. It is so natural for savages to believe a foreigner inferior until the day when that foreigner is manifest as the king that one adores! Save a thief from the gallows, and he

301

will damn you; condemn him, and he will anoint you. For the sake of prudence, the conspirators were only to meet again on the morning of the Revolt, for the distribution of weapons and ammunition. I could only express my hatreds, desires and hopes to myself.

I still saw Meloe, for fear of awakening her suspicions, but I was only happy when I was alone, and could display the future before my eyes in its diffuse beauty, a sheet of joyously floating light. My continual flight sometimes visited my kingdom, sometimes the other parts of the island. A good king ought not to be ignorant of the resources of his neighbors.

One day, I had wandered a long way. Drunk of speed and altitude, I glided through the cold and stimulating regions of the air. I arrived on an unknown shore, and I perceived two islands a short distance from Atlantis; I was curious to visit them.

I descended toward the first, but I stopped a paraca above the ground, listening and striving to see. The mewling of a tiger rose up, loudly, and the troubled atmosphere was heavy with the odor of wild beasts. Between two huge trees, a liana quivered and slid; my eyes, hesitant at first, recognized that living liana as a snake. Atlantis did not contain any dangerous animals; I was astonished to encounter that menacing fauna such a short distance away.

My hand on my belt, ready for any maneuver of flight, I examined the island of wild beasts from an adequate height. A heavy and violent object fell nearby, with a whistling noise. There was a noise of broken branches, and then the din of an explosion, and black fragments dispersed in a large bouquet of flames,

A bomb!

Sinister suppositions crossed my mind. Had the Atlanteans discovered the conspiracy? Would they hunt each of the conspirators down with improved weapons and packs of ferocious animals? That pacific mildness so vaunted by Makima might be nothing but a hypocrisy, which, vaguely sincere, would disappear at the first proof. Rapidly, I fled toward the other island.

I was twenty paracas at the most from the island of wild beasts when I felt my flight arrested by an invisible obstacle. There was nothing in front of me but the vast daylight, and yet my body rebounded. From what?

Instinctively, my hands made in the air the gesture by which a swimmer opens his way. As if they had come into contact with a resistant object, my body was pushed gently backwards. I tried twenty times to force a passage; twenty times I failed. I tried to change direction; the invisible object caused me to recoil lightly as if, on a dark night, I were groping against the concavity of a circular wall.

"A dirty trick!" I murmured. "Now I'm a prisoner in an invisible prison. Am I going to be condemned to live among the tigers, the snakes and the bursting bombs?"

At that very moment a projectile passed high above my head, perhaps thirty paracas up.

That clarified my mind.

"Thank you, bomb!" I said, with a nervous laugh. "That invisible wall, which doesn't stop you, doesn't rise all the way to the stars. As long as it isn't complicated by an invisible roof! But no, since you, dear bomb, can fall to the ground!"

I launched myself up to a prodigious height, and by a free route, I reached the unknown island that seemed to me to represent salvation.

I was exhausted by too much excitement and I hadn't eaten or drunk anything for a long time. Indifferent to all dangers, I let myself fall on to the sand of the beach.

XXXI

A curious people surrounded my fatigue. They seemed to be of the Atlantean race, but their mores offered a few singularities.

The men were dressed in a kind of black cloak with a black band around their heads. Some carried short rifles in their hands; others wore similar weapons slung over their shoulders. The women were bare-breasted, but the lower part of the body was covered by a yellow skirt tightened around the legs.

The crowd gathered on the ground and in the air, noisily. Many words appeared to be addressed to me. The people spoke the Atlantean language; at the beginning or end of sentences that seemed to be interrogating me I often recognized the word *nelti*.

I stood up and declared, with a gesture of impotence: "I'm French and I don't understand your language."

An old man flew down to land beside me and said: "Be my guest. Few people here will be able to converse with you."

He asked me rapid questions and translated my replies for the crowd as one throws scrap of meat to a pack of dogs. Then we headed toward his house, which was nearby.

The country was manifestly less rich and less fortunate than Atlantis. Life, however, had to be easy there.

I had the pleasure of sitting down at a table and eating a veritable meal. A young woman, the old man's daughter, served us different dishes, among which—oh joy!—was a fish with delicate flesh and an excellent haunch of roe-deer venison. I was finally back in the civilized world, then.

My hunger appeased and my host curiosity satisfied, I asked him in my turn for some information about the country and its inhabitants.

"This island," he replied, "Babrin Island, was completely uninhabited thirty centuries ago. Four thousand years ago, the Atlanteans, delivered from servitude and from cities, had attained the apogee of their intellectual power and moral beauty. Then their decadence commenced. Foolishly, they extended to animals the ideal of fraternity that are only just for the human race. Soon, the majority were abstaining from eating anything that had traversed life, and their senile tenderness gave animals the name of cousins.

"We, the Babrinans, are descended from those who were able to reject those sentimental follies. That minority, diminishing all the time, was increasingly scorned by the rest of the people. More and more frequently, at the starry gatherings, the women rejected our ancestors, calling them, with insulting intention, *flesh-eaters*, *eaters of life* and also, the poor contradictory souls, *eaters of death*—and even, the poor fools, *murderers*. Soon, those who abstained from eating the 'cousins' claimed that we carried and intolerable stink wherever we went, the 'odor or the tiger.'

"Furthermore, at every opportunity, the 'respecters of life' indoctrinated our female friends, our sisters and our daughters. Their propaganda, obtaining a facile success over the feeble reasoning of those scrupulous hearts, isolated us increasingly. A few, sickened by continual feminine defections, began to preach against women, and for a long time, in a clearing in Euemonia, here were starry gatherings in which only men assembled. Others proposed, in order that our people should not perish by virtue of the abandonment of the women, to separate us from the 'respecters of life.'

"The majority of the flesh-eaters therefore took refuge on Babrin Island. For three thousand years we have formed a nation that scorns the Atlanteans and waits patients for those cousins of animals to fall back into animality, as promised by reliable prophecies. Then, returning to the large island, we will repopulate it with humans."

I had been able to observe very little of Babrin. However, the intellect of my host appeared to me, in spite of my hatred of Atlanteans, to be obviously inferior to Makima's. I questioned him and learned that the Babrinans had not yet been able to discover the secret of the pantoscope and the oneirogene. The belts they manufactured were not as powerful as those of the Atlanteans.

Sometimes, they visited their neighbors in order to obtain a belt from a fraternity. They also borrowed foreign books, because they were unable to print at a distance. They experienced the greatest repugnance for such expeditions, though. The Atlanteans looked at them with intolerable smiles of superiority. They offered them the best of what they had, saying: "Take this one instead, *nasca*."

Sometimes, the Babrinans replied: "I'm not a cousin with four hands or four paws, *nelti*. I'm a man like you; I'm your brother."

But the other said: "You can become my brother, cousin, whenever you wish. In order to be human, you only have to consent to a human life. O voluntary *nasca*, rise to our full measure, realize yourself and be my brother."

Some allowed themselves to be seduced and did not come back. Mildness is a bird-lime from which it is difficult to escape.

Inferior in so many respects, the Babrinans possessed, by way of compensation, admirably ingenious fishing tackle and extraordinarily improved weapons.

"Why," I asked, "don't you go and impose your customs on the degenerate Atlanteans by force."

The old man made a gesture of horror. "Constrain a human being to do something!" he said. "But that's the worst of crimes!" He added: "Are the Atlanteans degenerate? Undoubtedly! Not sufficiently, however, to allow themselves to be constrained. I've read in French books that there are people in your country cowardly enough to yield to force, people cowardly enough to obey. I've never believed it. I've always observed in your writers imaginations so bizarre as to be impossible, and a mania for talking about humans as one talks about beasts. I've often supposed that your writers are fabulists and are ingeniously presenting animals to us with human names. There are domesticated animals, but I can't believe that, even in a savage land, domesticated humans exist."

"You never make war, then?"

"Are you insane, *nelti*?"

"Why, then, do you manufacture weapons?"

"To kill the murderers—tigers, lions and serpents—and also to hunt the animals to which human have not consented an alliance."

"You live primarily by hunting?"

"We live on bred, rice, fruits, fish and game."

"You're ignorant of the art of breeding and fattening co-mestible animals—poultry, pigs...?"

"We bred poultry because we like eggs. We have cows because we like milk. Horses and oxen aid us in our work. All those animals, which give us something and which live in community with us, are friends. You don't suppose us capable, I hope, of the treason of killing those dear and useful companions and devouring them. I have no duty toward wild animals; the natural relationship that the Atlanteans imagine between animals and humans is a childish dream of degenerates. On the other hand, friends of election, contracted alliances and mutual services create between us and domestic animals an artificial relationship that implies respect for the life and sensibility of our allies."

I smiled. These people, who believed themselves to be liberated from Atlantean prejudice, still appeared to me to be very timid and naïve. I straightened up in the mocking pride of a slave-master before the poor plebeian who believes himself to be free but who has no one to command.

"We civilized people are not so short-sighted," I declared, "and we raise animals in order to eat them. Some of them become deliciously fat and fleshy."

I felt the pleasant memory of a certain capon melting in my mouth.

The Babrinan cried: "But the animal I rear is my guest, and I don't betray my guest! If it gives me milk, eggs, wool or work, it also becomes my benefactor..."

"You furnish it with food and built its accommodation; you're quits."

"An exchange of services does not appear to you to create a solidarity between two beings? What bizarre thinking!"

"Your scruples mustn't make it easy to procure meat."

"We like meat, but not to the point of crime. Listen. I've read that in your homeland, gold is valued above everything else. Some of our birds are also madly fond of objects that shine. If your guest has a lot of gold, though, would you kill him for what you call his riches? And the man who, having rendered you a service and accepted a service from you, and has become your friend twice over—would you strike him, saying: *Scruples render the acquisition of gold too difficult*?"

"You make singular comparisons and have singular fashions of reasoning."

"You're not replying, however, having no reasonable reply to make."

"I never have any reply to make to absolute reason, or to absolute folly."

"I suppose, then, my generous guest, that your words express absolute reason and mine..."

I changed the subject without permitting the old man to finish the sentence. I told him about my visit to the island of wild beasts and the invisible obstacle I had bumped into on my return.

"Another folly of our Atlantean brothers!" he exclaimed. "They don't even kill dangerous animals. Fortunately, we used to mount expeditions to hunt tigers, lions and panthers. Looking at things realistically, it's to us that they owe their lives, those brothers who scorn us. Ten centuries ago, however, I don't know by what means, they exiled all bloodthirsty beasts from their midst. Our books recount the vast bewildered flight of the wild beasts before a moving wall of apparent fire, which didn't burn anything but terrorized the malevolent beasts.

"A strange community of life had habituated the others, the cousins, to imitate humans and only to flee if the Atlanteans fled. They understood those of our words that relate to material things, and kind words reassured them. Like the Atlanteans, they let that formidable innocent fire pass over them.

"The ferocious beats, fleeing in fearful silence, swam to Tababrin Island—the one you called the island of wild beasts just now. The Atlanteans then surrounded the island with what they call 'a circle of repulsive force.' One can only enter that circle or exit from it at a height of thirty paracas. The best Babrinan belts deflate well before that vertigo—with the result that our intolerant brothers have deprived us of the hunts that were the greatest joy of our ancestors. Fortunately, we have good cannons, and we launch bombs into the midst of the hostile creatures that hiss, roar and mewl."

XXXII

After my excursion to Tibabrin and Babrin, the sky of Atlantis was animated and saddened by strange bands of armed men dressed in black cloaks and headbands. I recognized them, with an inexplicable terror. Some instinct advised me to pretend astonishment and ask Makima for explanations.

"They're the inhabitants of a neighboring island," he said, "flesh-eaters and killers of murderers, demi-cruels who—to our shame, alas!—are descendants of the same race as us. I've never seen them in troops above the innocent land. Usually, it requires a very keen desire for a good belt or a new book for one of them to visit us.

"Once, carnivorous beasts lived in our forests and bands of these Babrinans came to hunt them. Our ancestors fled, weeping with humiliation, the odious spectacle in which humans behaved as malevolently tigers or panthers. A long time ago we exiled the wild beasts to Tibabrin Island, and the semi-beasts, the *nasca-nelti* of Babrin haven't appeared since.

"Animals that like blood have an extraordinary sense of smell. What are these looking for? Are we threatened by an invasion of ferocious beasts? If the wall of force had a breach, though, we'd have been alerted..."

He concluded: "Let's go and ask them!"

I didn't understand the conversation, which naturally took place is Atlantean. It frightened me, though. The Babrinans were all talking at once, with violent exclamations, and their threatening gestures were directed at me.

Makima took me far away from them.

"The love of blood," he said, "is a dementia that gives birth to dementias. These people, always dreaming of combats, or, as they put it, murders of murderers, easily hope to

309

find others worse than themselves. Semi-bestial, they willingly see other humans as complete beasts. The executioner desires to encounter the guilty; his imagination is a hasty matrix in which blood and monsters always seethe. The poor castaways that we have received fraternally and whom the great bath of prolonged innocence has already rendered almost as human as ourselves, these madmen identify as a frightful danger.

"It appears, Jacques, that you are forty vertiginous adventurers capable of killing eight hundred million human beings. Fortunately, these brave Babrinans are watching out for our salvation. One of them has affirmed by words and sniggers: 'You have chased away the tigers that tear apart at close range, but you have welcomed the tigers that can kill at a distance.' And he added, amid the joyful acclamations of his comrades: 'They'll soon give us an opportunity for a fine hunt.'"

The old man put his arm around me and hugged me. "Oh, *nelti*," he groaned, "people who like combat are very insulting madmen."

I thought it necessary to let the Captain know about the peril that was menacing us, but he rubbed his hands.

"So much the better, King of the Diaprepedans! That will shake up Atlantean patriotism. The entire country, waking up with a start, will rise up around us, alarmed and enthusiastic, to repel the foreign invasion."

XXXIII

The hour of action approached. In the air and on the terraces carved out in the side of the Azaid mountain, the dense crowd was innumerable. In the middle of the stage, around the altar of perfumes, the terrestrial demi-choir and the aerial demi-choir were circling in opposite directions. The terrestrial strophe was relating dolors, weeping plaints, but the aerial antistrophe was responding with joys, populating the sky with rising hopes.

Only the rhythms and attitudes were expressive for the conspirators. We had thought it necessary to form a compact group, and no indigene was in our midst to explain the words.

The two demi-choirs halted their dance and their song. Three individuals dressed in the Babrinan fashion—but I think they represented ancient Atlanteans, contemporaries of the Fortunate Separation—were uttering sonorous words through the round and grandiloquent mouths of masks when the Captain gave the agreed signal. As abrupt as a storm that bursts without warning, we ran on to the stage, shoving aside the actors and the choristers and tipping over the fuming altar. Alarmingly, there was nothing in the crowd reminiscent of a tumult, not a surge of curiosity, nor an impulse to flee. The Atlanteans waited, indifferently, to see what would happen.

The Captain started speaking. He painted a very black picture of the anarchy that reigned in Atlantis. Then he depicted the glorious future of the island under a paternal government, with an efficient organization that would multiply production a hundredfold. A broad and noble speech finally offered the regenerated Atlantis the scepter of the Earth.

When he fell silent, after the long echo of our acclamations, there were bursts of laughter here and there in a black silence, which rippled around like sparks. Then there was a vast rumor. Those who knew French were explaining to their neighbors. And the laughter multiplied from a thousand nuclei, then combined and rose toward the sky like a vast blaze of dementia.

A man, who was naked, like the rest of the crowd, but white-skinned, advanced through the air. He had difficulty clearing a passage. An Atlantean woman was gliding in his wake. We recognized Charles the renegade and jeered him unanimously.

When silence permitted it, he spoke.

The Atlanteans, he said, disdained to respond to our follies, but he thought it necessary, for the honor of the white race, that a white man should speak after the Captain. The pictures painted by our leader, he proclaimed to be "images of fantasy, or rather of dementia." He claimed to oppose to them "the simple truth." He praised the material prosperity and facile happiness of Atlantis and bewailed, not without exaggeration, the evils suffered by the Cruel peoples. We interrupted him continually with denials and insults, but the Atlanteans, whom he lauded, listened to him with the same indifference that they had listened to the Captain.

"Thus far," Charles went on, "I have only spoken to you; I have addressed myself to your base calculative reasoning, and my Atlantean brothers will doubtless criticize me for lingering so long on these irrelevant material considerations. I will try to say now what one of these people would say to you if they were in the habit of speaking to wild beasts."

I pointed my pistol at the insulter.

"Should I shoot?" I asked the Captain.

"Patience, King of the Diaprepedans!"

Charles went on: "What is our ambition? Do you want flavorsome aliments, rapid belts, harmonious and supple canoes, everything that makes the exterior of life smile? No one stops your hand as it reaches out to take the fruit of the tree or the handiwork of humans. Do you want gold? Take it: load yourselves down like the beasts of burden that drag unnecessary weights long the cruel roads. What more do you want, when everything is yours?"

"We want this land to produce all that it can produce."

"No one is preventing you from sowing and planting."

"We want the regulation, law and organization that can triumph over natural idleness and permit the multiplication of production."

"I hear that you want to give orders and be obeyed. But no one here understands the words that command or knows the attitude that submits. When human beings are liberated from all avidity; when they no longer tremble for riches stolen from all and mount guard against despoiled avidities; when they are no longer beasts that flee and hide before suffering and death; when they are no longer beasts that advance crawling and drooling toward pleasure, with what can you still

312

make them afraid and hopeful? With what can you domesti-cate them? Is it not the case, *neltis*, that none of you can be domesticated?"

This time, those who understood approved: "Yes, you're right. Yes, Charles, you are a true *nelti*." The young woman who had followed our former compatriot placed an exquisitely small hand on his shoulder, made him turn his head, and kissed him on the lips.

"At least have the modesty to rise toward the stars!" I shouted.

But Charles resumed his absurd exclamation. "Lovers of vile impossibility, impotent demons who dream of igniting the Inferno in Heaven itself, there is, however, one thing you can do. You can kill. You can kill innumerably. None of us will react to violence with violence, or avoid it by flight. Look—you are among thousands of Christs or thousands of followers of Epictetus, all capable of supporting physical injury and mortal wounds with disdain, all equally incapable of the cow-ardice of retreat and the cowardice of striking. But the mur-derer of a Christ or an Epictetus—do you not sense it?—only harms himself. You can cover yourselves with blood, but don't hope that torrents of shed blood will make a single Atlantean bend to you will. You will not have the infernal joy of extracting a scream or obtaining a fearful attitude. You will be weary of killing before we are weary of dying. Are you mad enough to commit so many futile murders?"

"Enough chat!" said the Captain, taking aim.

The pistol shot was the signal for a butchery that was fantastically horrible. With revolvers, daggers and sabers, we fired on the immobile crowd, we cut and we thrust. Our blows, hesitant at first, soon became firm and bold, then violent and exasperated. The odor of powder and the odor of blood intoxi-cated us. We uttered indistinct cries or whipped and spurred our courage with words.

"A few more dead," we affirmed, "and they'll flee; and those we overtake in the panicked stampede will beg us for mercy. Oh, the stubborn fools! They'll have to give in. Our perseverance and our fury will overwhelm their insensible patience."

Our anger increased, foaming, against the inert resistance.

"Are you stones then, that it's necessary to topple one after another, stones that feel nothing, which understand nothing?"

A shame rose within us that increasingly wanted victory. If they did not flee, if they did not beg for mercy, we would kill them all—yes, all of them. The insensates! Hundreds had already fallen, and none had yet avoided our blows.

The tempest of rage grew, and an amazement mingled with it. Not content with not recoiling, some Atlanteans came toward us, inviting wounds, inviting death, throwing themselves upon our weapons.

Suddenly, Meloe was in front of me.

"Strike!" she said. "I am thirsty for death."

I turned away. She followed my movement; she would not permit me to escape from her and to run to soothe myself with other murders. Her small hand took my armed hand and guided my blade to her left breast, quivering with an unknown emotion.

"Thrust!" her voice ordered.

I recoiled.

"Why don't you strike the one you hate the most?"

"Ah!" I cried. "My hatred is love. I love you to the point of crime, to the point of treason. Come, Meloe, be mine!"

"Strike, then; I shall only be yours when dead."

"Don't tempt me!" I wept.

And my boy tried to recoil, but my dagger, as if it had a will independent of my own, exerted pressure.

A drop of blood was, on the delightfully tawny body, a slightly redder pearl. I threw away my weapons, and my lips drank the blood that I had shed.

Then I groaned: "Forgive me—or rather, forgive yourself! Your disdain alone created my crime. Forgive me, love me, and I'll be cured."

314

"Madman!" she said. "Can I determine that you have not killed? Can I destroy your past?"

"You could, oh, you could determine that my future would no longer be the slave of the past that I detest."

But she shook her head in a gesture of impotence. "If you renounced evil for love of me, and not for hatred of evil, in what way would you be less wicked?"

Meanwhile, little Telo threw herself between us.

"I want to die," said that infantile voice. "I want to die by Jacques' hand, that my blood might be the flame that enlightens my friend. Strike Telo, Jacques, and be disgusted by murder!"

Suddenly, however, a strange obscurity descended upon us and frightful cries burst forth in the air.

"Fall back to the stage!" ordered the Captain.

XXXIV

Around the altar of perfumes, which was still fuming, having been tipped over, there were forty of us. We had no more bullets; we had no more powder. Our hands were clutching the hilts of chipped sabers and cutlasses. And the enemy army was hovering, numerous and formidable. Between two and three thousand Babrinans, rifles in hand, were taking aim at us, already extending a kind of sepulchral shadow over us. And there were muffled sniggers that made me think of the sound that earth makes as it is crumbled over coffins.

"We're doomed," I said. "It only remains to fall gloriously. Let's show that we're worthy of the great name of Frenchmen. Let's show the Atlanteans that Frenchmen also know how to die."

There were ten of us who stood up against the darkened sky, directing a stare and a rictus of defiance against the implacable enemy. There were ten of us; the others, dispersed, were slipping, narrow, petty and diminished, in among the Atlanteans, who were surrounding them, protecting them with

315

their bodies. "This way, *nelti*! Come; either your life will be respected, or they'll kill me before killing you."

I addressed the ten brave men, immobile and tense.

"Come on!" I said. "Toward death!"

"It's good enough to wait!" replied the Captain, severely.

Meanwhile, between the Babrinans and us, the entire innumerable people of the Pacifists launched themselves, forming a dense, quivering, buzzing rampart.

No, I ought not to accept the pity of enemies I had struck, outraging life! With a abrupt oblique bound I rose above the crowd, and I shouted: "Fire at me! A vanquished king has nothing to do but die."

Before a rifle could take aim at me, numerous Atlanteans surrounded me, enclosing me in a moving and tenaciously protective prison. Among them, very close, touching me, enveloping me with her body like an irritant kiss of mercy, was the inevitable Meloe.

"What right do you have over me, you who don't love me! Let me die. Don't you realize that you're injuring my pride? Don't you realize that you're more cruel now than in the treetops or behind Tacmar's corpse? Don't you realize that I need—oh, such a dolorous need!—to extinguish myself, no longer to be? Meloe, I beg you, let me fall in the bath of oblivion that alone can cure and soothe my fever."

Thus I raved deliriously amid emotions too strong for a human brain and heart.

But she, without having, as I had, the excuse of an agony that one desires and yet flees, spoke more madly still.

"No," she declared. "You believe that a violent death will equilibrate your murders. You'd depart in the pride of a debtor who imagines that he's redeeming his debt, for your stupidity still tells you that the present can absolve the past. I don't want you to die with that evil thought."

"What does my last thought matter?"

Then she pronounced this strange item of mystic dementia: "Don't you know that a last thought is a first thought?"

I shut up, crushed by a circle of humiliations and follies.

Telo was also beside me, implacably gentle. Perhaps in the hope of dispelling my grim ideas, she set about explaining what was happening.

Makima was negotiating with the Babrinans.

"Let us act," the killers of murderers were saying. "Since you allow yourselves to be killed, what illogicality entitles you to prevent us from killing them."

"Brothers," the old man replied. "Our fortunate death might enlighten these individuals accustomed to killing people. But you, who have respected human life for centuries, would be drawn further down into the hell of violence by this murder. Brothers, separated from us by a gulf that time and reflection will fill in, don't descend into the abyss from which one lifetime is never sufficient to emerge."

"Permit us to be just."

"It is never just to kill."

"You do not throw yourselves in front of our rifles to protect tigers, which suffer as much as these Cruels. Why defend these tigers, worse than those in the jungle? The beasts of the forest kill, innocently, because they are hungry, and we fight them as honest enemies. These, sated, have killed for no reason, have killed for the love of murder, have killed their benefactors. We want to purge the earth of these monsters."

"Brothers, rather purge your hearts of the love of murder. Hatred and vengeance cry in vain: 'Our name is justice.' Their ugliness makes them recognizable. Brothers, justice does not soil its hands with blood. Brothers, so long as you do not love, you cannot know what justice is, for those who know call justice the equilibrium of love. Brothers, you say, hatefully: 'They are tigers,' but the hope of my love replies: 'There is, lost in the moving dung-heap and compost of each of these tigers, the seed of a human being.' Respect the possible human. Respect the human being who might surge forth tomorrow, weeping over today. Brothers, the murderer who weeps is vanquished, but the murderer one kills is victorious: he has created another murderer."

The strange debate continued between the beings of brutal justice and the beings of gentleness and love. Love, you are a folly more obstinate than justice and vengeance!

The Babrinans ended up yielding. A part of the armed troop flew away, insulting the Atlanteans and peppering us with threats.

"Let them not come near the coast of Babrin is they value their skins!"

But many of the Babrinans hovered in the air, hesitantly. Sometimes, they seemed to want to rejoin their compatriots. Sometimes, they drew closer to the Atlanteans, who blew them kisses and appealed to the, with words that I could not understand, but the tone of which moved me, giving me, in the unstable nervousness that was tearing me apart, a reckless and tender desire to weep.

The Babrinans, after long uncertainty, bid their retreating companions adieu. They threw away their weapons. They removed the headbands retaining their hair, and took off their clothes. And while the wind carried those rags away, they—now similar in all respects to the Atlanteans—fell into the arms of their brothers, brothers retrieved, and tears of joy were shed on either side.

XXXV

The days that followed were abominable. Our former companions, furious with the Captain and me, could not see us without heaping insults upon us. But the indifference of the Atlanteans, who, as if they were unaware of our crimes, maintained the same attitude toward us as before, appeared to us to be more insulting than all the words, and made our hearts race with shame, rage and hatred.

In spite of the Babrinans' threats, we flew nostalgically in the direction of their island. That more similar humankind, those beings whose passions and justice we could understand, those warriors who were able to kill, like us, attracted us, like a fatherland from which we were exiled.

The Captain praised those brave people; then, talking about the Atlanteans, he shrugged his shoulders. "They're not human!"

"They think of themselves as *realized* humans."

"Yes, what people back home call angels. But anyone who wants to be an angel is an idiot. Then again, don't they sicken you, these wretches who, not content with letting themselves be killed in a cowardly fashion, let those who are dearest to them—wives, children, mothers—be killed? That's abysmal madness and cowardice."

In the vicinity of Babrin, we witnessed the most discouraging of spectacles: groups of Babrinans flying away from the little island, crossing the channel, throwing headbands, black cloaks and yellow skirts into the sea.

"They're becoming Atlanteans," I said. "Ah! Ignoble meekness is victorious!"

"Cowardice is the most contagious of diseases," added the Captain, harshly.

We resolved to quit the odious country. My companion proposed that we come back with an entire population of colonists. Instructed by experience, they would avoid the initial errors and faults. They would install themselves with their families in one of the most fertile regions. They would build a city, establish a government, and organize civilized life. The movement of a solid mass always attracts and annexes neighboring dust. The Atlanteans would inevitably be drawn to it, and the entire island would gradually be invaded, submerged by reason and order.

I made vague approving noises, because the Captain could no longer tolerate contradiction, but I experienced mute anxieties. Would not the colonists, contrary to the anticipations of the ambitious individual, be won over by the Atlanteans? A bad example is more contagious than a good one. A man who remains sober in a land of drunkards, or submissive and honest in a land of liberty, or laborious in an atmosphere of idleness, is a rare character, an exception that one ought to neglect in practical calculations. Where have I read the observation, shameful for human nature, that civilized men return voluntarily to savage life, but savages are only civilized by constraint and force? Even force could do nothing here, and in spite of my friend's generous dreams, the Atlanteans appeared to me to be irredeemably doomed.

Then too, the Captain was taking insufficient account of the dangers and obstacles of the Sargasso Sea.

How a canoe transported us secretly—in our belief, at least—all the way to the open Ocean; how, a short distance away from the last of the weed, we rose into the air involuntarily, and saw our craft gliding away, as if in a dream, in the direction of the island; how our weakened belts soon refused to raise us into the thinner air, but held us suspended us over the sea, disdainfully merciful, until a ship passed by; how they deflated, losing the last of their force as soon as we set foot on the vessel; and how the very fabric disappeared as soon as we fell asleep, I do not think it necessary to relate such petty events in detail. Nor shall I bother to relate the last obstacles to our return and the end of our adventures; my story would become as banal as a traveler's tale.

In France, the Captain tried to recruit colonists for Atlantis. He was arrested on a charge of fraud. He cited me as a witness, but I could not be found. The convinced strangeness of his story saved him from prison; the judges confided him to alienist physicians, who are in the process of driving him mad.

XXXVI

Although reinstalled in my dear homeland and my old habits, there remains deep down within me I don't know what disturbance, almost unhappiness—something like the bitter taste that lingers obstinately in the mouth of some convalescents.

Human beings are such contradictory animals! In Atlantis I missed the civilized life as a bird under a bell-jar lacks air. But that irrespirable existence, now, at the shock of certain ugly aspects of this environment, sometimes causes a momentary regret. Social organization, demanded by my education, my habits and my reasons, often comes into conflict with my appetites.

The man who desires happiness and calm of mind ought, I believe, to descend deeply enough no longer to perceive anything except the life to which he is condemned, becoming incapable even of imagining strange possibilities, or of not finding them foolish and ridiculous. Happiness is a matter of fusing, naturally or artificially, the ideal with the real. Whether it is the work of a God or of Progress, our reality ought to satisfy us, as the manifestation, the expression and the materialization of the ideal. Woe betide the man who no longer affirms the immobile solidity of his horizon.

I know a great principle: "Be like a beast," and an even greater one: "Put down roots." The vegetal advice of Barrès is even more profound than the animal advice of Pascal, and completes it marvelously.[40]

I shall make every effort to obey those two instructions to prudence, more and more.

I have written my memoirs in order to relieve myself of their obsession. I also thought that I might relieve the heartsickness of utopians by showing them that their ideal is a reality somewhere, a reality poorer and more irritating than ours. One corrects a puppy by taking it by the scruff of its neck and plunging its nose into its ordure; the dreams of future cities are excreta that poison the air of present society; I have plunged the mulish nose of the utopian into a little realized utopia.

Having concluded the work—it was necessary, alas!—I feel relieved of a crushing and unsteady weight.

---

[40] Maurice Barrès (1862) began his career as a left-inclined Symbolist writer but deserted that fold to become a pillar of right-wing propaganda and politics, embracing a strange kind of nationalism that venerated "*la terre et les morts*" [the earth and the dead]. Regarded as a traitor by his former friends, he was held up by more than one as a Horrible Example.

Henceforth, I shall be the sage who gazes at all his own things, who refuses to quit the solid point of view of a Frenchman and a man of the twentieth century. I shall never consider anything under the aspect of eternity, and I shall not content to the heart-rending and humiliating effort of looking at my life from Sirius or Atlantis. I know my duty: to shut oneself up in one's enclosure and one's moment, in order to work, between high and narrow walls, on one's dear little garden.[41] I like the brave people who admire their country and their epoch; I detest unsociable minds that deny their homeland or their century.

Glad to have neither genius nor aspiration, I shall increasingly become a good little Barrès, fearfully curled up in his shell.

I have made the most sincere of confessions. I have often deformed irrelevant exteriorities, on the instructions of my consciences, but I have always revealed my sentiments and their succession with equal and naïve frankness.

I had arrived in Atlantis conflicted by uncertain opinions, buoyed up by an excessive love of progress, weighed down by too much respect for tradition. I was dazzled for a time by the apparent happiness of those people. At the times when the seduction troubled me and dispersed me the most, however, I was able to proclaim that something central and immutable, a powerful rational framework, sane and French, always resisted and protested within me.

My eyes were opened completely and definitively by the insulting refusal of Meloe. My heart understood, that night, that the facile and broad life is not enough. We need above all an organized society in which we know our place. Where there are no classes, one is necessarily the most despicable and dolorous things of all, devoid of status.

---

[41] This remark deliberately recalls the conclusion of Voltaire's *Candide*, as the reference in the previous sentence to Sirius is suggestive of *Micromégas*.

To command is the primordial need to human nature. In our old lands, even the humblest is happy; he commands his wife. A servant elsewhere, served at home, he is always in a definite situation, always aware of his rights and duties. Our wives are happy; they command their children. Our children are happy; incapable of distinguishing the living from the inert, they joyfully command their dolls or their toy soldiers. Hierarchy and discipline distribute equitably to everyone the virtue of obedience and the joy of command.

I do not only imagine hierarchy with an emotional mind; it seems to me that I see it with my eyes, a noble equilibrium, a powerful pyramid of pleasures. Everyone rests, satisfied, on the step that suits his merit; everyone knows the pathways that permit him to climb, in accordance with his strength and his determination, and anyone who is discontented with his present lot strives toward more elevated joys and more dominating ambitions.

In Atlantean anarchy, by contrast, no social ascent and personal progress is possible. Morally, that country is a marsh, always flat and always fetid, in which no healthy path is traced by duty, but in which every step is bogged down like he preceding one and the next: a hellish labyrinth of tedium.

Among those eight hundred million people, the traveler is more alone and denuded than in the smallest hamlet. I do not know any village in which one cannot procure a woman with money. In Atlantis, there is no money; the great human power is suppressed, and a woman has no reason to yield to you, either by virtue of hunger, fear or the sentiment of your superiority. In that mild country she has no need of the protection of a strong man, and she is ignorant of marriage and the legitimate consideration that it brings.

Even the life of true savages appears to me to be preferable to that of the Atlanteans. A man can at least rape a woman there; he then has the joy of protecting her from other assaults and of feeling her huddle against him, fearful and grateful.

"Man is made for war," a great thinker has said, "and woman for the recreation of the warrior. Outside of that, all is folly."[42] In that lax island, where there is neither war nor warriors, all is folly,

I have indicated—and I still believe that I have done the right thing—a part of the scientific and industrial progress of the Atlanteans. Certainly, what I have said will not seduce anyone. The reader will not be jealous, in spite of the marvelous instruments that they possess, but which their folly renders so futile—poor beings who live naked, without commerce, and as indifferent and comfortable as the most inept animals. In any case, it will suffice for French scientists, minds so undeniably superior, that I have described the flying belt, the pantoscope and the oneirogene for them soon to make those admirable discoveries in their turn. I regret not being a physicist; I would have been able to give more precise information and more exact descriptions. I console myself with the thought that, thanks to my incompetence, the glory of my compatriots will be greater in due course.

I shall send my book not only to scientists, but to horticulturalists. Few years will pass before our agricultural shows are able to take pride in fruits as enormous and flavorsome as those I ate in Atlantis—those, at least, to which our climate is suited—and Makima will be jealous, via the pantoscope, of our flowers.

One final word. I am not signing this work and in narration I have masked my forename with one that is not mine. I have taken all possible precautions, and no one will ever know the veritable author of these pages.

Political necessities impose that prudence upon me. I am a socialist general councilor. I shall soon be a socialist député. Circumstances prohibit me from changing my electoral clientele, and my ideas, insofar as they can be divined from this book, do not correspond entirely with the program of my party. That confession I make proudly. If I do not sign it with my

---

[42] The quotation is from Friedrich Nietzsche's *Also Sprach Zarathustra*.

name, it is because the education of the electors is as yet insufficient. They do not understand that a politician defends a cause that all sorts of hazard might have chosen for him and for which he has the right of an advocate—provided that he is honest, disciplined and pleads eloquently—not to believe a word that he says.

SF & FANTASY

Adolphe Alhaiza. *Cybele*

Alphonse Allais. *The Adventures of Captain Cap*

Henri Allorge. *The Great Cataclysm*

Guy d'Armen. *Doc Ardan: The City of Gold and Lepers*

G.-J. Arnaud. *The Ice Company*

Charles Asselineau. *The Double Life*

Henri Austruy. *The Eupantophone; The Olotelepan; The Petitpaon Era*

Cyprien Bérard. *The Vampire Lord Ruthwen*

S. Henry Berthoud. *Martyrs of Science*

Aloysius Bertrand. *Gaspard de la Nuit*

Richard Bessière. *The Gardens of the Apocalypse; The Masters of Silence*

Albert Bleunard. *Ever Smaller*

Félix Bodin. *The Novel of the Future*

Louis Boussenard. *Monsieur Synthesis*

Alphonse Brown. *City of Glass; The Conquest of the Air*

Emile Calvet. *In a Thousand Years*

André Caroff. *The Terror of Madame Atomos; Miss Atomos; The Return of Madame Atomos; The Mistake of Madame Atomos; The Monsters of Madame Atomos; The Revenge of Madame Atomos; The Resurrection of Madame Atomos; The Mark of Madame Atomos; The Spheres of Madame Atomos*

Félicien Champsaur. *The Human Arrow; Ouha, King of the Apes; Pharaoh's Wife*

Didier de Chousy. *Ignis*

Jules Clarétie. *Obsession*

Michel Corday. *The Eternal Flame*

André Couvreur. *The Necessary Evil; Caresco, Superman; The Exploits of Professor Tornada* (3 vols.)

Captain Danrit. *Undersea Odyssey*

C. I. Defontenay. *Star (Psi Cassiopeia)*

Charles Derennes. *The People of the Pole*

Georges Dodds (anthologist). *The Missing Link*

Harry Dickson. *The Heir of Dracula*

Jules Dornay. *Lord Ruthven Begins*

Alfred Driou. *The Adventures of a Parisian Aeronaut*

Sâr Dubnotal *vs. Jack the Ripper*

Alexandre Dumas. *The Return of Lord Ruthven*

Renée Dunan. *Baal*

J.-C. Dunyach. *The Night Orchid; The Thieves of Silence*

Henri Duvernois. *The Man Who Found Himself*

Achille Eyraud. *Voyage to Venus*

Henri Falk. *The Age of Lead*

Paul Féval. *Anne of the Isles; Knightshade; Revenants; Vampire City; The Vampire Countess; The Wandering Jew's Daughter*

Paul Féval, *fils. Felifax, the Tiger-Man*

Charles de Fieux. *Lamékis*

Louis Forest. *Someone is Stealing Children in Paris*

Arnould Galopin. *Doctor Omega; Doctor Omega and the Shadowmen* (anthology)

Judith Gautier. *Isoline and the Serpent-Flower*

H. Gayar. *The Marvelous Adventures of Serge Myrandhal on Mars*

Léon Gozlan. *The Vampire of the Val-de-Grâce*

G.L. Gick. *Harry Dickson and the Werewolf of Rutherford Grange*

Edmond Haraucourt. *Illusions of Immortality*

Nathalie Henneberg. *The Green Gods*

V. Hugo, P. Foucher & P. Meurice. *The Hunchback of Notre-Dame*

Romain d'Huissier. *Hexagon: Dark Matter*

Jules Janin. *The Magnetized Corpse*

Michel Jeury. *Chronolysis*

Gustave Kahn. *The Tale of Gold and Silence*

Gérard Klein. *The Mote in Time's Eye*

Fernand Kolney. *Love in 5000 Years*

Paul Lacroix. *Danse Macabre*

Louis-Guillaume de La Follie. *The Unpretentious Philosopher*

Jean de La Hire. *Enter the Nyctalope; The Nyctalope on Mars; The Nyctalope vs. Lucifer; The Nyctalope Steps In; Night of the Nyctalope; Return of the Nyctalope; The Fiery Wheel*

Etienne-Léon de Lamothe-Langon. *The Virgin Vampire*

André Laurie. *Spiridon*

Gabriel de Lautrec. *The Vengeance of the Oval Portrait*

Alain le Drimeur. *The Future City*

Georges Le Faure & Henri de Graffigny. *The Extraordinary Adventures of a Russian Scientist Across the Solar System* (2 vols.)

Gustave Le Rouge. *The Mysterious Doctor Cornelius* (3 vols.); *The Vampires of Mars; The Dominion of the World* (w/Gustave Guitton) (4 vols.)

Jules Lermina. *Mysteryville; Panic in Paris; To-Ho and the Gold Destroyers; The Secret of Zippelius*

André Lichtenberger. *The Centaurs; The Children of the Crab*

Jean-Marc & Randy Lofficier. *Edgar Allan Poe on Mars; The Katrina Protocol; Pacifica; Robonocchio; Return of the Nyctalope;* (anthologists) *Tales of the Shadowmen 1-10*

Xavier Mauméjean. *The League of Heroes*

Joseph Méry. *The Tower of Destiny*

Hippolyte Mettais. *The Year 5865*

Louise Michel. *The Human Microbes; The New World*

Tony Moilin. *Paris in the Year 2000*

José Moselli. *Illa's End*

John-Antoine Nau. *Enemy Force*

Marie Nizet. *Captain Vampire*

C. Nodier, A. Beraud & Toussaint-Merle. *Frankenstein*

Henri de Parville. *An Inhabitant of the Planet Mars*

Gaston de Pawlowski. *Journey to the Land of the 4th Dimension*

Georges Pellerin. *The World in 2000 Years*

Ernest Pérochon. *The Frenetic People*

Pierre Pelot. *The Child Who Walked on the Sky*

J. Polidori, C. Nodier, E. Scribe. *Lord Ruthven the Vampire*

P.-A. Ponson du Terrail. *The Vampire and the Devil's Son; The Immortal Woman*

Edgar Quinet. *Ahasuerus; The Enchanter Merlin*

Henri de Régnier. *A Surfeit of Mirrors*

Maurice Renard. *The Blue Peril; Doctor Lerne; The Doctored Man; A Man Among the Microbes; The Master of Light*

Jean Richepin. *The Wing; The Crazy Corner*

Albert Robida. *The Adventures of Saturnin Farandoul; The Clock of the Centuries; Chalet in the Sky; The Electric Life*

J.-H. Rosny Aîné. *Helgvor of the Blue River; The Givreuse Enigma; The Mysterious Force; The Navigators of Space; Vamireh; The World of the Variants; The Young Vampire*

Marcel Rouff. *Journey to the Inverted World*

Han Ryner. *The Superhumans*

Pierre de Sélènes. *An Unknown World*

Angelo de Sorr. *The Vampires of London*

Brian Stableford. *The New Faust at the Tragicomique;The Empire of the Necromancers (The Shadow of Frankenstein; Frankenstein and the Vampire Countess; Frankenstein in London); Sherlock Holmes & The Vampires of Eternity; The Stones of Camelot; The Wayward*

Muse. (anthologist) *News from the Moon; The Germans on Venus; The Supreme Progress; The World Above the World; Nemoville; Investigations of the Future; The Conqueror of Death*
Jacques Spitz. *The Eye of Purgatory*
Kurt Steiner. *Ortog*
Eugène Thébault. *Radio-Terror*
C.-F. Tiphaigne de La Roche. *Amilec*
Louis Ulbach. *Prince Bonifacio*
Théo Varlet. *The Golden Rock. The Xenobiotic Invasion; The Castaways of Eros; Timeslip Troopers* (w/André Blandin); *The Martian Epic* (w/Octave Joncquel)
Paul Vibert. *The Mysterious Fluid*
Villiers de l'Isle-Adam. *The Scaffold; The Vampire Soul*
Philippe Ward. *Artahe*
Philippe Ward & Sylvie Miller. *The Song of Montségur*

MYSTERIES & THRILLERS

M. Allain & P. Souvestre. *The Daughter of Fantômas*
A. Anicet-Bourgeois, Lucien Dabril. *Rocambole*
A. Bernède. *Belphegor; Judex* (w/Louis Feuillade); *The Return of Judex* (w/Louis Feuillade); *The Shadow of Judex*
A. Bisson & G. Livet. *Nick Carter vs. Fantômas*
V. Darlay & H. de Gorsse. *Arsène Lupin vs. Sherlock Holmes: The Stage Play*
Séamas Duffy. *Sherlock Holmes in Paris*
Paul Féval. *Gentlemen of the Night; John Devil; The Black Coats ('Salem Street; The Invisible Weapon; The Parisian Jungle; The Companions of the Treasure; Heart of Steel; The Cadet Gang; The Sword-Swallower)*
Emile Gaboriau. *Monsieur Lecoq*
Goron & Emile Gautier. *Spawn of the Penitentiary*
Rick Lai. *Shadows of the Opera: Retribution in Blood; Sisters of the Shadows: The Curse of Cagliostro*
Steve Leadley. *Sherlock Holmes: The Circle of Blood*
Maurice Leblanc. *Arsène Lupin vs. Countess Cagliostro; Arsène Lupin vs. Sherlock Holmes (The Blonde Phantom; The Hollow Needle); The Many Faces of Arsène Lupin*
Gaston Leroux. *Chéri-Bibi; The Phantom of the Opera; Rouletabille & the Mystery of the Yellow Room; Rouletabille at Krupp's*
Richard Marsh. *The Complete Adventures of Judith Lee*

William Patrick Maynard. *The Terror of Fu Manchu; The Destiny of Fu Manchu*
Frank J. Morlock. *Sherlock Holmes: The Grand Horizontals; Sherlock Holmes vs Jack the Ripper*
Jean Petithuguenin. *The Adventures of Ethel King*
Antonin Reschal. *The Adventures of Miss Boston*
P. de Wattyne & Y. Walter. *Sherlock Holmes vs. Fantômas*
David White. *Fantômas in America*
Pierre Yrondy. *The Adventures of Thérèse Arnaud*

SCREENPLAYS

Mike Baron. *The Iron Triangle*
Emma Bull & Will Shetterly. *Nightspeeder; War for the Oaks*
Gerry Conway & Roy Thomas. *Doc Dynamo*
Steve Englehart. *Majorca*
James Hudnall. *The Devastator*
Jean-Marc & Randy Lofficier. *Royal Flush*
J.-M. & R. Lofficier & Marc Agapit. *Despair*
J.-M. & R. Lofficier & Joël Houssin. *City*
Andrew Paquette. *Peripheral Vision*
Robert L. Robinson, Jr. *Judex*
R. Thomas, J. Hendler & L. Sprague de Camp. *Rivers of Time*

NON-FICTION

Stephen R. Bissette. *Blur 1-5. Green Mountain Cinema 1; Teen Angels*
Win Scott Eckert. *Crossovers* (2 vols.)
Jean-Marc & Randy Lofficier. *Shadowmen* (2 vols.)
Randy Lofficier. *Over Here*

ART BOOKS

Jean-Pierre Normand. *Science Fiction Illustrations*
Raven Okeefe. *Raven's L'il Critters; Rave's Faves*
Randy Lofficier & Raven Okeefe. *If Your Possum Go Daylight...*
Daniele Serra. *Illusions*

HEXAGON COMICS

Franco Frescura & Luciano Bernasconi. *Wampus*
Franco Frescura & Giorgio Trevisan. *CLASH*
L. Bernasconi, J.-M. Lofficier & Juan Roncagliolo. *Phenix*
Claude Legrand, J.-M. Lofficier & L. Bernasconi. *Kabur*
Franco Oneta. *Zembla*
L. Buffolente, Lofficier & J.-J. Dzialowski. *Strangers: Homicron*
Danilo Grossi. *Strangers: Jaydee*
Claude Legrand & Luciano Bernasconi. *Strangers: Starlock*
Thierry Mornet & Juan Roncagliolo. *Guardian of the Republic*
J.-M. Lofficier, M. Garcia, F. Blanco & J. Pima. *Strangers in a Strange Land*

www.ingramcontent.com/pod-product-compliance
Lightning Source LLC
Chambersburg PA
CBHW022219010726
47493CB00002B/521